THE WRITING ON THE WINDOW

T. M. BENNETT

ISBN 979-8-9947153-0-7

For all of us who have faced what we may not speak openly of.

Table of Contents

Chapter 1

Alfred Featherbomb stepped onto his porch. Without needing to check to see whether his neighbor, Mr. Carter, was likewise venturing onto his porch, he lifted his right hand in a wave.

Observing the regular flow of the morning greeting rituals, he turned with a broad smile and called, "A fine day to say good morning on."

Mr. Carter, who was always dreadfully stuck in an older era, waved and returned, "It's swell. Good morning, Mr. Featherbomb."

Alfred clasped his hands on his hips and rocked back on his heels and pulled in the fresh air. It was one of those bright, crisp mornings that always comes between the surrender of spring cool and the onset of summer heat.

The moment of peace and revery shattered. Mr. Carter's twin boys raced from their house shoving and shouting at each other.

Mrs. Carter's voice rose shrilly as she sent it chasing after the two ten-year-olds, "Get back in here and get your shoes on. Oh! Your father will brand your hides if you stain your Sunday best."

The dark-haired boy bent, picked up the rolled-up newspaper and swung it at his light-haired brother. Mimicking his mother's shrill voice, he screeched, "Your father will brand your hide."

They ran back inside, upsetting Mr. Carter's balance a second time. He laughed silently and grinned at Alfred. "Girls are harder at this age they say."

Alfred was about to reply, but Mrs. Carter filled the doorway and glared at her husband. Mr. Carter frowned and immediately growled after his sons, "Now, see here, boys."

Alfred shook his head and reached down for the paper. As he stood, studying the front-page headline, he called to his neighbor across the street, "Good morning, Mr. Riley."

Mr. Riley, always gruff and somewhat impolite, replied, "Mornin', Featherbim."

Alfred smiled and lifted the paper in acknowledgement. Such was their relationship that they never talked about anything more important than the weather—and that they did only on rare occasion.

Several more neighbors called pleasantries to Alfred as he hiked back to his front door and eased himself inside.

"Clarabelle?" he called.

His wife hurried into the kitchen. She was holding her hair up with one hand and set a handheld mirror on the counter. "I'm sorry, Al, I haven't made you your coffee, yet. Let me get that for you."

Alfred sat at the aluminum-edged, Formica table and shuffled the paper, "You know, Clarabelle, nothing happens. The paper's always the same. Somebody's cat got rescued, a couple announces they're getting married and a sale is going on at the supermarket. Oh, and then the obituaries."

Mrs. Featherbomb stirred sugar into her husband's coffee, "I'm sorry, dear, maybe one day something exciting will happen."

Alfred chuckled, "No." He sipped his coffee, "I like it this way." Spreading the paper and scanning it, he exhaled and added, "Nope, this is just fine the way it is."

"Dad?"

Alfred grunted.

"May I have some money to get ice cream with Donna and some others after church?"

Alfred looked up from his paper and peered at his daughter through his black-rimmed glasses. Her long, pale fingers fidgeted with the corner of her jacket, and her round, brown eyes fell to the floor.

"Don't crumple your jacket, Barbara," Alfred chided before Mrs. Featherbomb could interject. He turned back to the paper. "It'll be this evening, right?"

"Yes," Barbara said, clasping her hands tightly in front of her waist and twitching as if physically resisting the urge to pull at her buttons.

"And boys won't be going with you?"

"Well..."

Alfred folded the top of the paper down and took off his glasses. The look he leveled at her sent her hand back to the corner of her jacket.

"Donna invited Will and James," Barbara tried to push her voice past a mumble.

"What? You're mumbling," Alfred said sternly.

Barbara tugged at her jacket, smoothed her dress and grabbed the pleated cotton. "Donna invited Will and James," she repeated as clearly as she could.

"You're too young for boys," Alfred grunted. He slipped his glasses back on and shook the paper to straighten it. "And stop crumpling your clothes."

He caught an appreciative look from his wife as she bustled back to her vanity to finish her hair.

Alfred expected to hear his daughter walk away, but her lighter footsteps didn't sound. The paper was too blurred to read anyway, so he removed his glasses and set them on top of the paper.

"Didn't your mother teach you to be respectful?" he asked quickly.

"Why can't I go?" Barbara pleaded.

Alfred stood and rubbed his eyes. "You're being rude and disrespectful. I've told you no. Your mother and I agree, not as long as there'll be boys present."

He watched his daughter bite her lip and blink back anger. Briefly, something tugged at his heart, but he suppressed it. Barbara was his only child, and he wouldn't have her ruined by boys even if they did go to the same church.

"Besides," he added in a mumble, "shops should be closed on the Lord's Day."

He thought about calling Clarabelle to tell her about the disrespect Barbara had just shown him, but a smudge on the kitchen window distracted him. Grabbing a towel, he reached toward the window, but when his hand was a few inches away a knock at the door shattered the tense stillness.

"I'll be a minute," his wife called from the master bedroom. Small glass bottles and metal cases clinked as she painstakingly applied makeup at the vanity, evidently having finished with her hair.

Alfred figured it was Barbara's friends. He could send them off without making a scene. They should know better than to run around on Sunday morning right before church anyway. Dropping the towel, he strode to the door and jerked it open. Words already wormed toward his lips as he saw the short figure, but then he stopped short.

A shortish man pulled his hand quickly from the position of knocking on the door and gripped his hat, pressing it to his chest with a little bow.

"Hola, Señor," he greeted Alfred.

Alfred stood stone still, glaring down on top of the slicked back, black hair.

The man straightened and held out his hand, "Llama—called Señor Jose."

Alfred glanced at the brown hand offered to him to shake and then at the smile filled with teeth that weren't quite as white as teeth should be.

"Lo siento, Señor," the Mexican backed up a step. "Sorry. Sorry."

"Who's at the door, Al?" Clarabelle called pleasantly.

"No one, Clarabelle," Alfred called over his shoulder.

"I need... I need," the Mexican worked his hands around the brim of his hat. "Necasito trabajo. Work?"

Alfred replied gruffly, "I don't speak greaser-language. Go look in town with some of your people. And don't knock on anymore doors. It's Sunday."

"Dear? Who's there?" Alfred closed his eyes as his wife asked again.

"He's just leaving," Alfred called into the house. His wife came up behind him and nudged his side.

"Oh!" Clarabelle exclaimed brightly. "He's dressed pleasantly."

Alfred eyed the pinstriped suit and the bow tie the Mexican wore over a stained, white shirt. The buckle on his belt, the cleanest piece of his getup, looked freshly polished and far too large.

"Did you ask him what he wants?" Mrs. Featherbomb asked. Before he could respond, she glanced toward the road and added, "Oh, and he's got his adorable family with him. Ask them to come to church with us."

"I'll do no such thing," Alfred growled. "Their kind doesn't even worship the same as we do."

Clarabelle paid no attention to Alfred and gasped as a little, brown hand waved at her from the battered car parked on the edge of the street. She returned the wave and then addressed the man standing on the bottom step.

"Come in. Come in and bring your family. I'll have lemonade ready in a jiffy."

"Sorry. Lo siento, Señora."

"Oh," Mrs. Featherbomb batted at her hair, "you don't speak English. ¿Limon?" She made the motion of tipping a glass to her lips.

The Mexican smiled and then glanced nervously at Alfred. At Mrs. Featherbomb's further beckoning, he hurried back to his car and returned escorting his wife and a little, bouncing girl with a head of thick, black hair. He lifted the girl into his arms and carried her through the door.

Alfred backed up as he attempted to hide his fury. He watched as his daughter stepped toward the little, Mexican girl and spoke to her. Little black dots danced in his vision. He made a mental note to tell her schoolteacher about his daughter's ability to speak Spanish. He felt the table bump against his leg and snatched his glasses and smashed them into place. He winced only slightly as a temple stabbed his left eye.

He watched helplessly as his wife opened the refrigerator and removed the pitcher of lemonade. She had prepared it to take to the Carter's barbecue after church. He wanted to shout and throw the Señor Jose and family out, but he couldn't move.

Barbara laughed as the little girl danced in a circle after tasting the lemonade.

"Gracias, Señor," the Mexican beamed at Alfred.

Why couldn't the man speak intelligibly?

The Mexican's wife smiled at Clarabelle and accepted a glass, then she cast her eyes back to the floor.

"Be careful of your dress," Clarabelle called as Barbara took the little girl out the back door to the yard. "Didn't I hear your father tell you not to crumple your jacket?"

Alfred frowned at the three people in front of him. Being late to church was something that he had not been since...well, since his parents had started dressing him up in a hand-me-down suit when he was a toddler.

"Of course, I'd appreciate the help with the gardening, and I'm sure some of our neighbors would like you to help them as well," Clarabelle was saying. "That is, if you're as good as you say you are. Don't you think, Al?"

Alfred fumed silently to himself.

"What do you think of Mr. Jose working in the gardens, dear? It would be only until he could find better work, but it would be such keen help."

"Why don't you show them the door and teach them how it works. We don't want to be late for church," Alfred gave a stiff nod.

Mrs. Featherbomb glanced at the clock on the wall and gave a gasp. "Come to church, won't you?" she said to the foreigners.

The Mexican grinned and bobbed his head.

"He doesn't have a clue what you're saying, Clarabelle. Show them out."

"Oh," Clarabelle didn't sound put out in the least. "Where's Barbara when you need her? Barbara?"

Barbara hurried back in holding the little girl's hand. She looked questioningly at her mother.

"Will you invite them to church for me?" Clarabelle asked.

Alfred watched his daughter as she wadded her face up in her search for the words. Finally, she simply said, "¿Iglesia?"

The Mexican held up a hand, "Oh, no, no, no. Gracias. Thank you. Thank you."

"Clarabelle," Alfred ground out between nearly closed teeth, "we'll be late."

With his wife in tow, the Mexican turned for the door. With incredible frustration and consternation, Alfred dodged the little girl's outstretched hands as she ran to plaster a hug on his own daughter's legs. He mustn't explode in front of the company—no matter that they were uninvited. Well, *he* had not invited them in, at least. He tugged at his tie as Barbara bent and hugged the little girl and then shuffle-stepped with her to the door.

"Hasta luego," the Mexican called as his family traipsed down the steps toward their car.

"Adios. Via con Dios," Barbara waved after them.

Alfred tugged at his collar again.

"Well, aren't they just delightful," Mrs. Featherbomb proclaimed, turning back from the closing door. "Al, straighten your tie."

Alfred spluttered, but nothing intelligible passed his lips. He waved his arms as if intending to break into a run, but his feet remained planted to the floor like he was standing in glue.

"These are new times we're living in, dear," Mrs. Featherbomb pecked him on the cheek. "And do straighten your tie. It's all askew and dead like a flag without any wind."

Alfred felt rage he couldn't describe burn hot inside him, but he grabbed his tie and pulled the little rabbit that had gone through the hole, grabbed his hat and the car keys and placed a hand on the doorknob. He sure hoped the Mexicans were gone.

"Come along, Barbara. We don't want to be late for church," his wife called.

Alfred opened the door and stepped out. He knew his daughter was either right beside his wife or right behind him. Clarabelle had certain phrases she used to call Barbara every time they had somewhere to go, and he had deciphered the code years ago.

Chapter 2

In the Buick, silence reigned for several minutes. Clarabelle adjusted her hair and inspected her jacket sleeves for lint. Barbara sat on her hands and peered out the side windows from the middle of the rear bench seat.

Alfred leaned forward at a stop sign and rubbed the windshield with his sleeve.

"Oh, really, Alfred," Mrs. Featherbomb shuddered, "do you know how long it takes to clean and press that blazer?"

A Chevy passed through the intersection, and Alfred sat back with a grunt.

"I'll refrain from letting my dander show with Barbara in the back, but would it hurt you so much to look at me?" Mrs. Featherbomb sniffed. "And to think we're on our way to the Lord's House."

"There's Donna," Barbara cried excitedly and slid to the right side of the seat. She waved out the window as if her life depended on her friend seeing her.

Alfred closed his eyes. He had forgotten about Barbara's request to get ice cream with Donna—Donna and some boys. Clarabelle expected him to lay down the law. He would take the blame for being old-fashioned and cruel, while Mrs. Featherbomb would somehow work herself into the position of savior. It was enough to make him feel like never speaking again except in grumbling grunts, which would cause his wife's ire to be directed solely at him. It would be best to pretend to have forgotten the entire incident.

He maneuvered the Buick into the church parking lot. Several families were walking toward the wooden doors. He glimpsed the sunlight striking the stained-glass windows above them. It was remarkable how, with just a few different colors of broken glass, the artist had captured Jesus' crucifixion and resurrection.

The Nicholsons waved as they led their two boys in front of them. Mrs. Nicholson carried their two-year-old daughter in her arms. Alfred was reaching for his glasses so he could clean them as soon as they parked, so he turned his reach into a wave and stretched his tight lips into a smile he hoped appeared genuine.

Alfred parked beside the Barnett's Ford pickup. Barbara hopped out and stood waiting respectfully for her parents after slamming her door.

"Does my hair look alright?" Clarabelle turned to him.

Alfred turned slowly, a thoughtful look muddling his expression as he cleaned his glasses on his shirt, "I'm sorry, Clara."

"It can't be that bad," Mrs. Featherbomb fumbled with the clasp on her handbag.

Alfred wanted to reach out and calm her scrambling fingers, but he slid his glasses back on and explained, "I was just too surprised by them."

Clarabelle inserted a pin into her hair, "A few loose strands brought under control can make all the difference."

Alfred grunted as though he was clearing his throat and exited the car. With his Sunday smile firmly in place, he opened his wife's door and let her loop her hand in his elbow.

"There's the Connors," Clarabelle whispered with a small tug on his arm.

Alfred looked up and focused on a family, a husband and a wife, walking stiffly across the parking lot. Between them, they seemed to be dragging a ten or twelve-year-old boy.

"Richard just turned eighteen," Mrs. Featherbomb explained. "The army got him. I heard he got drafted just last Thursday. Isn't it awful? We just won the World War and now they're fighting in Korea. I looked it up on a map. It's a little country clear on the other side of the world."

Alfred's brain felt frozen. He couldn't process all that information at once. He wanted his own life to go back to the easy predictability that had been shattered that morning with the visit of the Mexican and his family before he worried about someone else's life.

"Good morning, Mrs. Connors," his wife called to the family as they drew alongside. They were moving slowly, mechanically, as if built from clockwork.

Mrs. Connors turned puffy eyes toward Clarabelle and forced a smile, "Good morning, Mrs. Bombfeather."

Mr. Connors grunted without turning to look. Then, he reached out for a bulletin from the greeter and buried his attention inside it.

Confounded grieving woman, Alfred thought. *Can't she even get our name right? It's Featherbomb not Bombfeather.*

He was not inclined to feel empathy for the Connors. After all, he still hadn't figured out what needed to be done to keep those Mexicans from coming back every day. Once they received a handout, they were like a stray dog that you set food out for. The dog would return and whine as it stared at you with eyes so pitiful the only option was to succumb to the begging.

"What's the world coming to?" Alfred muttered under his breath.

"Good morning, Mr. Fritterbomb," Alfred looked up to see a boyish hand extended toward him.

He took the offered hand and shook it. As he glanced at the young man's dark eyes hooded by thick brows, he couldn't help but see Jose again. This man was much taller, however, and his skin wasn't so dark.

"Uh, good morning to you, too," Alfred looked toward the rows of thinly cushioned pews.

"You don't know me, and that's fine," the tall man grinned. "I'm a recruiter for the army." He lowered his voice conspiratorially, "I thought it best to meet a few people before setting up with my duds."

Alfred nodded and scanned the pews nervously. Clarabelle, with Barbara standing dutifully at her side, was still talking with Mrs. Connors.

"Yes, sir," the recruiter snapped to attention. "Name's McCoy—Sergeant Oliver McCoy. The boys get some good stuff if they enlist before the draft chooses 'em. Did so myself. Well, it's a nice church here, Mr. Fritter."

"Ah, yes," Alfred wanted to correct his last name with the man. However, he couldn't do anything except work his jaw like a hand pump. The action seemed to bring some words bubbling up from where they flowed underground far out of sight. "You might talk with the Prescotts. They're right over there," he pointed. "They've got two boys."

Sergeant McCoy saluted casually and sauntered over to the thin wisp of a man and the two, lanky teenagers. As the recruiter drew near them, Mrs. Prescott grasped her husband's upper arm as her face contorted into a worried wad laced with anger or maybe hatred.

Alfred felt heat rise in his cheeks as the older boy's gaze found his. Quickly, he shifted his gaze to the pews, which were filling rapidly.

He jumped as a hand linked through the crook of his elbow.

"Oh, these wars are so awful," his wife said quietly. "They take all the young men away and leave us mothers at our wits end, worrying about the awful things they put those boys through before ever even going overseas to fight. Richard's friend got his leg broken. His letter just arrived. Dreadful." She shuddered and pressed her free hand to her hair. "And there's an awful man in town. McConnel or McCoy or something Irish like that."

She squeezed Alfred's arm and gasped slightly.

He couldn't take any more hysterics. He wanted to find a seat and clean a smudge off his glasses before the service started so he wouldn't appear as though he wasn't listening.

"That's him over there," Mrs. Featherbomb hissed. "The devil of a man. Handsome as all get out, but full of dead man's bones on the inside. Mark my words."

Alfred peeled his glasses off and set to polishing the lenses with the cloth he always carried with him. Everybody became human shaped blobs floating around him in a fuzzy landscape.

"I think that's the minister," he blurted under his breath. "We should go to our pew."

"You didn't see who I was pointing at," Clarabelle insisted. "You can't see without your glasses."

Alfred slipped the black frames back into place and blinked. The smudge was still there. Thinking it could be a strange trick of the stained-glass windows, he cocked his head to make the light hit the lenses from a different angle.

"I can see just fine," Alfred grumbled, slipping his glasses back off. His wife, however, was not listening.

"Mom," Alfred overheard his daughter ask, "can I sit with Donna today?"

"I don't see why not, but ask your father."

His daughter turned to him as he pushed his glasses to the bridge of his nose. He wasn't sure what the big deal was, yet he didn't want to say yes.

"Dad, may I sit with Donna and her family today?" Barbara asked with what Alfred thought was a forced smile. It pained him to see her hesitant to talk to him, or maybe he was simply frustrated with how the morning had gone so far.

He didn't respond right away. After scanning the little groups of gossipers, who were breaking back into their family units and migrating to the pews, he murmured, "Why don't you call me papa anymore? It was cute the way you said my name."

Alfred glimpsed a frown on his daughter's face.

"Dad, it's not flip anymore to use papa," she said in a hushed whisper.

"Why can't you sit with us?" Alfred asked. He was genuinely hurt that his daughter no longer wanted to associate with her parents.

Barbara opened her mouth in exaggerated horror, "Dad, you're so square. Why can't I sit with Donna?"

Mrs. Featherbomb reached for Barbara's hand. "Sweetheart, don't make a scene that will embarrass your father," she said gently.

Alfred blinked several times. He hadn't told his daughter that she *couldn't* sit with her friend, yet he couldn't think of anything except that she had said he wasn't cool, if that's what the teens meant when they used "square." He rubbed his forehead, trying to shake the fear that he had failed in raising his daughter.

Mrs. Featherbomb's grip on his arm pulled him from his ponderings.

"Alfred," she scolded into his ear, "don't you dare have a cow here in church. We'll go to our pew, and I think it would be fine for Barbara to sit with her friend."

Alfred wished he could pull his words back into his mouth the instant he said them, but he said them anyway, "What happened to women and respect?"

Mrs. Featherbomb's face went hard for a moment, but then she smiled sweetly, patted his arm and said, "Go on,

Barbara, you can sit with Donna. Al, you ought to be ashamed of yourself. You're acting like an immature, little brat."

Alfred blinked. His wife surely was not telling him he was throwing a tantrum and pouting, was she? He plucked his glasses off and ran his palm down his face.

Barbara skipped to her friend's side, and they both squealed as she grabbed Donna's hand. He couldn't remember seeing his daughter ever smile so wide as the two girls giggled and fell into place beside Donna's parents.

Several older folks frowned at their antics. Alfred looked down as their disapproval found its mark on him.

Clarabelle linked her hand through his arm and steered him toward their pew. Donna's family was seated two pews in front, and Barbara turned around with a grin and waved. Alfred made an effort to return her smile.

The pastor's wife pounded out the opening chords to "I Know Who Holds Tomorrow" while the pastor rose from his chair on the stage and motioned for all to stand. Alfred sang the words and desperately tried to mean them, but the confidence he sang about found no place in his heart.

The singing ended with the ringing power of "How Great Thou Art." Then, the pastor led his congregation in a prayer pleading for the boys over in Korea. Many women sniffed, and a few sobbed. When Alfred opened his eyes, husbands stood ramrod straight beside their wives, who dabbed at their eyes.

"Now," Pastor Meyers launched into his oratory, "turn with me to the book of Luke, chapter twenty-one, and, beginning in verse five..."

They read nearly the entire chapter. Alfred marveled at how Luke had recorded so much detail.

The pastor reached a crescendo as he read verse thirty-four, "And take heed to yourselves, lest at any time your hearts be overcharged with surfeiting, and drunkenness, and cares of this life, and so that day come upon you unawares.'"

Pastor Meyers paused, letting the silence reign for nearly thirty seconds. Alfred reflected on the part of the passage he could remember, verse thirty-four. He chided himself for not being able to recall what Jesus had said in the earlier verses.

For the rest of the service, Alfred nodded along with what the pastor said, and he was particularly careful to remember everything he had heard with special attention to the passages from the Bible. By the time the service let out, he felt confident he could recite Pastor Meyers' sermon nearly word for word.

"You're acting excited for having just heard a warning about the last days," Mrs. Featherbomb whispered to Alfred as they stood.

She was right. He was giddy with enthusiasm. "I think I'll remember this sermon," he replied. "Especially the part about surfing."

"Yeah," Mr. Davidson said. He had a funny smile peeling up his lips on one side, "All those lost boys and girls going to hell because they love being on the water on a piece of wood." He shook his head and wrapped up his thought, "Cryin', pitiable shame. Well, I guess I better tell my boy to sell his board and move his sinful self back here."

Alfred did not laugh with Mr. Davidson. He didn't even chuckle. His fellow churchgoer didn't understand. How could the man joke so lightheartedly about a serious matter?

Mrs. Featherbomb laughed as Mr. Davidson caught her eye.

"It isn't funny, Clarabelle," Alfred insisted. "Mr. Davidson's boy isn't the only one on his way to hell. I've heard it said for years that those who surf are acting on the Devil's volition."

Alfred checked his tie to make sure it hadn't slipped loose and brushed a strand of his close-cropped hair off his forehead. That reminded him of another thing he was certain was preached against—long hair.

"Surfing's only getting bigger every day," Mr. Davidson chuckled. "Before you know it, some hit songs are going to be made about it." He raised a hand as if running it along script he wanted printed in a shop window, "I can see it now, 'Long-haired surfers sing Devil-anthem.'"

This was not a good Sunday to be in church after all. Alfred was certain of it. He ignored the urge to fight back. Besides, it looked as though Mrs. Davidson was about to have a word with Mr. Davidson. Alfred took his wife's arm and guided her to the aisle.

"Good to see you, Mr. Featherbum," Mr. Davidson called.

Alfred didn't turn around. He marched straight toward the exit. Clarabelle caught Barbara and towed her along. He was glad to leave the church behind with its mocking congregation.

Mrs. Featherbomb chided, "You're anxious to agitate the gravel. He was just having a bit of fun."

"You call *that* fun?" Alfred retorted as he pulled open her car door.

Barbara slipped into the back. Mrs. Featherbomb laid her right hand on his cheek, "We all get smog in the noggin from time to time, dear."

Alfred helped her in and closed the door. Lowering himself in on the driver's side, he asked tersely, "What do you mean by that?"

As she replied, he ran his shirt over his glasses. Another smudge had developed on the left lens.

"Oh," Mrs. Featherbomb patted her hair, "I think you should drive."

"God—"

"Uh uh uh. No profanity, Al," Mrs. Featherbomb raised an index finger. "Especially no cussing on the Lord's Day at the Lord's House."

Alfred scowled, started the car and threw it into reverse. Someone screamed, and Clarabelle gasped as Alfred shoved the clutch and brake to the floor.

Sergeant McCoy staggered and hobbled backward, brushing vigorously at his slacks.

A male voice shouted, "Run 'im over again."

Alfred scrambled to get out. Heat rose to his face, making it feel ten pounds heavier.

Sergeant McCoy held up a hand, "I'm all good. No harm done, old boy. Though, I might have the zorros for a few days around the rear ends of cars."

He should have looked in the mirror more carefully. If he hadn't been so quick with the clutch, the man would have had a dusty tire mark or two to wash out of his suit. Alfred wanted to put his hand in his pockets or throw them over his face. Maybe he needed a drink. Yes, that would soothe him. But, no, he had given that up when he joined Pastor Meyers' church.

Alfred returned Sergeant McCoy's wave and ducked back into the car.

"You almost ran that poor man over," Clarabelle chided.

"He's quite alright," Alfred snapped. "He waved me off. Look, he's not even limping at all. He's fine, I tell you. Just as he says he is."

"Let's go," Mrs. Featherbomb pressed her lips together. "There's a crowd watching."

Alfred glanced around as he slowly put the Buick in gear. His hands grew clammy on the steering wheel, and he bored his gaze through the mirror. The car crept back a few inches, shuddered, coughed and stalled.

"Oh, Alfred," Mrs. Featherbomb raised a hand across the side of her face to shield herself from onlookers.

Barbara, who had remained silently sitting on her hands through the whole ordeal, offered softly, "I'll watch for you, dad."

Alfred's vision tunneled, and his heartbeat throbbed in his ears. Mechanically, he restarted the Buick.

"Thank God the engine didn't flood," Mrs. Featherbomb murmured to no one.

"All clear, dad," Barbara called.

Alfred inched the car back.

When they were finally moving forward, Alfred avoided looking anywhere but straight ahead. He didn't want anyone to see how pathetic he was. He knew he should thank his daughter for the help in the parking lot, but his tongue refused to grasp the words and push them out of his mouth.

Poised to pull out onto the road, Alfred pushed his glasses up and rubbed his eyes with a thumb and forefinger. Repositioning his glasses, he flicked his fingers to the windshield. Someone had smudged a black streak across it. He let his anger flare as he mumbled, "Kids these days with no respect for other people's things."

"You weren't actually trying to run him over, were you?" Mrs. Featherbomb asked as he pulled onto the street behind a blue Ford.

Chapter 3

"Al, we're almost ready," Clarabelle called from the master bedroom where she was applying touchups to her makeup. "As soon as Barbara gets the last lemon squeezed. It's lucky we had enough lemons left to squeeze a new pitcher after our company this morning."

"Dad?" Barbara called loudly.

Alfred jumped and rushed to the kitchen, "What is it?"

"I can't get the ice out," his daughter said, holding the ice tray in both hands.

Alfred, afraid of being blamed for the delay, grabbed the tray and gave it a twist.

"Ow. Ow," Barbara cried.

"You didn't tell me your hands were frozen to the tray," Alfred growled.

Clarabelle bustled in. A handful of bobby pins clattered to the counter.

"Help her, Al," she cried. "I wish they wouldn't make these trays out of aluminum."

By the time Clarabelle had the water running in the sink, Barbara's body heat had melted the bond between her fingers and the metal. She yelped as the tray pulled away from her tender fingers.

"That electric ice box is too cold," Clarabelle fussed over her daughter's hands. "Al, I think we ought to have it adjusted."

"And have you complaining about going back to using a hammer and chisel and an ice box that leaks all over the floor?" Alfred glared at his wife. He was not about to go back to the era before electric ice boxes. That brought another thing to mind, "If there was a world war going on, we could turn that tray in for scrap."

Mrs. Featherbomb slammed her fists onto her hips and turned away from Barbara, who was bathing her hands in lukewarm water. "Well, aren't you just full of sunshine," her voice came low and slow.

Alfred backed away from the counter. He wouldn't admit it to anyone, but he was scared of his wife when she was angry. And this was no ordinary anger. This was something deeper he didn't think he understood. Most days, Clarabelle was even-tempered and even-keeled, but sometimes, things happened that blew her ship into a different hemisphere. He didn't know how he knew, but he knew he was the one to blow her off course nearly every single time—no, one hundred percent of the time he was to blame.

Mrs. Featherbomb broke her glare from him and turned her attention back to their daughter.

Alfred peered at the two from the doorway. Barbara had her head down and shoulders curled forward. He knew the stance. He had used it to try to hide every time his own parents had fought with him in the same room. He should tell her he was sorry. He was just about to open his mouth when Mrs. Featherbomb reached for the lid to the pitcher which had ended up on the table.

She paused, her arm half extended, "You could at least grab the cucumber canapes. We're almost ready."

"Look, I'm sorry," Alfred said. "I didn't know her hands were frozen to the tray."

Mrs. Featherbomb turned back to the counter, lid in hand. "Best not to talk about it," she sent over her shoulder.

Alfred took a step forward.

Barbara gave a small whimper she must have been trying to conceal and whirled around. She pulled up suddenly when she saw Alfred in the doorway. She put her hand over her mouth and all but sprinted through the archway at the opposite end of the kitchen.

Alfred wanted Clarabelle to turn around and tell him to go after his daughter to apologize. That or chew him up and spit him out again. Anything would be better than perfect silence and being completely ignored. She didn't even look his way as she whisked the refrigerator open, snatched the tray of carefully assembled cucumber canapes and began rearranging the already perfect circles.

He swallowed and reached up for his thick-framed glasses, trying to remember where he'd put his cleaning cloth.

He rubbed at the dirty lenses. Without his glasses his eyesight was poor but not terrible. He squinted at the kitchen window. That smudge from the morning was still there. He contemplated checking with Mr. Ashley, the janitor at his office, for some chemicals that would take the smudge off.

"Are you ready?" Mrs. Featherbomb asked without warmth or feeling in her voice.

Alfred pocketed the cloth, "I'll check with the cleaner at the office so I can get the smudge on the window there cleaned off."

The look Mrs. Featherbomb returned froze him stiff.

Then, she smiled and said primly, "Since we're all ready, let's not keep the Carters waiting. I'll fetch Barbara."

Alfred reached for the tray of cucumber canapes but drew back before laying hold. He brushed his hands on his pants and reached for them again. Once again, he could not get his fingers to grasp the tray. He wanted to help out to show that he was sorry for the trouble he had caused, but he could think of nothing but of how Mrs. Featherbomb would scold him for trying to sneak an early bite if she saw him holding the tray.

His hands did their hesitating dance two more times, and then he decided he would carry the pitcher of lemonade. With that the worst he could be blamed of was that he didn't want it given to a tramp family looking for work. He frowned as waves of anger flooded his body.

His wife and daughter's footsteps sounded softly as they crossed the living room.

"Why can't dad see there's no problem with Will and James coming along?" Barbara asked.

Alfred's anger pulsed and funneled toward his daughter. She'd learned nothing about respecting the rules.

Their footsteps paused. Alfred heard his wife reply quietly, "He's quite right about that. I agree with him. You're too young to be running around with boys."

"But Donna's parents—" Barbara didn't get to finish.

"Are raising her and her brothers as they see best. I may not see eye to eye with them, but I don't get to change how they raise their children. Now, you're sure your hands feel better?"

"They're fine," Barbara returned poignantly, "as long as I don't have to handle a square."

Alfred heard the clench in his wife's jaw as she snapped, "Barbara Ann, you should be grounded for that."

Alfred found himself agreeing. Kids had no respect these days. He pretended as if he hadn't overheard anything as Mrs. Featherbomb, sporting a game-winning smile, picked up the tray of cucumbers. His daughter shuffled in, saw him holding the pitcher and kept shuffling.

"Barbara, dear, pick up your feet," Mrs. Featherbomb chided. "Shuffling is no way for a woman to walk." Without so much as a glance at her daughter, she added, "Head up, don't slouch. And, for God's sake, don't cross your arms."

Alfred watched as Barbara opened her mouth to retort. He didn't even have a stitch of encouragement when she snapped it shut without making a sound and released her arms to swing freely at her sides.

"Al," Mrs. Featherbomb called, "you might let Barbara carry the lemonade. It'll be good practice for her. It isn't fitting for a man to do women's work."

Alfred's own mouth unhinged to retort, but he clamped it shut and let his daughter take the pitcher. He busied his hands by stuffing them into his pockets but quickly removed them before Mrs. Featherbomb could tell him how sulky that made him look.

The perfect family crossed the yards and traipsed into the chaos of the Carter's family of four.

Chapter 4

The following morning, Alfred nursed his coffee and read the paper. Somone in the classifieds had posted an ad for a red heifer. He rubbed his eyes, wondering where he'd heard about red heifers before. Finally, he decided it was from some sermon at church. The Jewish extremists wanted to sacrifice a red heifer, or was it a dozen? Either way it was best not to think of them as extremists. That would never do for him to be so derogatory to a people group.

Barbara floated in wearing a brown skirt and blue pullover. Alfred studied the back of his daughter's heels where bulges showed themselves beneath her stockings. Then, he felt her eyes on him.

"If you're going to say my skirt is too short," Barbara blurted before he could ask about the blisters, "mom said it's fine. She said she used to wear some the same length."

Alfred dropped his gaze to the bottom of her skirt. It hung at the top of her shins, and her knees were doing their best to peek out.

Barbara tipped her weight onto one foot while she grabbed her hip with her left hand. Rolling her eyes, she blew out, "Fine. I'll change."

Clarabelle walked in as Barbara blustered out. Alfred thought he heard his wife compliment how Barbara looked.

"What did you do to her now?" Mrs. Featherbomb asked.

Alfred laid the paper down and set to cleaning his glasses, "I didn't say anything to her." In further defense, he hastened, "She's just being a difficult adolescent."

Mrs. Featherbomb shuddered and gave him a patronizing glare, "She's not turning into a beatnik, Al. She's hardly doing half the things we used to do."

Alfred thought of a retort, but bit it back. Instead of arguing, he settled for something that he hoped would put her in her place, "You might do a better job of raising her or she will go beatnik on us."

"I didn't know you knew what radioactive terms meant," Mrs. Featherbomb said airily and left the kitchen, her chin pointing up.

Alfred returned to his coffee and grumbled about women. He was just about to pick the paper back up when a knock sounded. "Clarabelle," he called. "Door."

"I'm busy. Be a flutter bum and answer it yourself, won't you," came his wife's muffled voice.

Alfred growled low in his throat. If it wasn't his daughter dressing like a pinup girl, it was his wife refusing to help out.

The knock sounded again, quieter and less insistent.

Alfred set his coffee mug on the table, but before he removed his hand, he thought better of it and yanked it along with him to the door. To appear busy, he took a long sip from his coffee as he pulled the door open.

The Mexican from yesterday morning stood on the bottom step, working his hands around the brim of his hat. A smile played on his dark features.

"Buenas dia, Señor," he said with a slight lean forward that could have been a bow.

Alfred's mouth missed the lip of his mug, and lukewarm coffee dribbled onto his shirtfront. Immediately, he tried brushing the dark spots off, but it was no use. He glanced helplessly between the man at the door and the kitchen.

His voice reflected his anger, "What do you want? You made me spill my coffee."

The Mexican smiled wider, bowed and replied, "Si, Señor."

Alfred leaned out just far enough to see if the man had parked his car nearby. He didn't see any beat-up car or the man's wife and daughter.

"I walk...uh...this day," the visitor reached out a hand.

That was not good. If the man could walk to Alfred's house, he was stationed far too close. Alfred was about to close the door and ignore the knocking he was sure would ensue. However, at that particular moment, his wife stepped into the kitchen, and Barbara's muffled giggle reached his ears as her lighter step joined her mother's.

Glancing behind, he dropped his coffee mug. Brown liquid splattered the porch as white, ceramic shards exploded in all directions.

A passersby would have described the door as being slammed much like a cartoon representation of the door rotating around the frame a few times before finally settling closed while the whole cartoon slide shook violently.

"What...?" Alfred couldn't fit words to the rest of his question.

Mrs. Featherbomb swished her skirt around her thighs and kicked her right leg onto a chair.

"No self-respecting woman would do that, Clara," Alfred's voice lost all sounds of anger as his eyes traveled his wife's legs.

"I wore this while we were dating," Mrs. Featherbomb said seductively, tracing her forefinger up her thigh and letting it catch on the hem of her skirt to drag it up above her garter buckles.

Barbara's giggle made his face turn red. He swiped a hand over his face.

"No need to show me how I was made," Barbara said snidely.

"Barbara Ann," Mrs. Featherbomb snapped, "don't talk so vulgarly. Can't you see I'm helping you?"

Alfred couldn't take his eyes off his wife's leg, yet he wanted to rage about how his daughter should not be dressing like that. His wife had taken all the wind out of his sails in the most efficient way possible. He couldn't deny that Clarabelle had worn that skirt on several dates. In fact, he remembered it well.

He spluttered something about boys and how they would want nothing more than to lift Barbara's skirt even higher.

Mrs. Featherbomb huffed and declared, "There's no need for more of this vulgar talk."

At last, Alfred said, "I need to change my shirt." With that, he strode out.

By the time he made it back to the kitchen, his wife and daughter were deep in discussion about their worldly shopping trip they were embarking on despite having attended church just yesterday. Barbara needed clothes for the summer and upcoming school year. He knew more of those short skirts would be purchased.

All thoughts of the Mexican on his doorstep and the broken coffee mug had vacated their rooms and turned their keys in at the front counter.

Alfred kissed his wife's cheek. She turned and gave him a wet smooch on the corner of his lips. He said nothing and wiped her saliva off with the back of his hand.

"Get those quacking numbers all in their rows," Clarabelle called over her shoulder.

Alfred smiled or grimaced, even he didn't know which, and opened the door.

"Hola, Señor," the bright, accented voice of the Mexican nearly blew him off his feet.

Alfred struggled for balance. His office shoes suddenly seemed more like ice skates than earth-stompers, but he had never been ice skating in his life. His tie wrapped around his arm, preventing him from slamming the door.

The Mexican held out the white shards of the broken mug, "Clean for el Señor."

"No," Alfred blinked. "No. No, I don't..."

The Mexican smiled and nodded his head.

Alfred felt one of Barbara's small hands press on his back as she leaned around him to see who was at the door.

The Mexican smiled even broader and, tipping the broken ceramic into one hand, doffed his hat and called with a bow, "Buenas dia, Señorita. Pretty—pretty—chica americano bonita," he struggled for the correct words.

"Gracias, Señor Jose," Alfred felt his daughter smooth her skirt. Her hand brushed his backside. "¿Hija de usted?"

"Ah," the Mexican put his hat back in place to cover up the slicked back, black hair curling above his ears. "No hoy. Not this day."

Alfred wanted to make the man back off the porch and leave the neighborhood. Well, leave the country for that matter.

And his daughter. Barbara should know better. He would definitely have a talk with her teacher.

He began turning to address his daughter, but something jangled in his hands. That was funny because the Mexican had been the one holding the broken mug, and he, Alfred, had been holding the doorknob. But, sure enough, the white shards were in his hands, and the Mexican was walking around the house toward the garden shed.

Chapter 5

"Now see here," Alfred called after the Mexican.

His weak voice apparently didn't carry to the Mexican's ears because he kept right on his way.

Barbara went back inside, leaving Alfred standing alone, holding the door wide open and hollering at the dark-skinned man while holding the shards of the coffee mug.

"Stop. I'll call the police. Trespassing." Nothing he yelled changed the Mexican's gait.

"He probably doesn't speak a lick of English," he grumbled to himself. He considered adding a few cuss words that were common in the office. He suppressed the urge, however. Mrs. Featherbomb had good ears and would scold him to no end if he uttered them at home.

The Mexican returned to the garden beside the porch. He carried a trowel, cultivator rake and some other weeding implements. Kneeling in the damp grass, he hummed to himself and set down the tools.

Alfred almost dropped the broken ceramic as he lunged for the Mexican. He was going to chop apart his wife's favorite flowers. He had to be stopped!

A dark smudge on his glasses halted him mid-lunge. He could think of nothing more embarrassing than taking a misstep on his own porch and scraping his elbow. Maybe he would tear a knee open in his slacks, too. That would be embarrassing.

"Mornin', Featherbim," Mr. Riley's voice carried across the street.

"Morning," Alfred replied mechanically without looking.

He hurried down the steps, cocking his head slightly to see around the smudges on his glasses. He wished the things would just stay clean.

By the time he reached the Mexican's side, the dark-skinned man had dragged the gardening claw through the soil and was plucking a clump of scraggly weeds from the tines. Best not to get too close. Gardening claws could turn into weapons lickety-split.

"Pretty flower," the Mexican touched Clarabelle's favorite flowers and looked up at Alfred. "I make pretty more. No weeds." He showed Alfred the uprooted weeds as if they were a scalp like an Indian in the wild west films.

Alfred cupped the shards of his mug in both hands and looked down with a look somewhere between confusion, anger and pleasure.

Clarabelle and Barbara spilled from the house. Alfred nodded in satisfaction when he saw his wife had changed. His daughter, though, still wore the short skirt.

"We'll be back in a couple of hours," Mrs. Featherbomb called sweetly to him as if nothing had transpired a few minutes before. "I left you a check on the counter by the bowl."

She'd left him a check? What did she mean by that? Alfred ducked his head as he couldn't wave without dropping the remains of the coffee mug.

The Mexican twisted back to him and said, "I make work two…three hours, all day, and you say when return."

Alfred scrunched his face together as if squinting at the sun. Another clump of weeds lay dying on the lawn before he figured out what to say.

"I'm not paying you. You can't come onto my property, trespassing, and expect me to pay you for pulling some weeds out of the flowerbeds. You probably don't even know what I'm saying. You ought to have stayed in Argentina fighting bulls or whatever it is your lot does."

The Mexican, kneeling on both knees, cocked his head and straightened momentarily. "No. No hay corrida de toros en Argentina," he muttered to himself. "Soy Mexicano. Creo— I think you like work."

"Speak English, man. I don't understand your Meh-he-kahn-o," Alfred returned.

The sound of a car rumbling to life in the drive next door cut off further comments. Alfred nodded to Mr. Carter as he backed the chevy for the road. The Carters' twin boys shot out of the garage on their bikes hooting and hollering to each other as they argued over who could keep up with their dad the farthest.

"I make plants pretty more," the Mexican said as he kept working. "You like."

"It's prettier not pretty more," Alfred nudged his glasses with his biceps. "And I don't like it. I'm going in the house to throw this mess away. When I come back, I want you gone. Go back to Argentina or Meh-he-ko, or wherever you're from."

The Mexican turned and grinned at him, "Si, Señor."

"I don't see. I don't think you understood a word I just said."

"Si, Señor," the Mexican held up his dirt-covered hand and laid it on his own chest. "Llama Jose."

Alfred shifted his gaze to look through a different part of his glasses. Maybe he needed to call in and make a stop at the optician to get some new lenses. He hefted the broken ceramic in return to the Mexican's offered handshake.

The Mexican tapped the side of his nose, rolled his eyes at himself and shot a look of "how silly" skyward while opening his hand in a shrug. He went back to work pulling the garden claw through the sunbaked soil and removing the weeds that lost their grip on life.

Alfred needed to empty his hands and get to the optician before he, like one of those weeds, lost his grip on his sanity. How many dark smudges could glasses accumulate in one morning? He was decided to ask the techs why he couldn't get some of them cleaned off, as well.

Just then, he had a thought that stopped his foot mid-step. Cataracts? No, Clarabelle hadn't said anything. He was getting older, so maybe? No. He second-guessed his decision to go to the eye doctor. What if they did say his vision was completely failing? What if he lost his job? What if he went blind and crashed into everything in his house? What if Mrs. Featherbomb had to take him by the hand to guide him to their pew at church?

It was all too much for him. His brain simply squealed in place like a steam locomotive loaded too heavily slipping as it tried to start on an upward grade.

Had a fly just flown into his glasses? A fresh smudge, long and striated, appeared at the bottom right corner of his righthand lens.

Alfred raced to the front door. He nicked his finger on a sharp piece of the garbage in his hands as he twisted the knob. In a flurry of jerky movements, he emptied his hands into the wastebasket, flung his glasses on the table and ran to the bathroom mirror.

A sweating, middle-aged man with a touch of gray gracing his temples beneath well-kept, brown hair cropped close stared back at him with eyes somewhere between brown and green in color. The image in the mirror was slightly blurry. He definitely needed his glasses to see properly, but he needed glasses that would stay clean. Without the lenses over his eyes, no black smudges encroached his vision.

He sighed, patted his forehead with the hand towel and closed his eyes. The muffled sound of the Mexican weeding the flowerbeds filtered through the partially open bedroom window.

He hadn't been able to get rid of the man after all.

He opened his eyes, relishing the clarity of his smudge-free vision. He frowned and peered closer, mimicking the position his wife assumed if she used the bathroom mirror instead of her vanity to apply her petroleum jelly and coal dust to her lashes. No, he shouldn't think of her like that. Mascara wasn't made from those ingredients anymore. But she did get close to the mirror while applying the stuff. She must have grazed the glass with the applicator.

He swiped at the streaks with the towel. Nothing happened. Normally, such streaks were simple enough to wipe off. He frowned.

He slid his glasses on. A fly must have landed in black paint and crashed into the lenses as it tried to fly straight. Maybe it had seen the reflection of the yard in his glasses and that was why it had flown into them, leaving streaks of black paint behind.

He had plenty of chemicals that could strip paint, but he didn't want to attempt it without asking a professional. In the meantime, a new set of glasses would serve him well. He could probably get a stronger pair like he knew he needed but hadn't told anyone, especially not Mrs. Featherbomb.

Chapter 6

"That's the earliest we can have them ready for you, Mr. Flutterbum," the smiling receptionist tilted her head so the beads glued to her horn-rimmed glasses sparkled in the light. "There's simply nothing more I can do."

"But two weeks?" Alfred argued. "And my name isn't Flutterbum. It's Featherbomb."

"What was that?" the receptionist, Ms. Ogden her nameplate read, flicked her attention back to Alfred.

He could check on the other side of town, but that was a fat chance. For all he knew, the two optometrists in town were in cahoots. Maybe they'd even planned the shortage of lenses together to get a double shipment in just before school started and all those nosy teachers started sending kids home with notes that said their parents ought to get their child's eyes checked.

Alfred sighed heavily and relented, "I'll be back in two weeks. Is there anything I can do to get the paint off in the meantime?"

"Hello. Doctor Heinkel's Office," the receptionist pushed her smile into a shooing expression and waved to Alfred. "Yes, we have your glasses ready for you. Will you be in tonight to pick them up? We'll be open 'til five. Alright. Goodbye."

The receptionist's smile disappeared as she turned back to the man at her counter, "Mr. Fluffelmuffel—"

"Please, call me Alfred," Alfred said with masked annoyance.

"Mr. Alfred—"

The phone's shrill ring split the quiet office again.

"I can't help you anymore with your glasses. If you need to clean them to satisfy yourself, use some of your wife's window cleaner." Her voice shifted to cheery and sweet as she greeted the caller.

Alfred stuffed his hands in his pockets and crossed the beige tiles to the door. He needed lenses nearly twice as strong as the ones he had. The doctor had assured him he could still drive without fear of being slammed by the police, but he couldn't stop thinking about the incident in the church parking lot. Sure, he'd been upset and all, but nearly running someone over was something only near-blind people did.

A haggard-looking woman bustled toward the door. She balanced a little girl on her left hip and tugged on the hand of a whining boy of about six years.

Alfred tugged the door open and held it for the woman and her children. He prepared to smile and nod in response to her thanks. She never even looked at him, though.

The boy grabbed the doorframe and wailed about catching frogs in the creek. His mother almost toppled into Alfred who reached out to keep her from striking her head on the imitation marble stand which held a potted fern.

"Keep your hands off me," the woman shrieked. "Whomever looks at a woman to lust after her commits adultery with her in his heart."

Startled, Alfred withdrew with a jerk.

The woman stumbled and spun partway around. Her daughter struck her head on the imitation marble stand. The wail and sobs that erupted from her little mouth like the lava and ash of Mt. Vesuvius, which buried Pompeii, were enough to convince Alfred that the girl was in the throes of death.

Alfred ran his hand through his hair and adjusted his glasses. He shouldn't have let go of the woman. If he had held on until she stood straight, the toddler wouldn't be dying in front of him. He deserved all the anger and ire the girl's mother and the receptionist glared at him.

The receptionist dropped the phone on her desk and rushed toward the screaming, flailing girl. Her eruption singed Alfred a second time.

"If you're going to stand there like a ninny, gawking, just show yourself out," the receptionist hissed.

Alfred sputtered but couldn't make the correct words with his mouth. He wanted to say, "I'll get some ice. Where's your ice chest?" No matter what he told his mouth to do, nothing intelligible passed his lips.

"Good day, Mr. Fitter," the receptionist glared at him as she helped the mother ease the toddler to lay in her mother's lap.

Alfred stood where he'd been buried and watched an egg of a lump form on the toddler's upper forehead. It wasn't nearly as gruesome as the towers that formed on the cartoons' heads when they beat each other up, but the sight of the little girl's helplessness and agony weighed his head to the floor.

"I said *good day*, Mr. Filcher," the receptionist snapped.

Why were they so angry at *him*? The six-year-old boy, the real perpetrator, stood still and stared with an open mouth from six feet away. He was clearly not remorseful in the least. He probably just wanted his sister to stop crying so he could go catch his precious frogs.

The mother knelt on the entry rug, rocking her little bundle of calming toddler. The girl hardly sobbed as her mother leaned over her, murmuring and kissing her cheeks.

Alfred passed a hand over his face and tried to be angry at the women. Normally, it would have been easy to see how they were in the wrong, but today, he couldn't shake the feeling that he had been the one to hurt the innocent, little girl. If he hadn't grabbed the toddler's mother, the mother would have stumbled further into the office instead of bashing the little girl's head against the imitation marble. He had caused the accident. By grabbing the doorframe, the little boy was acting only as he normally did, so the mother had to have been able to handle him. She hadn't needed any assistance from him.

He adjusted his glasses and blew out an exasperated breath. Where was all the paint coming from? A new smudge ran across the left-hand lens. It started at the bridge of his nose and sliced the lens nearly in half. It was thin, like the line where he signed his name for the stronger pair of glasses, but it may as well have been a railroad spike driven into his eye and out the back of his skull.

He was falling apart. That was the only explanation for all the mishaps and the way he couldn't seem to say the right things to Clarabelle anymore. Oh, and, for that matter, Barbara was on another planet. No, that didn't sound right. He, Alfred, was the one who had jumped on one of those experimental rockets that picture films showed landing on foreign worlds where the earthlings ran for their lives as they were hunted by mechanical monsters and villainous reptiles.

Alfred tore his glasses from his face, rubbed his eyes and rubbed his glasses with his shirt. He was so intent on eliminating the smudges that he didn't see the car in front of him.

With a little, feminine-sounding cry of surprise he tumbled forward on top of the fender. His toe caught beneath the white walled tires, and pain shot into his shin.

Gasping, he pushed both palms against the car's hood and struggled unsteadily to stand.

"My God, man, are you drunk? It's not even ten in the morning," a man's clipped voice sounded from the car.

Alfred smiled and waved without making eye contact with the driver. He reached for his glasses. They'd miraculously taken up residence right in the center of the hood as if the car wore them as a secondary hood ornament.

He would have sworn he felt heat radiating from his red face with his hand as he pushed the black frames into place.

The car drove off, and Alfred limped to his car. He threw the door open, climbed in and slumped over the steering wheel.

Could the day possibly get better? He knew it most certainly could get a whole lot worse. Yet, maybe, just maybe, he could turn his space rocket around and return to earth.

Chapter 7

Alfred arrived home late that afternoon. Clarabelle met him at the door, a worried look on her face.

"Is everything shipshape?" she asked.

"What?" Alfred replied absently. "Oh, yeah. I stopped at the doctor before work this morning. Had to work a little late."

"Dinner's been getting cold for the past half hour, but I'll warm it up for you," Clarabelle gave a tug at his tie to loosen it. "You didn't phone to let me know."

Alfred didn't catch the strain in her voice as she told Barbara to take her needlework to her room. He was too tired to remove his tie the rest of the way. It flopped onto the table when he sat, and his wife tucked it against his chest before she sat across from him.

"How bad is it?" she asked.

"How bad is what?" Alfred responded. His mind seemed stuck in low gear. He smelled the roast beef and potatoes steaming on the plate in front of him, but he couldn't get his hand to pick up the fork.

"What happened?   You didn't have a doctor's appointment today, and you don't seem entirely alright."

Alfred watched his fingers grip the fork and slide underneath the creamy potatoes. The dollop of gravy flowed onto the plate as he lifted the bite halfway. "I'm tired, I guess," he said in explanation.

Mrs. Featherbomb placed a hand on his arm, "Something's eating you, and if you're about to flip your lid, well, I just want to know what's going on."

Alfred hesitated. The hand on his arm reminded him of how his mother used to try to calm him. It never worked very well. He took the bite and talked around it, "Went to the eye doctor is all."

"Oh," Mrs. Featherbomb sat back in her chair with a miffed air. "It has been a while since we've gone. Are they getting new glasses for you?"

"I can see just fine," Alfred muttered with a scowl. "What do you use on the windows?"

"Pardon?" Mrs. Featherbomb patted her hair.

"To clean the windows," Alfred forked another bite and talked around it. "What do you use?"

"I keep a pretty good house, sire. It's not as prim and hoity toity as some of those in the Heights, but, well, I'd have to have more to work with."

"I'm not talking about the way you keep the house," Alfred grunted in frustration. This woman could take anything and turn it into a plea for bigger, better, more expensive stuff. The kinds of things the pastor said showed the love of money. "I want to give my glasses a good cleaning."

"For whatever for?" Mrs. Featherbomb peered intently at his glasses. "They're clean as a whistle. Not a speck on them. Not even a fingerprint. You're so uptight about them, you'll never be called supermurgitroid."

Alfred fumed quietly while his wife slid her chair back and rose from the table.

"What the—"

His wife cut him off, "No cussing, darling. Please."

"That's not even a word," Alfred grumbled. He didn't want to continue the conversation. He knew he would never win. He shoveled a huge bite and choked once on it. "It sounds like some sort of disease."

"I heard some of the girls, Barbara's friends at school, use it. It was rather a compliment," Mrs. Featherbomb smiled and poured a glass of water. "You needn't worry yourself. You'd never catch it if it were a disease."

Alfred dropped his fork and froze. The anger that blossomed like an atom bomb fell like ashy snow around the chill that crept up his shoulders and down his back. Truly he wasn't seeing what he thought he saw. There was no way. No logical explanation.

He passed his hand in front of his glasses. The thing continued.

Snatching the glasses from his face, Alfred breathed hard and fast. He felt his pulse skyrocket as he rubbed his eyes. Then, he stared at his glasses. The left lens had a new streak forming right before his eyes.

"Alfred? Al?" his wife asked sharply. "Are you okay?"

Alfred didn't glance at her. He blinked and rubbed his eyes. Next, he tried looking out the kitchen window, but the same smudge formed in the lower, lefthand corner. He leaned back, and his hands fell limply to the table.

"Alfred," Mrs. Featherbomb shrieked. "What's going on? Are you having a heart attack?"

Barbara rushed in and froze. "Mom," she called unsteadily, "what's wrong with dad?"

"Call nine-one-one," Mrs. Featherbomb ordered.

Barbara spun, ripped the phone from its receiver and flung the dial to the right numbers.

Mrs. Featherbomb grabbed Alfred's hands and pulled them from the gravy-filled plate. Carefully, she dabbed them clean.

"Look at the window," Alfred said in a strained whisper. "Don't you see it?"

"Alfred. Alfred Featherbomb, you stay right here with me.   There are no angels coming through the kitchen window."

Alfred heard his daughter give their address in a tight, terrified voice. He tried to shake his head. He had to stop the emergency responders before they came to the house. He shuddered as he thought of the neighbors visiting and having to tell each one that he wasn't sick and hadn't had a heart attack.

But then again, what if he *was* having a heart attack? Did people have strange hallucinations as their heart stopped?

"Thanks, sweetheart," Mrs. Featherbomb said to their daughter. "Now, get the aspirin from the medicine cabinet."

Why could no one else see it? He wanted to close his eyes, tell himself he was looney and then open his eyes and not see the word that appended itself to the window.

No, that wasn't it. Words didn't write themselves. Some brat or neighborhood bully had taken it on himself to take on a target larger than himself. Alfred simply hadn't seen the hand clutching the brush or maybe the brush had been tied to a stick. Maybe the stress from the Mexican showing up was just making him see things. That had to be it.

With a start that sent his wife falling into her chair, Alfred pushed himself to his feet. As he strode toward the kitchen window, he mashed his glasses back in place.

He stopped.

Mrs. Featherbomb shrieked, "You're supposed to stay calm."

His quivering hand reached up and slowly peeled his glasses from his face. However the brat had managed to write the word on the kitchen window, he had also smeared it onto his lenses.

"What's wrong with you?" Mrs. Featherbomb demanded. "You should be sitting down or, for heaven's sake, lie down, Alfred. Alfred!"

"Mom?" Barbara's lips quivered, causing her voice to oscillate. "Is dad alright, mom?"

"We'll know soon enough, Barbara," Clarabelle returned flatly. "Alfred, what's all this about. You've given me the gringles, and you're scaring Barbara."

"Don't you see it?" Alfred uttered in a voice caught somewhere between existence and fantasy. A keen-eared listener might have stated that his voice possessed a winged quality that allowed it to flutter out of its cage and into the mist of a crashing waterfall. "It's right there on the window."

"What I see is a man making a fool of himself. Barbara, tell the ambulance we don't need them."

But it was too late. A siren gave its final wail in their driveway, and heavy footsteps pounded to their door.

Barbara let them in and then stepped into the nook created by the refrigerator to watch. Her father didn't take his eyes from the window—not even as the responders backed him into the chair he had vacated in his dazed madness.

Alfred sat heavily. The medics peeled open his shirt and inspected him with probing fingers and cold instruments. All the while, they pummeled Mrs. Featherbomb for information on his condition.

"He said he went to the doctor this morning before work," she recited. "He didn't have an appointment that I knew of, and he came home late and started asking about cleaning solutions."

"That ain't gonna bake a biscuit," the younger of the two responders commented as he counted Alfred's pulse.

Alfred tried to raise his arm to point to the window, but his arm was pulled down and pressed to his lap.

"Don't you see it?" he asked in the same dazed, lost voice as before.

"Mr. Flutterbum, you just live up to your name now and calm down," the younger responder crooned. "You've all the signs of a panic attack. Mrs. Flutterbum will have the windows clean in a jiffy, I'm sure."

"No," Alfred strained his voice, "she can't see it. Can't you see it?"

He was growing frustrated that no one else could see the word that he could read plain as day. Then, a thought took shape in his mind, deep, deep down in the deepest, blackest part of his mind. He chuckled silently as he realized it sounded like something Dr. Seuss would write about the Grinch. What if they were all joined against him? What if they could see it just as well as he could, but claimed they couldn't?

"Now, Mr. Flutterbum, we've all seen monsters under the bed when we we're scared." The responder folded up his stethoscope and laid it gently into his bag. Running his fingers through his hair he added, "I haven't been the same since the war either, and now, all this stuff with Korea and the Soviets has me livin' in gringlesville.

"I took a chunk of shrapnel to my leg on the Hornet. Lost a bunch of good boys to those Japs and their bombs."

Alfred watched the mistiness retreat from the man's eyes as he forced the memories of naval warfare from his mind. He hadn't joined the military. He'd managed to obtain a religious deferment and had used his extensive knowledge of finances to help run a soil conservation project for the government. After what he'd seen happen to his father when he came home from the Great War, he'd been angry and fearful of the World War.

"Where did you serve?" the responder asked.

"I d-didn't," Alfred answered. He looked down at the floor and felt his pulse rise.

"Why not, man? Nothing's wrong with you except nerves right now."

"I d-didn't serve," Alfred said again.

The responder slid his hands off his hips and picked up his bag while the other responder talked with Mrs. Featherbomb.

"Give him tonic and something stiff like brandy and humor him. Cleaning the window will help calm his nerves," Alfred overheard.

"And what about me?" Mrs. Featherbomb asked. "I feel a bit frayed thinking about how long this fit of imagination might last."

A bird darted across the view from the kitchen window. Alfred glanced up and froze, then he shouted, "No, I'm not. You rascals stop writing on my window. I'm not a coward."

Strong arms wrapped around him. He struggled momentarily and then let the responders shuffle him out of his house and into the ambulance.

Through the dark fog in his mind, he heard one of them tell his wife, "We'll take him in, get him calmed down and have him back in a jiff."

"Dad? Dad? Mom, what's going on?" Barbara ran after him.

"Hold up there, dolly," the younger responder said. "Your dad's gonna be alright."

Of course he was alright. They were the ones pretending not to see what he could see. Vaguely, he wondered why they were trying to make him flip his lid. He wanted to call out to his daughter and comfort her, but wasn't she in on the scheme too?

"Mom, why are they taking dad? Is he gonna be alright?" Barbara's voice reached a wail.

Alfred couldn't hear his wife's response. The ambulance doors slammed shut with finality. He lay on the stretcher and let cold and heat take turns washing over him.

Chapter 8

Nutter

That's what the window said when he opened his eyes after rubbing them for the fourth time. Alfred sat at the kitchen table, his coffee and the morning paper forgotten. Mr. Carter had looked at him quizzically. Alfred had lifted the paper in a wave and ducked inside before Mr. Carter's boys could explode out of his house and drill for oil in his trip to the hospital.

Alfred crossed the kitchen and lifted the curtain further to the side. Mrs. Featherbomb had drawn them in hopes that he wouldn't panic again.

Coward

It glared back at him. He didn't even feel a shred of warmth from the anger he wanted to wash through him. He *was* a nutter and a cowardly draft dodger. All those boys who had gone to war to fight were braver than him. His mouth curled with a sardonic smile. Most of them probably had fathers who had fought in the Great War as well.

Mrs. Featherbomb nudged Alfred's arm and grasped the curtain, gently tugging it back into place. "I'll have your blazer ready in a jiff. It's too bad it's going to be a stormy day."

Alfred silently stepped across the kitchen and sank into his chair at the table. Mrs. Featherbomb was acting as if nothing had happened. He decided to play along.

"Yes. I'll try not to wrinkle it," he said somewhat absently.

Alfred scanned through the classified ads. Someone had run the red heifer ad again. He thought to himself how silly it seemed. Israel had only just been recognized as a nation a couple of years ago. He froze. Hadn't Pastor Meyers said something about Israel becoming free and established in the end times? What if what he was experiencing was part of the end times judgment, and he was being judged early?

Barbara breezed into the kitchen, sliding on her socks.

"Sweetheart, don't slide like that on the floor," came Mrs. Featherbomb's rebuke. "You'll wear a hole in your socks."

"I haven't gotten one yet, mom," Barbara retorted. As she reached for a glass, she saw Alfred for the first time. "Dad," her voice held a slight squeak. "Are you feeling better?"

Alfred let his face slip into a brief frown, "Yes, I'm feeling quite alright." He looked down and then peered at his daughter, "What are you doing today, Sweet Pea?"

"Dad," Barbara said in exaggerated frustration. She seemed to change her mind and said, "Just don't call me that around my friends."

Alfred blinked and gave a slow nod.

"Donna said her parents let her buy a new record. I'm going to her house so she can show it to me."

Alfred took a sip of his coffee and beheld his daughter.

"What's wrong with that, dad?" Barbara asked, eyes narrowing. "You really can be such a square like mom says."

Alfred's coffee mug hovered in midair. He wanted to retort and negate what his daughter had said, but he could do nothing but blink.

"Mom," Barbara called, apprehensively backing away, "I think it's happening again. Something's wrong with dad."

Mrs. Featherbomb's muffled voice rang down the hallway, "I'll be there in a jiff. Make sure he doesn't fall and hit his head."

Barbara stopped inching away.

Alfred felt his eye twitch. Two smudges darkened his vision. Staring back at his daughter, he snatched his glasses. Coffee showered him and dripped from every inch of his body, pooling on the floor around his chair.

"Mom, something's really wrong with dad," Barbara yelled, fear painting her voice.

Mrs. Featherbomb hurried in. Her daughter clutched at her as they both stared at Alfred, still sitting in his chair rubbing his glasses with a coffee-soaked shirt. He didn't look up or acknowledge them as he scrubbed furiously at the lenses.

"Alfred?" Mrs. Featherbomb's voice was slightly shaky. Alfred gave no sign that he heard. She crossed the floor, careful not to step in any coffee puddles. "Alfred, you're scaring Barbara."

Just then a rap-tap sounded on the door. Alfred crammed his glasses onto his face and shoved his chair back, standing so fast he rocked the table.

"Alfred, you're in no shape to answer the door," Mrs. Featherbomb declared. "Let me get it."

By then, Alfred was already twisting the knob. He was sure his wife was right. He must look a miserable sight, but maybe it would scare the solicitor away. He really didn't want to talk with anyone at the moment. In fact, he had just decided to not swing the door open more than the few inches it already was when he heard an accented voice.

"Hola, Señor, Como—how you and you familia?"

Alfred, realizing it was too late to pretend the wind had blown open the door, held the knob and stared at the Mexican.

The dark-skinned man stood holding the brim of his hat and peering up at him with a quizzical light in his dark brown eyes.

The Mexican murmured under his breath, "Oh, Señor tienes problemas." Louder, so that Alfred could hear and with a quick glance toward the side yard, he added, "I work this day, yes? Flowers pretty and—and cut grass. Is long, no?"

Alfred wished the man would learn to speak English. It was a brisk morning, and the cool breeze found the coffee he wore, making him shiver. As he moved his gaze around the yard, he realized black smudges blurred the grass. It probably did need to be cut.

"No," he stated flatly. He started to turn back inside then stopped and looked at the smiling Mexican, "And I don't want to see you again. Take your 'sin-yor' talk somewhere else."

"Si, Señor, I do good work. You see," the Mexican snapped his hat onto his head and with remarkable speed stepped off the porch, making for side of the garage where Alfred usually let the mower lean against the wall.

"Now see here," Alfred hollered and started out the door. He was caught by Mrs. Featherbomb, however, and stopped midstride.

"Don't you dare go outside where others can see you. They'll think I threw the coffee on you, and I'd never see the end of their contemptuous looks," she said. "It's bad enough that poor Mexican saw you. He'll probably blab it to all of his kind. They're always talking about us."

Alfred fumbled feebly, trying to push Mrs. Featherbomb's hand from his arm. "Clarabelle, I don't want him messing up the yard."

"Nonsense," Mrs. Featherbomb soothed. "He did quite a bang-up job on the flowers yesterday. I think I like having him do the gardening."

Alfred stared at the Mexican as he pushed the mower around the corner of the house. He knew his face did not hold a single happy line, but he felt powerless to displace the frown.

The Mexican grinned and doffed his hat at his employers. Mrs. Featherbomb let go of Alfred's arm and returned the wave.

Alfred rung his hands together. He was free to charge out there and demand the man return the mower and get off his lawn. The longer he thought about it though, the clammier his hands grew, and he was sure he felt a bead of sweat on his forehead.

"Come inside, dear, you need a new shirt before heading off to work," Mrs. Featherbomb grabbed Alfred's arm like an usher. "I'll see what I can do about that stain," she continued in a carefree, whimsical tone, "but I don't think there's much that can help it. Oh well, I've been looking for an excuse to go out for a bit."

"Thanks, Clarabelle," Alfred said what he knew he needed to say.

"I think I'll see if Barbara wants to go with me," Mrs. Featherbomb stated. Alfred grunted as she called into the house, "Barbara, I'm headed out. Do you want to come with me?"

Mrs. Featherbomb busied herself, putting her shoes on while Alfred clumsily undid the first button on his shirt. He marveled as he did so. His wife usually spent several minutes minimum in front of the full-length mirror choosing which shoes to wear. Apparently, she was not observing that particular ritual today.

"Barbara?" Mrs. Featherbomb called again.

"Barbara, answer your mother," Alfred snapped.

He glanced at the yard where the Mexican was grinning and nonchalantly pushing the mower. Grass clippings flew everywhere. He took a half step toward the man, then he remembered he needed to get Barbara to answer Mrs. Featherbomb so she didn't stand at the door and call into the house for minutes on end. He turned back and stepped toward the kitchen.

"She's your daughter," Mrs. Featherbomb shot at him from behind.

Alfred felt his shoulders round and anger flare behind his eyes. He needed to clean his glasses.

Light broke through the kitchen window where the curtain did not fully meet in the middle. A new smudge darkened its early morning brilliance. Several cuss words filled his mind to describe the neighborhood pranksters who were marking up his windows. Yet, what if they were right? He was feeling like he was going crazy. What if the window now said he was a nutter twice over? He ducked, hoping Mrs. Featherbomb couldn't actually hear his thoughts like it seemed she could at times.

Undoing the final button, he pulled at his shirt only then realizing he had forgotten to take his tie off first.

"Barbara," he called, hastily yanking at the rabbit that went around the tree. The tie was wet with coffee and would have to be cleaned as well. "Answer your mother, please, Barbara."

Not a single sound came from Barbara's room. Alfred sighed a growl. After he changed, he would have to see why she was ignoring her parents. A glance at his watch told him he would have to drive over the speed limit to get to work on time; no time to waltz around.

"Barbara," Mrs. Featherbomb's voice carried from the front room.

Alfred groaned. This sort of thing happened far too often. He wondered why he was always expected to run and check on Barbara when his wife stood and bellowed from another room.

He attempted to suppress the thoughts that clawed into his mind. He really did love his wife he told himself as he buttoned his new shirt, refusing to glance up at the mirror. If the bedroom mirror had black streaks, or worse, words, pop up on it, he really would go crazy. He would be a nutter without a doubt then.

"Barbara Ann," Mrs. Featherbomb called again from the front room.

"Confounded woman," Alfred muttered.

He positioned his tie and glanced up. He stepped back and caught a glimpse of his eyes growing round as he grunted and tripped over the assortment of Mrs. Featherbomb's shoes that congregated in front of the mirror like sheep in front of the pastor at church. Mrs. Featherbomb always got nearly all her shoes out to choose a pair before going out, and she never took care of them until after she came back. That is, she took care of them if Alfred didn't get annoyed with them and place them back on their shelves before she got to them.

He often wished they could go back to being at war as a country so that Mrs. Featherbomb wouldn't be able to have so many pairs. Once the war had ended, she had been so elated to be able to buy rubber-soled shoes again that she bought nearly every pair she found that fit her.

Alfred lurched over the shoes, certain he was crushing many pairs, and fell heavily onto the bed. It slid across the floor a few inches, jostling the nightstand and banging against the wall.

"Al," Mrs. Featherbomb hollered from the front room, "you better not be crushing my shoes like an oaf."

"I'm alright," Alfred called back. He wanted to yell about cleaning up after oneself and not leaving a closet full of shoes on the floor. However, what stopped him was the innumerable times he had made that same exact blunder and received such a talking to that he vowed to himself that he would never say anything again. Of course, it had taken more than a few incidents for him to learn to bite his tongue. He continued to fume as he pushed himself up from the bed.

A glint of dark-colored glass caught the light in the closet. Alfred pulled his gaze away, trying to convince himself he hadn't seen the unmistakable shape of a bottleneck. Mrs. Featherbomb was a pious woman and not given to vices. He was the one who had gotten drunk as a young adult—not Clarabelle.

The Mexican pushed the mower by the window with a whir, but that wasn't what snagged his attention. In streaky, black lettering, the word

Oaf

stared at him from the dead center of the window. He froze as his mind skidded to a halt. That was exactly what his wife had just called him.

A second word coalesced into existence—or had he simply not seen it when he noticed the first?

Sot

The new word joined the description of his clumsiness and held his gaze like an anchor holding a ship in calm weather.

"No. No. No," Alfred muttered, hands going involuntarily to his hair and raking trembling fingers through it. "It can't be. How does he know. It's that Mexican. It's that—"

"No cussing, dear," Mrs. Featherbomb's voice cut through his mind like the brutal, retina-searing flash from a nuke.

Alfred growled and tripped to the window. Franticly, he grabbed the crank, but it didn't budge. He glared out at the man mowing his yard.

The next instant he leapt over the pile of shoes with surprising agility and sprang down the hall. He would let that Mexican know just what he thought of the pranks. The short man would probably end up calling all of his relatives in the surrounding counties, and, together, they would parade back to Mexico with their tails between their legs and their greased back hair caking with dust and drying out in the unrelenting, southern sun as they sweated and panted for water in the deserts.

Alfred pressed his lips tight. He intended to give the Mexican such a fat lip that he would have to wait a whole week for it to heal before he could say "sin-yor" again. It would delay their leaving, but it would be worth it, watching the Mexican try to speak.

"Alfred, where's Barbara? She's not coming when I call," Mrs. Featherbomb ignored Alfred's glowering countenance.

"How would I know?" Alfred growled. "Maybe she left for Donna's already."

"What's gotten into you?" Mrs. Featherbomb returned as Alfred stormed past. "It was just a bit of coffee. It can all be cleaned up."

Alfred spun. He felt spittle shoot from his mouth, "Pick up your d—"

"Uh, uh, uh. No cussing, dear," Mrs. Featherbomb said calmly, patting her hair.

"Pick up your shoes and stop telling that Mexican how clumsy I am to trip over your d—"

"Oh, you really shouldn't cuss, dear. The pastor would have your hide."

Alfred's vision darkened as if a cloud were passing over the sun. It took him only a moment to realize that it was a black smudge streaking across his glasses. With a frenzy he shot his arm up to grab at the hand that must be drawing the smudge. When his hand closed on air, he spun around, crouching into a fighting stance. With his fists poised to strike, he danced in a circle.

"Really, Alfred, what are you doing?" Mrs. Featherbomb said in a detached tone.

Alfred slipped his shoes on and hastily tied them.

"I'm putting an end to this," he said, snapping his fingers and pointing into the empty air. He jumped up and stepped to the door. His shoes were lumpy in the wrong places. He stumbled and caught himself with the wall.

Mrs. Featherbomb commented unaffectedly, "Dear, you've worked yourself into such a tizzy you put your shoes on the wrong feet. That's quite an accomplishment for an *adult.*"

Heat boiled up Alfred's already steaming cheeks. He was just about to yell when he froze. There, in the bottom right corner of his glasses someone had written

Turkey oaf

"Alfred, you're behaving like someone from Weirdsville," Mrs. Featherbomb chided. "Get your act together or I'll have to have Barbara call nine-one-one. Where is that girl anyway? Barbara?"

With a burst of dexterity, Alfred swapped his shoes to the correct feet and ripped off his glasses, nearly crushing them as he swung the door aside. He flew down the steps and tore into the yard.

Before he reached the side yard where the Mexican was mowing, Alfred waved his hands and shouted, "Get off my lawn. Get out of here."

To Alfred's great consternation, the Mexican slowly came to a stop and leaned an elbow on the mower handles. A passive, unreadable look settled on his brown features. Alfred didn't stop. In an exaggerated lunge, like those in the old silent films, he grabbed the mower, yanking it away from the Mexican.

"Get out of here," Alfred bellowed.

When he was met with a slow blink of the Mexican's dark brown, almost black, eyes, he cried, "Do you understand?"

To say Alfred was disturbed by the Mexican's response would have been a bit below accurate. He had expected the man to take off running as fast as he could the moment he'd come out of the house yelling.

The Mexican blinked once more, and his expression took on a slightly pained pinch, "Tranquilo, Señor."

"I know you are," Alfred snapped, "but you won't succeed in killing me. Oh no, not with this." He shook the mower. "Or with the insults you've been writing everywhere. I've got you figured out." Alfred felt his head shaking and a dribble of spit at the corner of his mouth, but he continued, "You're trespassing. Get off my property, greaser."

Alfred watched as the man's eyebrows scrunched together as he adjusted the wide-brimmed hat shading his eyes. The man really was daft. Anyone would have been able to understand his message clearly whether he spoke any English or not.

He stepped closer to the Mexican, and, annunciating slowly, said, "Get. Off. My. Property." He raised his hand and pointed toward the road.

"Si, Señor," the Mexican said without a single hint of emotion.

"The only thing I want to see is you hightailing it down the road," Alfred growled.

"Si, Señor," the Mexican said again.

Alfred stood and spluttered nonsense as he attempted to form a new way to tell the man off—one that he would actually respond to. Where was Barbara when he needed her? She'd be able to translate his wishes into Spanish.

That reminded him, he still needed to talk with her teacher.

Wiping his forehead, Alfred looked back at the Mexican. He stood with his hat off and drinking deeply from a glass of lemonade. When he saw Alfred looking at him, he lowered the glass, swallowed and smiled broadly.

"Intiendo," he said. "Trabajo no good. I work in flowers pretty atras la casa para Señora."

Alfred followed the Mexican's gaze to see Mrs. Featherbomb standing just outside of his peripheral vision.

"Clarabelle, what are you doing?" Alfred fumed.

Mrs. Featherbomb patted her hair and replied, "He's doing such good work with the flower gardens I asked him to tend the gardens in the back of the house since he hasn't gotten to them yet, and it's obvious you're unhappy with how he's mowing." She added in a lower tone, "Though, I think he's doing quite a bang-up job. He works so hard."

Alfred refused to look at his wife as he heaved out a frustrated breath in defeat from somewhere deep inside him, "See to it that Barbara tells him he's not to come back. I don't want him here, and we don't have any work for him."

"It seems you've already told him that," Mrs. Featherbomb said, patting her hair and accepting the empty glass from the Mexican. "Besides, it doesn't seem like you want Barbara speaking Spanish."

Alfred grunted and clenched his fists. He would not lose his cool again. At the same time, he would regain the privacy of his own lawn. "Have Barbara say it in a way this buffoon will understand."

"Really, Alfred," Mrs. Featherbomb stared aghast at him.

"I don't want him here when I get back from work, and I don't want to see him again," Alfred risked a cross look at his wife as he stalked back to the house.

Chapter 9

"Good mornin', Mr. Featherbomb," Ethel, the receptionist, called as Alfred strode into the office.

"Good morning, Sunny," Alfred returned, using her popular nickname.

Ethel stood and straightened her yellow blouse. The sequined buttons reminded Alfred of a cowboy's oversized belt buckle. The young woman rounded her desk and bent toward Alfred.

Conspiratorially, she whispered, "Mr. Davis won't want you lookin' like that for the mornin's meetin'." Sunny's voice was caught somewhere between a middle-Louisiana lilt and a rapid foreign language. "Why don't you freshen up a bit before you walk in there."

"Sunny, I'm late already," Alfred fumbled with his briefcase.

He had fought traffic the whole way, and the Buick had been stifling hot. He had nearly sweated through his shirt before he realized he had bumped the heat when he put his briefcase on the passenger floorboard.

Then, he'd seen

Pathetic buffoon

form slowly on the passenger window. It had glared at him so intensely he had bumped the car in front of him at a red light. The driver had gotten out and looked ready to blow Alfred and his Buick back to where he'd come from. However, once he saw no damage had been done, he'd waved to Alfred, who hadn't been able to get out of his seat, and called, "No harm. No foul, old boy." Alfred had managed a shaky wave as the man returned to his car.

Then, the smudges started appearing on his glasses again. He'd tried to drive without them, but when he bounced onto the curb, he'd put them back on, cocking his head to see out of the cleaner sections.

Alfred came to. Sunny waved her hand in front of his face and called, "Yoohoo."

Alfred blinked, "I'm sorry. What?"

Sunny presented her cheek to him, "I said you owe me a kiss for cleanin' up after you."

Alfred brushed his hand across his face underneath his glasses. Looking down, he spied grass clippings attempting to colonize the fake tile linoleum. He shuffled uneasily. He hoped Mrs. Featherbomb would never find out about Sunny's antics.

He gave her a swift, light peck on her cheek the way everyone did if Sunny caught them messing up her floor. Mr. Davis had, after all, given her complete ownership of the reception area. Alfred glanced around glad to see nothing else had turned yellow from Sunny's interior decorating.

"There, you see. All cleaned up," Sunny swept a shortened broom and dustpan over the grass clippings before whisking the tools back under her desk.

"Thank you. I'm really sorry, Sunny," Alfred hefted his briefcase and prepared to take a step.

"Not many people mow their lawns in the mornin'. Do you have big plans tonight," Sunny asked, straightening his tie and brushing the shoulders of his jacket. It felt like something only a wife or perhaps a girlfriend should do.

Alfred batted Sunny's hands away, "I don't want to be any later."

Sunny placed her hands on her hips and gave him a wink, "Mr. Davis won't have anything to complain about," she glanced at his shoes, "at least if you don't insist on spreading mulch around his conference room."

Alfred looked down. Sure enough, grass clippings continued to release their hold on the hem of his pants and fall to the floor. Sunny knelt down, careful to keep her skirt tucked over her knees. Before Alfred could say anything, she had his pants brushed off and the clippings swept into the dustpan.

"That's another one," Sunny said, giggling as she tilted her cheek for him to kiss again. "At this rate, if you keep mowing your lawn in the mornin', I might not be able to buy enough foundation and blush."

Alfred scrubbed the back of his hand over his lips and checked it for makeup. The last thing he wanted was for Clarabelle to have a reason to suspect him of cheating. The thought had never crossed his mind, and the playful teasing Sunny gave him was what she did to all the men at the office.

Sunny laughed, "Don't be such a scrooge. Let some sunlight in."

She turned smartly and sat at her desk. Grabbing her coffee mug with both hands, she winked at Alfred again, "You smell like coffee, Mr. Featherbomb, but it's a bit bitter."

Alfred tried to retort but could think of nothing. He wasn't a scrooge, was he?

"Now," Sunny made a shooing motion, "get to your meetin'. Mr. Davis doesn't like to be kept waitin'."

Alfred stumbled into a hasty stride. One of his coworkers leaned out of his office, plucked the half-burned cigar from his teeth and whistled, "Two for Sunny. Zero for the Featherbomber. You look like she stole your sunny rays from you."

Alfred grunted, "Don't ask."

"Woah," the coworker bit his cigar and talked around it, "we got ourselves a scrooge today."

Alfred's right eye twitched. He reached up to massage the spasm away. Then it happened.

"No. No. No," he muttered as he stared in horror at his glasses. He tore them from his face, but it didn't stop what was happening.

Black smudges grew like tentacles on the lenses. The smudges contrasted with the light flooring, making them easy to see. They formed with no hand or writing utensil. What had been clear glass moments before transformed into dark, cloudy smudges like black ink brushed onto coarse paper. Alfred felt the blood drain from his face as the smudges continued to take shape. Slowly, almost like watching an airplane you know is flying fast from far away, the smudges coalesced into a word.

"God," he stopped. He could hear Mrs. Featherbomb telling him not to cuss.

Scrooge

The new insult faced him from the lenses of his glasses.

"Hey, Featherbomber, you alright?" someone called.

Alfred stood statue-still, staring at the word his glasses mocked him with. First, Sunny had told him not to be a scrooge, and then he'd been called a scrooge by Codgens.

Alfred swallowed and shakily placed his glasses back on his face.

Apparently, he *was* a scrooge.

"Something's gotten into the Feathbomber. Codgens, what'd you say to him?" Alfred heard his coworkers discussing him.

"He was being stingy with his kisses for Miss Sunny after he messed her floor up twice. Stingy like a scrooge," Codgens ground out around his cigar.

"Who wouldn't want to kiss a doll like that?"

"You just wait until she gets a man, then every kiss will cost you a black eye," Codgens let a grinding laugh loose.

"I'm gonna go ask her out," a nasally voice some would call whiny piped up.

"You asked her last week," Codgens chuckled.

"So," the whiny voice retorted.

"Miss Sunny doesn't want a whiny weasel like you. Or don't you remember how she took the flowers you gave her and whacked you upside the head?" Codgens leaned out of his office.

"Oh, I remember," whiny-voice said. "I'm still nursing the scratches. There were roses in there. Miss Sunny will go out with me...once I find what she wants to do, won't you, Sunny?"

"That's Miss Potter to you, Mr. Albright," Sunny called from the reception area.

"Sounds like I'm making progress," Mr. Albright said.

"Yeah, you are," Codgens grunted. "You'll have her swooning in your arms in no time."

Alfred yanked his glasses off with a shaking hand and scrubbed at the lenses. Nothing changed. Sweat beaded on his forehead.

"Hey, the Featherbomber's getting the zorros about talking with Mr. Davis this morning," Codgens called across the office.

Alfred shook his head, mumbling, "It's nothing. I just wish I wasn't late."

His coworkers' discussion of his behavior continued as he cleaned his glasses one more time and continued toward the huge oak door of the conference room. The nasally monotone escaping the room was undoubtedly keeping the occupants so captivated they wouldn't notice him slip in. He sighed and pushed the left-hand door.

"What? Did the paper boy run you over or something?" Mr. Davis grunted out of the corner of his mouth as Alfred found an empty seat.

All eyes were on him. He swallowed, shoving his briefcase under the table. "My apologies, gentlemen," he said, trying to sound nonchalant.

The speaker rambled on about line item five. Mr. Davis leaned over to Alfred, "It's a real doozy. If you don't fall asleep in here, I want you to research item three."

Mr. Orton, who sat between Mr. Davis and Alfred spun a document toward Alfred and pointed to the item.

"And while you're at it," Mr. Davis continued, "see if you can find this guy a music teacher. The only note he can hit is E flat."

Hardly able to wrap his mind around what his boss was asking him to do, Alfred stared at his glass lenses certain that another word would show up at any second. And so, it was with crossed eyes that he looked at Mr. Orton to see how he should react. Mr. Orton was grinning and nodding his head with Mr. Davis, but when he saw Alfred, he elbowed Mr. Davis, pointed to Alfred's eyes and let out an audible chuckle.

Mr. Davis flung himself back in his chair and laughed silently but deeply. "Alfred," he reached around Mr. Orton to cuff Alfred's shoulder, "you're alright, man."

Alfred propped his glasses up and rubbed his eyes with thumb and forefinger. More laughter ensued. He knew they weren't necessarily laughing at him but at his coincidental reactions to their discussion. He felt his face start to burn all the same, and he was too scared to let his glasses fall back into place.

The way he felt must certainly ensure another word was forming. How was the Mexican doing it? He must have used some sort of invisible ink that became visible with heat. But when had he had access to Alfred's glasses? Alfred concentrated hard on recounting to himself every place he had left his glasses out of his sight. He couldn't rule out the man entering his house while he slept either.

"The Featherbomber didn't make it," Mr. Orton's voice intruded on Alfred's careful recollections. A few others joined Mr. Orton in a chuckle.

"I don't blame him," chimed in the voice of Mr. Radcliffe.

Alfred opened his eyes he hadn't realized he'd closed and wiped at them. With a sinking feeling, he felt his glasses fall back into place. Shielding his glasses from view with his hand, he peeked his eyes open. Another word stared back at him. It matched how foolish he felt at having appeared to have fallen asleep during the presentation. Just reading the insult made Mrs. Featherbomb's reminder not to cuss play in his head.

He pulled his glasses off and rubbed the bridge of his nose, hoping he appeared at least somewhat normal. He didn't want to feel any more conspicuous or foolish, like the idiot the new word on his glasses called him in different words. He wondered how the Mexican even knew that word and how he had managed to get it to show up at the exact time he was turning red with shame at appearing to be a nutjob.

"You alright, Alfred?" Mr. Davis asked quietly.

Alfred nodded and kept rubbing his nose. "My glasses are just hurting my nose."

Mr. Davis replied in a half mutter, "These plastic frames aren't as comfortable as the old wire ones, but progress is progress. They'll figure it out."

Alfred nodded, enthusiastic that his boss was willing to understand.

"Look who must be cozying up to the big man," Mr. Orton joked. The room erupted in laughter.

Mr. Davis turned and addressed his subordinates, "Now listen up you gorillas, it's time we got back to work. The morning's been enough of a bust already. I may have to send Sunny for a new record player to help me recover my ears."

The room laughed again. Then, they filed out. Conversations about various work topics sprang up as coworkers coagulated by the projects they were on together.

Alfred, who was not part of a group project, retreated quickly to his office, sat at his desk and began energetically cleaning his glasses.

At long last, he gave it up and stepped out of his office. His right hand rose immediately to remove his glasses. He couldn't let anyone else see what the Mexican called him. It wasn't true, after all, was it? He doubled back, practically diving behind his desk.

He looked at the stack of mail on the far, left corner of his desk. He needed to open the letters and sort out the important ones. He wrung his hands together and reached for his glasses. The words were still there plain as day. His hands shook as he redirected them to reach for the letters.

His hands fell to the edge of his desk. He gripped it with white knuckles. Alfred glanced out the window by the door with wide eyes. No one seemed to be watching him. He breathed in relief. He had to keep what the Mexican had done a secret.

But he also needed to clean his glasses.

Alfred picked up his cleaning cloth and scrubbed the lenses vigorously. Nothing changed. He started to swear but stopped when he heard Mrs. Featherbomb telling him, "No cussing, dear. It wouldn't do for Barbara to copy you. I don't want to be alone in heaven."

Alfred froze. He had sworn and cussed like some of the best—or was it worst?—of them as a teenager, hiding it from his parents. Did that mean he was a heathen? Was he destined for Hell?

His right forefinger twitched and then spasmed uncontrollably. Making the best fist he could, he crammed his malfunctioning finger against his jaw and closed his eyes. He still could not conceive how the Mexican had done it, but somehow, he knew that when he opened his eyes, he would see that the Mexican had anticipated this very moment and written another word in invisible ink that materialized at just the right moment.

He needed to open his eyes though. If he kept them closed, not only would he not get any work done but he would also appear to be sleeping or, with all the uncontrollable twitching, someone might think he was having a seizure or a mental breakdown. Or, what if they thought he was having a heart attack like Mrs. Featherbomb had done and called the emergency responders to look him over? He really wasn't keen on the idea of having two medical interventions in as many days.

Alfred positioned himself upright in his chair and prepared for what he was sure to see. Blowing out his breath in an attempt to calm his nerves, he opened his eyes a sliver at a time. Nothing peered accusatorily back at him, nothing new leastways.

He breathed deep. He had escaped the Mexican's ink this time. The foreign man hadn't anticipated this after all. He turned to glance out the window to make sure none of his coworkers had seen his instability.

His gaze never left his office.

On the window beside the door in big, black letters that looked smeared on by a giant paint brush a new word glared back at him. He whimpered and ducked his head. Sweat beaded above his eyebrows, his heart raced and blood drained from his extremities. Fight or flight kicked in in full force. One desperate need dominated his thoughts. His coworkers could not see the word. He would be ruined if anyone knew how the Mexican described him.

The Mexican. He *had* anticipated this after all, and he had already been here before Alfred got to work. The man was a hard worker Alfred had to admit, but why was he working so hard to ruin him?

None of that mattered at the moment. Alfred jumped from his chair but, thinking better of attracting so much attention to himself, slowed to a hasty walk as if he were calm and collected but still had an important task.

Sunny kept her reception room spotless. She would know which cleaners to use. Of course, he would probably have to kiss her cheek ten times or so for her help. He needed some real help though. Nothing he had tried so far had worked on his glasses or the windows in his house. He strode to Sunny's desk.

She was just placing the phone on its receiver when he walked in.

"Well, I'll be," she said with her hand moving to cover her surprised gape. Then she hopped up and took Alfred's arm, making as if to sit him down in one of the waiting chairs. "Are you unwell, Mr. Featherbomb?"

Alfred let himself be guided to a chair. "I," he paused as he realized he didn't know what he was going to say. Sunny wasn't much of a gossip despite her personality and appearance, yet he could not let on that someone was out to make him go insane by writing words on his glasses and windows. He ripped his glasses off and blinked at Sunny, hoping she hadn't seen the words smeared there.

"I broke a pen and can't get the ink cleaned off the window in my office. What do you use to keep it so clean out here?" Alfred gathered himself hurriedly.

"Is that all, Mr. Featherbomb," Sunny placed her hands on her hips and then threw one palm up in the air as she grinned. "I'll help you grab the supplies." She cocked her head and stifled a giggle, "The way you looked, I thought one of those buffoons, Mr. Codgens or Mr. Orton, must have put somethin' a bit bigger than a thumbtack in your chair."

"N—no, ma'am," Alfred stammered.

"Well, c'mon," Sunny reached for his hand.

She led him to the janitor's closet. Pulling out an unlabeled bottle with a spray nozzle, she said, "Use this. It's powerful stuff so don't let it sit on anything longer than a few seconds. You have a clean cloth, don't you?"

When Alfred didn't nod his head or reply right away, she took out a stepstool and reached to the top shelf. A white towel fluttered onto Alfred's head, covering his eyes.

"Catch me," Sunny called in mock urgency.

Alfred held out his arms. Sunny stepped off the stepstool. Her foot landed on his own, and she tipped backward. Alfred compensated by leaning the other way. He wished the towel wasn't disrupting his vision. He wanted to make sure Sunny wasn't going to hit her head on anything, and the towel smelled of chemicals.

"Well," Sunny breathed heavily. "You can put me down now."

Alfred tried to move his foot so he could place her gently on the floor. Her foot, however, remained firmly planted on top of his. If he let go of her, he would fall. He didn't want to appear weak, but what could he do?

"Miss Potter?" Mr. Albright asked in confusion. "Are you—are you trying to put the moves on the Featherbomber?"

Alfred felt Sunny twist in his arms. Now, he was thankful for the cloth and hoped it covered every inch of his reddening face.

"Mr. Albright," Sunny gasped. "This isn't what it looks like. I ain't tryna put the moves on Mr. Featherbomb. He asked me for help cleaning some ink up in his office. I slipped off the stepstool, and he caught me."

She lifted her foot off Alfred's, allowing him to move his feet without toppling over.

"If you say so, Sun—I mean, Miss Potter," Mr. Albright said unconvinced.

"You have everything you need, Mr. Featherbomb," Sunny said, brushing his blazer back into its pristine lines. "Would you be a flutter bum and close the closet up?" Then to Mr. Albright she said haughtily, "I'll let you escort me back to my desk."

"Of course, Sun—I mean, Miss Potter," the elation in Mr. Albright's voice was as thick as the whipped topping used in ambrosia salad.

Alfred reached up to pull the towel from his face.

"Working late I see, Mr. Ashley," Mr. Davis's voice boomed behind Alfred. "Keep up the good work. I don't have a single complaint. How's the wife and boy doing? How old is he again? Two or was it three?"

"Pardon me, sir," Alfred squeezed out as he pulled the cloth off his face along with his glasses.

"Oh, it's you, Mr. Featherbomb. I mistook you for Mr. Ashley," Mr. Davis explained unnecessarily. "What are you doing? Moonlighting as a janitor?"

"No, sir," Alfred said. "I broke a pen and came here for something to clean the ink up."

"You're alright, Mr. Featherbomb, I like when a man can admit he made a mess and sets to cleaning it up himself." Mr. Davis glanced toward the reception area, "Did you notice if Sunny was busy on your way over here?"

Alfred shook his head, "Well, I mean she helped get the cleaner and headed back to her desk."

"Thank you," Mr. Davis said, stepping around Alfred and the stepstool.

Relief flooded Alfred's body, making him feel weak. Mr. Davis hadn't asked him about his glasses, and he hadn't shown any signs of having seen what was written on Alfred's office window.

Feeling like a cartoon character with extraordinarily long, melty arms, he clumsily stuffed the stepstool back into the closet and took off for his office.

He kept his head down and muttered under his breath, "Don't see it. Don't see it."

The smeared word didn't come off from the inside. Alfred sprayed and scrubbed and sprayed and scrubbed. The cloth became soaked with the cleaner. He knew Sunny would be worried of it dripping onto the floor or the windowsill, but he had to get the word off before anyone else saw it.

In frustration he turned from the window and spun once in front of his desk. That was it he realized. It would have been far easier to write the word on the window from the outside.

In a flurry of motion that upset the topmost papers on his desk, Alfred flung the door open and jumped out. His hand was already moving in scrubbing circles before the cloth touched the glass. He scrubbed vigorously and used half the bottle of cleaner.

"No, this can't be. What kind of ink did he use?" Alfred murmured as sweat dribbled down his nose and forehead. His hands were clammy, and the armpits of his undershirt were soaked. Still the word persisted.

"Featherbomber?" Mr. Codgens asked from behind.

Alfred would have cussed right then and there, but he heard Mrs. Featherbomb tell him not to cuss. He jerked upright and spun to look at his coworker, hoping he had the word hidden behind him.

"Are you taking over Ashley the Vampire's job? It might suit you if you didn't spend so much time on one window," Mr. Codgens chuckled. "Can't you see how clean it is? If you scrub it anymore, you'll have a mail slot instead of a window."

Alfred's heart sank. His frenzied work had been pointless. Everyone would see what the Mexican had called him.

"Can't you take a little teasing, Featherbomber?" Mr. Codgens playfully punched Alfred's shoulder. "Albright," Mr. Codgens called to the man as he walked by.

"What? Hmm?" Mr. Albright said listlessly.

"What do you make of this window?"

Alfred wished he could slither away like a snake and hide under his desk until his coworkers left for the day. Maybe he would just be fired. He didn't know how Mr. Davis would react when he was shown, but he knew it wouldn't be good.

"It's the cleanest window I've ever seen," Mr. Codgens continued. "But if the Featherbomber here keeps at it, he'll dissolve it right into a hole in the wall, won't he?"

"Maybe," Mr. Albright replied with only a cursory glance at the window.

"Say," Mr. Codgens' tone changed, "isn't Sunny wearing bright red lipstick today or did she give it all to you?"

"What makes you say that?" Mr. Albright wiped at his bright red lips.

"She full on kissed you, didn't she?" Mr. Codgens accused.

Mr. Albright's eyes lit with fear, and he made to back away. Mr. Codgens grasped his arm before he could flee and turned to Alfred, "Good job on that window, Featherbomber. Would you do mine next?"

Shaking Mr. Albright and lifting his arm up like a prize fighter, Codgens called in a subdued shout, "Gentlemen and lady," he glanced at Sunny where she leaned against the door frame leading from the reception area, "we have ourselves a winner. The illustrious Miss Ethel 'Sunny' Potter has pledged her love to Mr. Bright-as-a-Light-Albright! May we have a round of applause."

Sunny laughed and grinned at Mr. Albright's embarrassment, but to the whoops and cheers of the whole office she strode up to Mr. Albright, grasped his cheeks with her hands and deposited her freshly reapplied lipstick onto his lips and then smacked a giant kiss mark on his cheek.

Mr. Davis elbowed Alfred, who hadn't heard his boss walk up. "It's good to see them finally getting together, isn't it? They danced around one another so long I thought I was going to have to bring my wife in to set them straight. Great job on the window by the way."

Chapter 10

"None of them could even see it," Alfred told Clarabelle.

"Well, it sounds like they were pretty distracted by that girl kissing, what'd you say his name is? Lightbulb?" Mrs. Featherbomb brushed Alfred's concerns aside as she pried further to hear the story of Sunny and Mr. Albright again.

"Albright," Alfred corrected halfheartedly. He then proceeded to explain again how no one else had commented about the word on his office window.

"Really, dear, please don't start bringing all that up again. It's just like the kitchen window. You claim someone wrote on it, but there's nothing there. You're just seeing things and scaring Barbara in the process. Do you know how long it took me to find her?" Mrs. Featherbomb patted her hair and rose from the table. "Besides," she said morosely as she fingered a plate drying on the counter, "what will I do if you have another panic attack when we have guests. They'll think my husband is looney, and they'll stay away."

Alfred could see he would get no sympathy. Mrs. Featherbomb had a point. No one else seemed to be able to see what he could. That meant they were all in it together, or he really was looney. He would have to be more careful with whom he told, and he really needed to figure out something that could remove the words and smears.

That was it! He needed to hire professional cleaners, say he needed to keep an eye on them while they worked and discover what they used on the windows. It was genius. He would be free.

"Alfred?" Mrs. Featherbomb interrupted his thoughts. "You never did ask where I found your daughter."

If he hadn't been so preoccupied, Alfred would have known to tread carefully with Mrs. Featherbomb's calling Barbara *his* daughter. He could add "inattentive" to the list of ways he failed as a husband and a father.

He shook his head and grunted, "Where?"

"Well, she and Donna apparently got Joey Chadelle to drive them into town to buy tickets—"

"Joey Chadelle?" Alfred asked, making sure he had heard correctly.

"Yes, stop interrupting me. That's not the worst part. Anyway—"

"But he's barely old enough to drive, and he just got his driver's license," Alfred's anger boiled at the foolish and unsafe choice his daughter had made. "Doesn't she know we don't want her taking chances like that. What if Joey wrecked with them in the car?"

"I was trying to say," Mrs. Featherbomb placed her hands on her hips, "that Donna and Barbara convinced Joey Chadelle to drive them into town so they could buy tickets to see some new artist. Elvin or Elves, something like that, Presley."

"Elvis?" Alfred asked.

"Yes, that's it," Mrs. Featherbomb patted her hair. "Elvis Presley."

"I've heard of him," Alfred stated, deep in thought.

Mrs. Featherbomb's eyes narrowed, "How do you know about him?"

"I don't think there's any harm," Alfred waved his hand. "I will have to talk with Joey Chadelle's parents though. He shouldn't be driving young girls around. He needs more experience behind the wheel."

"How do you know about Elvis Presley?" Mrs. Featherbomb demanded. "As soon as I heard, I called a few of my friends to get their impressions. I must say, that Elvis Presley is repulsive."

Alfred grunted to himself. He had learned over the years that talking with a few friends meant she had called no less than twenty women, both friends and acquaintances from church, and talked with them, sharing all sorts of legitimate and illegitimate facts, until each woman had gotten riled up and said they agreed with her.

"You really must have a talk with *your* daughter," Mrs. Featherbomb said tersely.

The list of people Alfred needed to have a talk with was growing long indeed. He would have to start writing the names down and checking them off, otherwise he would most definitely forget someone.

"He has drums in his music," Mrs. Featherbomb said as if the statement would shatter the earth or at least the kitchen table. "And we all know what the Heavenly Father thinks of that." She placed her hand on Alfred's shoulder and continued in a lamenting tone, "All those young people heading straight to the gates of Hell."

Alfred grunted his agreement, but he also wanted to scoff by pointing out that Korea was referred to as such as well.

"So," Mrs. Featherbomb added, "no more nonsense about words showing up on windows or your glasses. No one else has been able to see them, so you must be making it up for some reason. Besides," she pulled Alfred's glasses off and peered through them at the light, "your glasses are the cleanest I've ever seen them, dear.

"Let's focus on the things that matter. I won't have your daughter making these lousy choices. Devil music and bad boys, she's going to make me flip my lid, and the Good Lord help me."

She pushed his glasses back onto his face, but they tilted down like those of the old librarian who wore hers on a beaded string when she didn't have them perched on the tip of her nose. Alfred adjusted them with a familiar backhand nudge.

He was about to make a reply to his wife when he caught sight of the kitchen window.

Crazy ape

stared back at him, mocking him and proclaiming his insanity to the world. How could Mrs. Featherbomb not see it? Why did everyone else pretend it didn't exist?

Only one answer made sense to him. Indeed, only one answer could explain it. He was an ape gone nutty. No doubt could dispel the simple fact that he was going mad. His actions with the Mexican all but proved it. How could he have made such a spectacle of himself in his own yard? Then, he had proceeded to track all those grass clippings into Sunny's pristine reception area. Not to mention, he had made a fool of himself at the meeting afterward. Everyone at work had every right to call him mad. No, everyone at work did call him mad. That's why they'd nicknamed him "The Featherbomber." It wasn't a term of endearment or of camaraderie. It was an observation of the truth.

"And you'll be over this," Mrs. Featherbomb was wrapping up something Alfred hadn't paid attention to, "this attention-seeking in time to have a normal dinner with the Larsons after church this Sunday?"

Alfred reached up to adjust his glasses. No one believed him. No one would believe him. His hand trembled, and he ended up shoving the glasses to the side of his face. He felt Mrs. Featherbomb's stern eyes on him as he pushed his glasses up and wiped at his eyes.

"Yes. Yes, of course," Alfred shuddered, pressing his hands firmly against the table so their shaking wouldn't be seen. Under his breath he added, "Just gotta keep that—"

"No cussing, dear. I hear you whispering under your breath," Mrs. Featherbomb chided.

The infernal woman. He couldn't take care of his yard the way he wanted, nor could he make a truthful observation about the foreigner his wife had hired to take his place.

Mrs. Featherbomb stepped behind Alfred and rubbed his shoulders. "You've been under a lot of stress with the buyout or merger or whatever it is that you're doing for Mr. Davis. Maybe you should take a day off and go fishing, or Barbara and I can say you had a work event scheduled—that they already bought tickets for Sunday afternoon that couldn't be missed. You could go fishing then while Barbara and I go to the Larsons."

A million letters floated and swirled in Alfred's mind. Everything his wife had said about being under stress at work was true, but did she even know what hobby he indulged in? Finally, the letters formed words and fell from his tongue.

"Clarabelle, I don't fish, and I never have. I golf," he said, cringing with how each word sounded like a harsh reprimand.

Without missing a beat, but with a notable withdrawing of her hands and an audible huff, Mrs. Featherbomb replied in an arrogantly aristocratic tone, "Oh, is that what you call it? I heard you spend so much time fetching your balls out of the water that you would put a whole fleet of fisherman out of business if you carried a net with you."

Alfred's anger flared. He was not that bad at hitting the little, white ball into the little holes. He suddenly had an indescribable urge to hit something.

Mrs. Featherbomb went back to rubbing his shoulders. He tried to put her mockery out of his mind.

"My you're tense," Mrs. Featherbomb laughed. "Don't take it so personally. It was just a bit of teasing for fun."

If that was what she considered fun, Alfred did not wish to be the butt of one of her serious jokes. He shrank under his wife's massaging hands. He had been the butt of her jokes more often than occasionally, but, just like her comment about comparing his golf game to fishing, there was a slight bit of truth to everything she said, albeit a bit exaggerated. And this time she hadn't made the comment in front of their friends or fellow churchgoers.

Alfred took his glasses off, placing them on the right side of the table. He rubbed his eyes and kept his gaze angled toward the floor. He knew he should take Mrs. Featherbomb's advice and not take her jabs so personally, but she had jabbed him where it hurt.

"I'm not that bad at golf," Alfred mumbled.

"So that's where Barbara gets it from," Mrs. Featherbomb crossed the kitchen, picked up the morning's paper and dropped it into the basket that the Boy Scouts had given them to collect old papers for a project they were doing.

"I wasn't done with that," Alfred said weakly.

"Perusing the classifieds can wait until tomorrow," Mrs. Featherbomb leaned against the counter and looked at him. "Are you going to have a talk with your daughter?"

Fear gripped Alfred's heart. If there was one thing that he feared more than his wife, it was having a talk with his adolescent daughter. He was left no choice, however.

In resignation to his fate, he crammed his glasses on and left the kitchen, being certain not to make the slightest noise that could be interpreted as a grunt or a sigh or a grumble or anything else that had an overtly negative connotation. He had made that mistake for the last time years ago and would not be repeating such a misdeed ever again.

Alfred stopped in the archway, his right hand reflexively reaching for the wall. A new smudge glared at him like a monster from under the bed when he was just a kid. It wasn't real he knew, but telling himself that hadn't worked when he was a kid either. When you had to tell yourself that something wasn't real, it seemed only to make it more real as if denying it gave it life.

He waited for Mrs. Featherbomb's condescending remark that was sure to follow his strange action. When it didn't come, he glanced back into the kitchen. Mrs. Featherbomb stood at the sink, hands on the sliver of counter between the edge and the sink. She peered out the window, and Alfred thought of turning around and comforting her.

Maybe she had finally noticed the words on the window. If she could see them, he was vindicated. But no, he needed to talk with Barbara. His wife would just chew him out for wasting time if he didn't have that conversation with their daughter right then and there.

The hallway leading to the bedrooms was dark and so were Alfred's contemplations as he drew up to Barabara's door. He knocked. Slowly, the door opened, and Barbara turned stiffly as if she were an eyeball in the world's biggest eyeroll. When she saw Alfred, she ended her quiet growl of frustration and stepped back.

The two looked at each other for a long moment before Barbara broke the silence, "Dad, are you alright?"

Alfred knew that Mrs. Featherbomb wouldn't be satisfied he had had a talk with Barbara unless she heard him yelling something, but he couldn't bring himself to slip into that act. Not tonight. He stepped quietly into his daughter's room and closed the door. The light was on, and the heavy scent of nail polish filled the room. He wrinkled his nose and then rubbed it when that didn't help.

Barbara backed up to the window and cranked it open a crack.

"Your mother says you got Joey Chadelle to drive you?" Alfred asked softly.

Barbara nodded. looking guilty and scared. "He didn't try anything. He's not like everybody says he is. He's really nice."

Alfred listened to his daughter's defense and tried to think of a response. Why was it such a big deal? He and Clarabelle had been part of the crowd that did the exact same sort of things as teenagers. But maybe that was the issue, both he and Clarabelle knew what kids were capable of.

"Donna didn't tell me it was Joey," Barbara tried to ease the punishment she had good reason to expect. "She just told me she'd found us a ride into town. We met everyone else at Rhonda's."

Rhonda's was the most common name for the tap dance studio downtown. A few days out of the week they would host a matinee concert for fledgling artists in hopes of being able to add another photograph to their bragging wall if the artist blew up. Despite being such a small venue, they had photos of Betty Hutton, Bing Crosby, Woody Herman, Count Basie and many others. Their brag, "You heard them here first," was not entirely unfounded but neither was it entirely accurate.

Alfred looked down, trying to think of what he should do. Then, he glanced up at his daughter. She chewed her lower lip nervously. She was in quite a bit of trouble. He just needed to figure out exactly what the trouble should be.

Alfred's eyes widened.

Barbara winced.

"Wait," Alfred said thoughtfully, "you said you met everyone else at Rhonda's Taphouse? What were you all doing there? It doesn't take more than one person to buy tickets."

"Don't tell mom," Barbara didn't even try to defend herself. She sat on her bed, crossed her arms over her stomach and curled forward as if injured. "Don't tell mom," she whimpered again.

Alfred caught the fear in his daughter's voice, but he also could do nothing to silence the rage welling inside him. Here was his daughter, his own flesh and blood, sneaking off to a heathen concert. If he didn't at the very least raise his voice, he would never hear the end of how he wanted his daughter to go to Hell in a handbasket. Mrs. Featherbomb would not let it go. In fact, she would probably request a larger handbasket for him to follow his daughter.

The window was still open, and a breeze rustled the curtains. A long moment of silence stretched. Neither looked at the other.

"Barbara," Alfred began and paused when she winced. He ran his hand through his hair and peeled off his glasses to rub his eyes. "Barb," he started again, "you scared your mother near to death. And," he hoped no one but his daughter could hear the next part, "and I would rather have taken you than have you ride with Joey Chadelle."

Barbara looked up at him. Something flashed in her eyes. Was it more fear? No, it looked like the uncertain wonder of surprise. He definitely was handling this differently than most other times. Maybe he was being affected by all the words showing up on his glasses and windows at the office and at home.

"He needs more experience behind the wheel before he gives rides, especially to young girls."

He glanced at the window. It was too blurry without his glasses to make out anything. His daughter smeared at her nose as he pushed his glasses into place.

He crossed the room in an uncoordinated leap. Barbara screamed. A torrent of venomous words shot from his mouth as he grabbed the windowsill and feverishly cranked it completely open.

"No cussing, dear," Mrs. Featherbomb's prim voice filtered into the room. Despite his anger, Alfred could see her in his mind's eye, patting her hair as she said it.

Alfred stuck his head out into the gathering night. He couldn't see anyone darting from shadow to shadow, and he couldn't hear a sound except the pounding of his heart sending blood to throb in his ears. Sweat beaded on his forehead, but he did nothing to stop it from trickling into his eyes.

The door squeaked behind him. Mrs. Featherbomb flew to the bed and sat beside Barbara, who held out her arms and whimpered like a toddler that had gotten knocked down by an overly friendly dog.

Alfred ran his hand through his hair. Barbara would have listened to him before, but it was plain to see she wouldn't hear him now.

"I think you've done enough here," Mrs. Featherbomb stated without looking at him. "You and your obsession with someone trying to scare you by writing on the windows is scaring my daughter again."

As if to corroborate Mrs. Featherbomb's statement, Barbara flinched and pressed her face into her mother's shoulder.

"There, there, Barbara. Your dad's gonna get ahold of himself, and everything will be just fine." Mrs. Featherbomb rounded on Alfred with a look like a slave driver's whip.

"She's grounded for a week. No going into town with her friends," Alfred held up a finger that felt small and utterly insignificant. He stuffed his hands into his pockets, "I'll get Ned's Cleaning to clean the windows."

"Oh, really, Alfred, must you be so harsh," Mrs. Featherbomb talked as though cooing to a baby. "I mean look at the poor girl. Frightened nearly to death. I'll add a couple extra chores for her to do. That should help take her mind off

92

what happened tonight and how you about lost your marbles again."

"Lost my..." heat swirled into Alfred's words. "Look here—"

"Shush, dear," Mrs. Featherbomb held up a hand in a gesture to wait, "can't you see she needs rest. She's trembling again she's so scared. Go and busy yourself with whatever it is you do in the evenings."

"You threw away my paper," Alfred muttered under his breath. He was seething about something. Something had happened back there where it felt like he was to blame for everything from Barbara running off to town with Joey Chadelle to them actually going to the concert instead of simply buying tickets. How was it all his fault?

"Just go," Mrs. Featherbomb whispered.

Alfred eased the door closed with a muffled squeak and thump. Mrs. Featherbomb started softly singing an old song she used to sing to get Barbara to sleep as an infant. He rested his hand on the door frame and then trudged to the living room.

There on the plate glass window, in large, black letters, another word was scrawled in smeared lettering.

Alfred tore from his house and galloped down the sidewalk. He didn't know where to find the Mexican, but he knew the man was close.

Blood would be spilled this night, and vengeance would be realized.

Chapter 11

Alfred came to a stop at the corner of the block. He hadn't seen a single sign of his target. His breath rasped in his dry throat, and the night was setting in dark with only a sliver of a silver moon peeking through scattered clouds.

Maybe he shouldn't hurt the Mexican. That would be a crime after all. He did want to rough him up a little bit though. Maybe something like what the Mafia did all those miles away in Chicago. He'd heard stories and read plenty of only slightly embellished accounts in the papers.

Placing his hands on his hips and grimacing against his loss of breath, Alfred struck out in a brisk walk. He didn't want to get blisters on his feet was the excuse he told himself in between panting breaths.

The neighborhood had very few streetlights. It was located on the edge of the suburbs, not quite rural and not quite city, but it did have plenty of sidewalks thanks to the city planning committee who didn't want the roads congested with pedestrians as the number of automobiles increased. A few houses had garbage cans sitting by the road for early morning pickup the following day. Here and there an old couple rose from creaky rocking chairs and shuffled across groaning front porches, the evening's visiting hours all but spent.

Alfred glanced around. He must look a fool to all those old folks who had seen him. None of them had called to him though. That was good…unless it meant they had heard about his episode with the ambulance. His shoulders slumped. It was likely they had heard. That was something about the front porch visitors, they always passed along what they saw and heard to each other. Truly, the only reason they needed papers was for large, national news. Anything that happened locally made it through the porch post well before it could be typeset and printed for the following morning.

"You fool," Alfred muttered to himself. "You've got people thinking you are a nutter."

"Hola, Señor," a bright accented voice called.

Alfred whirled. He couldn't see anyone in the gathering gloom, yet he thought he recognized the foreign accent and words.

"Noche hermosa," the voice said with a satisfied sigh.

Alfred turned toward the sound, better able to pinpoint it with the second phrase. A dark man approached, blending into the night until all but the whites of his eyes were lost. He took a wide-brimmed hat from his head and smiled. His teeth glinted like his eyes.

Alfred's heart pounded, though he was sure it was more from fright than from his exercise. "Do I know you?" he tilted his head, trying to see the man in better light.

"Si, Señor," the man said.

"No, I don't see, and that's the problem. It's too dark out here. Who are you?"

"Is me, Señor Jose."

It was the man. The nemesis himself. What had he come to do? He hadn't really expected to find the Mexican. Alfred stood, frozen and blinking repeatedly, trying to think of what he would do. An image of him grabbing the Mexican and yelling at him to stay away played like a silent movie in his mind. He couldn't hear what he was yelling in the movie. He could only see that his mouth was open and the cords of his neck were stretched taut.

"¿Señor?" the Mexican asked. "All is okay?"

Alfred blinked unable to get his body to do anything else.

"I'm fine," his voice grated like stone on ice.

The Mexican grunted and bent down. A little voice giggled. He lifted his daughter to his shoulders and hummed playfully as she kept giggling to his bouncy steps.

Alfred cocked his head, angling his gaze toward the retreating form of his enemy. He should have acted. At the least, he should have told the man not to come around anymore; that he didn't have work for him. Why hadn't he stood up for himself like a real man would have?

A real man. The phrase hit him like a baseball bat to the head. He hadn't acted like a man. He'd just behaved like a milksop.

"No. No. No," he grunted, pressing his eyes shut and ripping his glasses off.

How long until his new glasses were ready? Probably a couple of weeks. What had the optician's receptionist said? He couldn't wait. How the confounded Mexican was writing on his glasses was a mystery and would remain unsolved because if the man came back, and Alfred suspected he would, he would have a way to get rid of him for good.

Alfred checked his watch. He couldn't see it in the dark, but if he hurried, he estimated he still had time. Old Mr. Faustner surely had the supplies in his hardware store, and he had a habit of staying open late because he fell asleep by the fridge he had built under his sales counter. If the lights were on and one could wake him up, he would never turn down a customer.

He glanced at his watch again. It would be quicker to walk instead of backtracking to grab the car. But he should be home and not galivanting around waging war.

"No cussing, dear," Alfred muttered to himself.

Was that what he was doing, waging war?

He turned, walked briskly back toward home for five steps. Then he stopped. He needed those things from Faustner's if he was going to stop the Mexican from coming back. The man was the whole problem. Nothing had been going wrong until he had shown up.

Alfred turned. Five steps toward the hardware store, then he about-faced and took five steps toward home. He couldn't let Mrs. Featherbomb see everything he was going to buy.

What if Old Mr. Faustner didn't have enough left? He spun and broke into the nearest thing to a sprint he could manage. He, Alfred Featherbomb who hadn't run since grade school, pounded the sidewalk with speed. His shoes were not made for such exercise, and he would most definitely have several blisters as his reward. If he could just get to the hardware before everything was sold out...

Mrs. Featherbomb would most definitely blame him for scaring Barbara again. Once she woke up and saw what her father had done, she'd be terrified. He should really think about how this was affecting her more.

Alfred's gaze drooped to the ground. He was a fool. A weak fool who couldn't take care of his family. His steps slowed, and he came to stop in an intersection, puffing and gasping with hands on knees.

He glanced back toward his house. What was wrong with him? He couldn't even make up his mind and stick with the decision.

Alfred pivoted on one foot. He faced home, then he turned back toward the hardware store.

Bright light engulfed him.

Tires screeched, and a man shouted, "Get out of the middle of the road you fool."

There it was. Confirmation. Alfred rubbed his eyes and put his glasses on without thinking about what he was doing. The night grew noticeably darker, and the meager light from a far-away streetlight dimmed with dark, blurry lines crisscrossing it.

Alfred's hands shook, and his knees trembled. It was happening again. Something new had revealed itself on his glasses. Had that been the Mexican that drove past and yelled at him? The voice hadn't sounded accented. Could the man be faking his Mexican accent when he came over to work? Alfred shook his head. He had just come across the Mexican a few minutes ago. He had been walking with his daughter. Not enough time to go get their car and try to run him over.

That was something. If he could prove that the Mexican had tried to run him over, the police would have to remove him. All of his problems and frustrations with the Mexican would be over.

He needed to get to the hardware. At the same time, he needed to get home. Maybe he needed to call the police too.

Like a dog chained to a tree, Alfred Featherbomb lunged first one way and then lunged the other. He never made it more than a couple of steps toward the hardware. Likewise, he was unable to take more than a few shuffles toward his home.

He may have continued acting like a chained animal had he not closed his eyes and kicked at an invisible anthill in his percolating frustration. His shoe flew off into the dark. It sailed down the road in the direction of the hardware.

He couldn't head back without his shoe, and the momentum gained by retrieving it propelled him forward enough that he reached the hardware just as someone was leaving the shadowy interior.

After the figure took three steps, Alfred recognized him as Mr. Faustner.

"No cussing, dear," Mrs. Featherbomb's prim voice rang in Alfred's ears.

He was too late. Old Mr. Faustner had closed the hardware and wouldn't want to open it up for pennies worth of stuff. He didn't need his glasses or kitchen window to point out how slow he had been. How long had he pivoted in the middle of the street in indecision?

"Hello there," Old Mr. Faustner's slightly slurred voice called through the darkness. "Ya'll got a repair emergency?"

Alfred scratched his head and called back, trying to mask the shakiness in his voice, "No. I need some signs."

Old Mr. Faustner grunted and huffed, "Well, you're here now. Step on in. We'll just get you rung up in the dark. No sense throwing the lights. I know where ev'rything is."

"That's fine," Alfred sounded too relieved. Without the lights, he wouldn't have to see what the Mexican had managed to scrawl on his glasses. "And I need some of the strongest glass cleaner you have."

Old Mr. Faustner grunted again and shouldered the door open. A little bell jingled, and two shadows burst from the door.

"Don't mind them. I'll just have a brood of kittens looking for homes most likely," Old Mr. Faustner grumbled. "Here we are," he grabbed a jug from a shelf. "You want a kitten for that little tot of yours?"

Alfred forced his body to relax from the fighting stance it had slipped into when the cats had brushed past him. He couldn't see anything in the near pitch blackness. "Do you mean Barbara? She's not a toddler anymore," Alfred tried to loosen his tight voice. "She's a teenager."

"Is she now?" Old Mr. Faustner sounded distant. "I can't remember stuff the way I used to back before my Sarah… Well, what kind of sign ya'll say you were after?"

Alfred told him and tried to keep from reminding the old man about his late wife. She had died almost ten years ago, and the old man had never remarried.

Alfred bumped into the counter. The ancient cash register plinked as a few coins settled. The hardware smelled of oil, dirt and kerosene. He would have looked around at the walls all covered in tools and clocks, but it was so dark only little glints of light here and there offered anything other than darkness.

Grunting and dragging his feet along the worn, dusty floorboards, Old Mr. Faustner set the purchases on the counter. The cash register dinged. The drawer slid out with a sound like a sword being drawn.

"Your total comes to two dollars and thirty-seven cents," Old Mr. Faustner's voice sounded muffled and then clear again as he rummaged below the counter. A paper bag rustled, and bottles clinked together. "It's a long walk back home, ain't it? Here's one for the road."

Alfred reached out for the bag. "No thanks," he said about the beer.

"No," Old Mr. Faustner grunted. "My pa taught me never get yerself a beer in front of company without offering them the same."

Alfred paused and then grabbed a bottle.

"Not that one," Old Mr. Faustner whistled. "Ya'll drink that and your innards will come out looking like a piece of white lace window curtain. Be careful with that stuff."

Alfred didn't want the beer, but Old Mr. Faustner had been kind enough to reopen his hardware for him. It would be incredibly rude to refuse the drink. He could hear Mrs. Featherbomb telling him off for drinking it. Maybe he could "forget" and leave it on a shelf on the way out.

Two caps popped off.

Maybe he could pour it out and toss the bottle in a ditch.

"Did I ever tell you how I got shot in the Great War?" Old Mr. Faustner sounded like he was settling in to tell the whole story. Alfred had heard it a couple of times.

The gurgling sound of Old Mr. Faustner pulling a big gulp of beer from his bottle seemed amplified by the quiet store. Alfred resigned the idea of getting rid of the beer. He couldn't throw the bottle in a ditch on the way home. There were no ditches, only sidewalks and yards. Maybe his host realized this and that was why he was offering to entertain him while he finished his beer. He couldn't be impolite and say no, especially now that the bottle had been opened.

He took a tentative sip and grimaced at the strength of the bubbly liquid. Old Mr. Faustner knew how to make nearly anything. Apparently, beer was one of the things on that extensive list. It was thick and yeasty with plenty of alcohol.

Chapter 12

"Dad? What are you doing on the couch?"

Alfred stirred and felt for his glasses. He'd put them on the nightstand, hadn't he? Unsuccessful in his attempt to find them, he opened his eyes and beheld his daughter. She stood frozen in mid step partway into the living room as though she'd intended to walk through but stopped abruptly upon seeing him.

"Is everything okay?" Barbara asked. Her voice was pinched and wrought with fear and worry.

Without his glasses, everything was slightly blurry. He had intended to get up at dawn and put the finishing touches on his plan. The Mexican would not be able to legally come onto the Featherbomb's property. He let that satisfaction pull him from the couch.

He'd gotten back late from the hardware, spent hours out in the yard and then hadn't wanted to wake Clarabelle so he'd lain down on the couch.

"Everything will be," Alfred said, peeking out of the window instead of looking at his daughter. "Everything will be just fine."

The sun was just peeking over the treetops. Thin, bright rays stretched over the neighborhood above the trees and houses. Songbirds called to one another as they flittered from one perch to another and pecked at seeds or prodded at bugs. It was an ordinary morning, but to Alfred it felt like an extraordinary change was in the air.

A set of footsteps stopped behind him. Alfred turned to see Clarabelle standing where Barbara had been. His daughter was backing away down the hallway toward her room.

"What were you doing on the couch out here?" Clarabelle patted her hair. "I fell asleep waiting for you, but when I woke up, I found you out here."

"A man's place is to protect his family," Alfred grinned. "I didn't want to wake you when I got back from the hardware."

Alfred turned back to look out the window. Clarabelle moved into the kitchen.

"Yes, sir," Alfred proclaimed with immense satisfaction, "today will be a good day."

"It is a beautiful day," his wife called from the kitchen where she poured water into the coffee percolator, "but you don't want to be late to work."

"Yes, yes," Alfred muttered to himself. "I'll get changed."

After changing and slipping on his office shoes, Alfred opened the blinds to allow him a view of the front yard and driveway. He was so engrossed with the anticipation of his plan working that he didn't even notice the black smudges on the glass.

He was just finishing his first strip of bacon when Barbara burst in. Alfred didn't take his eyes off the driveway as she asked breathlessly, "What's on my window? Did you tape something there last night, dad?"

Alfred waved a hand to show it wasn't a problem, "It's all part of the plan."

Mrs. Featherbomb and Barbara bustled to Barbara's room. A few minutes later, they silently marched outside and looked at the house. Alfred could see them, their gazes roving from one sign to the next. Yes, it would work. You couldn't help but notice.

Movement at the end of the driveway snapped him away from his revelry. Right on time, his target was striding up the driveway. He had him.

Alfred shoved his chair back and ran for the door.

The two Carter boys raced across his lawn. Each one had a huge frog in his hands, and they were calling with high pitched excitement for their father to come out and see their catch. Once on their own porch, the light-haired boy started yelling that he was going to have frog legs for breakfast.

Alfred glanced across the street. Mr. Riley had venetian blinds in the front room of his house, and Alfred caught him peering out of a gap pushed wider between the blinds. Their eyes met, and Alfred smiled and waved.

It was going to be a good day. His neighbors would see him win. He would be the talk of the neighborhood. People would tell the story of how the Featherbombs got rid of the scourge of the Mexican.

He strode confidently, hands relaxed in his pockets and chin held high, to the center of his driveway. He felt like whistling he felt so good about his victory.

"Hola," the Mexican called with a wave and smile. "Good morning, Señor."

So, the man was learning English. No bother.

"Can't you read?" Alfred called back. He watched the Mexican's dark eyes take in the signs plastered on every surface. Alfred grinned. He had spaced the signs no more than four feet apart and made sure each window had one taped to it. He'd even taped one to each of the ornamental rocks alongside the driveway. There was no way someone could claim to have missed them.

"Si, Señor," the Mexican replied, still walking calmly up the driveway. "I read."

"Well, don't you know what it means?" Alfred called, feeling the heat of anger rise to his face.

"Si, Señor, I know this one," the advancing enemy declared.

"Then, you know I can have you arrested," Alfred grinned smugly. He was winning. The man was walking right into the trap.

Mrs. Featherbomb walked slowly to Alfred's side. She eyed him with eyebrows raised and her lips pressed into a distinctly thin line.

She broke her gaze of displeasure off and greeted the Mexican, "Hello, Mr. Jose, thank you for coming out." Her tone darkened a little, "You're a bit early, but maybe that's for the best. Hopefully that tape won't leave too much residue."

"I clean todos las windows, Señora," the Mexican grinned and gestured with his hands, presumably indicating all the windows on the house.

"What are you doing?" Alfred growled low enough the Mexican shouldn't be able to hear him. "Can't you see I can call the police and have him arrested? He's the one who's writing on the windows, and somehow, he's gotten into my office and even managed to make fun of me by writing on my glasses."

Mrs. Featherbomb patted her hair, "Don't get your ruffles in a duff."

Alfred made to answer, but before he could he caught a glimpse of Mr. Riley entering his house. His neighbors must all be watching. Could they hear too?

"I hired—"

"Yes. Yes," Mrs. Featherbomb interrupted with a hiss, "and they're much more expensive than Mr. Jose here. Besides," she added in a lofty tone, "he's been doing such a fine job I don't understand why everyone doesn't hire him."

Alfred wound himself up to reply. He really didn't need to put much effort into looking or sounding angry. He needed to put work into being calm enough to be understood. Mrs. Featherbomb ruined his efforts, however.

"Now. Now. No cussing, dear," she said with a pat to her hair.

Movement at the front door snagged Alfred's attention. He just caught his daughter whirling away, an unreadable expression on her face. He knew he'd probably upset her again. She didn't like it when her parents argued or, what was more common, when Alfred spluttered for words while Mrs. Featherbomb told him not to cuss.

Mrs. Featherbomb's explosions were like a bomb that had hit the ground. You knew it would go off, but you couldn't tell when. You couldn't even tell if the detonator had been activated or if the bomb needed to shift an eighth of an inch before exploding. Alfred couldn't blame his daughter. It happened far too often, and, lately, he'd been wishing he had a room he could run to and hide in just like her.

"Get him off our property before I call the police," Alfred recovered enough to grind out from inside a stiff jaw.

"Whatever for?" Mrs. Featherbomb countered. "I hired him. Why can't you be a flutter bum and get around for work. I'm sure Mr. Jose will be finished by the time you're back."

Mrs. Featherbomb was a couple inches shorter than Alfred, but he felt like he had to crane his neck to physically look up at her, "He's trespassing. He's not supposed to be on our property."

Mrs. Featherbomb crossed her arms and gave her husband an incredulous gaze, "I know what trespassing is, dear. I hired him because he does a bang-up job at a much more reasonable cost. I'll get Mr. Jose started on the front lawn here. Oh, it's dreadful to think of how many people must have driven by and seen what you did." She shook her head and stepped toward the Mexican, "I better not get any phone calls about all this. I'm surprised you didn't tape any signs to the flowers."

Alfred wanted to shout after her and put her in her place, but where was that exactly? He didn't know anymore. Maybe she was right. Maybe he really did need to acknowledge that he was going crazy like one of the trains coming off the rails in the westerns that were becoming popular. The truth was he had wanted to put up more signs, a lot more signs, but had run out too soon.

"Hullo! Mr. Fritterbump, isn't it?" a loud, young man's voice called from the sidewalk.

Alfred glanced down the driveway and saw a young man with dark sandy hair sporting an army uniform. The recruiter he'd nearly ran over at church. He froze. What could the man want? Surely, he couldn't press charges now since the incident had been several days ago.

"Well, I've at least got your attention," the recruiter smiled widely. "Mind if I come up there to ask you for help? I'd like to not get in trouble for trespassing."

As the man trailed off, Alfred felt his right eye twitch. Involuntarily, his feet bore him down the driveway toward the recruiter.

The recruiter looked down the street to his right and shaded his eyes even though he stood in the shadows of the trees lining the street and the sun hadn't yet reached the point of giving its warmth. He carried his cap in his other hand and pinned it under his arm as Alfred stopped in front of him. He stuck out his free hand.

"Sergeant Oliver McCoy," he said, once again smiling widely.

"What do you want?" Alfred felt his mouth move and heard the words, but the worry in his mind kept him from feeling present in the situation.

"I just need some help with my old gal," the recruiter stated, still holding his hand out for Alfred to shake. "She blew a tire, and my spare's gone flat as well."

Could he be late to work a second day in a row? Alfred didn't know what Mr. Davis would do, but he did know that his boss would likely say he understood helping a man with a flat tire and then have him stay late.

"I need to get to work," Alfred said reluctantly, "but I'll give you a ride into town."

Sergeant McCoy snapped a salute and said, "Thank you, sir. I won't hold you up. I'll have that tire ready to toss in your trunk in a jiffy."

Alfred nodded and spun with a grunt. He scowled when he saw the Mexican peeling one of the three "No Trespassing" signs off the living room window. How was he supposed to have known that his wife would undermine him and hire the Mexican while canceling the real cleaners? No, he mustn't think like that. Mrs. Featherbomb would not be happy to hear a thought like that.

Heat filled his face. He pulled off is glasses before another word the Mexican had scrawled there in some sort of invisible ink could react to the heat.

And what was he thinking, giving a ride to the one man everybody in town hated collectively? Church would have to be avoided this weekend. Unless...yes, unless he could spin it so the recruiter had told him he was leaving town and had gotten the flat tire. In that case, Alfred would be seen as a hero ridding the town of its scourge. Now, to just get the recruiter to say he was leaving town so that—

"No cussing, dear," Mrs. Featherbomb's voice played in his head.

Alfred scowled and smashed his glasses onto his face. That Mexican would not be able to call him a liar.

Chapter 13

"Hey, Featherbomber," the gravelly voice of Mr. Codgens talking around his ever-present cigar made Alfred jump. "You're early today, old boy. Well, the younger generation calls it on time."

"Mornin', Codgens," Alfred said softly as he reached for the door handle.

Mr. Codgens leaned forward conspiratorially, "Don't you mess Miss Sunny's floor up this morning, and don't be stingy with those kisses neither."

Alfred grunted, heaving the door open. Sunny was leaning over beside her desk. She kept several tall, leafy potted plants there and cared for them every morning.

"Good mornin', gentlemen," she straightened and called in her strange, too-fast-to-be-a-drawl drawl. "Which one of you fine gentlemen would be willin' to fetch me some water? I've got some thirsty plants wantin' out of the desert."

"Featherbomber volunteers," Mr. Codgens said, slamming his briefcase to the floor so he could reach an unencumbered hand into the bowl of mints Sunny kept beside her phone.

"Mr. Codgens," Sunny pressed her hands onto her hips, "aren't you ever goin'a learn to ask first before helping yourself to my mints?"

"You set them out here for me. Admit it," Mr. Codgens flung his head back and dropped several of the candies in after whisking his morning cigar out.

"I'll admit no such thing, you overgrown ankle-biter," Sunny shouldered the man away from her desk and swiped at a few gray ashes that settled there like ducks landing on a pond. "Shoo. Take your filthy cigar with you and get."

"But don't I owe you a kiss?" Mr. Codgens showed no intention of listening to Sunny.

Alfred opened his mouth, preparing to help Sunny get rid of Mr. Codgens, but before he could say anything, the front door opened and Mr. Albright stepped in.

Sunny didn't see the new arrival and replied to Mr. Codgens, "Now don't it seem a little inappropriate for me to let you kiss me?"

"You always did before," Mr. Codgens insisted. He wasn't far from the truth.

"Why do you think I made such a fuss when you men stomped in here and made a mess?" Sunny's eyes narrowed slyly and then she opened them wide and innocently, "It certainly wasn't so *you* could kiss me. I had to have an excuse for Ed to kiss me. He was always so nervous around me that I could make him think he'd made a mess even if he actually hadn't."

Mr. Codgens started talking around the mints he hadn't managed to swallow yet, but before he got more than a word out, a bouquet of bright yellow flowers wrapped in crinkly tissue paper smacked him in the face.

Sunny gasped, and Mr. Codgens sucked in a startled breath and choked.

"Oh, Ed, do save his life. Not all fools deserve to die," Sunny cried.

As Mr. Codgens stepped back, Mr. Albright wound up a massive slap that thudded into the choking man's back. With a sound like a bass drum, Mr. Codgens spit a mouthful of half-chewed mints onto the floor. His face was red and eyes watery. He tried to rasp something but had no breath with which to articulate it.

"Here. These are for you," Mr. Albright stepped forward and held the rumpled bouquet out to Sunny. "They're your favorite color. Leastways, I've seen you like to wear yellow. I'm sorry they're all broke up, and—"

"They're wonderful, Ed," Sunny accepted them eagerly and planted a solid kiss on Mr. Albright's mouth. Then she peeked at Mr. Codgens who grasped her desk and leaned over to regain his breath. "I don't think they're nearly broken enough."

With that she lifted the bouquet and brought it down on Mr. Cogden's head. The man looked stunned, and his cigar fell to the floor.

Sunny and Mr. Albright embraced and kissed again. Alfred opened his mouth to ask where the watering can was, but Mr. Davis walked in from the offices.

"Alright, break it up you two. Private rooms, not public reception areas, are for that kind of thing." Mr. Davis looked at the floor and at Mr. Codgens, "Codgens, give our Sunny some help cleaning this place up and then clean yourself up. You look like you tried to outrun a dog and failed. Albright, I expect a full day's work out of you. I don't want to see reports with doodles and sketches of Sunny on them. Yes, she's the most beautiful thing in this cave when my wife isn't here, but we're here to work not to draw pictures and compose poetry."

Mr. Davis turned to Alfred. Alfred looked back. Neither one said anything.

"What about you, Featherbomb? What are you doing here?"

Alfred finally located the watering can and sought to save face, "I was going to help Sunny water her plants, but I couldn't find the watering can."

Sunny gave Mr. Albright a lingering, salacious look, broke away from him and scooped up the watering can from beside the trash can. Giving it to Alfred, she said, "Half a can for the big pots and just enough to wet the dirt on the small ones. My Susans," she appraised the somewhat mangled flowers Mr. Albright had given her, "are goin'a need a whole watering can to themselves. I don't have a vase for 'em, so I'll have to use the watering can to hold 'em." She smiled at Mr. Albright, "The broken ones, I'll pull out and press so I can put them in a frame. That was fun knocking some sense into Mr. Codgens."

Mr. Albright smiled back at Sunny, but Mr. Davis was the one to speak, "It may have been fun, but all the sense he gained must've dripped out his ears.

"Alright, gentlemen, and lady," he looked pointedly at Sunny, "we are open for business. Let's make this place look like we know how to handle people's money and not just fight over a bit of gold." He winked at Sunny and strode back into the offices.

Alfred hurriedly delivered the water to Sunny's plants and left the watering can full beside her desk.

"You do that for your wife, and she'll swoon every time," Sunny called after him.

Alfred couldn't help but wonder whether she intended him to hear her or if she were simply trying to convince Mr. Albright to help her out with the tasks she set for herself. After all, choosing to keep plants alive indoors was a difficult undertaking.

He drew close to his office and kept his gaze firmly fixed on the floor. The old words and any new ones the Mexican had managed to paint on his window could wait.

"Maybe if you weren't so stingy with your kisses for Sunny you'd be bright-as-a-light like Albright," Mr. Codgens growled at him. "Look at that blighter. He's got 'er fawning all over 'im."

"I'm married, Codgens," Alfred replied simply.

"C'mon, you sourpuss, dream a little. What'd it be like to have a young doll like that just dancing in your arms," Codgens didn't look at Alfred. Instead, his eyes were fixed on the new couple who appeared to not have heard or not have understood what their boss had just told them about a private room.

Alfred made a motion he had learned from his grandfather. Every time his grandfather didn't want to waste time on a conversation he deemed to be stretching the facts, he raised his hand by his cheek and made a quick motion shoving his hand down. Alfred did not join the gesture with his grandfather's customary assertion that the story was hogwash and should be stuffed. He figured the meaning was clear.

Reaching for the handle on his office door forced his eyes from the floor. There on the window. What had Codgens just called him? How had the Mexican known? How had he known he would be called that this morning? The Mexican must have told Codgens to call him that. That was the only explanation. How else would he have been able to paint the insult on his office.

Unless he had it all wrong.

Maybe it was Codgens all along. Codgens could have bribed the Mexican to paint the insults on his house and office windows. It made sense. Alfred wasn't Codgens' supervisor, but he was slightly above him in the order of things. Alfred reported directly to Mr. Davis, while Codgens reported to the head of his department whom, in turn, reported to Mr. Davis.

That made sense. All except one thing. But it was the thing that refused to make sense no matter who was behind the rotten prank. How had the perpetrator gotten everyone to say they couldn't see the words? Further, how had they managed to smear and paint his glasses? He had them on him most of the time. A pickpocket? That seemed not entirely farfetched. A second pair of glasses identical to his could be swapped back and forth when he put his glasses on the nightstand at night.

He needed to get that new pair of glasses from the eye doctor. No, he needed to outsmart his enemy and get an entirely new pair of glasses from an eye doctor he'd never been to—one on the far side of town. Yes, a plan was forming in his mind. He would outsmart the man responsible for his humiliation.

What was it that the little Belgian detective with the mustaches, Hercule Poirot, was always proclaiming in those Agatha Christie novels? Something about motive. Yes, once you knew the motive, you could determine the murderer. Codgens possessed the motive. He wanted Alfred's job and was going to extraordinary lengths to make him seem crazy and unstable so that his credibility would collapse. It was an elaborate scheme, but it had also been working.

"Not anymore," Alfred hummed to himself. "I'm onto your motive. This is one murder you won't be able to commit. I won't be going down."

Alfred settled into his chair, still humming to himself, and pulled the first contract he had to rectify for the day. It was a more complicated assignment. One of those that would require several letters and the involvement of the opposition's commercial attorney.

What was it that Codgens had told him to do? Dream a little? Codgens knew Alfred was married, yet he had tried to convince him to imagine going out with Sunny.

A new fear reared its head in his mind. It was dark and formless until he put the pieces together. Once he saw the creature, he couldn't unsee it.

But surely his wife would never go along with something like that, right? And with *Codgens*?

Chapter 14

Alfred pushed himself back from his desk. He wanted to believe the best, but the realizations were adding up. Recently, he and Mrs. Featherbomb had been arguing more.

The contract lay forgotten in front of him. Just getting rid of the Mexican wouldn't solve everything. He might be able to buy some reprieve from the insults showing up on his windows, but that wouldn't resolve the real issue.

If it had been as simple as Codgens wanting his job, he could leave for a different job or, most likely, simply inform Mr. Davis, who would look into it, find it was true and fire Codgens. He couldn't do any of that though. He had to play it very carefully. He couldn't let on that he knew what was going on. All he had to do was outsmart them one at a time.

He downed the last of his water and felt sweat clinging to his armpits. The Mexican had a lot to gain from the fallout as well. He would probably get Alfred's house and move his brothers, uncles, aunts, cousins and grandmas and grandpas all into it, making it an entire village instead of a single-family residence.

Barbara would undoubtedly go with her mother wherever she went. Alfred tossed his pen on top of the contract and stood, eyebrows furrowing, face flushing.

His office was not large, but it was big enough that it took him three steps to reach the door. He could then take five steps to the back wall, which was the building's exterior wall. He couldn't remember the last time he'd paced, but he paced now, and he paced with vigor.

Several times on his rounds he almost wrenched the door open, but he didn't want his coworkers to see him like this. Also, with his anger barely contained as it was, he could easily see himself walking up to Codgens and walloping him good.

He could see it now. Codgens would play dumb in front of the others until Alfred had landed one too many punches, then Codgens would take advantage of the situation and speed up his plans. Alfred would probably be fired and hauled away by the police to cool down.

He had to think of something truly indelible.

Back and forth he paced, the room feeling smaller and smaller with each step. The Mexican was at his house right now under the guise of cleaning the windows. Most likely, he was measuring for where his relatives would soon occupy.

He flung himself into his chair. Pacing wouldn't do. He had to appear calm and unaffected if he was going to outsmart these people. He closed his eyes and pulled his work toward him. His right foot waved from side to side, toes pointing first to the left and then to the right. That was alright. Alfred rolled his shoulders. His desk hid his lower half with a modesty panel.

Rolling his shoulders again and tapping his chin with the pen, Alfred presumed to read over the faulty contract again. His mind couldn't have been further from the demanding task. It was still scheming and planning.

A knock sounded on his door. With a start he sat back and stared at the door.

"Come in," Alfred said with no vocal inflection. He didn't want to talk with anybody at the moment.

The door opened with only a single creak at the very end of its swing. Codgens stepped in, a sheaf of papers decorating his hands.

"These just came in, Featherbomber," Codgens said. Spotting the open part of Alfred's desk, he stacked the documents. The top one was creased as if it had been folded and mailed in a letter envelope. "The bossman says they're beyond my department and asked me to deliver them to you. Said you'd know what to do with 'em once you saw 'em."

Alfred stared at Codgens as if he were staring down the Devil himself. The pen rested against his chin, forgotten.

"Right, you're busy, Featherbomber," Codgens said, holding up his hands. "Do your old lady a favor before you go home."

Alfred's mind froze. This was it. Codgens was going to make his intentions clear. His left hand, the one hidden beneath the desk, balled into a fist.

"Wash that ink off, unless you're acting the part of an Eskimo in a play after work." Codgens grinned smugly and turned to leave.

Alfred continued to glare at him. His intense anger had the opposite effect than he expected. It froze him to his chair, keeping him from rising and shoving his enemy out of his office perhaps with a well disguised punch explained away by stressful work and trying to close the door.

The latch clicked shut, and Alfred blew out his breath. Little droplets of black ink sprayed across his desk, covering the faulty contract and other documents Codgens had brought in with tiny, black specks.

He jerked the pen away from his chin and glanced at it. The writing tip stared back at him. He'd been tapping his chin with the ink-covered tip. In horror, he rubbed his chin and pulled his hand away. It was smeared much like the smears that formed insults on his glasses. Desperately, he dug through the drawer on his left where he had stuffed the box of tissues Mrs. Featherbomb had insisted he take to work when he had a sneezing fit months ago.

Under the cover of wiping his nose, he scurried to the restroom. The mirror revealed the damage. His entire chin was pockmarked with black spots. Gray smears ran between the spots. His chin looked like some child's attempt at drawing a fake beard to impress his friends.

Ten minutes later and feeling self-conscious of the red and raw hue of his chin, Alfred returned to his office. Thankfully, no one had seen him. But ten minutes had been sufficient time for his nemesis to strike again. What was his world coming to when he couldn't leave for a few minutes and come back to his office the way he'd left it?

Dimly, Alfred noted that Mr. Ashley hadn't been able to scrub the window clean from the other black smears. Now, joining them, a new insult was scrawled in the same smeared handwriting. Even though he knew it to be true—he was a dolt after all—it infuriated him. Well, maybe what angered him was the fact that he hadn't been able to strike his enemy, yet his enemy had struck him another blow.

Alfred hung his head and plodded to the window overlooking the sidewalk and street outside. Parting the blinds, he peered out and wondered what it would take for so many people to be working together. How could everyone at work pretend not to see the insults accumulating on his office window? What about Sunny? The young woman seemed far too nice to be playing along with Codgens' plan.

"No cussing, dear," Alfred heard Mrs. Featherbomb's voice in his head as his thoughts progressed.

What about Barbara? Surely, she hadn't joined in. However, she had claimed on multiple occasions that she could not see the words showing up on their windows. She was severely affected by Alfred's insistence that the words were there. Her reactions certainly could not be an act, could they? In an off-handed way, he admitted that if she was indeed acting, she should definitely go out for an acting career.

Alfred exhaled and shuffled back to his desk. The room spun slightly as he dropped into his chair. His downcast gaze fell to the stapler. It was a special tool in his office. Mr. Davis had given it to him in front of the whole office two years ago. It was engraved with the phrase "Because you make them stick." Alfred had weeded out the loopholes that were being exploited in a particularly lucrative contract. Mr. Davis had given him that stapler, a large raise and named him employee of the year. Now, it had turned into a lofty pedestal to hang a target on, and they were all taking shots at him.

Alfred's thoughts spiraled down dark stairways. He tried to bury himself in the numbers and legal jargon, but it didn't suck him in as it usually did. He remained in the shallows of the lake. At this rate the contract would take all week for him to correct, and he wouldn't be sure he had fixed it sufficiently.

Sometime after midmorning, Sunny knocked on his door. He waved her in, and she placed a sheet of paper with a short note on his desk, smiled and retreated out of his office.

Alfred picked up the paper and read the note. He didn't have a phone in his office, so anytime Mrs. Featherbomb needed to call him at work, she would call the front desk. Sunny would answer and handle the phone call accordingly. This time, Mrs. Featherbomb had requested that Alfred stop at the butcher's and pick up a beef roast.

Driving to the butcher's would take him a good ten minutes out of his way. Mrs. Featherbomb was trying to hide something. Alfred leaned back in his chair. He felt his brow bunching above his nose and the corners of his mouth turn down.

That Mexican was supposedly cleaning the windows today. The extra time would allow him to write more of his insults in that strange, invisible ink of his. Alfred considered heading home a few minutes early, stating he either hadn't received the message from Sunny or that he had simply forgotten. He could also claim the car had trouble starting so he had driven directly home to avoid breaking down at the butcher's.

Alfred rose, dropping his pen on his desk. It was a solid pen and made a loud thud as it hit the thick oak. Hands shoved deep into his pockets, he paced to and from the outside window. Normally, he could solve problems like this one rapidly. Well, normally, he didn't suspect foul play. His marriage wasn't as bad as others he'd witnessed. He and Clarabelle never fought—not in public at least. She still made him breakfast and coffee the way he liked it each morning.

It was normal that she liked to gossip and tell her friends that he was a grouch. He'd overheard countless other women talk the same way about their husbands. Other men, though they rarely talked about it in more than passing comments, also shared that nothing they did seemed to be good enough for their old lady.

Up until today, he hadn't been alone, but now that he understood the inner workings of the evil dynamics at work around him, he was truly alone. He was just like the orphans in the stories looking through shop windows and being driven off by an owner scared of the urchin making off with his wares.

His chair creaked as he sat and picked up his pen. Savagely, he attacked the contract, making so many notes and adjustments to the phrasing that he was in danger of running out of ink in his pen and drafting a completely new contract that could void the existing relationship between the two companies.

Mr. Albright cracked his door open, poked his head in and knocked on the door frame. "Sunny's running out for sandwiches. Mr. Davis is buying. You want anything?" he asked.

Alfred glanced at the boyish grin on the man's face. He had been that way when he'd first met Clarabelle. He held his pen on the paper too long, and a large puddle of ink formed. It would be rude to refuse. At the same time, he needed to order something inexpensive so there was no further "proof" of him costing the company exorbitant, unnecessary debits.

He grunted and replied, "I'll take a club. Extra mayo please."

Mr. Albright nodded. Alfred knew the man would deny seeing anything on the office window, but he could trust him with lunch, couldn't he? If the plan was to poison him, they'd have done it already, right?

Mr. Albright started closing the door and then flung it back open partway. "What flavor soda?" he asked.

"Water," Alfred barked.

Mr. Albright swallowed, ducked his head and retreated.

The contract stared at Alfred, but his hands lay limply on the desk. His mind was like a cold, fall day. He didn't usually snap like that. The man had simply been trying to help him get his lunch ordered.

A forest fire started in the wet wood of the cold, fall bracken. It smoked and smoldered in the wet leaves of his mind where it could stay for a long time before turning into a disaster.

"Alfred, old boy," he murmured to himself, "you need to get rid of that Mexican, and figure out some way to keep Codgens away."

He smirked as a plan formed. He would not be so easily removed, and he most certainly would not let others think he was going mad—because he *was* going mad, wasn't he?

Chapter 15

"Oh! What are these?" Mrs. Featherbomb exclaimed.

"Those, my dear, are roses," Alfred forced himself to smile.

Mrs. Featherbomb pulled the crinkling tissue paper from the cut stems of the roses and smelled the lovely scent of the dark red blooms. She sighed with an air of satisfaction.

"I have missed the bouquets you used to lavish upon me," she stated and stepped to the corner cabinet and began digging for a vase. Twisting suddenly, she asked, "You didn't forget the roast, and now these flowers are to say you're sorry, did you?"

Still holding his smile that was a little too rigid, Alfred placed the wrapped meat on the counter. Mrs. Featherbomb hadn't thanked him for the flowers like he'd hoped. Instead, had that been an insult about how he hadn't bought her cut flowers for several years?

Barbara walked in, clearly on her way to the door.

"Oh, you got mom roses!" she gasped as she watched her mother cut the stems and drop the flowers into a vase. "What are you apologizing for?"

Alfred held up his hand, but no words came. It was as if his brain were the carburetor on an engine. The spark plug was sparking but no gasoline was getting to the cylinder. He opened his mouth and closed it again.

"Barbara Ann," Mrs. Featherbomb scolded, "that's no way to talk to your father, and," she continued in a gentle, teaching voice, "if you want men to buy you flowers, you had best not assume flowers are only for apologies."

"Kendra's dad always buys her mom flowers after he's been out too late," Barbara muttered.

Mrs. Featherbomb's eyebrows shot up. "Young lady," she said severely, "the Good Lord knows that man has a drinking problem, and it'll be only so long before he's dealt with. We needn't gossip about the man's problems. The Good Lord will judge him."

Mrs. Featherbomb gave her head a satisfactory nod as if to say the lesson was finished for the day. Grabbing a placemat, she placed the flowers in the center of the table. Next, she rotated them until giving a satisfied nod.

Barbara eyed her mother and edged toward the door.

"Where are you off to now, young lady?" Mrs. Featherbomb asked without looking at her.

Alfred watched his daughter sigh and look down as she responded, "Donna and a couple other girls asked me to get malts with them."

"Where?" Mrs. Featherbomb straightened, hands on hips.

"Piper's Pier," Barbara said reluctantly.

Mrs. Featherbomb stared at Barbara with a look that would have made a tough, growing-in-a-crack-in-the-sidewalk weed wilt.

"Good choice," Alfred offered. He glanced at Mrs. Featherbomb who turned her poisonous glare on him. He

126

fumbled for his voice, "I—I mean to ask, how are you getting there? It's on the other side of town."

Barbara shrugged.

Mrs. Featherbomb took a large breath, the primer for a storm.

Alfred, in an attempt to curb the building explosion, hurriedly asked, "Are Donna's parents taking you?"

Barbara glanced back and forth between her parents. She looked like a helpless animal stuck in the middle of the road with oncoming traffic bearing down from both directions.

"Barbara Ann, you are grounded," Mrs. Featherbomb was so upset her voice was a menacing whisper like the wind before a dangerous thunderstorm. "You march yourself to your room right now, and don't come out unless I call for you." Mrs. Featherbomb continued, gaining volume with each syllable, "You'll stay in there as long as it takes for you to learn to respect your mother and father."

Barbara winced with each word. Alfred knew how she felt. There was no opening for a counterargument. Trying to say anything only increased the fury of Mrs. Featherbomb's judgement.

"And," Mrs. Featherbomb was just reaching her first crescendo, "you may not use the telephone until I say so."

At that, Barbara burst into silent tears. She turned a watery, pleading gaze to Alfred, her father. He should have stepped in and helped calm Mrs. Featherbomb down. He shouldn't have let his daughter be yelled at like that.

Mrs. Featherbomb was still going strong with her terms of grounding, but her tempest melted into the background. Alfred gazed at his daughter.

"You heard your mother," he tried to sound gruff, but lifeless was the only description that could be accurate.

Barbara fled.

"Keep yourself locked in there," Mrs. Featherbomb yelled after her, "and if I ever catch you riding with Joey

Chadelle again, you'll be grounded until you're an old spinster."

Alfred glanced at his wife. She could be so strict with their daughter he wondered if it would have been better to not have had any kids.

He turned his gaze out the window. Black smudges covered the smooth glass, but a car parking at the foot of the lawn pulled his attention beyond his broadcasted shortcomings. After all, he had expected the Mexican to have painted more insults on every window, so it did not surprise him.

It was Mrs. Wyman who drove the car. In the back seat of the late model sedan sat a row of smiling girls. He imagined he could hear them giggling from where he stood. Not a single boy in sight. He kept watching as the girl by the door waved toward Barbara's bedroom window. A moment later the girl's smile faded, and she beckoned one more time.

The rasping click of Barbara's window being cranked open sounded. Mrs. Featherbomb marched toward the bedroom. Alfred heard Barbara call to her friends, saying she couldn't go. When the girl in the car asked why, Barbara said she just couldn't and cranked the window shut again. Mrs. Wyman pulled the car away a few minutes later.

What had he done that had been so wrong? Surely, had he handled the situation differently, his daughter would have been able to skip out the door with a smile and a cheery goodbye. He had blown it. He had put his daughter in the crosshairs of Mrs. Featherbomb's punishment.

Alfred remembered the first couple of years he and Clarabelle had been together. They had been some of the most blissful, fun-filled years of his life. He couldn't think of anything he'd done to change that. He'd finished school, landed a decent paying job and bought their first house with money he'd saved as a teenager.

Back then Clarabelle had been the doting wife he'd always wanted. Sure, she was always gossiping with her friends, but she hadn't spoken too ill of him back then. Now, it seemed no matter what he did, she found fault and gossiped openly about him. This latest explosion followed by his inaction would become the most relevant topic in Mrs. Featherbomb's gossip circle. She would tell the story of how Barbara had disrespected her parents and Alfred had done nothing but encourage her, going so far as to say Barbara was right in what she'd done.

"Hang in there, old boy," Alfred murmured to himself and slipped his glasses off to clean them.

He was just sliding them back into place when Mrs. Featherbomb walked into the kitchen. Alfred glanced at her and quickly pretended to be occupied with loosening his tie.

"I don't know what's gotten into your daughter," Mrs. Featherbomb stated.

Alfred grunted. He didn't need to look at her to know she was patting her hair and didn't want him to say any of what was on his mind. He really couldn't have said what was on his mind even if he had been asked though. His eyes didn't bulge, and his heart didn't slam out of his chest the way characters in cartoons did when they were frightened, but he was jumpy and wanted only to not do anything that would unleash Mrs. Featherbomb's wrath upon him.

"Sooner or later that girl has got to learn what we do for her, wouldn't you agree?"

Alfred wanted to go change out of his slacks and put something more relaxing on. Instead, he took his glasses off and stood, grunting now and then to let Mrs. Featherbomb know he was still in the room. The last time he had left the room while she was having one of her one-sided dialogues had led to no less than two months of hearing Mrs. Featherbomb complain to her friends about how her husband was insensitive and didn't talk with her.

Mrs. Featherbomb continued, "I don't know what you've done to her, but she won't listen to me. She's not spoiled like those Alverson brats, but she sure acts like it. I know I shouldn't cuss, but one of these days, your daughter is going to make me lose my inhibitions."

Alfred felt what little energy remained in him drain like water gushing out of a sink with no plumbing installed. He didn't know where it came from, but he did not fight the urge to interrupt.

"There weren't any boys in the car," he said under his breath.

"What was that?" Mrs. Featherbomb turned sharply. "You had better stop teaching Barbara to mumble like that. I could barely hear you."

"Mrs. Wyman came to pick her up," Alfred said, still feeling exhausted. "There weren't any boys in the car."

Mrs. Featherbomb patted her hair, "Well, why couldn't the girl say so. You know, all the trouble she gets into, she brings it on herself. If she weren't so densely selfish at times, I wouldn't have to be so hard on her."

Alfred had given up arguing with Mrs. Featherbomb long ago. Suffering in the restraint of caging his words had proven to be a more peaceful reprieve than behaving as though he had an opinion that was acceptable to share.

In that moment, standing in the mire of fatigue and wilting under the heat of Mrs. Featherbomb's glare that was so intense it would put the atom bomb's explosion to shame, something happened inside Alfred that he didn't understand. It wasn't that he had taken all he could take. He would have recognized that. It was something deeper and more instinctive, an ingrained attitude of rebellion to anything that threatened his personal wellbeing. Mrs. Featherbomb was blaming him for all of Barbara's shortcomings, and it just wasn't true. He wasn't a good father. At the same time, he wasn't a terrible father. He knew he could spend more time with his daughter, but that just wasn't acceptable in the culture. He provided for their needs and then some with his salary. She had friends and kept her grades up in school. If anyone was to blame for corrupting his daughter, it couldn't be him.

"Maybe she would have told us if she'd been given a chance," Alfred said in a deadpan. He dropped his gaze to the floor and braced for the renewed tempest. When Mrs. Featherbomb reacted, he knew the storm would rise several categories in destructive force.

Mrs. Featherbomb exhaled sharply, and Alfred looked up in time to see the hem of her skirt disappear around the archway into the next room. He sat heavily in his chair at the table and wondered what was going to happen next.

Chapter 16

Alfred's stomach growled, and his neck hurt when he moved his head to the right. He rubbed his eyes and put his glasses on. The living room came into focus. The curtains were drawn, and slivers of gray light pushed into the room around the edges. Sweat formed on his brow as he considered opening them.

Standing, he noted the deplorable state of his clothes.

He walked down the hall to the master bedroom and tried the handle. Still locked. He'd slept on the couch after finding it so last night. Mrs. Featherbomb hadn't made a sound since she left the kitchen during their conversation—confrontation? War? He didn't know what to call it. All he knew was he had overstepped and was reaping the just rewards. Mrs. Featherbomb's actions and silence were just, and that was fine. That's what he told himself anyway.

Alfred rubbed the back of his neck. He didn't have the answers. The more he thought about it, the only thing he knew beyond a doubt was that his glasses were dirtier than ever, and the windows would be in the same state.

His stomach rumbled again. That's what he got for upsetting his wife he supposed, sleeping on the couch with no dinner.

He wouldn't go to work without breakfast though.

Passing by Barbara's door, he heard her rummaging through her dresser, sliding drawers in and out. The sounds came quick and sharp. Alfred moved on not wanting to get on his daughter's bad side. Besides, she might not be dressed. He definitely did not want to open that can of worms.

Bacon, toast and eggs sounded good to him, and it couldn't be too hard to make. He'd grown up watching his mother slide bacon and eggs onto his plate from the heavy skillet, and he'd bought Clarabelle a toaster oven a few years ago.

Alfred rummaged in the cupboard until he found the pan Clarabelle often used for breakfast. He set it on the range and began heating it. Next, he cracked three eggs onto it, thinking sunny side up eggs sounded like they could banish some of the gloom. Bacon joined the eggs on the other side of the pan, and its savory smell lifted his spirits somewhat.

"What are you doing, dad?" Barbara asked quietly.

Alfred set the coffee can on the counter beside the percolator. He wasn't sure how to use it just as he wasn't sure how to respond.

"You're burning the eggs," his daughter crossed the kitchen in a rush and grabbed a spatula from the drawer.

After attempting to slide the spatula underneath one of the eggs, she asked, "Didn't you use butter to keep them from sticking?"

Alfred opened his mouth, but nothing came out. How had he forgotten?

Barbara flipped the slide on the toaster. Blackened hunks of bread popped out. The cloying odor of burnt bread stung his nose.

"Go read your paper," Barbara told him. "I'll get this cleaned up and make you something edible."

Alfred stared at his daughter. She was behaving more like a wife than a daughter, but he couldn't argue with her. He was hungry, so he did as he was told.

He stepped out the door and bent for the morning paper. The paperboy had gotten it right on top of the mat. The boy was getting so good he should go out for baseball.

Alfred recoiled. The paper flopped to a stop three feet away. Giggling came from the hedge between his lawn and the Carter's. Alfred lunged for the paper. Again, it jerked and flopped away several feet.

Loud guffawing erupted from the hedge. One Carter boy yelled at his brother to be quiet.

Alfred made one last dive at the paper with the same result.

Mr. Carter stepped from his house, steaming mug of coffee in hand, and yelled, "You boys give Mr. Featherbomb his paper before he tans your hides while I watch. And put my fishing pole back where you found it."

The two boys shuffled from the hedge. With downcast expressions, they untied the paper and handed it to Alfred.

Mr. Carter waved to Alfred as the two boys raced to the garage, shouting at each other. "Sorry about that, neighbor. You know boys."

Alfred waved back. He really didn't know boys. He didn't think a son would be in the kitchen right at that moment making him breakfast because his wife was too mad at him to act as if everything was alright.

"You look like a giant cat caught you and tossed you around all night instead of eating you," Mr. Carter said, narrowing his eyes slightly. "Everything swell?"

Alfred nodded, "Forgot to change out of my clothes last night."

Mr. Carter appeared to find nothing else amiss and lifted his coffee. "Have a swell day, neighbor," he said with a smile.

Alfred sat at the table, smelling the breakfast Barbara was making for him. The thick scent of coffee wafted over him as she plinked two mugs onto the table. Next, she slid a plate of perfectly cooked over-easy eggs, bacon and toast in front of him. She sat across from him in front of her own plate.

Alfred watched silently as his daughter poured milk into her coffee and followed it with two heaping scoops of sugar.

"What?" Barbara asked, shrugging her shoulders and raising her eyebrows.

"I didn't know you like coffee," Alfred stated.

"Don't," Barbara replied. "Some of the other girls told me to add milk and sugar so I could drink it without making a face. Boys seem to like a girl that drinks coffee."

Alfred sat back, shocked. Barbara suddenly seemed to realize what she'd just said. She slammed a hand over her mouth and stared wide-eyed at him.

This was an opportunity, Alfred knew, to be more present with his daughter. Thinking of how cool Mr. Carter handled his boys, Alfred winked at his daughter and said in a conspiratory whisper, "I won't say a word." He followed the statement with a minute nod toward the master bedroom.

Barbara's eyes grew rounder. She shot a fearful glance down the hall.

"Don't scare me like that, dad," she hissed.

Alfred took a bite of the eggs. The flavor burst in his mouth, buttery and salty.

"Dad, you didn't bless the food," Barbara scolded.

Alfred felt heat crawl up his face. Then he remembered a comment he'd overheard at a diner the other day.

"'Food this good is already blessed,'" he quoted.

However, he complied and bowed his head. He had to admit that he felt better after offering thanks for the breakfast. That nagging feeling that he was sinning diminished considerably.

Several times while they ate, Barbara looked up as if she were going to ask a question, but each time she looked back down and continued eating in silence. Alfred was so accustomed to eating breakfast alone that even when he tried to think of something to talk about with his daughter, he remained silent for fear of embarrassing himself.

Barbara finished eating and gathered up the empty dishes. After placing them in the sink, she pulled the ironing board and iron from the closet.

"Dad, choose something to wear," she called quietly. "I'll iron it for you."

Alfred looked up from the paper. He had resolved to deal with whatever criticism he received for his appearance.

"Those are all dirty," he stated absently.

"I know," Barbara said apologetically, "but you can't go to work wearing the same thing you did yesterday. C'mon, you don't want to be late."

Had his daughter just transitioned from being his daughter to his wife and now his mother? Alfred stared dumbfounded.

Barbara smirked and giggled, "No wonder Donna's mom says men would perish if women didn't take care of them."

Alfred gave the table a bewildered glance. It was the other way around. Women needed men to go to work to make the money the family needed. He didn't want to make the same mistake with his daughter that he'd made with his wife last night though, so he remained silent. Barbara urged him to pick something again.

Women. Why did they put so much stock in clothes? Frustration ate into Alfred's voice as he replied, "Just give me some slacks, shirt, tie and a jacket."

A few minutes later, after the creaking of the ironing board ended. Barbara held out a pristine suit of clothes draped over her arm.

"Wear your brown shoes with these and don't cinch your tie as tightly as you usually do," she said as Alfred stood and slid the clothes from her arm. "Oh, and if you want to wear a tie pin, use your gold one shaped like a leaf."

The clothes were still warm, and no moisture remained on them that would wrinkle as it dried. New smudges dotted Alfred's glasses, but he was getting more accustomed to positioning his head to see through the open spots. He already knew he was utterly helpless and didn't need to read an insult for confirmation.

Awestruck by his daughter's ability, Alfred said, "Thank you."

Barbara shrugged and turned toward her room. Halfway there she stopped and turned back. Alfred hadn't moved yet.

"I'll lay on the apple butter for mom. Maybe she'll be a little less moldy when you get home from work."

Alfred's brow furrowed as he struggled to sort out what his daughter had just said for a good thirty seconds or more before wiping his forehead and stepping into the bathroom to change.

He'd just pulled on his shirt and buttoned his sleeves when someone knocked on the door. Fear grasped Alfred at first, but once he realized whoever was at the door wouldn't know what had transpired between him and Clarabelle, he draped his tie around his neck and opened the bathroom door.

He'd taken only a single step into the hallway when he heard the voice. The somehow deep and still slightly nasally voice with a thick Mexican accent.

Anger pulsed in Alfred's ears. His nemesis stood on his very own front porch.

"Hello, Jose," Alfred heard his daughter greet his enemy.

"Hola, Señorita," the Mexican replied. "I trabajando—I working in el campo this day."

"Okay," Barbara replied. "¿A donde su hija?"

The Mexican chuckled and said something in Spanish Alfred didn't understand. Involuntarily, Alfred's hands clenched. He could be rid of the man. Today would be a good day to kick him off his property. The man hadn't been invited to work. He had just shown up as if he were reporting to a full-time job he'd been hired for. The police would prosecute him for trespassing.

Alfred hid in the hallway behind the corner, listening to his daughter converse with his enemy. Something withheld him from barging to the front door and confronting the Mexican. If he had been asked about it later, he may have said that he'd felt too small and incapable to do anything about the Mexican, and he'd say something about not wanting the Mexican to discover his realization of the truth—how the Mexican was working with Codgens.

Alfred slumped and slunk back into the bathroom. All anger left him except for a burning despondence with himself. He wasn't a big man. He was a puny little thumbtack of a man. The worst he could do was be a mild annoyance to those around him, and that wasn't because he was sharp and could draw blood. Even a killer with a thumbtack could kill a person if they stabbed them enough times in the right places. No, Alfred was a bent and dull thumbtack that wouldn't go into the cork easily and always fell out after a short time.

Alfred pulled the rabbit through the hole, glancing at his dull expression in the mirror as he did so. He threw away useless thumbtacks all the time. They were so cheap they weren't worth keeping around.

"What makes you worth keeping around?" he murmured to his reflection.

Alfred combed his hair and shrugged into his jacket. The lines and dark colors looked crisp and clean. Barbara had done a good job choosing what he should wear. He hung his head and flicked the light off.

He couldn't even dress properly without help.

Grabbing his brown shoes from the closet by the front door just as Barbara had told him to, Alfred ducked through the door and hurried for the car. He wanted to get away as fast as he could. Barbara didn't need a goodbye, and that Mexican, well, he didn't want to see him ever again. Maybe he could simply ignore him and that would be sufficient.

Alfred glanced in the rearview mirror. Mr. Riley, his neighbor across the street, waved. Alfred rolled his window partway down and held his hand up for a second. He found himself wishing the Buick had tinted windows like a Mercury Romango.

All the way to work, new smudges coalesced onto his glasses and the Buick's windows. Maybe they weren't new, and he simply hadn't noticed them before. Or, maybe, the Mexican had painted them that very morning before knocking on the door.

"No cussing, dear," Mrs. Featherbomb's voice played like a thirty-three skipping, which made it repeat the same section of the vinyl over and over.

The gall of that Mexican that couldn't even speak proper English. Alfred slammed his hand against the steering wheel. He still needed to talk with Barbara's teacher about teaching kids to talk to dangerous strangers. For all he knew, with his ability to sneak around and break into any building without leaving a trace, the Mexican was a psychotic spy for the Soviets.

The Buick's tires screeched in protest as Alfred threw it into a sharp U-turn. He may not be much of a man, but he still had to save his family or die in the attempt.

The tires screeched with another U-turn. A horn blared. Alfred fixed his gaze straight ahead. He headed for work. He didn't want to be late, but he had also remembered an ad that had been run in the daily paper. It said to remain calm and not alert a suspected commie spy that they were found out. The ad went on to list several government agencies with their phone numbers so that the authorities could capture the threat.

Alfred would be rewarded for doing his duty as an American. He got no satisfaction from that realization, however. He knew he wouldn't be recognized. He wouldn't be considered a hero. He would still be a nobody that nobody cared about. A blunt, bent thumbtack that ended up in the wastebin.

Chapter 17

A black smudge on his glasses hid a bottle from view as he whipped the Buick into the parking lot.   Alfred grimaced as he heard the crunching shatter of the glass bottle shooting from under the tire and breaking against the concrete curb.

Another smudge on his windshield made him misjudge how close he was to Mr. Albright's sedan.   He nudged the bumper on his coworker's car.   Hearing Mrs. Featherbomb trill about no cussing, Alfred threw the Buick into reverse and quickly parked.   He desperately hoped no one had seen.

Mr. Codgens pulled in as Alfed closed the Buick's door and strode for the office.

"Hey, Featherbomber, slow down," Codgens called as he stood from his car. "There's plenty of work for all of us, and it'll be there tomorrow. What's gotten into you, man?"

Alfred didn't slow. He called a good morning over his shoulder and rushed into the reception area.   He barely noticed Sunny's smile and the bright bouquet of fresh carnations on her desk.

"Good morning," Alfred called.

"Did you remember something ya'll forgot yesterday?" Sunny asked, mouth slightly agape at his haste.

"Got a phone call to make," Alfred stated. He stopped, "Do you have this morning's paper?"

Wordlessly, Sunny reached under her desk and pulled out a rolled-up newspaper.

"Your country's going to thank you," Alfred grabbed the newspaper and kissed the startled young woman on the cheek. Alfred was through the door before she could respond.

He dropped his briefcase by his desk and thumbed through the paper until he found the article he sought. He couldn't wait, and he needed privacy. That meant he wouldn't ask Sunny to borrow her phone. A phone booth would have to do.

Outside his office he heard Codgens addressing anyone who would listen, "The Featherbomber ran in here like he was running from a fire. Doesn't he know you're supposed to run out of a building that's on fire?"

Without missing a beat, someone cut in, "Codgens your cubicle is the only thing in here that's on fire. If the fire department rushed in there to save you, they'd all become trapped victims. Have you ever considered cleaning up after yourself like Eddy Albright does?"

"That lovebird," Codgens laughed, "only cleaned up his space so that little songbird would have a place to sit and watch him work."

Amidst the stares, Alfred flung the front door open and pretended not to hear the questions fired at him. He fumbled in his pocket for the phone booth fee and inserted a nickel into the slot. Muttering the agency's number as he rotated the dial, he glanced around nervously.

"Hello," a grainy voice said.

"Ah, yes," Alfred held a hand around the mouthpiece of the phone, "I need to report a suspected spy." He glanced out the clear sides of the phone booth and spoke quietly. Every word felt like the whole world could hear it.

"And he's at your house right now you say?" the representative asked.

"Yes. I handle contracts for large companies for Davis and Fitch," Alfred hoped they were nabbing the Mexican as he spoke.

"Has the man deviated from his routine of working at your house?"

Alfred wiped his eyelids, pushing his glasses up to his forehead. "No. He's showed every day this week."

"Okay, sir," the agency rep said. "I'll have someone look into this."

"My family is in danger," Alfred hissed into the phone.

"I understand, sir. Thank you for the tip, and don't hesitate to call the hotline if you see anything suspicious."

Alfred formed another retort, but the click and hum of an ended call cut him off. He pressed the phone onto the receiver and backed slowly out of the phone booth. With both hands he rubbed his eyes. The day was just starting and already the weight of responsibility was proving too much.

When was the last time he'd gone on vacation? Had it been when they'd gone to New York? Had that been two years ago or had it been longer? Barbara had been a little girl at the time.

Alfred hurried back to his office and managed to sneak in without anyone demanding to know about his absurd behavior.

He'd just sat at his desk and opened his briefcase when the sharp crack of knuckles rapping on the door broke his daze. Alfred snapped his focus to the door as Mr. Orton pushed it aside and stepped in.

"Did you hear, Featherbomber?" he said in his brisk, over-excited voice.

Alfred searched his desk for a memo he might have missed. "Hear what?" he responded.

"The boss got the big dog," Mr. Orton grinned at Alfred's confusion. "That project you and I worked on a few months back. Well, it went down so well, Daddy-O is giving us both a bonus, and," he paused as if waiting for Alfred to ask.

He obliged. "And what?" Alfred asked, feeling a strange fear and sinking feeling sliding down his spine.

Mr. Orton rubbed his hands together, "Daddy-O is giving us each a stay at the ritz with our families. Says he'll treat us to a round of golf too."

"That's," Alfred stumbled for a response that felt adequate. He should be excited. He knew that was the normal response, but he couldn't shake the feeling of dread leaking into his soul. If others found out what was going on at home, well, he dared not consider that.

"Say," Mr. Orton scrunched his brow, "something's gotten into you, Featherbomber, you're dressed sharper than normal. You're swingin' today. You're not jealous of Mr. Bright-as-a-Light, are you? Man, she's too young for you."

Alfred opened his mouth to object.

"Say," Mr. Orton continued, "aren't you married already?"

Once again, Alfred tried to respond but was not quick enough. He was not jealous of Mr. Albright hitting it off with Sunny. Mr. Orton was right; he was already married and was most definitely *not* looking for the problems that would grind him further into dust if he were to pursue Miss Potter.

Mr. Orton made to leave, saying as he reached for the door, "I just thought I'd step in to say Daddy-O is happy with our work. I'm sure we'll be working on some more topnotch projects soon."

"Yes," Alfred stood and gave an awkward, little bow.

Mr. Orton squinched his eyebrows and left Alfred's office, leaving its occupant to drop back into his chair exhausted.

Alfred picked up his pen and absently rubbed the smooth, wooden cylinder. What part had he played in that project Mr. Orton had mentioned? What part did he play at Davis and Fitch for that matter? There had been a time when he had been proud of his work and the way he screeded faulty contracts into level-headed agreements between businesses.

Now, he would be going a little too far to say he thought he was doing a good job. Everything he touched felt wrong, and the amount of time he spent second-guessing himself felt like solid ground for firing him. Despite all that, Mr. Davis wanted to reward him? He didn't deserve it.

He sighed. If he was on his way out, he might as well stay busy. He pulled the latest contract closer and began scanning it again.

Why can't Clarabelle and I get along? he wondered.

It wasn't like they fought tooth and nail, but he wished they could have some blissful moments like they used to have early on in their marriage. Maybe their contract was faulty. If that was all, Alfred could fix it just like he did all day at work. After all, the companies that went to Davis and Fitch wanted to work together, but in today's world of leaps and bounds in all sectors—and not to mention the fear the Soviets imposed—no one wanted to be, pardon the cliché, up the creek without a paddle if the commies attacked or a nuke wiped out half of the population.

That brought Alfred's attention back to the Mexican. Surely, they'd captured him by now. Alfred wanted to feel exuberant that at least one of his pressing problems had been removed, but he felt nothing. All he felt where such satisfaction should be present was profound emptiness. He'd heard of spies grouping together and pretending to be a family. What if that Mexican's wife and daughter really were his family and not some facade to get him to trust him? It was all overwhelming, and his mind felt like popcorn. A thought popped over there and then one exploded close at hand. He rubbed his eyes.

His door creaked open, and Sunny spoke timidly in her strangely brisk southern drawl, "I'm sorry if I'm disturbin' you. Your door was ajar. I thought you might have stepped out again."

Alfred discarded his glasses onto his desk and waved his hand, "Mr. Orton didn't close it."

"Mr. Davis wanted me to give you this," Sunny held out a white envelope.

It had his name on it.

So, the man couldn't fire him face to face. No matter, he would take his things and leave quietly. He stood and quietly accepted the envelope.

"Thank you," he said in a whisper.

"Eddy dresses real fine," Sunny observed, "but you're dressed to the nines. I'll have to have him take notes from you before we go to the square dance this weekend."

Alfred pressed his mouth into a courteous smile and nodded once.

"Anyway, I'm sorry to have bothered you," Sunny said.

"It's been nice working with you," Alfred finally found words. "You have been a golden ray of sunshine every day."

"What?" Sunny's face contorted in confusion.

Alfred grimaced. "Nothing," he shook his head dismissively.

"Mr. Davis dictated that over the phone," Sunny pointed to the envelope still in Alfred's hand. "He's not able to make it in today or tomorrow, and he didn't want to make you wait." Sudden realization played across her face, "Oh! You thought...he's not firin' you. There's quite a lot in there I think you'll be mighty thrilled about."

Alfred glanced at the envelope. His name stared up at him in blurry squiggles without his glasses. "Oh, thank you," he tried to sound genuinely enthusiastic.

Sunny gave one of her huge, genuine smiles, "I hope I'm not steppin' over no bounds. You really do look swingin' today."

Blood rushed to Alfred's cheeks. "Yes, ma'am," he said, searching for anything else to say. "You're looking quite pretty yourself."

Sunny crossed her arms and shifted her weight onto one leg. In an obstinate voice she stated, "Now, Mr. Featherbomb, that's quite enough from you. You're married to a fine woman, and this old thing," she spread her hand down her long, brown skirt, "ain't worth the air it takes to compliment it."

Alfred froze, blinking repeatedly. Warning bells and lights went off in his mind as if it were Fort Knox in the middle of a break in.

Sunny giggled, "I'm just messin' with you. You needn't kiss me. I'll take your payment from a certain fine, young gentleman I know." She held up her hand, "Not that you aren't a gentleman, Mr. Featherbomb."

Alfred knew well what she was talking about, but he couldn't form words to comfort the young woman.

"Well," Sunny said slowly and softly, "I'm sorry I made it awkward. I guess I need to be more careful with those types of jokes." She continued in a surrendered tone, "That's probably just what I get from working around so many men all day."

A response similar to something Mr. Davis would say left Alfred's lips before he realized he even thought it up. "It's fine. You light up Mr. Albright like no one else can."

Sunny smiled, and a dreamy look glazed her eyes. "Good day, Mr. Featherbomb. If you need me to take a note for Mr. Davis, let me know. He doesn't want to be disturbed today if it can be helped."

Alfred nodded and sat down. Sunny, accustomed to the nonverbal language of the office, took the cue and stepped out, closing the door behind her.

Alfred picked up the envelope and stared at it. No matter how long he looked at the flowing, black letters, they didn't grow any clearer. He gained slight reassurance that Mr.

Orton hadn't been pulling his leg, but he still didn't want to open it. If his boss wanted to reward him for a job well done, he should be able to receive it readily. What was wrong with him?

With a frown etching itself onto his face, he nudged the envelope a few inches across his desk. The completely normal business envelope somehow felt like poison. He needed to wash his hands and air out his office after handling it. There was no doubt about it, he was an ingrate. But he couldn't have others see how his wife was treating him.

He needed to wash his hands. Wiping them on his slacks, he reached for his letter opener.

As his fingers closed around the silver handle, he stared in disbelief. His fingers were twitching as if his hand had forgotten to shake and they needed to make up for the hand's inability. With a loud crack, Alfred slapped the letter opener on top of the envelope.

He needed to wash his hands.

He hurried from his office and locked himself in the bathroom.

Several minutes later, and lacking several layers of skin on his hands, he approached the letter on his desk again. Sunny had assured him that Mr. Davis wasn't firing him, but Alfred thought to himself that he would prefer that over the threat of embarrassing himself by not having the family everyone thought he had.

Listlessly, he pulled his chair from the corner it had slid into upon his hasty exit and righted his wastepaper basket. The actions bolstered his sense that everything was alright.

Before he could second-guess himself again, he grabbed the envelope and letter opener. The crisp paper gave way easily.

Sunny's neat, concise handwriting outlined Mr. Davis's gratitude and planned recognition. A trickle of sweat crept down Alfred's forehead as his eyes darted over the note.

Maybe the date of the golf outing would be far enough in the future to allow him the time to sufficiently make up to Mrs. Featherbomb.

The note slipped to his desk. Enterprising as always, Mr. Davis had already booked the hotel and golf reservations for the Monday and Tuesday of the following week—only a few days away.

Chapter 18

"Dad, what happened to Señor Josc?"

Alfred slowly pushed the door shut behind him. He was not ready for his daughter's energy. He needed a drink—maybe a trip to the hardware store to see Mr. Faustner or, if Mrs. Featherbomb was out, he could see what she had stocked in her closet.

He closed his eyes and failed to push the nagging thought from his mind. Now that he acknowledged what he knew he had seen, he would never be rid of the image of the bottles spilling out of their hiding place.

Setting his briefcase down by the wall, Alfred raised his tired eyes to meet Barbara's wide eyes. Her mouth was open, most likely with a repetition of the same question. She closed it and stared at him. He dropped his gaze to the floor.

Barbara pressed quietly, "Mom doesn't know, and she won't say what she thinks."

Alfred closed his eyes and winced.

"Oh, right. Sorry," Barbara said, her voice sinking to a more dismal sheen.

"Everyone at the office liked the clothes you picked for me, Sweet Pea," Alfred said. He eased into his accustomed spot at the table and then remembered that Mrs. Featherbomb would not be getting him his accustomed glass of lemonade. He made to get up, but Barbara told him to stay seated and whisked to the refrigerator. A moment later, a cold glass of freshly squeezed lemonade sent tingles along his tastebuds as the glass began its arduous task of collecting condensation.

"That's great, dad, but what about Señor Jose?" Barbara pulled back the chair next to her father and tried to sit primly. However, she bounced her legs and swept her arms across the table before locking them in place by crossing them.

Alfred stared at his lemonade and took a sip. "This is good lemonade," he said.

The smile he offered his daughter did nothing to address her demand. She raised her eyebrows and pushed her head forward to reiterate her question.

"I made it this afternoon. Donna's mom dropped off a whole bag of fresh lemons. I had to walk to the store to buy sugar. I think mom forgot to buy more last week," Barbara said conversationally. Then she took a different tact, "So, when will you be ready to tell me why they took Señor Jose away?"

Alfred set his glass down and swallowed loudly. He wished the answer he could use would be something that equated to never being ready. However, he knew his daughter wouldn't be put off so easily.

He cleared his throat and hurried through the explanation he had concocted, "You're familiar with the threat we're under with this cold war. You have to do drills at school. Must be the Mexican did something that looked suspicious. He could be a communist agent."

"Mom seemed to think you had something to do with it," Barbara said as if thinking out loud. "How could he be a spy if he has a family?"

"Barbara," Alfred said, wishing he was talking about nearly anything else with his daughter, "that's the best cover a spy can have. He blends in that way. They're nothing but a fake family."

Alfred stopped. He had just called the Mexican's family a fake family, yet they behaved and treated one another with perhaps more warmth than most of the families Alfred knew. Barbara was still talking, but he wasn't hearing her. He considered the golf outing Mr. Davis had given him and his family. He was so scared of going on it because he didn't want others to see the real relationship he had with his family. Didn't that make them the fake family?

"Dad? Dad?" Barbara questioned more adamantly with each repetition.

Alfred's thoughts muddled, and his vision swirled until it focused. He was staring at the middle of the table.

"Don't worry about it, dad. There's nothing you could've done. You were at work," Barbara rubbed her upper arm with her right hand and tucked a stray strand of hair behind her ear.

There had been something he could've done. He'd done it—or, rather, he'd done the thing that caused the Mexican to be arrested.

"I'm sorry," Alfred mumbled. "I guess I wasn't listening."

"You do that to mom a lot," Barbara quipped without a hint of annoyance. "So, are we gonna go find his family and make sure they're okay?"

Hadn't she heard what he'd said about spies having fake families? What else had she said that he hadn't heard? And she was right; he did apologize to Mrs. Featherbomb quite often for having drifted off in his thoughts and having not heard what she'd been saying.

A ray of hope shone in his mind. Maybe that's what he'd done. Maybe Clarabelle had said something important that he had seemingly ignored.

Instinctual self-preservation rose up inside. He was a better listener than nearly every other man alive.

His hands began to shake, and he ripped his glasses off. He could feel the smears forming a new word, a new insult—a new truth.

"Dad, are you okay? You're acting weird again," Barbara asked, voice edged with mild panic.

"I'm fine," he said quickly and made a chopping motion with his left hand. With his right he placed his glasses in his shirt pocket.

His daughter stared at him. He could see the doubt and questions she kept at bay swirling like a tornado behind her eyes.

"I'm fine," Alfred repeated softly with more control.

The truth, and he knew it well, was that he was far from okay. His new glasses hadn't come in yet, and even with the Mexican locked away, he was still terrified of discovering more insults that the man manipulated like magic. He most definitely was not okay. He was cold and shriveled inside like Scrooge in Dickinson's "A Christmas Carol" staring down at his own grave.

"Has your mother been normal today?" Alfred asked. He really didn't want to assume anything, yet the prolonged silences Mrs. Featherbomb was capable of forcing on him were inconvenient at best. He refused to think about the worst case scenario with Codgens' involvement.

Barbara huffed out a breath, turned to the side and stabbed a hand onto her hip. "If you mean talking on the phone all day and going to get her nails done with Mrs. Evansley, then yeah, I guess she's been pretty normal," she said.

Alfred winced. "Is that where she is now?" he glanced at his daughter and then stared at the top of the table.

"Yeah," Barbara said, deflating slightly. "She wanted me to tell you there's food in the refrigerator."

Alfred grunted. Maybe that was a good sign. Mrs. Featherbomb wasn't going to let him starve as she had that morning. He rubbed his eyes and pulled out his glasses. A glance out the living room window showed lengthening shadows reaching for the opposite side of the driveway. He swallowed a lump in his throat. He was a man who was supposed to know how to fix things. Well, he might as well have pasta for brains because all he'd been managing lately was creating problems.

"Have you eaten?" he turned to his daughter.

Barbara laced her fingers and shrugged her shoulders, "I guess I'm not hungry." She paused, looking down and rubbing her toe against the leg of the nearest chair. "I don't like it when you and mom aren't getting along," she stated quietly.

What had he done now? Alfred felt anger flare to life inside him. Just as quickly, he metaphorically took it in his hand and donned it like an overcoat. His daughter couldn't blame him for the current state of his marriage.

Alfred glared sharply at Barbara. She glanced into his eyes and stood still, seemingly trying to appear smaller as if she were attempting to slide behind the wall dividing the dining room and living room.

He was not that man. Alfred knew it. He was not the man who would take his anger out on his children, or, in his case, on his daughter. The overcoat remained, weighing down his shoulders. A look of pain and sorrow washed over his face. He had just glared at his daughter as if he wished she weren't there. He was a lousy father, and a teeny tiny, little bent thumbtack of a man.

They stood that way for a full minute, father staring with a look of self-loathing and daughter standing like a blade of grass in the calm before a storm.

At long last, Alfred slumped under the weight of his anger and despondence. Shoving his hands into his pockets, he stepped up to his daughter. She shrank and trembled slightly.

"I," Alfred began, but with that one syllable, Barbara shuddered and spun around as if to run down the hall to her room. Without thinking, Alfred caught her arm and pulled her tight. She started sobbing before he could finish wrapping her awkwardly in a hug.

With deepening sorrow and remorse, Alfred realized he couldn't remember what it felt like to hug his daughter. When had he last hugged her? Had it been on her sixth birthday? He couldn't remember. He had failed at being a loving father.

He was a failure. No wonder his daughter didn't want to be around him.

"I don't want you and mom to fight," Barbara squeezed out in between sobs.

Alfred felt the wetness of her tears through his shirt and undershirt.

"Why can't we just be happy together?" Barbara turned large, water-filled eyes up to him.

Alfred looked into his daughter's eyes and saw pain. Deep pain that could not be described, only felt. He had no answer for it.

"No cussing, dear," Mrs. Featherbomb's voice directed in his head.

He couldn't solve anything. He wanted to cuss and scream—or maybe scream and then cuss. Either way he had something inside that he desperately needed to get out and some combination of screaming and cussing seemed the only way to release it.

Barbara unfolded her arms and wrapped them around her father. Alfred froze. Something happened inside him that he had never felt before when he had received a hug. The feelings of wrongness and darkness that demanded release quieted. To him it felt like a snake coiling into the basket as the snake charmer played his flute.

He rested his cheek on top of his daughter's head and hugged her tighter. She cried and mumbled a few other things about not wanting their family to fight.

A knock sounded on the door, breaking into the quiet solitude. Alfred glanced at the door while his daughter gave a cry and immediately swiped at her tears and sniffed loudly.

Alfred moved to the door as a second series of knocks were thrapped.

Upon opening the door, he stood stunned in disbelief. A little girl with a dark mop of hair scrambled in and latched onto Barbara. A short, dark woman, the little girl's mother, standing on the step released a torrent of rapid Spanish and animated hand gestures.

Then, the woman looked at Alfred and said what seemed to be the only word she knew in English, "Sorry. Sorry. Sorry, Señor. Marie, ven aqui, ahora."

The little girl was now in Barbara's arms tracing the lines the tears had made on her face and not paying heed to her mother. For an instant Alfred considered how the woman and the girl might not even be related. They were merely a cover for the Mexican spy. And then, the Mexican woman addressed his own daughter in Spanish.

"¿Donde Jose, mi amor?" she asked.

Barbara thought for a moment and responded, "No se, necitamos buscamos para Señor Jose."

"What's she saying? What are you telling her?" Alfred demanded. His voice had an edge to it. He couldn't completely shake the idea that the Mexican *was* a communist spy and was also the reason for the ongoing insults buffeting him.

"She's asking where Señor Jose is," Barbara stated flatly, shifting the little girl to her hip.

"How should I know?" Alfred barked.

Barbara looked at him with fear tugging at her eyes, but she swallowed and said, "That's why I think we should go look for him."

The Mexican woman, still standing on the porch, glanced back and forth between Alfred and Barbara as they discussed her husband.

"You said he got taken—arrested, yes?"

Barbara nodded and said, "They came here and just took him away."

"Who?" Alfred watched in irritation as the little Mexican girl hugged Barbara and rested her head on her shoulder. Barbara responded by hugging her tighter and resting her head on top of the little girl's.

"The police, I think," Barbara said softly.

"Policia. Ay-yai-yai. No, Señor. Por favor," the woman on the porch uttered. "Marie, ven aqui."

The little girl looked at her mother. Sadness played across her dark features. Barbara snuggled her and set her down.

Marie wrapped her arms around Barbara's leg and said adamantly, "No, Mami. Find Papi."

The woman on the porch flashed a stern look and then smiled, "Si, si. Papi. Ven aqui."

Marie repeated, "No, Mami. Find Papi." She looked pleadingly up at Barbara.

Alfred could do nothing. He didn't know Spanish, and could he really bring himself to phone the police and have them take away the woman and the little girl? The longer he observed, the more certain he became they were legitimately mother and daughter.

Barbara knelt and talked softly with the little girl.

Marie shook her head, sending her dark, wavy hair dancing around her. "No," she said again more forcefully, "Find Papi."

Barbara attempted to unclasp the girl's grasp on her, but Marie only clutched her hand and pulled her toward the door.

Alfred caught the silent plea for help in his daughter's eyes as the little, Mexican girl dragged her toward the door. The mother was making an entire apologetic speech interspersed with commands for her daughter, and Barbara was nearly out the door when he spoke.

"Tell them to get in the car," he said in a defeated tone.

"What?" Barbara apparently couldn't hear over the racket the mother was making.

"Tell them to get in the car," Alfred raised his voice. "I'll drive them to the police station."

At the mention of the police, the mother went into a fresh onslaught of demands for Marie to "Ven aqui" and numerous exclamations of "Ay-yai-yai" interspersed with "Dios mio."

Alfred slid his shoes on and grabbed the car keys. He reached for his daughter's shoes, but she managed to snatch them before nearly tumbling out the door. Once she recovered, Alfred heard his daughter speak commands in Spanish.

The little girl understood right away. She dropped Barbara's hand and raced to the car. She yanked the door open and was standing in the middle of the back seat before her mother had made it two steps.

Alfred sighed. He didn't look forward to cleaning the car or paying someone else to clean it.

"I'll ride back here with them," Barbara said as she slid in behind the driver's seat.

Alfred grunted.

With the little girl jabbering excitedly about finding Papi, Alfred steered the Buick to the road and turned right. It would take only twenty minutes to get to their destination.

Chapter 19

"You just missed 'im," a roundish officer in dark blue said as he bit into a bagel loaded down with more cream cheese than it could hold. "He put up quite the fuss, but no one could understand 'im. The interpreter's out sick, so when they said to put 'im on the bus with the other prisoners headed up north, we obliged."

Alfred blinked and slapped at a twitch in his left eyelid. Behind him, in hushed tones, Barbara translated for the Mexican's wife.

"Where's Papi?" Marie whined.

"We'll find him," Barbara tried to reassure the little girl.

"¿Donde Papi?" the girl responded.

This time the girl's mother shushed her and spoke in rapid undertones. The girl let out a muffled wail and cried, "Quiero Papi. I want Papi."

Alfred had to steady himself. He couldn't remember a time when Barbara ever would have wailed and thrown a tantrum to be with him. Did that make him a bad father?

Probably. No, it most definitely did mean he was a bad father. Once again, he was the one with the fake family while the Mexican had a real family who wanted to stay together.

Señor Jose. Was it really that hard for him to think of the Mexican as a man with a name and, evidently, a real family?

"Seems like that little rascal misses her father," the officer said, making the last of the bagel disappear but leaving a smudge of cream cheese at the corner of his mouth. "The Mexican was brought in for suspected espionage, but I've never seen a spy with a fake family so attached whether they're greasers or not. Don't think I've ever actually seen a real spy.

"Tell ya what I can do," the officer reached for a pen and paper. "I'll take your number since you can at least understand English. I'll phone up north. When they see your friend, I'll give you a holler. How does that sound?"

Alfred glanced at the woman and daughter. There was no way they would understand. The man's wife would probably stay up all night worrying, and the little girl... Well, she would ball her eyes out until she wore herself out, and then, when she woke up, she'd be so cranky he'd want to leave her behind.

Wait. What had he just thought? No, not about leaving the little girl behind all alone, but the fact that he would be able to leave her behind at all.

Barbara looked at him expectantly. Somehow, he had missed her transforming from a little girl, not all that different from the Mexican's daughter, into a grownup. She stood with poise and a calmness that few adults even managed to exude. He shook his head.

"No," Alfred turned back to the officer. "I don't think that will work. Where up north did you send him?"

"I had nothing to do with it," the officer sputtered. "I was just coming on duty when the bus left."

Alfred bit his tongue. He hadn't intended to insult the man.

"I want Papi," Marie murmured. Her mother shushed her and cooed to her in their language.

"Where up north you ask," the officer said. "It's about an hour from here. They left over an hour ago, so they made it there by now."

Alfred pushed his glasses up so he could rub his eyes. He did not want to drag the Mexican family all over the place. He wanted dinner and his own bed with his wife on speaking terms with him again.

"Take Sheller's Road out there by the old Smith place, you know the one with the barn that has the sign painted on it for Faustner's?" the officer began drawing a crude map. "It's nearly a straight shot up from there. It's a pretty remote area, so be sure to fill up on gasoline before you leave town."

"Thanks," Alfred reached for the map.

As they left the police station, Alfred felt Barbara's arms around him. She hugged him for the second time that day.

"Thanks, dad," she said so only he could hear. "I know this is the right thing to do." She went on overexplaining, "We don't know them very well, but they don't seem to have anyone else in town. At least, Señor Jose doesn't seem to have anyone else to work for. I know he'll be grateful. And Marie might be so happy you helped her find her Papi she might start calling you Abuelo. Wouldn't that be cute?"

Barbara's hand slipped into his. For a moment, they were both several years younger. She was telling him she could slide down the tall slide when none of the other girls were brave enough. It had been after her first day at school. He'd taken her to the park after picking her up, having left work early to make it a special day for her. He'd lost so much that he would never get back and never be able to replace. A black smudge clouded the bottom portion of his glasses.

And then, Barbara was stroking Marie's wild locks of wavy, dark hair and talking encouragingly to her. The little girl lifted her head off her mother's shoulder and stared at Barbara with eyes glassy and unfocused from exhaustion.

As they climbed into the car, the mother said something that sounded like a question. Barbara asked for the map Alfred always kept in the glove box and explained in halting Spanish. The woman nodded and sank into the backseat, shoulders slumping.

Alfred rubbed a spot on the windshield and nosed the Buick toward the nearest gas station. He glanced in the rearview mirror as headlights glinted off dark smudges in the gathering dusk.

The words glared back at him bold and black. But he wasn't he told himself. What he was doing right now was neither selfish, inconsiderate nor barbaric. He was selflessly driving this woman and her daughter to find their husband and father respectively. What more could he do? The answer didn't creep up on him. It had been in plain sight all day. Ever since he'd made that phone call, it had been staring him down, daring him to acknowledge its presence.

The next question his mind entertained was more morose. Would the Mexicans ever forgive him if they ever found out what he had done? Pastor Meyers' voice rang in response, telling him how he had done evil and needed to repent. It would come at great cost to his pride, but it would ultimately be well worth the pain to come right with his fellow man.

Fellow man? Is that how Pastor Meyers saw all the migrant workers and even the Chinese who looked just like the Koreans?

"No cussing, dear," Mrs. Featherbomb's phrase sounded in his mind. He shut his mouth. He wasn't going to say it out loud. Maybe a whisper, but surely not loud enough for anyone else to hear.

"Dad," Barbara's voice contained a twinge of urgency, "don't drive past the turn."

Alfred shook his head and recentered his attention on the road. In the quickly descending night, the sun-faded colors of the garish sign proclaiming that Faustner's had it all stood out like bas relief for an instant as the headlights swung over them.

"Did you bring any water?" Barbara asked.

Alfred cleared his throat and adjusted himself in the seat. "No," he said. "We can get some at the depot."

"Okay."

Alfred glanced at his daughter in the rearview mirror. She curled her lip and contorted her face.

"I don't feel super good," she stated and rubbed her stomach. "I think I'm gonna hurl."

Alfred slammed on the brakes and slid the car to a stop alongside the road. Dust billowed up around them, and the sounds of Barbara yanking the door open introduced her moaning. She didn't puke or even dry heave, but Alfred sat frozen in the driver's seat unsure how he could help and wondering whether he was even capable of helping.

Barbara had always been a healthy child. He couldn't remember the last time he'd seen her sick. He wondered what he had to offer her. Finally, he remembered the blanket he had stowed in the trunk in case of a breakdown in the middle of nowhere during cold weather. He jerked himself out of the seat. As he rounded the car, he saw Barbara standing but curled over on herself with her arms holding her stomach.

"It's not too bad," she held up a flailing hand. "It's just really bad cramps."

Alfred paused, his hand on the trunk. He stared at his daughter and continued watching helplessly as the Mexican woman, Señor Jose's wife, exited the car and draped an arm around her. The two attempted to converse in Spanish, but Barbara kept shaking her head and looking slightly confused. And then his daughter made a noise that she'd been making much more often as she passed into puberty. She growl-sighed and gently pushed herself away from the woman. She massaged her stomach as Señor Jose's wife sidled up to him.

"Su hija, you da...daughter," the English words came slow and were twisted with the woman's accent. "Help...her. You," she made a shooing gesture with both hands. It was the most animated he'd seen her behave outside of her hearing mention of the police.

Alfred stood inert—maybe helpless was the better description. He decided he was using that word too much. He needed something more potent to describe his inability.

"You," the Mexican woman shooed at him again. "You go. You…no help."

She didn't wait for him to walk away but rummaged in her purse and approached Barbara. Barbara listened, clearly understanding only a small portion of what the woman was saying.

Alfred watched the strange gestures the woman was using until he finally shrugged and plucked his glasses from his nose and walked toward the front of the car. He kept walking and contemplating the woman's insistence that he was no help. Of course he was no help. She didn't need to point it out to him.

Glancing back, dread slammed into him. Somehow, he knew that as soon as he got back into the car, he would see some new insult smeared on the windshield. There really was no peace for the wicked. He was obviously wicked. Why else would this be happening to him, and, not to mention, he didn't need any further evidence than what he'd done to Señor Jose.

His daughter and the Mexican's wife stood up from where they had squatted down beside the car. The Mexican woman beckoned him back, but Barbara looked bashful even in the meager light.

Once they were all back in the car, Alfred decided to not ask any questions.

"I'm fine, dad," Barbara blurted suddenly. "Stop looking at me like I might break."

Alfred grasped the steering wheel and stared straight ahead, straight through black smears that were darkening and growing into a new insult right in front of his eyes.

Absently, he responded, "I wasn't even looking at you."

"Sorry, dad," Barbara apologized.

Señor Jose's wife jabbered something in Spanish.

"We can keep driving now," Barbara barked.

Alfred slowly forced his hands to shift the car into gear and his foot to press the accelerator.

"I'm sorry, dad, I don't mean to be so snappy," Barbara apologized again.

Alfred made no reply as the car bounced over the imperfections in the road. Whatever had just happened, he was no help and no better than a vegetable after a lobotomy.

The miles ticked by beneath them, and Barbara remained completely quiet and pressed up against the corner every time he glanced at her in the rearview mirror. She didn't even get out to stretch when they fueled up at the depot.

Every so often, the little girl stirred, murmured that she wanted Papi and then restarted her string of drool she was depositing on her mother's arm.

The sun had fully set by the time the glow from the facility's lights came into view. Alfred wove the car around the few vehicles in the parking lot and did his best to see around the black smudges obscuring the parking stall lines.

"I want Papi," Marie muttered. Her eyes were still closed, and she clutched at her mother's arm.

Barbara lifted her head from where she'd rested it on the door for the past twenty minutes and yawned. She opened her door and went to get up, but halfway through she turned red and extricated herself in an odd contortion that kept her facing the other passengers. Alfred wondered at her for a moment but put little thought into her strange antics as he pulled his glasses off and cleaned them on his shirt.

Pushing the door shut, he pivoted on his heel, turning this way and that way. An oppressive silence hung over the facility all the way from the tall fence capped with barbed wire to the guard towers positioned around the facility every hundred feet or so.

The lights in the parking lot were bright, highlighting the insults on his glasses. He heard Mrs. Featherbomb tell him not to cuss as he vigorously snatched his glasses off and scrubbed them again. He knew it was a fruitless endeavor, but the act of managing dirty glasses made him feel slightly better. The new ones would be ready anytime he kept telling himself. Maybe he would receive a call from the optician tomorrow.

Barbara tied her thin jacket around her waist despite the chill settling around them and asked, "Where do we go?"

Alfred had no answer. He thought he should look for a main entrance with an awning or guards or something, but he could do nothing except pivot on his heel and look around. He cleaned his glasses again and rammed them back onto his face.

"Dad," Barbara's sudden sharpness startled him. He replaced his glasses midway through pulling them off again and settled his gaze on his daughter. "You just cleaned your glasses. This place gives me the gringles too. Where do we go?"

Señor Jose's wife clambered from the car. She held Marie on her hip, and the little girl buried her face in her mother's neck.

"Looks like Snazzy-Duds doesn't know where to go," a young, masculine voice said from the darkness some ten feet away.

Alfred jumped and reached for his glasses. He barely restrained himself from crying out in surprise like his daughter and the Mexican woman.

"Who are ya here for?" a young officer stepped into the light. The tools on his belt glittered coldly just like his badge and polished boots. He rested his hands on his belt in a way that was supposed to be relaxed but instead looked challenging like an Old West gunfighter preparing for a showdown.

"We," Alfred found words escaping him. "We...uh...did you get a busload of prisoners today?"

The officer's eyes narrowed, "Yeah. Why?"

Alfred fumbled for what to say, "We're here for a Mexican—I mean Señor Jose. We were told he was brought up here."

"What's he in for?" the officer tipped his hat back so the badge fastened just above the brim flashed in the electric lights.

"He, well, he didn't really do anything," Alfred wiped at sweat forming above his eyebrows. "I think someone told the police he was a communist."

"A commie, eh?" the young man asked with an incredulous expression. "They don't get let out."

The Mexican woman clearly understood more English than she let on to because she inhaled sharply and spoke soothingly to her daughter as she laid her head on top of Marie's crazy hairdo.

"He her husband or something?" the officer tipped his head at the Mexican woman.

"Yes," Alfred rubbed his eyes and could hardly believe the words that came from his mouth as he continued. "He works for us, does gardening and yard work."

"Does he now?" the officer leaned his head back again, looking down his nose.

Alfred couldn't meet his judgmental gaze.

"He won't be working for you anymore," Alfred didn't look at the man, but he felt the cold coils of demented glee snake through the air.

Alfred combed his right hand through his hair and pulled his glasses off with his left. What had he done? Had he ruined a family's life with a single phone call? A single lie?

Somewhere deep down, he'd always known the Mexican wasn't a communist spy. He had just wanted to keep the man from writing his insults all over his glasses and windows. But the insults still showed up, didn't they? Even when the man was locked away, the black smears and smudges still showed up on his glasses and the car windshield.

Alfred swallowed. He had been wrong and acted wrongfully.

"Jensen, what are you telling these folks?" a grandfatherly voice preceded a tall man with a lined face partially hidden by a mustache stepping into the light. He was similarly attired as the young officer, but his uniform had a worn and relaxed nature about it that made the old man look calm and confident.

"Bradley Sloak," he said as he shook Alfred's hand. He tipped his hat, "Ladies."

Turning only partially toward his fellow officer, Sloak spoke from the corner of his mouth, "Deputy Jensen, your badge seems to have pricked your tongue when you put it on."

The young man's eyes flashed, but he saluted and replied, "Yes, sir."

"As for you folks," the old officer turned back to Alfred. His gaze lingered briefly on Marie. "What are you here for? Are you looking for her father?"

Alfred nodded, "We think someone reported him as a communist spy."

Officer Sloak's eyebrows arched, "Well, it seems you better come inside. Visiting hours are over, but we can take a look at the records and see if he's here like you say."

Alfred phrased his question carefully, "If he was—If the report that he's a spy is wrong, can we take him back with us?"

The old man grunted and pulled open a door leading into a dark entryway. "He'd have to be released for you to be able to do that. That's not likely to happen for a good while. Does he work for you?"

Alfred nodded, swallowing the embarrassment that rose from his stomach at not knowing how prisons worked. The old officer asked him again with a gaze.

"Oh, yes," Alfred felt heat rise to his cheeks.

"Well, you'll probably have to do without him for a few days to a few weeks," Officer Sloak stepped behind the receptionist's desk and thumbed through a ledger. "If he's clean, like you say, the best we can hope for is that he'll be classified as a nonthreat. He won't get deported that way. Do you have any evidence that he's clean? It might be useful."

Alfred swiped at his eyes. When he replaced his glasses, he bugged out his eyes in an attempt to see better. No matter how wide he opened them, the old officer looked only like a dark smudge in the middle of a shadow.

"Well?" Officer Sloak turned fully to them.

Barbara nudged her father, "Dad, do you think we can call the neighbors and have them corroborate? He's worked for us for a while now."

Alfred shook his head and slid his glasses off. Doing the strange bug eye then squint thing people do upon taking their glasses off after wearing them for a long time did nothing to clear his normal blurry vision. However, the dark

172

smudges weren't creating thick shadows in his line of sight. Perspiration slicked his forehead. Someone was going to figure out he was going crazy. Maybe out here they would have a doctor on hand and wouldn't have to telephone an ambulance. He grimaced. He'd probably end up with a cell for a hospital room.

"How long is a while, little miss?" Officer Sloak's voice took on a softer edge.

Barbara fumbled for words, "Um...I don't know. He weeds the gardens and mows the lawn. Oh, and he cleaned the windows." Barbara looked down, and a sad tone dominated her quiet words, "Mom says he did the best job she's ever seen. Dad didn't like it though."

Alfred glanced at the officer, catching the raising of his eyebrows.

"You folks have any paperwork. Maybe a document signed stating that he's working for you?" Officer Sloak asked.

Alfred shook his head, "No. He just showed up and—well, he has done good work. My wife just hasn't... I didn't let her know I'd hired a window crew already."

Officer Sloak hummed a rumbling noise to himself and kept digging through the ledger. He licked his thumb and asked, "We've got a few names in here that look gringo to me. I don't think I heard the man's name."

"Jose," Alfred offered.

"I want Papi," Marie murmured more asleep than awake. Her leg kicked back and forth against her mother's legs, and the shoe on that foot was about to fall off.

In a rapid flurry of syllables Alfred grunted to his daughter, "The girl's shoe is going to fall."

Barbara glanced at her father and then dove toward the shoe. She caught the shoe as it teetered on the end of Marie's toe and gently pressed it back onto her foot. Jose's wife beamed at Barbara.

"Here we are," Officer Sloak called out. "Jose Gardea. He came in on the transfer this afternoon. Says here he helped settle a dispute between another gringo and an officer."

At the mention of her husband's name, his wife perked up with an apprehensive, inquiring look.

Marie added sleepily, "I want Papi."

Barbara moved to the mother and daughter and held out her arms, offering to take the little girl. The mother gratefully pressed Marie against Barbara and stretched her arms. Then, she folded her hands and smiled. Her smile, however, did not mask the worry in her eyes.

Alfred breathed deep, trying to force his body to relax. He hoped his forehead, slick and glistening with sweat, did not betray him too readily. He didn't trust his voice, so he blew out his breath softly and swung his hands at his sides.

Officer Sloak scratched at a pad of paper. Tearing it off he said, "Best I can do is ask you to come back tomorrow during visiting hours. Ask for Teddy Grant," he pointed to part of the swirled scribble. "He's the most likely to help you and not give lip like Deputy Jensen did."

He shifted his finger to the lower portion of the note, "Visiting hours start at nine o'clock. I don't think it'd be good for you to come earlier. No one will help you. Lots of the other guys—they're good guys in their hearts, but they don't like foreigners. Call 'em greasers and want to lock them all away or send them back."

He glanced at Jose's wife. Evidently, she seemed to not understand the conversation, so he continued, "I know it ain't right what either side is doing, but I'm just warning you to be careful if you want your friend to have a chance of bouncing his daughter on his knee again."

Alfred nodded, taking the note.

"We'll get him out," Officer Sloak winked. "Long as he's clean."

He ushered Alfred and the others to the door and pushed it open.

"I want Papi," Marie wailed. She flailed so violently that Barbara nearly dropped her. She probably would have fallen to the concrete had the child's mother not reached out and pulled her back into a tight cuddle, crooning softly to her in Spanish.

Chapter 20

Alfred frowned into the darkness. At least, he noticed with a grunt, the dark smudges blended into the night, rendering them all but invisible.

The little girl had fallen silent and hadn't even murmured for the past half hour. Barbara, looking small and tired, sat up front beside him. She looked at him, and he quickly set his gaze back to the road.

"Where are they going to stay tonight?" she asked.

She twirled a thin strand of dark brown hair around her pinky. He had noticed she used her pinky instead of her index finger like most other young women he'd seen engaging in the same behavior. Vaguely, he wondered what it might be like to twirl hair around a finger. He had never let his hair grow long, not even when he couldn't afford to pay to have it cut. He'd hacked at it with a pair of borrowed scissors until one of his friends insisted that he let her cut it. He had relented and walked around with a cut just like Moe from the Three Stooges. That had been before his hair had started thinning.

He gripped the steering wheel more tightly and pushed against it. "Well," he glanced at his daughter, "I figured we'd drop them off wherever they're staying."

"Oh, that makes sense," Barbara said quietly as she looked down.

He'd done it again. His daughter was ashamed because of how he'd treated her. But that was just part of life, wasn't it? Surely, she hadn't expected him to say they could stay with them. Mrs. Featherbomb still hadn't talked to him since going silent over the Piper's Pier incident. Had Barbara forgotten that her parents were technically still fighting?

As if she could read his thoughts Barbara said, "Mom's not going to be happy, is she? I mean she's going to be even less happy." She stared straight ahead through the windshield.

Alfred grunted unintelligibly. Out of the corner of his eye, he caught Barbara taking a long glance at him.

"It got dark fast tonight," Barbara stated.

"Yeah," Alfred mumbled. "Might be a storm."

"I haven't seen any lightning."

When had he and his daughter fallen into being adults who were too scared to talk—actually talk? Anybody could make small talk about the weather. Maybe that was why strangers in westerns always commented about the sun or the clouds or the dust.

He stifled a fake yawn. "I don't feel right making them walk home."

"Yeah," his daughter agreed. "Did Señor Jose tell you where they live?"

"No," Alfred responded slowly. He didn't think the man had. If he had, he clearly hadn't been listening.

"I'll ask them," Barbara twisted in her seat.

In halting Spanish, she asked the mother where they lived. It all sounded like mashed up syllables and tongue twisters designed to make the speaker spit.

"I think they live over by the supermarket," Barbara said. "At least she mentioned a supermercado a few times."

There were few times that Alfred could be considered a pragmatist at home. Most often he was thorough about considering all aspects of a problem at work. However, no matter what he thought of the Mexican family, he remembered they had shown up that first day in a car.

"What about their car?" he asked without straying his eyes from the road. They passed the outermost houses and other buildings of town. "Jose always walks, yet they had a car to start with."

"I'll ask," Barbara replied. "¿Donde su coche?"

The mother responded in a torrent of Spanish and a gesture of tossing something out.

Barbara turned back to her father, "I think they had to sell it, or it broke down or something."

Alfred pressed the brake to stop at the all-way stop at the intersection of Oak and Fourth. A streetlight rained yellow-orange light down, bathing them in a surreal glow. He didn't want to care, yet just as the light entered his eyes through his corneas, a feeling entered his mind. It seeped into his heart until he felt guilty and ashamed that he hadn't willingly helped the Mexican family.

No, he was just being pathetic. They had no right to impose themselves into his life. Jose had refused to take no for an answer.

A new smudge streaked across his glasses. He tilted his head to look around it.

They deserved the plate they'd been served. So, what if he had been one of the utensils used to serve misfortune.

"Are we taking them to the supermarket?" Barbara asked.

Alfred gripped the wheel. He didn't want to see where the family was living, and he didn't want to care that it was most likely not much different from a pigsty. It was probably a lean-to built with old mattresses and oil drums placed illegally against a building.

"We should have taken Fourth Street back there if we are," Barbara sounded like Mrs. Featherbomb.

"I'm not driving wrong," Alfred snapped. "I know where we're going."

Out of the corner of his eye, he caught his daughter flinch. He hadn't meant to bite back at her. The reaction had just rushed out of him. He knew he should apologize. That was, after all, the standard he would demand of his daughter. Instead, he excused his actions.

"You said they live behind the supermarket," he said sternly. "If we take Third Street, we'll circle around right behind the supermarket."

Barbara made no reply. She sat quietly gnawing on her bottom lip.

"Barbara," Alfred said in a low tone, "don't question me. We aren't going to do anything more than drop them off. We need to get home. It's late."

Barbara nodded once and glanced out the window. She crammed her hands under her legs and shifted around until finally resting her hands in her lap.

Out of the side of the windshield, the multicolored glow of the supermarket's neon sign stabbed Alfred's eyes. Perhaps what hurt more than the sudden brightness was the plethora of black smudges on the windshield and his glasses. The darkness had hidden them.

As the car kept moving, the glow of the sign gave way to the less obtrusive light of the streetlamps. However, he couldn't shake what he'd managed to read in that short second of illumination. The black smudges formed words which, in turn, because they were packed together so tightly, formed a confusing maze, but one word had jumped out at him. It was a euphemism for a hypocrite who also betrayed a close friend.

Judas

played on repeat in his mind like a jukebox that someone kept restarting after the first few notes of a song.

Alfred glanced at his daughter. She was clearly uncomfortable, and he couldn't blame her. Hadn't he just treated her the exact opposite of how he wanted her to treat others and himself?

"Dad!"

Alfred shifted his eyes back to the road just in time. The car tires crunched over the gravel alongside the blacktop as he spun the wheel. The car slid to a stop on the shoulder at the edge of the supermarket's side lot. A bead of sweat, powered by a spike of adrenaline, slid down Alfred's forehead. Ahead, a mere two or three inches from the Buick's bumper, a weathered telephone pole looked large enough to be the side of a barn.

"Need new glasses," Alfred muttered to his daughter. "They're supposed to be getting them in soon."

Someone shouted in intensely slurred Spanish. Looking to his left, Alfred beheld a lurching, upright carpet waving a bottle at him with a long, thin arm. The carpet shouted another slurred statement that ended in a long, grunting buzz. The man, wearing a long poncho, lilted to the side and stumbled into the middle of the road.

"That's why they shouldn't be here," Alfred murmured. "They can't fit into society. They're a danger."

A rear door clicked open. The Mexican woman mispronounced the English phrase. "Sank you," she said.

"¿Nos vemos aqui mañana?" Barbara said haltingly.

Alfred shot a glance at her and then glared at the Mexican woman. The little girl held tightly to her, and she bobbed her head and asked, "¿Que hora?"

His daughter turned to him with a question in her eyes.

"What?" Alfred grumbled. "I don't speak pig latin."

"Dad!" Barbara wailed. Then, she composed herself, "What time can we pick them up to go get Jose?"

"We can go after work."

Barbara gave him a disappointed frown and then fumbled with the Spanish words to convey that.

The woman looked dejected, but she nodded and said goodbye—at least, Alfred assumed it was goodbye, but for all he knew, it could have been some sort of foreign expletive to describe unsympathetic white people who couldn't drive safely. Well, being able to drive legally at all was more than she appeared to be able to do. Further, Alfred doubted Jose drove with a legal license that one day he had brought his family to the Featherbomb's with that broken down jalopy.

Somehow, Alfred didn't feel any better as he nudged the car into reverse and gripped Barbara's seat to twist himself backward to scan the street for more drunken carpets.

The ride home took place in perfect silence. Barbara stared out her window and moved only to clasp her hands in her lap or wedge them under her legs. That would have been fine with Alfred, who didn't feel like carrying on a conversation, if it hadn't been for the fact that his daughter was undoubtedly deeply disappointed and angry with him. He had let her down, and she was simply expressing how she felt toward him. It was so similar to what his wife was currently doing he wanted to swear and cuss not so under his breath. He wanted to declare his frustration out loud. Maybe he would just do it with the windows up instead of down.

"No cussing, dear," Mrs. Featherbomb's voice played in his mind.

He shook his head. Why couldn't he get rid of that inhibition? Mrs. Featherbomb wasn't even sitting beside him.

"No cussing, dear."

She wasn't even talking to him for the time being. How long had it been? Over twenty-four hours he realized. He glanced at his daughter as he remembered the breakfast she'd cooked for him. She yawned and glanced back at him. Simultaneously, father and daughter turned their gazes away from each other.

In the back of Alfred's mind, a little, dark creature gnawed at his sense of peace. His daughter had no right to judge him so harshly. He was already bending over backward for the Mexican family. He let the man work for him, and he had just driven halfway across the state with the man's family to try to bring him back from prison. What more could he do? He wasn't even getting compensated for his efforts. If Pastor Meyers saw what he was doing, he would say something like, "What you have done for the least of these, you have done for me."

Alfred knew he should be thankful for the time he was able to spend with his daughter and the simple fact that he was able to help fellow humans. He would just have to forget the glaring fact that he had been the one to call the authorities and falsely inform them about Señor Jose.

He shoved the parking brake and rested his feet on the floorboard.

"Dad," Barbara's voice was barely audible, "how did you know someone had declared Señor Jose was a spy?"

She hadn't talked the whole way home. Now, she wanted to bring up the very thing that was eating him up the most? Anger flashed as he thought of a nonincriminating reply.

Alfred's voice cracked, so he cleared his throat, "The communists are trying to take over our country. One of the neighbors must have called them about Jose. He fits the bill for the kind of man we need to be on the lookout for."

"No one's even seen a communist," Barbara muttered and yanked her door open.

"Barbara Ann," Alfred shouted.

His daughter whirled to face him but kept backing toward the house. "What?" she shot back.

Alfred realized he could scold his daughter for the disrespect she'd just shown, or he could do his best to smooth things out and thank her for her help translating and such. His hesitation lasted long enough for Barbara to reach the door.

Anger won.

"Learn some respect, young lady. That is not how you talk to your parents," Alfred didn't shout this time, but his voice was stern and held a cold edge.

Barbara looked at him. The wan light from the single porch light formed dark shadows on her stricken features. And then, her face contorted from a look of pain to one of anger.

"I think I know why mom doesn't talk to you sometimes," she said.

She twisted and ran through the door, leaving it swinging behind her.

Later, once he made it in, Alfred heard her sobbing in her room. But Alfred stood in the driveway for some time. His shoulders slumped and all the anger toward his daughter dissipated. In its place, a furious despondence with himself rose like one of those rubber-skinned monsters from the movies rising up from behind him and consuming him while onlookers stared in disbelief at the hulking thing.

She was right. His daughter had told him exactly what he knew to be true. Mrs. Featherbomb did not want to talk with him as an angry, obstinate man who was mean and inconsiderate. Further, he didn't deserve the attention of a loving wife.

He blew out a breath and placed his hand on the cold doorknob. As the latch clicked into place behind him, he couldn't help but feel he had just stepped into a prison cell.

Chapter 21

Alfred managed to make a couple pieces of toast, burning only one side to a crisp. The accomplishment brought him no satisfaction, and, despite a copious amount of butter, his tastebuds rejected what he tried to convince himself constituted a sufficient breakfast.

As he crunched through the dry toast and felt crumbs sprinkle down his chin, he longed for his daughter to make him breakfast again. As far as he could tell, she hadn't stirred yet. He had been too hard on her the previous day.

He had spent the night on the couch again, and Mrs. Featherbomb had acknowledged he was home only by stepping to the archway leading to the living room, staring at him for a minute or two in complete silence and then turning and walking back to their room. She hadn't yet left their room, and Alfred didn't expect her to do so until after he had left for work.

Fresh clothes would be nice, but he didn't have time or desire to apologize profusely and do penance for his crime of standing up for his daughter when she wanted to get ice cream with a bunch of her friends. No boys were going with them, so it shouldn't have been an issue. Mrs. Featherbomb had acted too quickly in grounding Barbara. That wasn't the problem, was it? He had acted out of line the way he shared what he'd seen—how it had been Mrs. Wyman who'd come by to pick up Barbara.

He turned slowly from the door he had every right to use. It hadn't been only the Piper's Pier incident that had set his wife off. Indeed, the longer he contemplated his behaviors, the more deeply he was convinced that he would be unable to live in the same house as himself. Mrs. Featherbomb was truly remarkable for putting up with him for so long.

Thoughts of hunting down Joey Chadelle and draping his corpse on the car hood like a redneck hunter proudly displaying his kill jumped into his imagination. It would be a peace offering from him to his wife. It would take a weighty worry from Mrs. Featherbomb's shoulders. Perhaps... Perhaps then she would be less harsh on Barbara.

The sensible side of his mind took over. He wasn't a killer and never would be. Besides, killing the troublesome boy would accomplish nothing but getting him thrown in prison alongside Señor Jose. He smirked to himself. Jose would be let out after the tensions with the Soviet Union eased, while Alfred, a murderer, would be sentenced to the electric chair. That would be a reversal of fate.

Alfred glanced at his watch. His stomach grumbled about the burnt toast. If he drove quickly, he'd have enough time to snag some eggs and bacon at the diner on the corner. He needed coffee too.

Fighting the weariness chaining him to the floor, he lifted his feet and slid them into his shoes. He laid his hand on the doorknob. He should do what he could to make peace. After all, Pastor Meyers taught on how Jesus said, "'Blessed are the peacemakers.'" Alfred shook his head.

"No cussing, dear," Mrs. Featherbomb's voice sang.

He looked up, expecting to see her standing in the hallway. It wasn't fair what she was doing, not talking to him. He worked hard and tried to lead his family the way he knew was his obligation. She, Mrs. Featherbomb, was just always there contradicting him and undermining what he said at every turn.

He removed his glasses as if not having to look through the black smudges and truth spelled out in criticisms would help his voice reach Mrs. Featherbomb.

"Goodbye, dear," he said facing the door to the bedroom. "I love you and will be thinking about you at work."

There, he'd said his piece and made his peace. He could do nothing more.

His shoes clunked forlornly on the wooden floor. The door slapped shut behind him. The car coughed and grumbled to life.

The curtain in his daughter's room swept aside. His daughter gazed out at him with a blank expression. He waved and pointed to his wrist, trying to convey that they would leave later to go back to the prison to get Señor Jose out. She did not react, and the curtain was back in place by the time the Buick's back tires hit the road.

From the metal waste bin parked at the end of the driveway, a bright orange sign fluttered in the gentle breeze. That's what had become of his stroll to the hardware store. Garbage. Did anything he did have more significance than creating more garbage for society? He knew the answer so well he didn't bother answering the question.

He put the Buick into gear and turned the wheel. An image sprang to mind. It was like he was childish Betty Boop dancing like a toddler next to Rosy the Riveter carrying an airplane propeller on her shoulder. The best he was capable of fell pitifully short every time.

A car horn tooted twice. A dark car passed him. In the driver's seat, a man in a crisp uniform waved to him. The army recruiter. How long did recruiter's stay in a town? Hadn't he told Alfred when they'd talked at church?

He definitely needed to avoid church this Sunday. He wondered what he could use for a cover, an excuse, for why he skipped Pastor Meyers' message when he clearly needed to hear it more than ever. Would saying he had to pack for the golf outing be sacrilegious?

"The—"

"No cussing, dear," Mrs. Featherbomb's voice cut him off before he started.

Mrs. Featherbomb was still not talking with him, yet she effectively controlled his inhibitions to cuss.

He slammed his hand against the steering wheel. Time was running out. Somehow, he needed to get Señor Jose out of prison, make it up to his wife—whatever "it" was—and practice his swing and figure out how to clean his glasses so he could see. Maybe his new glasses were in. He should call on them.

The paperboy coasted past on his bike. White rolls of news flew to the left and right as the boy's expert aim landed the morning paper at people's doors.

Alfred glanced down at his watch and then at the speedometer. He'd made it out the door before the paperboy had delivered his paper, yet he needed to drive fast if he was going to get breakfast at the diner. Grinding his teeth, he pushed the accelerator.

A rolled-up newspaper thumped against his window as he sped past the paperboy. The boy yelled something at him that Alfred couldn't decipher. His tires screeched at the stop sign as he braked, then they squealed again as the engine roared.

Loose gravel from a shoddily filled pothole skittered the Buick a couple inches sideways as he spun the wheel to guide the car into the tiny parking lot. The neon sign flickered at the "n" as it always did, causing it to read "dier" instead of "diner" for a split second.

Alfred threw the parking brake and flung his door open.

"Well, hullo," a man climbing from a dark sedan called cheerfully. "You agitated some gravel catching me up. You got a kid who wants to join?"

Alfred didn't look at the recruiter, and the only reply he offered was a grunt that could have sounded like he was saying he was hungry or maybe that he was in a hurry.

The recruiter tucked his cap under his arm and reached for the door. "Let me get the door for you," he said in his cheerful brogue. "And good morning to you too, old timer," he called to someone behind Alfred.

Alfred glanced back. Old Mr. Faustner raised his hand in a weary salute and flung his hand back to his side. His leg was evidently giving him quite a lot of trouble judging by the way he lurched forward with his opposite hand out and then dragged the leg as if it were too painful or too weak to lift.

"Always a pleasure to serve a man who's gone to the deepest pits of hell and returned," the recruiter saluted.

"Ya'll don't know nothin' about it," Old Mr. Faustner growled.

"All together?" a bright, female voice called. Before Alfred could answer that he wanted a table alone, the young woman, who looked about the same age as Barbara except for the makeup and heels, bustled them to a table that sat four and dropped menus in front of them. "Start you gentlemen off with some coffee?"

No one answered, but the young woman returned in about twenty seconds with a steaming pot of coffee and proceeded to pour it into the mugs waiting on the table.

As Alfred sat, a shadow darkened the window to his right, mirroring the shadow that darkened his already dark attitude. Smudges grew like crystal forming at high speed. Mrs. Featherbomb would have scolded him for cussing had he read it out loud. As it was, her voice played on repeat as he stared.

"I'll take the tallest glass of orange juice you got," the recruiter replied to something the waitress asked. "And if I can get a second glass with a phone number in it, I'll be a happy man."

"You've asked for my number every day this week. Got any other lines?" the waitress said without breaking from her cheery brightness.

"And for you?" Alfred heard her voice directed at him, but he kept staring at the window. It was impossible. The Mexican couldn't have known he would be at the diner today. He couldn't have used that infuriating ink that only Alfred could see to write on the window. Even if the man had been released after they'd left the prison last night, he couldn't have made it more than halfway back to town on foot.

"And for the nervous man looking out the window?" the waitress tried again. "Bacon, eggs and toast sound good? I'll do sunny side up for you. Looks like you could use a bit more sunny."

"Huh?" Alfred turned around just in time to catch the waitress's hair settling back into place after she spun and nearly jogged to the kitchen with their orders. "Yeah, that'll be good."

"Service here is so fast it almost makes ya want to scarf your food down and get out so they can fill your seat with another customer," Mr. Faustner remarked with a frown.

"I've seen you in here every day, old timer," the recruiter commented.

"What's that?" Mr. Faustner demanded. "A man's got to eat. Can't live on beer and bread alone. The Good Lord woulda said that if he'd known about beer."

The two men chuckled while Alfred revisited the window. Black smudges continued to erode the pristine glass. A new thought struck him, and he wondered whether the diner workers would have to spend hours scrubbing the windows or whether the smudges would disappear when he left. He felt even more conspicuous and uncomfortable.

"My—"

"No cussing, dear," Mrs. Featherbomb's voice in his mind made him wince.

What if the black smudges and insults followed him around? What if they showed up on the windows at the country club Mr. Davis had reserved for him and Mr. Orton?

"What's got you so fascinated like a cat with a three-legged mouse?" Mr. Faustner's gruff voice made Alfred flinch.

In a falsetto, the recruiter said, "Oh, it's a wittle tweety bird."

Alfred peered more intently, trying to see the bird through the words blocking his view. A flash of color shot through the letters.

"We used ta feed the birds over in France so we could catch 'em," Mr. Faustner referenced his war years. "Didn't make much more than a mouthful and was all crunchy with the bones."

"Sylvesters. All of you," Seargent McCoy grinned.

"You'da eaten 'em too if you'da been there. Rations were hardly worth the effort it takes to open your mouth to shovel it in." Mr. Faustner narrowed his eyes and cut a look at the younger man. "Something tells me you've never been in a real battle."

The recruiter held up his hand, "I wage war against emptiness in the army's lines and emptiness in young men's heads. The army'll pay your way through college if you volunteer. It's a bit of a harsher program if you're drafted. You could benefit from it if you weren't so full of rations that it was oozing out your ears."

Mr. Faustner took a long time to reply. "You're so full of government crap that you could make a skunk wrinkle its nose. It don't matter whether the boys volunteer or wait for the draft, it's all hell, and then, if they make it through, they get the same measly pittance."

"Digging your trenches all over again," Seargent McCoy took a sip of his black coffee. "I tell the parents what they want to hear."

Mr. Faustner raised his eyebrows, "You are part man. A lilly-livered government goon wouldn't be able to stomach that without dumping half the sugar bowl in first."

Seargent McCoy set his mug down and patted his belly, "If there's one thing bootcamp teaches you, it's how to eat just about anything."

"Ain't that the truth," Mr. Faustner agreed. "What about you, Fritter? You frettin' over drinkin' the coffee over there?"

"What? Hmm?" Alfred forcefully peeled his gaze from the window. "The coffee's fine."

The waitress slid to a stop beside their table, deposited steaming plates piled with bacon, eggs, toast and hash browned potatoes and then topped off each of their coffee mugs.

"Anything else you gentlemen need?" she asked, pulling a notepad and pencil from her apron.

All three shook their heads.

"Alright, you gentlemen enjoy while it's hot."

The waitress turned. A piece of paper fluttered into Alfred's lap. He picked it up and read: "If the commies are chasing you, we can call the cops."

He felt his face go red.

"What's that?" the recruiter asked, mouth full. "She give you her number? Why would she give it to you? Why not a fine, dashing specimen in uniform?"

"You go stand out there, and I'll fetch my rifle an' we'll see how dashing you are," Mr. Faustner laughed.

Seargent McCoy joined him, though a little nervously.

Alfred made no reply and stuffed the note to the bottom of his pocket. Focusing on his own plate, he began eating without looking up. The food was good he could tell, but the embarrassment of being assumed that he was

190

nervous because he thought the communists were trying to get him made the perfectly cooked eggs taste like mud on his toast which was like sawdust on his tongue.

Señor Jose. He couldn't forget what he'd done to the man. And Barbara. She had looked at him with such a look of dejection, he was sure she would never talk with him again.

"Mr. Frittworth," Mr. Faustner said around a mouthful, "you alright, man? You're lookin' a bit piqued."

Alfred didn't look up. He grunted and gave an insignificant bob of his head.

"The man eats like he hasn't seen a plate of food in a week," Old Mr. Faustner commented.

Alfred glanced at the other two men's plates. Sure enough, their plates still held most of their food while his was over half gone already. It was true, he was hungry, but he couldn't let anyone else discover the reason for his hunger.

"Is that how you boys ate once you didn't have to eat your boot leather any longer?" the sergeant asked Mr. Faustner.

"What in the tarnation, you fool," the older man spluttered and set down his coffee. "We didn't eat our boots. Not after dragging our sorry backsides through that mud and filth. That woulda been a surer way to die than being shot by the Huns. What's our fool government teaching you imbeciles?"

Alfred swallowed his bite of toast topped with sunny side up egg and cut into his hash browned potatoes. He didn't want to look at the clock, and he didn't want to get dragged into one of Old Mr. Faustner's long-winded putdowns of the government, which, judging by the antagonism the sergeant was giving him, was bound to happen.

He wiped his mouth and stole a hurried look at the clock. It was mounted on the wall between two of the large, plate glass windows. Just as quickly he ducked away and buried himself in scraping up the last few forkfuls from his plate.

Imbecile

burned like an after-image of the sun in his eyes, however. He still saw it scrawled across the window in dripping, black ink.

"He wasn't calling me that," he murmured. A bead of sweat dribbled down his forehead. His reassurance made no difference. He felt like an imbecile. He was an imbecile according to his wife...and according to his daughter, too. He was a foolish imbecile. Wasn't that a redundant statement? Further proof he was a foolish imbecile. He was too dumb to figure out how to make his family happy. He had to get out of the diner before others learned what he knew about himself.

Leaning back, he reached into his jacket for his billfold. Sergeant McCoy lunged across the table. His hand brushed Alfred's coffee mug as he extended his arm to press Alfred's billfold back into its pocket.

"I'll cover it. I owe you one for the tire," the sergeant said.

The coffee cup spun like a saucer set to spinning and wobbling just right. Alfred was just withdrawing his hand from his billfold when the mug wobbled off the table. He shoved himself backward, trying to avoid the few mouthfuls of coffee flowing out of the mug as it fell.

A sharp cry erupted behind him followed by a loud crash and a symphony of shattering dishes.

The waitress whimpered and swore in a tearful voice.

Alfred spun, standing.

"Ow, you oaf. My hand," the waitress shrieked.

Alfred lifted his foot. The waitress snatched her hand from where he had stepped on it and held it to her chest. Tears streamed down her cheeks, mingling with bright red blood and staining her uniform. Her bottom lip quivered as she surveyed the mess. Then, as if the pain had only just registered, she raised her untrampled hand to her temple and looked at her blood-covered fingers. She looked at Alfred slowly as if he'd just shot her.

"Here, miss," the sergeant held a wad of napkins out to her. She accepted them and pressed them to the side of her head. She looked around again. Incomprehension made her eyes shift from disbelief to emptiness.

Alfred didn't know what to do.

Old Mr. Faustner pushed him, "Don't just stand there, man. Get your flummoxed behind to the first aid kit."

Alfred took a step backward.

"She hit her head pretty hard," Sergeant McCoy said, wrapping his arm around the waitress's back to keep her upright.

"These tables is not forgiving neither," Old Mr. Faustner added.

Another waitress rounded the counter from the kitchen. She took one look, covered a gasp with both hands and grabbed the first aid kit from the wall and raced to her coworker's side.

Alfred couldn't move. Blood, broken dishes, ruined food all over the floor, puddles of coffee and a crowd of people who all seemed to know what to do may as well have been a prison just like the one Señor Jose was in.

A third waitress hurried up with a broom and dustpan. She and a bystander began cleaning up the mess. Alfred found himself pushed toward the door.

After several minutes, the sergeant and the second waitress eased the injured girl from the floor and helped her into the back.

Chapter 22

Alfred was quiet at the office. Sunny tried to get him to talk, and Codgens made fun of him to no end, announcing, "Here comes the Featherbomber," every time he strode through the office.

Alfred sat at his desk, averting his eyes from all windows. He'd removed his glasses as well and buried his face in paperwork, but he couldn't focus on the words that he managed to read through his blurry vision. It was as if each word he read was scooped out of his brain with a ladle after reading it, leaving him to read and reread a paragraph and then just a sentence over and over without comprehending what he'd just read.

It was exasperating. However, that was nothing compared to the guilt of knocking the waitress into the table and then stepping on her hand. He hoped she didn't have any broken fingers as a result. He sighed and rubbed his eyes for the umpteenth time. How bad had the cut on her head been? He'd seen the vacant incomprehension in her eyes. That usually meant a concussion.

His office door burst open.

"Out! Get out!" Alfred shouted. His voice was so loud his ears rang, but he didn't care.

"Featherbomber," Codgens tried to console him, "you're not stable, old boy."

"No cussing, dear," Alfred heard Mrs. Featherbomb's voice sing.

He overcame the inhibition in that moment. Codgens received a blast of profanity which struck him so hard he stopped his advance, and the grin melted from his face.

"Whatever you say, Featherbomber," Codgens swung around but stopped halfway through the door. "Maybe I can send Sunny in to help you calm down? Sounds like you need some sunshine."

Alfred did something else he later regretted. Codgens ducked and quickly vacated Alfred's office as the stapler, the one engraved with the description of how he made things stick, slammed into the door right beside where his head had been. Alfred threw the stapler so hard it left a gouging dent in the oak door.

There, Alfred fumed, *tell me not to throw staplers too.* In his mind's falsetto voice, imitating Mrs. Featherbomb, he called in mock sweetness, *No throwing staplers, dear.*

He felt good at having done something destructive. He wished only that the stapler had opened its jaws and left one of its pointy fasteners quivering in Codgens' forehead like an arrow shot into a wooden plank. He rolled his shoulders and returned to his work.

Sunny never came in to discuss his outburst. In truth, the only thing Alfred ever heard about the incident was whenever he closed his office door. The dent would look down on him, telling him how immature he'd been. For a few weeks, Alfred was afraid of being confronted by Mr. Davis, but it seemed that Codgens never circulated any stories about nearly taking a staple to the face.

Alfred ended up working through lunch, so, by the time he guided the Buick into his driveway, he was famished. Ducking into the kitchen, he saw his daughter rummaging around in the refrigerator. Fear seized him and ground him to a halt.

He had let her down. He would do it again.

But he was the father, the man of the house as Pastor Meyers put it. He laid down the law and decided what was okay. His eye twitched. Pastor Meyers had specifically pointed out that that common belief was not what God had raised men up to be. Not to mention, Mrs. Featherbomb was doing anything but listening to him. The woman hadn't even spoken to him in—how many days had it been?

Barbara straightened and closed the refrigerator door, a casserole dish clutched in her hands. She froze when she saw him.

His daughter's expression went blank, completely void of any emotion whatsoever. Alfred thought his own face probably showed the wide-eyed stare of fear. He didn't know because a new smudge was forming into a new insult, a new truth, on his glasses. His eye twitched as he yanked the black frames from his face and rubbed the lenses vigorously with his shirt.

He watched the somewhat blurry form of his daughter step to the counter and set the casserole down. When she pulled the lid off, a strong, sweet odor overpowered his olfactory senses. It was some sort of cheese and potatoes. His mouth watered.

"You look hungry, dad," Barbara said serenely.

Alfred finished cleaning his glasses and pushed them onto his nose. Cocking his head so as not to be looking directly through the latest representation of his shortcoming as a parent, he nodded and said, "I had to work through lunch."

"Mom told me to make this," she opened the oven. "I was supposed to get a roast ready too, but I don't remember what to do and mom wouldn't answer any of my questions."

It was Alfred's turn to freeze. He blinked and snatched his glasses.

"What's going on? Why is mom acting like this?"

Alfred rubbed his eyes and replaced his glasses. The thick, black frames felt like blinders on a horse, but he saw his daughter's tear-streaked face clearly for the first time since stepping into the house. He opened his mouth, but no words, comforting, angry or otherwise, tumbled out.

"Are you mad at me too, dad?" Barbara's face contorted as she hiccupped a small sob. "What did I do?"

An image of Señor Jose picking up his little daughter and comforting her with snuggles pricked Alfred's mind. That night he'd walked to the hardware store and crossed paths with Jose and Marie replayed like an old silent movie.

"Why don't you and mom love me anymore?" Barbara crumpled onto the floor, tucking herself into the corner created by the cabinets and the wall by the arch.

Alfred felt like an outside observer looking through a tiny plate glass window at the scene his daughter was creating. She pulled her knees up to her chest and wrapped her arms tightly around her shins. Staring straight ahead she let first one tear and then another slip down her cheeks. Then, she ducked her head, swiping the tears away with her skirt pulled tight over her knees.

Alfred needed to say something—assure his daughter that he loved her. He needed to make sure Barbara knew Mrs. Featherbomb loved her too. He took a step closer and sank into a squat. His knee popped loudly, and he winced.

Barbara stared at him through pools of salty tears. Slowly, she scooched herself a few inches away.

A white-hot torrent of anger spilled into him like a waterfall crashing down onto rocks as if trying to break them apart. He was trying to comfort her. Why was she misinterpreting his actions and shrinking away from him?

"Don't be foolish," he snapped. He winced as he heard himself. It only added an influx to his anger.

Barbara pressed her hands onto the floor and pushed herself further away. Her expression morphed from one of intense emotional pain to one of terror.

"Barbara," Alfred let out an exasperated breath. He tried to quell his anger. At first, he thought he was succeeding, but then

Recreant

scrawled itself across his glasses. Man, he needed those new glasses. He tore the infected devices from his face and flung them into the corner.

Barbara let out a whimpering cry.

With his blurry vision, Alfred saw his daughter had tucked herself as deeply into the corner as she could. His glasses clung to a fold in her blouse until she brushed them off like they were some sort of grotesque spider infected with a flesh rotting disease. He blinked and sat there. His daughter cried silently, cheek pressed into the wall.

She cringed as he reached for his glasses. He turned them over in his hands, looking down at the smudged lenses, but he didn't really see them.

"I know I'm not a good father," he grunted and slowly rose. In a haze of thick mental fog, he stumbled out the door and strode slowly to the backyard.

Chapter 23

Behind him, the door creaked open and closed softly. It only closed softly when someone forced it to close slowly by holding it. Alfred didn't turn to look. He sat on the porch and stared at the fence where it seemed to sprout from the grass. The Mexican hadn't been able to make it all the way around the fence when he trimmed the grass so, like a tuft of green hair left long on a buzz cut, the grass at the fence's foot stood out.

Alfred heard his daughter take in breath as if getting ready to speak, but instead she stepped off the side of the porch. She didn't face him as she asked so softly the gentle breeze nearly drowned her out, "Are we still going to go get him?"

Alfred absently polished his glasses with his shirt. The "him" was of course the man he'd had apprehended on a lie. Señor Jose had spent his first night in prison away from his family. Little Marie had probably pestered her mother the whole day by demanding to see Papi. Would Barbara behave the same if his and Jose's roles were reversed and he had been falsely accused and thrown in jail? He desperately wanted to ask, but something held him back.

Barbara shifted uneasily beside him.

"That might be the only thing I can do right," Alfred crammed his glasses on and pushed himself wearily to his feet. He stole a brief glance at Barbara. She wasn't looking at him. He should apologize. His tongue clung to the roof of his mouth as if it had been cemented in place.

"I put the casserole together, but it took me so long I didn't have time to bake it," Barbara said ruefully.

Great. Another problem. Alfred held the door open and replied, "Jiminy Slim's?"

No answer. Alfred looked over his shoulder. His daughter met his eyes for the briefest of moments and nodded.

Alfred shuffled to his bedroom door. He didn't know whether Mrs. Featherbomb was inside, but he didn't ask his daughter. He raised his hand to knock and rehearsed what he was going to say. He and Barbara were heading to Jiminy Slim's for burgers, then they would be gone the rest of the evening driving up north to bail Señor Jose out. That sounded like the right things to say. Perhaps he should add something about the golf outing the following week. After all, that was only a weekend away.

Barbara watched silently from the end of the hall. Her shoulders were hunched, and her face was already pulled tight in preparation to cringe. Alfred lowered his hand. No sense in sparking a fresh fight with his wife. He would just have to let her come out of her silence on her own terms. Maybe this time she would tell him what to apologize for.

He attempted a smile for his daughter, and her shoulders slumped a fraction of an inch.

All the way to Jiminy Slim's, silence reigned in the Buick.

Once they had their food, Alfred took a bite of his greasy burger piled high with sliced pickles.

He should try to make up to his daughter.

"The first time we brought you here," he said around his mouthful, "you would eat only the pickles. You didn't touch the french-fries or your burger. You insisted that you needed four pickles because you were four."

Barbara grimaced and took another crunchy bite of her second giant pickle. "Dad, that's so square. Don't say that so loud. I don't want my friends to hear about that," she said, glancing around.

"You were the cutest little four-year-old with your pigtails and," he paused for a second. He didn't know where these fond, albeit embarrassing, memories were coming from. He hadn't thought about them in years, so why did they come up now?

"Dad, don't say it. Don't be square."

Alfred didn't register what his daughter said until after he finished his thought, "Spelunking for gold nuggets in your nose."

Barbara gasped, "Dad!"

Alfred glanced up from his reminiscence. Barbara looked like she was trying to fold herself under the table to hide. "Huh?"

"Do you want my friends to think I'm square? Someone might tell them," Barbara scanned the small, nearly empty smattering of tables. The drive-in portion of the joint bustled with cars constantly pulling in and backing out.

His daughter was concerned with her image, but what Alfred heard was that she thought he was uncool. He swiped his glasses off and vigorously cleaned them. His greasy fingers left foggy smudges, so he cleaned them again. Anger flared as he checked them. They were still smudged and screaming insults at him.

"Dad," Barbara begged. "Dad, please stop." She shrank further under the table and glanced around like a hunted animal.

Alfred heard his daughter telling him to stop, but he had to get his glasses clean. He couldn't go around seeing the world through piles of insults.

"I need to get my new glasses," Alfred snapped.

"Oh no," Barbara lifted her glass of dark soda, pretending to study the bubbles, "there's Rhonda and Jimmy. Dad, can we go now?"

Alfred rubbed at a dark line on the left lens and grunted. His daughter had asked him something, but he needed to get his glasses cleaned.

"Can we go before they see us?" Barbara requested urgently.

"Can't you see I'm cleaning my glasses?" Alfred barked. He felt the rising red as blood flushed his face. His daughter should know better than to be so inconsiderate.

"They'll see us," Barbara insisted, setting up the menu the waitress had forgotten as a barricade.

"Barbara Ann," Alfred snapped, smashing his glasses back onto his face. His daughter froze, staring at him. Her mouth hung partway open, and her eyes pooled dark with fear.

One type of heat drained from Alfred's face. Its place was immediately taken by another type of heat. He had just yelled at his daughter.

"I'm sorry," he shuffled his remaining French fries around. "I'm sorry. Finish your food and we'll go."

Barbara set her glass down and folded up the paper around her half-eaten burger. "I'm full," she stated flatly. Her gaze settled onto the ground somewhere to Alfred's left.

"You didn't finish," Alfred trailed off. He didn't really need to chide his daughter on not finishing her food, did he? He crammed the longest of his remaining French fries into the dollop of ketchup and bit the ends off.

Around the greasy potatoes he muttered, "We'll go in a minute."

Barbara gave a disgusted sigh and shot, "I'm going to go wait in the car."

With that and tipping her head forward so her hair covered her face, she all but ran to the Buick and lowered herself into the back seat until she couldn't be seen.

Alfred finished off the last few bites of his burger. They were tasteless after what had just transpired between him and his daughter. Then, he left cash with a small tip on the table and hunched his way to the Buick. He wasn't trying to hide from the young couple who had started kissing. Instead, he was trying to avoid the world.

"Alright, Barbara, you can sit up now," Alfred called over his shoulder once they were three blocks from Jiminy Slim's. He watched in the rearview mirror as his daughter cautiously peered over the lip of the door.

"That was so embarrassing, dad," she muttered.

A few minutes later Alfred guided the car to the same spot he'd dropped Jose's wife and daughter off the night before. This time, no staggering drunk yelled at him, and he didn't nearly ram the car into the telephone pole.

He was just about to say they should go find the Mexicans' house when Barbara opened her door and called a greeting in Spanish.

A nervous, fidgety and sunken-eyed version of the small Mexican woman from last night climbed in. She was followed by her daughter who wore a dour face and clutched a balding teddy bear that smelled like restaurant trash basking in the sun.

"We have Papi now," Marie ordered obstinately.

Barbara climbed into the back seat once again, "Si. Voy por el Papi."

Marie stared at her for a moment before nodding her head and repeating, "Voy por mi Papi."

The girl's mother asked in a rapid but quiet string of syllables, "¿Ve a buscar a Papi?"

Marie nodded and grinned confidently, "Si, Mama. Vamos a buscar a Papi. Mi Papi. Te amo, Papi."

Alfred released the clutch and pushed the accelerator. The long car edged back onto the road. He held his head at an awkward tilt to the right so less of his vision was obstructed by the smudges on his glasses and windshield.

He frowned suddenly. He had heard distinct words in the rapid language from the back seat. Glancing at his daughter in the rearview, he saw she had started playing some game with the little girl, passing the stinky teddy bear back and forth. He opened his mouth to reprimand her about dirty toys transmitting diseases.

Before he said anything, he clenched his jaw and stared at the black streak appearing on the windshield. It started at the bottom left corner and grew until it ended at the top in the middle of the clear glass. No word formed, but the slash of black may as well have been a slash to his chest. He felt physical pain as if he'd forgotten to wear armor while fencing and had received a wound running from shoulder to hip from his opponent.

Anger welled like tears. Who was his opponent but himself? He could do nothing right, and here was yet another reminder of his failure. He was a despicable man and deserved to be looked down on by society.

He locked his gaze forward and fed his anger as the miles rolled slowly by.

Chapter 24

Somewhere along the boring, gently curving road, Barbara had stretched into the front seat and tuned the radio to a rock and roll station. The drums reverberated through the car, and Alfred found his hand slapping the steering wheel in sync with the accents.

He didn't know how long he had been enjoying the music when he remembered Pastor Meyers' sermon from over a year ago condemning drums and electric guitars.

"You like this stuff, Barbara?" he asked, glancing at his daughter through the rearview.

Barbara met his gaze in the mirror momentarily. "It's what everybody listens to now," she replied softly, shrugging her left shoulder.

The last thing Alfred wanted was to get into another fight with his daughter. He also didn't want to keep listening to the ungodly music. If he kept listening, he knew he was going to have another black smear mock him. The insults always showed up when he felt the way he was feeling. It was like guilt but deeper, more powerful and hurt like raw flesh being massaged with gravel.

"It's a little loud, Sweet Pea," he said, twisting the knob a few degrees. There, he could say he'd dealt with it, couldn't he? His hand went back to thumping the steering wheel along with the bass drum and snare.

Bill Haley just wrapped up a loud, fast song as the prison came into view. The tall fences and the guard towers rose like a villain's castle from the barren hills rolling gently in all directions.

"Don't forget we need to talk to the Teddy Grant guy, dad," Barbara said.

Marie attempted to burrow into her mother as they pulled up to the guard shack. Alfred thought he could feel some of the same fear that her huge, brown eyes shot in all directions. He was the guilty party here. If he hadn't lied, her papi would never have been incarcerated. He should be the one behind the fence and locked doors.

After a brief exchange with the guard, Alfred piloted the Buick through the retracted gate and parked. The main fence and the squat buildings of the inmate housing filled the windshield.

Marie whimpered as her mother carried her from the car. "I want Papi," leaked out from her mouth as she pressed her head tight against her mother's shoulder.

Alfred drew his wallet from his breast pocket as they approached the door and wondered whether Jose's wife had brought any identification.

When the guard asked for his driver's license, he made a show of handing it to the man, hoping the Mexican woman would catch on. Sure enough, she dug around in her tiny, drawstring purse and drew out a tattered card.

"Oh, these ain't wetbacks," the guard flashed a grin, "but I'll bet you're here for one, aren't ya?"

Alfred grunted, "Where can we find Teddy Grant?"

"Old Tedster?" the guard cracked a peanut and used the shell to toss the peanut's flesh into his mouth. "He's got an office on the north side of the hall. Take a right down there and then look out for his name card. Five or six doors down."

"Thank you," Alfred said, repocketing his wallet.

"¿Buscar a Papi?" Marie asked hopefully. Her mother snuggled her, and Barbara confirmed her question with something whispered in Spanish.

"Are you folks here for a wetback?" a voice boomed behind them.

Alfred turned and ducked. A huge man strode toward them. His uniform looked like it would split open if he had to wrestle an inmate back into his cell, and the black leather belt cinched on his waist was filled with a variety of pouches, handcuffs and an embossed holster holding a shiny revolver with an ivory-white handle. The man's hand dwarfed a coffee mug. His name patch beneath the polished badge on his left pec read "T. Grant."

"We're looking for Ted—Officer Teddy Grant," Alfred adjusted his glasses. "Officer Sloak said he could help us."

"Bradley's a good man," Officer Grant held out his hand for Alfred to shake. The man's hand felt like an entire ribeye wrapping around his hand. "I'm Teddy. What can I help you with? And who's this little angel?" he asked as Marie stared at him and then buried her face in her mother's neck.

"Perhaps we should discuss our situation in your office," Alfred hoped he wasn't being rude by demanding they get out of the hallway.

Teddy grinned and waved them on to lead the way. He circled around them after they piled into his office and sat at his expansive desk. Setting his mug down on a coaster, he peered at Alfred for a moment before asking, "This is some serious stuff, isn't it? Would you or any of yours like some coffee or water?"

To Alfred's chagrin, Barbara piped up, "I'll take water and Marie would like water I'm sure. ¿Quieres café o agua?"

Jose's wife glanced at the enormous man behind the desk then looked down and replied, "Nada, por favor."

"Entonces, café con leche y agua tambien," Officer Grant smiled and rose from his leather chair. "Sit tight for a minute. I'll be two shakes of a rattler's tail."

Alfred pulled his glasses off and swiped at them with something approaching bestial fervency. His daughter gently grabbed his hand and held it until he stopped rubbing the lenses. Officer Grant stepped back into the office, and Alfred smashed his glasses back on.

As he sat in the creaky, leather chair, he placed six mugs in front his guests.

Marie immediately reached for the nearest mug filled to the brim with milk. She drank deeply and then breathed out heavily from beneath a white mustache.

Officer Grant smiled and leaned back in his chair, crossed his right foot on his left knee and asked, "So, what can I help you folks with?"

"We're—I," Alfred stammered.

"Mi Papi," Marie exclaimed and then pressed herself against her mother as if she scared herself with her exclamation.

Officer Grant chuckled and looked at Alfred.

"Yes," Alfred swallowed. "Señor Jose was wrongfully reported as a spy—a communist spy."

"I see," Officer Grant's tone turned serious. "And we have him here?"

"We came here to pick him up and get the charges cleared," Alfred couldn't meet the man's eyes.

"This is a serious situation," the officer said. "Do you have some ID for Señor Jose? What kind of work release does he have?"

Alfred looked at Jose's wife and then at his daughter. Barbara caught the plea for help in his eyes and asked, "¿Tarjeta con foto? ¿Y...Y Tarjeta verde para Señor Jose?"

The woman flashed a nervous smile and dug into her purse. After a minute, she produced a driver's license for Jose Gardea, and the license was shortly followed by a stained card of green cardstock. Officer Grant leaned forward and accepted them.

After peering at the cards for a moment, he said, "These appear to be legitimate. I'm surprised. Most Mexican workers don't get a green card. They use the Bracero mostly—temporary, seasonal work."

"Does that mean you can help us?" Alfred asked.

"Well," Officer Grant handed the cards back to Jose's wife, "I can't make any guarantees. Being reported as a communist spy is a serious issue. Do you have proof that he was wrongfully reported?"

Alfred's eyes explored the desk without acknowledging anything he saw. "I called him in...didn't have any evidence though," he said in undertones. Then, gathering strength, he went on, "But I work a high-level finance job, and he was trying to spy on me."

Officer Grant grunted, "That's a serious offence. This man's basically a citizen. Is there any evidence that he was trying to spy on you?"

Alfred rubbed his neck at the heat that crept into his face. At first, he thought he would have to admit he did not, but then he remembered, "When I reported him, I thought it was him breaking into my office and writing insults on my windows. They were just like the insults on the windows of my house and those on the Buick's windshield. I thought he was even writing them on my glasses."

Alfred shrank down as much as he could. That had been too much. He wasn't just going to sound crazy. He would be proven crazy, and they would take him away to a place with white cushioned walls.

Beside him, his daughter cringed and clasped her hands tightly around each other until her knuckles turned white. He felt certain he could feel her holding her breath.

What was she thinking of him? Her looney father was more of a criminal than the man they were bailing out of prison.

"And you reported these break and entries and destruction of property?" Officer Grant asked in a conversational tone.

Alfred shook his head and fought to open his eyes and not rip his glasses off and clean them. How was he to say there hadn't been any breaking—only entering? It would sound ridiculous for him to claim the perpetrator was a master lockpicker and all he had done was deface property. And that, in a way that only Alfred could see. The whole thing sounded utterly preposterous when you couldn't see the writing.

"Mr. Featherbomb, are you feeling alright?" Officer Grant asked.

Alfred stretched his neck from side to side and grabbed his glasses. He pushed them back on his face and then grabbed them again, grabbing the loose fold of his shirt to rub the lenses.

The huge officer sat forward in his chair. The leather squeaked in objection to the man's weight.

"I seem to be the only one who can see it," Alfred muttered as though he was talking with himself.

Officer Grant sat back. Silence followed the squeaking protests of his chair. After a full minute he cleared his throat and said slowly, "I think I'm beginning to understand. This man starts working for you, and strange things start happening. With the contentions with the Soviet Union, your mind jumped to an extreme scenario. You strike me as a rather high-anxiety individual, Mr. Featherbomb. Young folk might say you got a bad case of the gringles."

Officer Grant leaned his elbows onto his knees, scraping his chair backward in the process. Clasping his hands, he peered at Alfred, "I'd like to help you, Mr. Featherbomb, just as I want to help what sounds like an innocent man, and I'm going to do what I can. I need you to sign a few papers, hire a lawyer and turn the news hour off."

Alfred did his best to compose himself. What he was hearing didn't make sense to him. "I probably just need to get my new glasses," he glanced at Officer Grant.

The big man ducked his head in acknowledgement and reached for his credenza. "That may be." He pulled a small sheaf of papers from a file and presented them to Alfred. "Here. I need you to sign these. Sloak told me something along the lines of what you've told me about Mr. Gardea, so they're all filled out. I can't get the bond lowered any further, but once you receive Mr. Gardea's hearing date, go to it, explain how you overreacted, and that should be the end of it."

Alfred found he couldn't meet the officer's gaze. Nodding, he accepted the offered pen and scribbled his name on the appropriate lines.

"I needn't remind you," Officer Grant said firmly, "false allegations help no one. Taxpayer dollars get spent and people like this little snapper," he motioned to Marie, "feel abandoned by their papi."

Marie looked at Officer Grant with questions burning in her dark brown eyes and then buried her face in her mother's neck.

Alfred understood what the officer was saying, "It won't happen again."

Chapter 25

The reunion had been filled with screams of joy from Marie and tears of relief from Jose's wife. Alfred glanced in the rearview mirror.

Marie sat on her papi's lap and snuggled into his chest. A placid look smoothed her face. Every few minutes she jerked back to look at her papi and ask him a question or to simply say, "Papi," and return to hugging and cuddling him.

Alfred glanced at Barbara. His daughter had been quiet and either stared out the window or down at her hands in her lap. He felt he needed to say something, but the words that came to mind felt all wrong.

As if feeling his gaze on her, Barbara turned to look at him. He tried to offer a smile, but it was shadowed by the shame slipping like a knife between his ribs. His daughter gave a slight smile before looking down.

"I'm sorry, Barbara," Alfred said as the Buick bounced through a pothole. "Maybe I did overreact. I shouldn't have… He's back now."

"Is mom going to talk to you now?" Barbara didn't blurt it out, but it came out in such a rush that she must have been contemplating it for some time.

Alfred glanced at her and gripped the wheel tighter. A fresh black smudge spread from the passenger side of the windshield. He tried to pull his eyes from it, but it was like a magnet pulling him toward itself. He couldn't look away as terror made his body erupt in sweat. In no uncertain terms, the new phrase captured his nonfeasance as a husband.

A car horn blared dimly on the edge of his attention.

"Dad!" his daughter shouted.

Alfred dragged his eyes back to the road just in time to pull the wheel to the right and swerve out of the oncoming traffic. A convertible zipped by. The driver yelled something that was lost in the motion, but Alfred was sure he was demanding to know where Alfred had gotten his license.

"It's happening again, isn't it?" Barbara was white-faced and held herself braced against the dashboard and door.

"I'm fine," Alfred snapped, maneuvering the boxy car back into the correct lane.

The family in the backseat made no comments, and Alfred spent the rest of the trip with his eyes glued to the task of driving. He couldn't shake the sense that something was incredibly wrong and that everyone except him could see what it was.

Barbara got out and spoke a few, halting words with the Mexican family as they exited the Buick behind the supermarket. Jose's wife hugged her and grasped her hand in farewell.

Alfred refused to look at Jose as the Mexican leaned down to look at him through the passenger window. "I work mañana—tomorrow?" he asked.

Alfred couldn't think of a response. Finally, he shook his head. "Tomorrow's Saturday," he said.

When he looked out the window, Jose had his daughter in his arms and was walking away with his wife wrapping an arm around his waist and leaning on his shoulder.

Barbara slipped into the passenger seat. She stared at him for a moment. He didn't react.

"Are we going to go home?" she asked after several silent seconds. "It's pretty late."

Alfred blew out his breath and rested his forehead on the steering wheel. He had never shown so much of his inner struggle to his daughter before. How was she going to make fun of him for the drama?

"I'm tired too," Barbara stated softly.

"Why is everything I do the wrong thing?"

Barbara shifted uncomfortably and looked out the window as the supermarket's neon blinked out.

They rode in silence for the few minutes home.

As Alfred dragged himself from the car, Barbara called, "Let me tell mom we're home."

He grunted and followed his daughter toward the door.

He hadn't taken two steps before the door was flung open. Before he could see the door flinger, an angry river flooded the driveway.

"Where have you been? Why didn't you have Barbara back at a sensible bedtime?" Mrs. Featherbomb shrieked. Then, she jumped to Barbara's side and began checking her over. In a quiet, maternal voice she asked, "Are you hurt? Were you kidnapped? You shouldn't be hanging out with those boys. I swear I'll kill that Joey Chadelle."

Barbara tried to regain her personal space, "Mom, it's none of that. We had to pick him up from the prison."

"Oh my God, what are you talking about? Who? Joey Chadelle? What happened? Why didn't you just leave him there?"

"Señor Jose is back with his family now," Alfred wasn't sure where his burst of courage to explain came from. Perhaps it was just stupidity.

Mrs. Featherbomb paused her torrential questions to glare at him.

Yes, definitely stupidity. He tried to shrink down into something unseen.

"You keep him off our property and don't you dare mention him again," Mrs. Featherbomb caressed her daughter, brushing Barbara's dark hair out of her face. "Not after what he's done to my sweet pea."

Alfred, who had been shuffling slowly toward his house, did a full stop and stared at his wife. Confusion, anger, shame and a deep sense that he had done something unforgiveable warred inside him. He interrupted Mrs. Featherbomb's ongoing, protective murmuring.

"Clarabelle, what do you think he did?"

Mrs. Featherbomb shot another glare at him. With a pat to her hair, she grabbed Barbara's shoulders and steered her inside.

Alfred thought of Old Mr. Faustner and his stock of liquor. The woman he had married was so unreasonable. What had he done this time? Or, maybe, what hadn't he done?

"No cussing, dear," Mrs. Featherbomb's voice played in his head.

"I wasn't about to cuss," Alfred muttered.

Mrs. Featherbomb shot him a venomous look. "What were you saying?" she demanded.

"Just talking to myself, Angel," Alfred dug deep inside for a calm smile and hoped adding it to the nickname would appease the tension threatening to burst into an inferno.

Mrs. Featherbomb drilled her gaze into him as if her eyes were two barbed spears with razor sharp tips. He would've been fileted had her gaze been able to cut.

Her stab narrowed ever so slightly, "You haven't called me that before."

Alfred froze, his right foot hovering over the threshold. Maybe he'd gone too far. Yes, trying to smooth things over with a new, endearing nickname was foolishness.

He should have bought flowers and maybe a roast or something.

Mrs. Featherbomb patted her hair and turned back to their daughter. Barbara, however, had slipped away from her mother while she was surgically operating on her father, and the click of a doorknob latching echoed down the hall.

Mrs. Featherbomb patted her hair again and stated, "You've upset your daughter."

Alfred hesitantly stepped inside and gently pulled the door shut behind him. He was tired and thirsty. All he wanted was to sleep in his own bed instead of on the couch. The truthful insults he'd been seeing everywhere kept playing through his mind until all he saw was the writing on his glasses, the writing on the Buick's windshield, the writing on his office window.

"No cussing, dear," Mrs. Featherbomb's voice sang.

Alfred shook his head and pulled off his glasses. Dishes clanked in the sink. Squeezing his eyes shut in an attempt to block out the truth that kept buffeting him, Alfred called, "I'll take care of them, Angel."

The dishes stopped clattering, and the water was turned off. "Sure you will. Just like you left them on the counter," Mrs. Featherbomb said flatly.

"No, I don't mind," Alfred winced as he stabbed his left eye with the temples of his glasses. "I know how to do them. I was the one that dirtied them."

Mrs. Featherbomb scoffed, "You look ready to keel over and die."

"Thanks for noticing, but I'm not a sailboat," Alfred said and then held his breath and readied his arms to block any hard objects that might find themselves airborne.

That's when it happened. Something that hadn't happened in so long, Alfred hadn't realized he'd forgotten the sound. Mrs. Featherbomb laughed an actual uncontrolled laugh. It was far different from the giggle she used when talking with her friends, and it was deeper, more guttural.

Alfred's heart rose and fluttered like a hatchling just discovering it could fly. And then, it crashed headfirst into the ground.

"If you were a sailboat, dear, I wouldn't ever wonder where you'd gotten off to. You'd always be right where I left you. So much easier than trying to help you see what I need," Mrs. Featherbomb kept laughing and murmuring about seagulls being the only issue apart from storms.

Maybe that was the issue. He was more like the Titanic—huge and immoveable. She had just put an iceberg in his way, and he had run into it and sank to the bottom of the ocean. All it had taken for her to laugh was a few days of not talking with him and not being around him.

"I'll take the trash out then," he offered as he stepped toward the waste bin.

Mrs. Featherbomb laughed again, "It won't do any good. It's empty. Do you want to know why it's empty? I took it out. I do much rather prefer it empty to spilling over."

Alfred tried to recall how full the waste bin had been, but all he saw was black smudges crawling across his glasses.

He turned. Barbara peered wide-eyed from around the corner. Here was his daughter watching his wife, her mother, treat him like a fool while seeming genuinely happier than she had been in the rememberable past.

He didn't see it coming. The plate didn't break until it slammed onto the floor and shattered, but his glasses, which took the brunt of the impact, snapped and fell in two pieces on top of the jagged wedges of porcelain.

"You see this?" Mrs. Featherbomb held up a flyer with lively colors depicting a girl on horseback tearing around a barrel. The block letters were big enough for Alfred to read without his glasses. "Your daughter got this from that Mexican, and now she wants to go to a rodeo. A rodeo!"

Alfred blocked another plate and took a step backward, his foot crunching on the broken porcelain already scattered on the floor. Barbara gasped and spun back to her room. His brain fired like an engine without a carburetor.

"Don't just stand there," Mrs. Featherbomb wailed. "Clean up this mess, you freak. I will not have my daughter living in a rundown tramp camp just as I will not have her going anywhere near one of those filthy, dusty, vermin-riddled, smelly, dung-covered, noisy trash heaps they call a rodeo."

All the while she had been describing the rodeo, which Alfred thought she had forgotten to mention expensive, Mrs. Featherbomb had been tearing the sodden flyer into ribbons and the ribbons crosswise into confetti.

Alfred bent to begin picking up the shattered plates and jumped.

"And what's more," Mrs. Featherbomb's voice rose nearly a whole octave, "my daughter will not be going anywhere with a boy. You hear me, Barbara Ann? No boys."

Alfred straightened and found that instead of picking up pieces of the plates he had managed to grab both halves of his glasses.

"Do you hear me?" Mrs. Featherbomb cried. "What did I say about boys?"

She didn't wait for an answer. Pulling the whole dripping stack of plates and silverware from the sink, she turned toward Alfred. Wild fury poured from her eyes, and she laughed again, a twisted, poisonous laugh.

"You think you can ignore me and live like I don't exist."

Smash. Another plate multiplied into many smaller plates.

"You think I don't know how you've been encouraging my daughter to want to do what those foreigners do with their devil music and dirty rodeos?"

Smash.

"You think you can trash my house and sweep it all under the rug by calling me Angel?"

Smash.

"You don't have a guardian angel that can protect you tonight, mister."

Alfred felt the doorknob dig into the small of his back. His hands were up in a defensive position. Another plate shattered on the floor. A spoon, hurled by the plate's inertia, flung soapy water up his slacks. Mrs. Featherbomb pulled another plate from the stack.

"Stop it," Alfred shouted. "Stop."

Something changed in Mrs. Featherbomb's countenance. Where she had been alight with wild fury before, she turned dark and cold. Ice, sharp and slick, formed like shards as she stared him down.

"Please stop," Alfred begged. "We can talk about it, can't we?"

Mrs. Featherbomb raised the stack of plates above her head. Alfred glanced at them and found relief that there were only two left.

"Clarabelle," Alfred plead.

"My daughter is not going to be some lowlife living in a hovel while nursing some stupid boy who got her pregnant and then got his back broke."

Smash. The plates crashed down. Shards and splinters glanced off the walls and Alfred's legs. He curled up, standing on one leg, arms wrapped protectively around his head.

Silence reigned for several seconds. Then, as the ringing in his ears subsided, a new sound trickled from the hallway. Suppressed gasping sobs vibrated the air.

Mrs. Featherbomb patted her hair and crunched over the broken plates with a stiff, dignified bearing to her stride. She opened the closet door, removed a broom and dustpan and shut the door. With swift, solid movements she pushed the clinking porcelain shards toward the center of the kitchen.

Alfred stood bewildered and too scared to move lest he incite a worse tirade.

The sorrowful clinking and Barbara's sobbing continued in melancholy orchestra. Alfred hardly dared breath.

"I want you to leave."

Alfred wasn't certain he'd heard correctly. He waited, lowering his arms a hair.

"I said get out," Mrs. Featherbomb screamed. "Get out. Get out. Get out."

Alfred's hands slipped on the doorknob as he scrambled to escape the incoming broom Mrs. Featherbomb brandished. He wasn't quick enough, and the broom came down on his shoulder and then his back.

At last, he stood outside with the front door safely closed between him and the vicious creature that had taken over his wifc.

He was mad, yet some part of him was finally satiated. Mrs. Featherbomb had finally told him to his face what she thought of him. He didn't need to fret and worry about what she might be thinking of him any longer. It was painfully clear just like the bruises forming on his body.

Chapter 26

With a jerk on his blazer to straighten it and a few brushes to the arms, Alfred turned and shoved his hands into his pockets. Slowly, he withdrew his hands and found the halves of his glasses in them. He must have shoved them into his pockets with his instincts of survival before reaching for the door even though he couldn't remember doing so.

Cautiously entering the garage, he grabbed a roll of adhesive tape and pocketed it. He would do his best to repair his glasses later. Finding a safe place for the night was top priority.

He started running through a list of places he could go when the sound of a window popping open broke the still night air. Muffled sobs followed. How could he help Barbara? He was no better than the horse dung at a rodeo according to his wife. He hadn't even thought of helping his daughter until he heard her crying. What a lousy piece of—

"No cussing, dear," Mrs. Featherbomb's voice ricocheted inside his head.

He shook his head but could not get rid of her nagging voice.   He reached for his glasses to clean them before remembering they were broken in his pockets.

He snuck out of the garage and, like a frightened deer, tiptoed across the walk leading to the front door. Barbara's sobs were clearer now, but she was gaining control of them. Something thumped onto the grass in front of him.

He looked up at Barbara's window. She had the light off in her room, but the crack of light filtering under the door painted her profile as she swung a leg over the windowsill and looked back.

The room behind her flooded with light. A shriek of fury drowned out Barbara's whimper.

Glass crashed to the ground. Alfred was close enough that a jagged chunk glanced off his cheek. A warm droplet of blood dribbled down like a tear.

More glass shattered as Barbara landed on the ground.

"You'll cut yourself," Mrs. Featherbomb screeched. Then she added, "Fine, run off. See if I'm still here for you when you come back."

Alfred bent toward Barbara. His face bumped a long, smooth object. He reached up to push it aside and found the broom handle protruding through the broken window.

"Dad?" Barbara's voice shook.

"I'm here," Alfred groped in the dark. "I'm here."

Barbara's arms wrapped around him and she cried, sobbing uncontrollably into his shoulder with great, silent gasps.

He hugged her to him, saying over and over again, "I'm here. I've got you."

As he comforted her, he picked his way through the yard to the sidewalk. It wasn't where he wanted to be with any neighbors arriving home late able to see him and his daughter, but he didn't know what else to do. His daughter needed him, and he needed distance between himself and Mrs. Featherbomb.

They walked that way, Barbara leaning into him and sniffing as she slowly regained some semblance of composure, for a few blocks. Alfred hoped the neighbors that noticed would simply think that they were just a father comforting his teenage daughter after a breakup.

"What happened to mom?" Barbara's voice shook. "Why was she doing that?"

"Shh, Sweat Pea," Alfred's mind was running so fast he didn't have the capacity to answer such questions.

"Why haven't you and mom been getting along?"

"Shh. Shh," Alfred hugged her tighter. "We've just got to give her a few minutes to cool down."

Even as he said it, he doubted that a few minutes would make much difference. In truth, he felt he was the one who needed to cool down. Anger coursed hot and heavy through his veins, and he couldn't shake the unfairness of being forced out of his own home.

What would Pastor Meyers say about their situation? Further, might it be best to ask the pastor for help?

Dread settled like silt at a river's mouth, slowly depositing one grain or pebble at a time. He couldn't tell anyone or risk having the congregation find out. He had to keep hidden the difficulties and fights between him and Mrs. Featherbomb. He needed to protect Mrs. Featherbomb's image. If everything and everyone appeared normal and happy, their reputation as an exemplary family would be sustained, and there would be no reason for Mrs. Featherbomb to throw plates at him again. The status quo would remain unchanged, and, therefore, family stability would remain intact.

Alfred grimaced to himself and then forced his anger to cool. He had a plan, and a plan meant everything was going to be alright.

"Dad?" Barbara asked. "Where are we going?"

In his mind's eye, his daughter transformed from a teenager struggling with the cusp of adulthood back into a toddler struggling to keep up as they walked through a park on vacation. She was so young and innocent that he needed to protect her from the sharp stones and splintering sticks. He needed to watch her carefully lest she trip and scrape her knees.

Alfred said, "We'll find a good place."

The toddler Barbara would have let that answer stand and gone on playing as if she hadn't a care in the world. However, the teenage Barbara asked with a worried, pinched voice, "What about clothes and breakfast? You forgot my bag back there on the ground outside my window."

Anger flared like an atom bomb detonation in Alfred as his daughter blamed him for forgetting her bag. *She* had forgotten it and hadn't said anything about it until now. He thought of snapping that they would just wear what they had on and then get breakfast at a diner, but, instead, he clenched his jaw and grunted.

He didn't need to be wearing his glasses to see the ugly description of himself in black smears. His imagination called up several ugly names, each describing his failure as a father.

Barbara let go of him and retained their physical connection only through holding his hand. Pain lanced through Alfred at the withdrawal. His daughter was sending a clear message she didn't want to be around him. And then she offered a sledgehammer blow.

"Can I stay at Donna's?"

The sidewalk surely had an uneven section that tripped him up when she asked that. Alfred struggled to regain his stride. His hand swing was off though, causing his hand his daughter still held to pendulate against her rhythm.

"It's okay, dad," Barbara said quietly. "I know it's late."

Alfred was about to confirm by saying they should really call first, but a heavily accented salutation cut him off.

"Hola, Señor Featherbomb," the unmistakable voice of Señor Jose called, "and Señorita Barbara. Mira, Marie."

Out of the darkness a towering figure materialized. Alfred blinked against the blurriness. At last, he made out Señor Jose smiling broadly as he carried his daughter on his shoulders. Marie stared at them he guessed, but her eyes were so dark he couldn't tell exactly where she was looking. She had her arms wrapped around Jose's forehead like a turban.

Barbara moved closer to him as if she were shy and responded, "Hola, Señor Jose y Marie."

Marie yawned loudly in reply and Jose laughed, "Chiquita." He extended his hand to Alfred, "It is time to...to cama, bed, no?"

Alfred shook Jose's hand and tried to smile. He couldn't look at the man even in the dark. Didn't he know Alfred had been the one to get him arrested?

"Ah," Jose drove the awkward silence away, "the air fresh. Is good."

Again, Alfred nodded.

"Good night for walking," Jose continued as if trying to illicit some conversation. "I make work mañana—tomorrow?"

Alfred wanted to curse. He'd already answered that question. Instead, he said, "Look, you've still got a court hearing, and my wife would like a few more days without work being done at the house." Alfred forced a chuckle. It sounded so fake he was certain even a foreigner would recognize the insincerity immediately. "Tomorrow's Saturday, the weekend, anyway. Don't you Mexicans take the weekends off?"

Jose smiled, revealing a flash of white teeth in the thin light of a distant streetlamp. "Ah, forget." He made a gesture beside his head as if to say it wasn't functioning. "Fin de semana, mami," he looked up at his daughter who responded with a small giggle and hugged her father's forehead more snuggly. Jose bounced her up and down while humming the opening theme to *The Lone Ranger*. Marie giggled gleefully.

Alfred gazed at the man and his daughter and tried to recall whether he had ever had such simple fun with his own daughter. Barbara tucked her hair behind her ears and looked down at her toe as she shuffled a pebble around on the sidewalk.

Finally, Alfred put two and two together. Looking at his daughter he asked, "Is the rodeo this weekend."

"Yeah," she responded quietly. And then she blurted, "Joey wasn't gonna take me. I told him no. Donna and I were talking about trying to get Will and James to take us."

Normally, Alfred would have found an out by telling Barbara to ask her mother about attending the rodeo, but, given the current situation, it was completely up to him. He thought of several ways to start a reply, but he discovered he didn't know what he wanted as an end result. His daughter glanced at him with nervous tension tightening her cheeks as he thought.

Finally, he responded, "Your mother is not going to be happy about it. What do you say to going with your old man?" Alfred kicked at the sidewalk, "I'll try to not be too—how do you put it? Square?"

He hid a frown and hoped the darkness obscured his bunched-up brow. For some reason, letting his daughter know he was willing to take her to the rodeo felt wrong like he was hiding something devastating from his wife. Mrs. Featherbomb wasn't there, and she wouldn't find out until after the fact. Was that just simplistic, juvenile justification? Sweat beaded on his forehead. He reached for his glasses, trying to snatch them off before another insult could form on them.

"Thanks, dad," Barbara said. "You'll always be a bit square, but maybe I can find Donna there as long as her parents let her come."

Alfred was taken aback. He couldn't decipher whether Barbara was truly appreciative of his willingness to take her or whether she was saying she was glad to use him as a means to get where she wanted to go.

Jose spun like a bucking bronco with Marie on his shoulders. The little girl laughed and cried in Spanish, "¡Otra vez, Papi! ¡Otra vez, Papi!"

Barbara hugged him, and Alfred's racing mind calmed for a second.

"Sometimes squares are nice," she said.

Alfred stood stunned. He didn't realize it then, but later, once things became clearer to him, he could see how his daughter had needed stability with the way Mrs. Featherbomb had upended their family, and leaning on him, square though he was, was an anchor for her to feel safe and grounded.

Jose waved, "Adios. Ah, goodbye."

"Buenos noches," Barbara said, returning the wave.

Alfred, still too dumbstruck to speak, lifted a hand awkwardly.

With the distraction of friends—friends? Yes, he decided. With the distraction of friends removed, the weight of their situation settled back onto Alfred's shoulders. He slumped and ran a hand through his hair. What did a father do in a situation like this?

Taking stock of the most important things they needed was the logical way to go about surviving. However, Alfred was stuck in recalling and replaying everything Mrs. Featherbomb had said and done to him. He reached up and gingerly touched and prodded his face. The darkness hid the bruise, but it would be a nasty black and blue in the sunlight at the rodeo. He didn't move like a cowboy or dress like a cowboy so claiming that a bronco had thrown him was not a feasible alibi.

"Does it hurt?" Barbara asked.

He looked at her. Nodding, he responded, "It'll be a real shiner tomorrow."

"Just tell everybody you walked into a door," Barbara said.

Kids. How were they that smart? Or maybe she was just that smooth at lying?

"If I had my bag, I could probably cover it up pretty well with some makeup," Barbara stated, peering through the darkness at his face.

"How long have you been wearing makeup?" Alfred asked, appalled that he didn't know this about his own daughter.

"Mom got it for me when we went shopping for school clothes," she replied. "I haven't worn it much. It doesn't feel nice on my face."

Alfred grunted. He would rather explain a bruise away than explain makeup. He could only imagine what the smudged, black letters would spell if he did wear makeup. The explanation that he'd walked into a door in the dark sounded better and better the more he thought about it.

"So, are we going to sleep at the motel?" Barbara asked. There was a nearly imperceptible edge of fear and uncertainty in her voice.

"What?" Alfred shook his head to clear Mrs. Featherbomb's angry words from his mind. "I don't know. Maybe we should head back. She might be cooled off by now."

"No way, dad," Barbara shrank away, shaking her head vigorously. "I'm not going back there tonight." Tears broke through her strong façade, "She threw the broom at me. It didn't hit me, but it shattered my window. She smashed your face too. I saw her do it."

Alfred reached for his daughter, but she backpedaled again. He stood with his hand outstretched and replayed the plate soaring toward him. He hadn't had time to react.

"No," he mumbled. "She probably isn't done blowing off steam."

"Was it because she found the rodeo flyer?"

Alfred couldn't make out his daughter's expression, but her voice was laced with remorse. He didn't have an answer.

"Why has she been ignoring you until now?"

Again, Alfred searched futilely for a reply. He was tired, and he didn't want to be taxed with coming up with an excuse to explain Mrs. Featherbomb's behaviors as logical.

"I'll go to Donna's if you head back there tonight," Barbara said. It wasn't a threat. It was merely her informing him what she would do.

"We have to go back sometime," Alfred scrambled for a reason. Finding none, he looked down and wondered what outcome he wanted. At least, that was somewhat easier to identify. He wanted life to go back to peaceful coexistence without plates being thrown at his face and without brooms being swung like swords at him or thrown like spears at his daughter. Then, he realized, he could take the occasional plate or broomstick to the face just as long as Barbara was not attacked again.

What a long night, and probably weekend, this would be.

He patted the breast pocket in his blazer. "I have my billfold with me. We can find somewhere close to stay. We'll have to walk. I seemed to have dropped the car keys at home."

Alfred caught a look of disgust on his daughter's face as she muttered, "I'll be so grody tomorrow my friends won't want to hang out."

"What?" he asked. He didn't know what the slang term meant, but he could tell it was something negative.

"Just keep being a square, dad," was her reply.

Barbara was silent as they walked to the motel a dozen blocks away. Alfred's mind was anything but silent, however. With each step he took, he thought of another way he had failed as a husband. By the time they reached the motel, he had a list that would rival any cartoon's scroll rolling to the floor and out the door and down the street.

Thankfully, no questions were asked by the motel manager, and the key to the room worked on the first try. Two beds greeted them with a floor lamp between them and a desk and chair on the opposite wall. Barbara walked toward the bathroom while Alfred locked the door and checked the curtains for gaps. He kicked off his shoes and sank onto the nearest bed.

"You're not going to snore tonight, are you, dad?" Barbara asked as if trying to distract herself.

Alfred grunted, pulling off his blazer and tie.

"You do snore."

Alfred heard his daughter peel open the second bed. Fabric rustled as she slid into it.

"It smells funny in here," she stated.

Alfred wiped his forehead and rubbed his eyes. It felt nice to sit and have the promise of a comfortable bed beneath him. He took a fearful glance at the window, but the curtains blocked his view of what he was certain was written there.

Feeling the pieces of his glasses in his blazer, he briefly considered not repairing them. That wouldn't do though. After all, he needed to be able to see when they were at the rodeo tomorrow or he would undoubtedly end up stepping in horse poop or something worse.

He stood and strode to the bathroom. In the doorway he stopped and turned toward Barbara. He was overcome with something he hadn't felt strongly since she'd been little. There, peering at him with her red-rimmed eyes, he saw not his teenage daughter, but the toddler he had carried piggyback to cheer her up after scraping her knee on the driveway.

"Goodnight, Sweet Pea," he said as a smile tugged at the corners of his mouth.

"Goodnight, dad," came her reply.

Alfred returned to his bed and yanked the chord on the lamp, plunging the room into darkness.

He was exhausted and ready to welcome sleep, but he couldn't find it. He lay in bed, which he decided was ten times better than the couch at home, and saw afresh all the mistakes he'd made.

He also couldn't shake what the mirror had called him.

Good-for-nothing riffraff

He already knew he was good for nothing but to be called such a demeaning term as someone who stole from the dead was on a level that made him feel like cussing and yelling angrily at anyone or anything that would listen.

"No cussing, dear," Mrs. Featherbomb's voice sang.

The urge to shout obscenities doubled. He heard Mrs. Featherbomb's voice again. The urge increased. He wanted to shout for her voice in his head to shut up.

"No cussing, dear."

He adjusted his pillow.

"No cussing, dear."

Why couldn't he scream and swear like he'd done to Codgens? The man had left him alone after that.

"No cussing, dear."

Throwing off the covers, he rolled out of the bed and grabbed the pillow. He lifted it above his head and slammed it into the mattress.

"Why is nothing good enough for you?" he ground out.

Wham. The pillow smacked the bed again.

He was about to lose his meager restraint and blast the bed with all of his anger, but he heard something that made him freeze. He'd forgotten his daughter was in the other bed just a few feet away. She made another frightened, squeaking cry. He dropped the pillow from his limp hand. Barbara whimpered and fabric rustled as she pulled herself into a ball.

Alfred stood stone still. Had he just scared her the same way the broom thrown by her mother had? What kind of father was he to forget his daughter was trying to sleep? She was probably terrified of him now. First, her mother had all but kicked her out of the house, and now, he was beating up a pillow and shouting.

Barbara whimpered and cried softly. He should go to her. He knew that, but he couldn't get his body to move. He couldn't do anything for her. He couldn't do anything right. He was worse than George Bailey contemplating suicide. If he were to pull a George Bailey, Alfred was certain he wouldn't have a Clarence Odbody to talk him out of it.

His daughter was crying and terrified. Terrified of him. He was a—

"No cussing, dear," Mrs. Featherbomb twittered.

One last, minute piece of resistance built up inside Alfred. He would not keep scaring his daughter. Sure, he was a recreant. Yes, he was a good-for-nothing. Absolutely, he was a lily-livered idiot who could do nothing right. But there was one thing he would not be. He would not be an abusive and dangerous parent.

Just as soon as he made that decision, he remembered how he had failed as a father over and over. Each time, Mrs. Featherbomb had been there to rescue Barbara and comfort her. He'd grown so used to not being needed he had stopped seeing himself as a father he realized. He sank to his knees. In his mind's eye he saw a disembodied hand making another checkmark beside this latest realization of his failure.

Jose's little daughter, Marie, had looked so content and trusting with her papi. Alfred knew he would never be as good of a father as he was.

"I'm sorry, Barbara," he forced out.

His daughter cried.

Alfred turned and sank to the floor, leaning back against the bed.

His daughter was right; the place did smell funny. What kind of father got his daughter kicked out of the house and took her to a motel? He rubbed his eyes and hung his head.

A sudden urge took him. He needed to know what described him, and he needed to know right then and there. Reaching for his blazer, he dug out his glasses and the roll of adhesive tape. Then, he flung himself across his bed and pulled the lamp cord. Vaguely, he was aware of Barbara cringing and curling into a tighter ball as if to protect herself—protect herself from him no doubt. He grunted an apology that not even the best neanderthal etymologist would have been able to interpret with years of study.

A few minutes later, he had the two halves of his glasses taped together. The lump of tape rested on the bridge of his nose causing the frames to ride a little higher than he was used to, but he could see who he was. Smeared, black lettering tracked trails of insulting descriptions all over the lenses. He didn't fare well in any of them. But—

"No cussing, dear," Mrs. Featherbomb's voice drowned out the words he was forbidden to use.

No matter, he was essentially an unusable piece of slag pulled from the dirtiest mine and couldn't be discarded properly because he was contaminating the entire world.

As he read, a new fear struck him. He wondered how he could protect Mrs. Featherbomb's image. Anything he did would reflect poorly on her. She had chosen him, and he had let her down.

His eye twitched. Something was off; however, he knew that line of reasoning was right. All of their marital, familial and financial problems were due to him. He couldn't meet even the basest of standards.

New words scrawled across his glasses.

"No. No. No," he found himself muttering. "I know it, but it still can't be."

He was powerless to reject the truth. He was everything that the words said about him.

"Dad," a small, terrified voice reached toward him, "what's going on?"

Alfred shoved his hand under his glasses and wiped his eyes. His fingers came away slick with sweat. The writing filled so much of his vision it was like glaucoma closing and narrowing what he could see into a pinprick of a tunnel. He tried to face his daughter, but it was like looking into a pitch black well with no flashlight.

"Dad?" Barbara's voice carried deeper fear. "Dad? You're scaring me again. What's happening?"

Alfred opened his mouth, but no words came out. His mind was stuck in place just as his feet felt stuck to the floor. He needed to assure his daughter everything was fine, and there was no reason to panic. His heartbeat sounded in his ears, heavy and fast.

"Dad?" Barbara clutched the blanket so hard her knuckles whitened. "Dad?" her voice was almost a shriek.

Alfred's eye twitched. He slapped at it to make it stop. Taking the brunt of the slap, his glasses popped off his nose and skewed to the side. His vision was unobstructed once again. He lowered himself to the bed.

"Did you see something like you did in the kitchen at home?" Barbara asked quietly after a few moments of silence.

Alfred stared straight ahead at the curtained window. His pulse remained elevated, but he could hear his breathing slowing down to normal. His daughter had asked a question, but it wasn't a question that could lead to her helping him. It was a question about his sanity. She was wondering whether she needed to call the authorities to cart him off to a white padded room and a straitjacket.

Anger and fear and duty played tug of war inside him. He wanted to snap and say he was alright and nothing was wrong with him, yet, at the same time, he knew something was dreadfully wrong. He didn't know much about mental illness, but he was certain he was going clinically mad. That was the only explanation that made sense. He wasn't fit for society.

He grabbed his glasses, rubbed his eyes and nodded his head, admitting to his daughter he had indeed seen something that no one else could or ever would see.

"I'm sorry," he stated flatly. "And I'm sorry you have me for a father."

Fabric sighed and footsteps slapped the floor behind him. Water ran in the bathroom sink. Then, Barbara stood in front of him offering him a glass half full. He stared at the water and at his daughter's hands, but he couldn't raise his eyes to meet hers.

"I don't know what's going on," she said. Her voice undulated as if she were on the verge of intense panic. "I don't know why you and mom don't get along. I don't know why she doesn't think I can take care of myself and do things on my own. I don't know why you're having these fits."

Alfred reached out slowly for the glass. Barbara wrung her hands together as she stood in front of him. He drank half the water and lowered the glass to his lap, clutching it gently between both of his hands. He swirled it and stared through it toward the floor. He didn't know why he was seeing things either.

The bed sank on his left side as Barbara sat and leaned against him. Her head rested on his shoulder. "I love you, dad." She breathed in a shaky breath, "I wish mom was going to the rodeo with us tomorrow."

Chapter 27

Out of habit, Alfred awoke as dawn was just beginning to lighten the sky. He lay in bed exhausted from his churning mind. He wanted nothing more than to grant himself distance from his problems. Enjoying the rodeo with his daughter and not thinking about Mrs. Featherbomb and her tirade sounded like the best possible way to spend the day.

He wasn't particularly fond of rodeos and hadn't been to one since he was a kid with a single digit age. Barbara clearly wanted to go, and that was reason enough for a reasonable parent. He *was* a reasonable parent, wasn't he?

Reluctantly, he shoved the covers to the side and eased himself out of bed. Pain flared from his nose and cheek as he instinctively rubbed his eyes. He winced and trudged to the bathroom.

The faint light prying its way through the curtains illuminated Barbara's smooth features. He had never seen her sleep before except when she was an infant. Without his glasses, his vision was blurry, but he still made out a slight frown pulling her lips down just a hair. Even in sleep she carried the weight of her parents' shortcomings.

Alfred's heart dropped. He had wanted to give her the world even when she cried and wailed with no end in sight as a baby. What had changed? Why hadn't he thought of her at every stage throughout the past dozen years? Why hadn't he protected her better from the cares and problems of their family life?

A profound sadness he would later come to recognize as grief attached lead sinkers to his feet as if the mafia had cemented them and dropped him into a harbor somewhere. He loved his daughter. There was no doubt about that. But...did she know it?

The face that stared back at him from the mirror was that of an ogre he decided. It was something Codgens would have a heyday mocking him about. There would be no end to the comments about how Alfred wasn't cut out to be a boxer. If Codgens made fun of him, Alfred would tell him to stuff it. Then, he remembered it was Saturday, and he was taking his daughter to the rodeo. He splashed cold water on his face.

He refused to look at the smudged writing in the bottom right corner of the mirror and squinted against the blurriness as he studied the Picasso Mrs. Featherbomb's projectile had made of his face. Just as Barbara had said, the most darkly bruised line running from his eyebrow and down his cheek like a pirate's scar looked like he had indeed run into a door. The eye was partially swollen shut and hurt like someone had embedded a stone under his skin.

The next moment, he chided himself. He was making too much of his little bruise he decided in retrospect of the injuries and mutilations that soldiers were coming home with. He really had nothing to complain about.

As he wrapped up in the bathroom, the business of the day pressed on him. He needed to have everything set so Barbara wouldn't need to worry about anything. Where they were going to get breakfast was first and foremost. Coffee

would do him wonders. The next thing was transportation.
He didn't feel like walking several miles each way to attend
the rodeo, and Barbara would probably protest if he
recommended it.

Barbara was still asleep, so as quietly as possible,
Alfred dug the phone book from the desk. He could have a
taxi pick them up at a diner and take them out to the rodeo.
It would be expensive, at least, it would be expensive
compared to driving their own family car.

Alfred set the phone book on the counter. Thoughts
raced through his mind, and his hands shook as he pulled his
glasses out. Self-preservation rejected the idea of wearing
them ever again.   At the same time, self-preservation
observed the need for him to have clear vision. He rubbed his
eyes. Either he could have blurry vision and avoid a large
portion of the insulting, black smears or he could put his
glasses on and constantly peer through the words in hopes
that he had enough of a tunnel that he could read and see
clearly.

That's how his daughter found him. His glasses were
halfway to his face, his hands were shaking and perspiration
beaded on his forehead.

"Dad? What happened?"

Alfred turned toward her unable to move his hand or
stop it from shaking. He swallowed, "Do you see anything in
the mirror or on my—on my glasses?"

"Have you been reading creepy books?" Barbara
laughed nervously and tucked a strand of hair behind her ear.

Alfred let his face fall and shuffled like an old man
struggling to coordinate his feet. "I need some coffee," he
stated.

Barbara brushed past him and grabbed the towel by
the sink. "Here. I'll just wipe the mirror clean for you," she
called as she vigorously scrubbed at the mirror.

Alfred stared as the towel passed over the words
several times. They were unaffected and shouted as starkly

as they had before his daughter tried to banish them. Worse was that she didn't see them. She spent too much time scrubbing the center of the mirror where no words resided.

With a sudden surge, Alfred rushed forward, grabbed the towel and scrubbed at the lower corners of the mirror. Barbara's hand was pinned under his, and she protested.

"Dad, what's going on? It's clean. I cleaned it."

"No, it's not," Alfred barked.

Mrs. Featherbomb's voice sang in his head, and he muttered, "Shut up. Shut up. Shut up."

Barbara whimpered. She yanked at her hand with enough force to pull it from under her father's grasp. Momentum from the sudden escape sent her stumbling across the small bathroom. Her calves hit the tub, and she fell into it, knocking her breath away.

Alfred stared, frozen, as his daughter gasped for breath. He hadn't meant to hurt her. He hadn't meant to make her feel that she couldn't clean the mirror correctly. Surely, Jose would never treat his little Marie the same way.

He had to pull it together. His daughter needed him to be strong and not show his reactions to the insults.

A black line formed in front of his eyes. He hadn't realized he'd put his glasses on. The line arced smoothly and flowed into several more lines.

Coward

stared back at him. It was true. Only a coward would be unable to hide his fears. Only a coward would treat his daughter like he'd treated Barbara.

"Barbara, I'm sorry," Alfred lurched forward, doing his best to overcome his terror of hurting his daughter further. "I didn't mean to scare you."

Barbara held up her hand and rasped with an incomplete breath, "I'm fine. I didn't hit my head."

Alfred reached for his daughter. The best he could do was help her out of the tub and figure out how to be the father he needed to be—show nothing but the strength she needed from him. Barbara took his hands and rose shakily.

"See," she said with an overexuberant smile. "No sweat," she was recovering her breath, and her voice wasn't rasping so bad. "I'm all peachy."

Alfred apologized again and grabbed his glasses. He scrubbed them with his shirt as Barbara ushered him out the door.

She was blocking him out. He scrubbed harder.

"I'll be out in a minute," Barbara assured him. "Can we get breakfast at Tiff's?"

Alfred nodded and kept scrubbing. The door latched behind him as he walked toward the room's door. He should have thought of Tiff's. It was only a few blocks away and she always had early morning hours no matter what day it was. Tiff's was also Barbara's favorite place to eat on the rare occasions they didn't eat at home before Jiminy Slim's opened.

As he waited, he checked his wallet and counted the cash. He was relieved to still have a check tucked away. Maybe Tiff's would let him write it over so they could avoid a trip to the bank.

Barbara emerged from the bathroom a moment later, a nervous smirk playing at her lips. Alfred gave his glasses a final swipe and placed them on his face. Something was different about her hair, and her ears were more visible. Alfred pulled his glasses off and immediately scrubbed at them again.

Barbara had her hair pulled back in a ponytail. As he stared, she turned her head slightly and ran her fingers through the loose strands bouncing above her neck.

Alfred knew Mrs. Featherbomb would have a conniption of a fit if she saw their daughter with a ponytail. He was her father. Did fathers these days let their daughter's sport such styles? His glasses cleaning intensified.

"Fine," his daughter said indignantly, "I'll change it."

Alfred fumbled for words, "No… It's fine… It's probably the style at the rodeo."

"Thanks, dad," Barbara grinned and slid her shoes on. "I know mom wouldn't like it. You won't tell her, will you?"

Alfred rubbed his eyes and put his glasses on. "She's going to find out one way or another just like she'll find out I took you to the rodeo. You know how she and her friends gossip."

Barbara frowned, and Alfred thought he heard her mutter something about wishing she could do as she pleased without having to please everyone around her.

They checked out of the motel and walked the few blocks to Tiff's. Only one car drove by, and Alfred didn't recognize the driver. Barbara was silent the whole way.

They sat at an empty table beside the corner booth. In a matter of seconds, coffee and fresh squeezed orange juice were provided by a waitress with dark circles under her eyes. Her smile was genuine as she took their orders and asked what they were up to on such a fine Saturday.

Alfred bit his lip before replying. What he was going to say felt like a big, fat lie. "We're headed to the rodeo," he ducked his head. "May I use your phone to call a taxi? I misplaced the keys to the car."

The waitress snatched a glance at the bright, sunny morning and smiled, "Of course you can. Would you like to call now or wait 'til after breakfast?"

Alfred resisted the urge to clean his glasses and replied, "I think we'll enjoy breakfast first. The rodeo doesn't start until later this morning." He hoped he was right. He glanced at his daughter, but she offered no instruction. He pulled his glasses off and asked, "Do you have a flyer we can look at? Ours went with the car keys."

The waitress nodded and smiled, "Of course. I'll bring it out with your order. They left a stack for us to give to customers."

Alfred looked over the flyer as they ate. A *Wild West Showdown* caught his eye. It was scheduled for ten o'clock. He was about to mention it to Barbara when she pointed at the event immediately following.

"They have a *Wild West Fashion Show*. That's where Donna and I talked about meeting."

Alfred cleared his throat.

Barbara looked at him, "What? You don't like the fashion show or you don't want me meeting Donna? What's wrong with hanging out with Donna?"

Alfred sat back in his chair. He hadn't expected to be blasted with half the cylinder of a six-shooter. He had cleared his throat simply because he was uncomfortable with people they knew seeing them at the rodeo without their family car.

"I didn't mean anything," Alfred said.

Barbara didn't look up from the flyer.

"It's fine meeting Donna."

"Oh," Barbara studied his black eye and bruised face, "you don't want people to see your bruises. I'll ask the waitress if she has some makeup."

"Barbara," Alfred attempted to dissuade the possibility of his face being painted.

"It's fine, dad, people hide stuff with makeup all the time. Then, you might not have to say anything about walking into a door."

His daughter said it so matter-of-factly he didn't bring it up again. However, he failed to hide his relief when the waitress said that she did not have any makeup with her.

Alfred called a taxi service and thumbed through the cash the waitress had let him write the check over for. They stood outside in the shade of a large maple.

"We need to be sure to head back to the arena after the bull riding," Barbara stated.

Alfred searched through the flyer's schedule until he came to the six o'clock mark.

"'Bob Wills and his Texas Playboys: music and dancing for the whole family,'" he read aloud. In his mind, he heard Mrs. Featherbomb screech that Barbara was not going to go to some dance with some boy.

He narrowed his eyes and thought for a second. Then he asked, "What type of dancing is this? It says it's for the whole family, so are you trying to meet any boys there?"

Barbara scanned the road both ways before replying. "No," she said. "Donna mentioned that she thinks Will and James will be there though. I wish you and mom wouldn't worry so much about boys. They're not all bad."

Alfred blinked. Another description of his failure as a father scrawled across his glasses. Sighing, he removed them and set to scrubbing the lenses. It wouldn't help, but he had to try.

"Barbara," he said after thinking for a while. His daughter turned to him and studied his expression—unless she was just staring at his black and blue eye. "The draft is still going." He hated talking about such serious things, yet he didn't want his daughter to experience the heartbreak of friends being killed or changed in the war.

"I know, dad," Barbara responded softly. "Will and James don't talk about it much, but they want to serve our country. They promise they'll come back and still be themselves. You don't need to worry about them either. Right now, they're just friends. Good friends. I might like them, but I don't think it's love—not like what mom talked about when she met you."

Alfred winced.

Barbara huffed an exasperated breath, "I'm sorry, dad. I know things have been rough, but you and mom can work things out, right?"

248

Alfred had never figured out why women put so much emphasis on keeping a relationship full of smiles and doing things that made them look good to other families. Sometimes, it dawned on him in that moment, he felt like little more than a prize or a trophy to be toted around and displayed for all to see as if to say "look how much my husband makes" or "look at what we can afford." After all, that was his place as the husband: work a job so he could provide for his family.

Alfred nodded. He was saved from further discussion by the taxi pulling to the curb alongside them.

Once seated and instruction to take them to the rodeo was given, Alfred began cleaning his glasses. Barbara fiddled with her hands and glanced out the window occasionally.

After four blocks, she turned to him and asked, "Why doesn't Jose work a normal job?"

Sunlight filtered through gaps in the trees lining the street on both sides, creating a strobe effect as the taxi driver drove well over the speed limit. On the sidewalk, starlings pecked at little stones and bugs and then flew away as the taxi came abreast of them.

"I don't know," Alfred finally admitted.

"It seems like they could use more money. He's good at a lot of things. I wonder why he wants to work for our family. We're not rich," Barbara glanced at him. "I mean, we don't have a mansion where we'd need to hire a full-time groundskeeper."

Alfred nodded to show he was listening, but just beneath the surface he was dissolving. His daughter expected him to make more money so they could be rich and own a mansion and hire maids and groundskeepers and chauffeurs. He was failing to meet her expectations.

"Dad," Barbara asked, "do you think they have a house? An actual house?"

Alfred scrambled to turn his spiraling thoughts to his daughter's latest question, but he got hung up on the implication that she was obviously saying he should buy Jose's family a house. He adjusted his back against the worn seat and scrubbed harder at his glasses.

"Sure they do," he said, sounding like a strangled dog. "We dropped them off by their house yesterday."

Barbara responded immediately, "I don't think they do. There's a community of Mexicans that live back there behind the supermarket, but I don't think they have their own house. Would you do whatever it took to buy our family a house if we didn't have one?"

Alfred felt less like a strangled dog and more like a mouse someone had kicked into a stoney whitewater section in a river. He provided well for his family. They had a house, a car, money in the bank, and they had enough that they could pay Jose for the work he did for them.

"Of course I would," his voice sounded a bit too sharp.

Alfred glanced out the window. They were getting close to the fairgrounds and the rodeo. Barbara gazed ahead around the driver's shoulder.

"Dad," she turned to look him in the eye, "when did you and mom start fighting?"

Alfred swallowed and shot a glance at the driver. The driver hunkered lower in the seat, but Alfred caught the flash of his eyes in the rearview mirror. He was glad all over again that he didn't know him.

sinful brute

formed from smudges on his window. Alfred worked harder at cleaning his glasses and shifted his gaze to the seatback in front of him.

Barbara shoved her hands under her legs. Her face reddened, "Sorry. I guess I have too many questions," her voice slowed as if she were saying something that was only then making sense, "since mom's not hovering over me."

Alfred shot another glance at the driver and then met his daughter's eyes for a moment. "That's enough, Barbara," he said, shifting his gaze back to the seatback.

"Are you going to buy a cowboy hat?" Barbara asked.

She was clearly extending an olive branch in hopes of smoothing things out. It worked. Alfred found himself grinning lopsidedly as he replied, "I'd look ridiculous in one of those things."

"Can I get a Stetson?" Barbara asked unabashed. She quickly added, "And maybe you can try one on, and we can get a photo. You wouldn't have to buy it."

Alfred was about to say that he wouldn't be caught dead in a cowboy hat. However, something inside him wanted to know what he would look like if he were to play in a western. Maybe it was some boyish curiosity that had managed to not get done in by adulthood. Then, he thought of Jose and what he would do with his daughter. He realized he had a choice—a rather uncomfortable choice.

It shouldn't be this difficult to do the right thing, he berated himself.

His black eye was another issue. He didn't want to remember it or have anyone notice it. Would it mean that much to his daughter for them to get a photo in cowboy hats together?

"Just promise me you'll keep the photo in your room under lock and key."

"Deal," Barbara smiled. "Look, dad! That Ferris wheel is huge. Being at the top would be a bash."

Chapter 28

"Well, look who it is," a brash voice rose above the music and mechanical clanking of the Ferris wheel.

Alfred paid no heed. The rodeo was not crowded this early in the morning, but there were dozens of people making their ways across the trampled and dying grass. He read a sign advertising Bob Wills and His Texas Playboys as the main musical attraction. They would be performing right before the bucking broncos as well as playing for the square dance that evening.

At the edge of his conscious range of hearing, Alfred heard the same brash voice explain, "This is the man that ran me over and almost cost the government his entire life savings."

Alfred glanced around. Sergeant Oliver McCoy stood a couple steps away, a pretty blonde hanging off his right arm and a petite brunette hanging off his left, both in short skirts that ended well above their knees. He was in civilian clothes but still held his military bearing. If he'd had time to react, Alfred may have groaned and thought of some line that said he was too busy to chat. As it was, McCoy disentangled his right hand from the blonde's grip and extended it to Alfred.

"Mr. Fritz, I hold no hard feelin's," he announced. The two girls swooned over him.

"Hello, Sergeant," Alfred tried not to mumble or show his black eye.

"Who-eee, that's some shiner," McCoy whistled. Scooping up the blonde's arm, he said in a broadcasting voice, "I give you the greatest bull-rider that ever lived. Here he stands with his head held high and his latest injury from his death-defying ride of the Bull of Death." This awarded him with the attention he sought from the girls.

"Actually," Alfred said quietly and laid his right hand on Barbara's shoulder as she moved in closer beside him, "it was just a door. Walked straight into it and got this."

"And he's also the most modest, humble man alive," McCoy broadcasted. He shared a laugh with his female companions.

Outwardly, Alfred smiled and portrayed a good-natured ability to laugh at himself, but inwardly, he was seething. How long was he going to have to keep this act up? He didn't want to be rude and walk away, and neither did he want to engage in conversation with the man mocking him just as Codgens would do.

"It isn't good manners to laugh at someone's calamity," Barbara interjected.

Alfred's face froze. He snatched his glasses and set to cleaning them feverishly.

McCoy and company laughed heartily. "What a little spitfire," he stated. "We're going to ride the Ferris wheel. Why don't you join us?"

McCoy disentangled his arms from each of the girls. They both squealed and jerked as they caught their balances as he laid a solid, flat-handed smack on each of them only a few inches above where their skirts ended.

The brunette recovered first and, slapping McCoy on the chest, chided, "Not in public, Oliver."

The blonde bit her lip and pressed herself up against the sergeant. "I do like a man in uniform, and if he's not gonna get all shot up," she breathed, "that's even better."

"Aww, shucks, ladies," McCoy grinned. "These isn't even my glad rags." Pretending to tip an imaginary hat, he said, "See ya around ya rippin' bronc buster." He winked and turned his full attention back to the girls hanging on him.

Alfred smashed his glasses back on, saw they were still smudged and went back to cleaning them. He caught his daughter staring after the trio. Even without his glasses, he thought he recognized a contemplative look in Barbara's eyes. He needed to make sure she didn't start throwing herself at boys like those two flappers.

"He seems like a completely different guy without his uniform on," Barbara stated in an almost dreamy drawl.

Alfred shook his glasses at the three. "They're no good. Those two probably throw themselves at anything that has warm blood. And Sergeant McCoy is...well, he's got a lot of growing up to do. He's not fit."

Alfred stopped. Normally, he would have listed out every reason he could think of and then think up a few more, but he was not getting through. Barbara still stared at them as their car slowly rose from the loading platform.

"I have to admit," Alfred sniffed and put his glasses back on, "he is a bit more handsome than your old man. I promised to not be too grouchy."

"You're not grouchy, dad," Barbara said. She stepped to his side and looped her hand through his arm. "I would trade you for a boy my age, but I'm not allowed to date yet," she looked up at him with enormous, pleading eyes of the softest brown.

Alfred cocked his head to see around fresh smudges darkening his glasses. "Where'd you learn to do that?" he asked gruffly.

"Oh, mom calls it a womanly charm," Barbara said flippantly.

"I had thought of letting you dance the square dance, but if you go pulling stuff like that, every boy in town will want to ask you out. What else is your mother teaching you?"

"You really think so?" Barbara asked with a tone that could have been playfulness or excited hopefulness.

Protectiveness welled up inside Alfred. He didn't know where it came from or why he hadn't ever noticed it before. The world was a lousy, ugly place sometimes, and those who took one step down a dark corridor usually never stopped. They got sucked in until, in their confines, light was only a memory in their dreams. He wanted his daughter to have the world and to have it fully lit.

As they moved deeper into the attractions, Alfred realized his protectiveness was not so different from when Barbara had been an infant in need of constant looking after for her mere survival. Just as he hadn't let anything hurt her then, he would protect her now.

"So, dad," Barbara tugged on his arm, "are you hungry or thirsty?"

Alfred took stock of his hunger and thirst. He hadn't considered needing anything until it had been suggested to him. A quick scan revealed no food vendors in the immediate vicinity.

"I just wanted to check," Barbara informed him. "Let's go look at the horses."

Alfred was supposed to be leading Barbara around with her on his arm, however, it was clear that she was the one leading, guiding him with little tugs on his arm or pressure on his side.

They wended their way through the crowd and soon were face to face with a sweating, snorting mustang. Dust billowed in the air around the horse.

Alfred had never been so close to such a powerful and wild animal. Although his heart hammered in his chest, he was drawn to the creature and found his hands clasping the thick boards used to construct the paddock.

Barbara grabbed at his hands, "I don't think we should be this close, dad."

Alfred, still mesmerized by the horse, grunted but let himself be pulled back a step. Just as his left foot planted firmly in the sandy dirt, the mustang threw its head to the side. Wildfire burned in its eyes. Racing toward a group of four or five other horses, its hooves kicked dust into the air. It raked its teeth along the rump of the first horse it approached. The victim threw its hind hooves at its assailant, but the mustang was already nipping the shoulder of the next horse. This drove the frenzied animals into a whirling storm of trotting, stamping, snorting and kicking. All the while the mustang kept up its assault, raking and biting.

"Oh my gosh," Barbara gasped. "Dad, there's someone in there."

Alfred scanned the paddock. Dust hung heavy in the air, and the horses created such a whirlpool of sweaty, snorting horseflesh that only brief glimpses of the ground were manageable. Sure enough, the body of a lanky teenager lay motionless in the center of the paddock. The horses' hooves thundered around him, but he was completely oblivious to them as they came closer and closer to trampling him.

Alfred watched in horror as the mustang drove his herd to wheel around and thunder inches from the boy's head. He knew nothing about horses, and he was terrified to get into the paddock and haul the boy to safety. Most likely he would end up as another casualty. He snatched his glasses but then slammed them back in place. He saw no one else around. Brushing his daughter's grip from his arm he hauled himself up onto the bottom rail of the fence.

The horses wheeled and careened past. He snatched back his fingers before they could be crushed by a dark brown horse scraping against the fence as it ran with the herd.

"Si, Señor," a shout rose above the thundering hooves. "Keep caballos busy. Un momento mas."

Alfred had no idea what had been conveyed or whether the speaker was talking to him. He clutched the fence and hoisted his weight up to the bottom rail again.

The mustang bit at his herd, turning them back toward Alfred.

"Cuidado, el diablo," the voice shouted. "Devil horse."

In some strangely composed part of his mind, Alfred acknowledged the horse's nickname and thought it fitting.

A dark-skinned, Mexican man ducked through the fence on the other side of the paddock. Alfred waved his hand and yipped like he'd seen cowboys do in westerns. The horses veered away from him.

"No. No, Señor," the Mexican raced back to the fence. "Silencio!"

Alfred lowered his hand and watched. The mustang forced the herd into a corner and turned toward the open paddock. The Mexican raced from the fence toward the motionless boy. The mustang pinned its ears tightly to its head and spun, raking its teeth on two of the unfortunate horses.

They whipped past Alfred and wheeled around the Mexican. The man showed no sign of fear as he gave the teenager a cursory examination before grabbing him under the armpits. Once the herd ran past again, he heaved the teenager to the fence and fed him under the bottom rail.

He wasn't quick enough in following the unconscious boy. The herd thundered by. The dark brown horse scraping the fence caught him, crushing him against the rails.

As the dust cleared, the man staggered to his feet, rolled through the fence and dragged the teenager several feet away from the paddock.

Barbara tugged on his arm, and they raced around the paddock.

The Mexican breathed heavily but shallowly as he examined the boy and muttered, "Pendejo," as they stopped beside him.

Alfred didn't know what to do to help, and he felt like a sack of flour as he stood beside the Mexican. He repeatedly pulled his glasses off to clean and then replaced them without having cleaned them. His heart beat madly, and his breath puffed heavily even though he was no longer in imminent danger.

A young girl with a head of bouncing, dark hair stopped at the rescuer's side and stared at the boy's face.

Alfred realized then that it was Jose, and the little girl was Marie.

"Dad," Barbara sounded awestruck, "that's Joey."

"Joey Chadelle?" Alfred took a closer look at the unconscious boy.

"Yeah," Barbara confirmed.

Jose continued to work with Joey, feeling his arms and legs and pressing on his ribs for anything that appeared to be broken. Blood, coated in a thick layer of dust, stuck like potter's clay to his left temple, matting his hair and attracting flies.

Jose shooed the flies away and muttered to himself, "Necasito agua y una toalla."

"He needs water and a towel, dad," Barbara translated.

Alfred stared at the boy. He needed to do something instead of standing around and gawking.

His daughter's words finally landed. Yes, water and a towel. He could manage that much.

Alfred saw Marie bite her lip and hug herself. Where was the girls' mother? "Barbara," Alfred instructed, "I'm going to find water and a towel. Take care of Marie, won't you."

Barbara nodded and immediately stepped to the little girl's side and knelt. Marie opened her arms and hugged Barbara, then she clung to Barbara as she stood.

Alfred snatched his glasses and scrubbed them with his shirt. Glancing around, he realized he didn't have the faintest idea where to find either of the items Jose needed.

"Amigo," Jose turned to him, "water and toalla, please, Señor." He mimed washing and drying his hands.

Alfred already understood and nodded. Jose went back to caring for Joey. However, when Alfred didn't leave to fetch the items right away, he turned back and instructed, "Pregunta...question el cabelleros—gauchos—cow—boys."

Alfred nodded and searched for a cowboy close by. Even with all the commotion, no one was around. Alfred placed his glasses back on. His surroundings settled back into focus as did a new insult.

Dunce

He grimaced. He was a fool. Who couldn't help an injured boy? All he needed to do was find water and a towel to wash the boy's wound.

"Come now, dear," Mrs. Featherbomb's voice played sing-song in his head, "everyone knows you struggle with simple tasks like this. Just call a professional and let them handle it. No. No cussing, dear."

Alfred gritted his teeth. This time, his wife's voice had the same effect on him as nails on a chalkboard. He walked hurriedly for a few steps and then broke into a slow jog toward the attractions. One of the food vendors was bound to have a jug of water and an extra towel they wouldn't mind donating to the cause.

"Now, why would anyone want to save that horrendous boy? He's getting what he deserves for messing with the horses," Mrs. Featherbomb's voice sang again.

Alfred was puffing and gasping by the time he reached a small hamburger stand. The cook quickly handed him two cups of water and a clean towel once he deciphered Alfred's breathless account of why he needed them. The cook went even further and instructed a bystander to phone an ambulance.

Hurrying back to Jose and the injured boy, Alfred wondered whether the ambulance was for him. He hadn't run like that since becoming an adult.

Alfred handed over the water and towel and leaned hands-on knees, gasping for air. Sweat trickled down his face, and his shirt clung to his back.

"Here," Barbara was at his side, "take your jacket off. You look about ready to expire."

Alfred attempted a weak chuckle and let his daughter help him out of his blazer. He immediately felt lighter and less like grilled chicken. He sat and watched Jose work gently on the gash on Joey's head.

Barbara tugged Marie onto her lap and sat beside him. "He must have gotten kicked," she stated without taking her eyes off Jose's work. "Why was he in their anyway?"

Alfred peeled his glasses off and scrubbed at them.

"Dad," Barbara reached over, grabbing his frantic hands.

He looked at her and slowly lowered his glasses to his lap and rubbed his eyes. "Just need my new glasses," he grunted.

"No one was here for him to show off for," Barbara continued.

Alfred glanced around. He wasn't looking for a girl hiding in the shadows that Joey may have wanted to impress. Instead, he was trying to silence Mrs. Featherbomb's response to anytime he said he didn't know something. She would pat her hair, then pat him on the shoulder and say, "It's okay to be a bit of a dolt sometimes. If we all knew everything, where would we be?"

He shook his head and replied, "I don't know."

"Yeah," Barbara was unfazed. "I guess we just need to help him."

Alfred was saved from responding by four people running up and kneeling beside Jose. The woman claimed to have been a nurse during the recent World War and rummaged through her purse until she pulled out a small, glass bottle and a tightly rolled bandage. Jose exchanged a few words with the new helpers, and together they bandaged Joey's head. Once that task was accomplished, the nurse took his pulse and checked his other vitals.

Jose stepped back, letting the woman and the three men take over. Wincing, he blew out his breath and sat beside Barbara.

"I get him out of horses," he glanced at Alfred and then hid a pained grimace as Marie settled into his lap. "Him be okay. Knocked out," he mimicked getting hit on the head and falling asleep. "But him be okay. Gracias. Uh…Thank you."

Alfred replaced his glasses and glanced at the Mexican. Jose was smiling tiredly, but Alfred could not return the gesture.

Dweeb

spelled in large, black letters, covered the entire right lens of his glasses.

Dolt

reciprocated the sentiment of his stupidity on the left lens.

He felt himself going pale.

"Señor?" Jose asked.

Alfred felt his eyes crossing as he tried to pull his gaze from the latest proof of his inability.

"Dad?" Barbara shrieked, waving her hand in front of his eyes. "Help! He's going to faint."

The next thing Alfred knew was he was being lowered to the ground by several hands and the war nurse was bending over him, checking his pulse and pulling his eyelids open.

A minute later, she announced that it was just panic. She'd seen it a hundred times if she'd seen it once, and he would be fine in a few minutes. She instructed Barbara on what to do and went back to monitoring Joey.

Barbara spoke softly to him as he grasped at his scattered thoughts. Slowly, he found himself returning to his normal state. His hands felt slightly numb as if blood flow had been cut off to them, so, with a jerky movement, he grabbed his glasses from his lap. Holding them out to his daughter, he said, "Can you see anything on them?"

Barbara took the glasses, peered at them for a moment and put them on. Alfred searched her blurry, magnified eyes for any sign that she was surprised, but her expression didn't change. His heart rate rose again, his pulse pounding in his ears.

"I don't see anything on them," Barbara handed the glasses back. "There's only a small scratch on the bottom of the left lens."

Alfred accepted the glasses and frowned at them. Plain as day, he read a dozen insults scattered over the lenses. He was the only one that could see them just like in his kitchen with the window.

Silence stretched long. He could sense his daughter wanting to ask whether he was alright.

"I'm fine," he stated without conviction. He realized he needed to get the attention away from himself while he sorted out the mess that had been bothering him.

"How did you know just what to do?" he questioned Jose.

Jose made a contemplative noise, "Ah, Señor. When a boy, mi papi walk in mountains. I go with him. All day we climb and look for food, water," he acted out scanning all around him for such. "Sometime, get hurt. Papi teach how help body heal. We take no food, water with us. We live on what mountain give us."

Alfred wondered about a childhood like that. It sounded dangerous, but somehow fun in a masculine sense.

Two men dressed in crisp uniforms hurried up and laid a stretcher beside Joey. After a brief exchange with the war nurse, they carefully transferred the teenager to the stretcher and carried him away. The nurse followed them, and the three men wandered back to the surrounding attractions.

"Ah," Jose said. "All is good." He shifted, and Marie hopped off his lap. "Ayudame, por favor," Jose said with a wince. Marie pulled on his extended arm until he was standing.

"Dad," Barbara whispered, "I think he's hurt."

"If he wants help, he'll say something," Alfred replied under his breath.

Barbara stared at him for a long moment before rising and bending down to help him up. Alfred waved her hand away and struggled to his feet.

"Alfred Featherbomb, is that you? Fancy finding you here."

Alfred groaned and reluctantly turned to face the man who addressed him.

Chapter 29

"Mr. Carter," Alfred greeted his neighbor stiffly. He stood slightly angled in an attempt to hide the bruising on his face.

"You escaped the wife too, did you?" Mr. Carter reached for a handshake. "Left mine with a gossip group back by the entrance."

Alfred felt his neighbor's scrutiny on his injuries. "Walked into a door," he offered quickly.

"Looks like the shiner my younger boy gave the older. Said four minutes didn't make him old enough to boss him around and walloped him with a stick," Mr. Carter kept eyeing Alfred's face. "You didn't see them run through here, did you? The rascals told me they wouldn't run off, but not two steps in here and they split like peas."

Mr. Carter chuckled at his own joke. Alfred grabbed his glasses and glanced nervously between his neighbor and his cleaning project.

"So, how'd you manage it? Getting away from the misses."

Alfred cut him a sideways look, wondering how much his neighbor knew of the fight he and Mrs. Featherbomb had had the night before. Could he have heard the plates shattering as well?

"Took a taxi," Alfred shrugged.

They walked alongside long barns and paddocks where horses and cattle chewed lazily while cowboys milled around, oiling leather or swatting away flies. The grandstands rose on the other side like a giant skeleton of wood and steel. Every now and then a dust devil whirled into existence before it was banished by some unseen force.

"Dad and Señor Jose saved Joey Chadelle from the broncos," Barbara interjected.

She was usually quiet around adults, but Alfred was relieved by the change in subject and how it shifted some of Mr. Carter's attention away from him. Guilt started welling inside him until he said, "I couldn't get into the paddock. Jose here, he pulled the boy out and saved him from being trampled."

Alfred followed Mr. Carter's gaze as he appraised the dark-skinned Mexican. Jose's attention, however, did not waver from his daughter and the story he told her quietly in Spanish, fluid hand gestures acting the parts of horses and cowboys.

"The migrant you've had doing your yard work and some exterior housework?" Mr. Carter evaluated Jose. "Tell me, has his kind been stealing from you?"

Alfred, anger flaring, almost snapped a negative. There was no way the man they had bailed from prison and who had saved Joey was a thief.

Mr. Carter backpedaled, "I ask only because the fuzz pulled up to your house as the family and I were leaving."

Alfred winced. His anger turned to shame. No doubt the police had made a call regarding the upcoming legal hearing to clear Jose's name. It was strange they'd make an in-person call on a Saturday though. He pulled his glasses down to clean them. His false allegations must have had a bigger impact than he'd yet realized.

"It's okay, dad," his daughter rested a hand lightly on his arm. "Jose will be fine. Anyone can see he's not a communist."

Mr. Carter observed quietly. Alfred still felt the need to respond. Fear silenced him, however, as he worried about what insult was going to show up on his glasses.

Marie giggled and hugged her father's leg. He lifted her to his back even though it was visibly painful for him to move his arms in the needed path.

"Nothing's gone missing. Jose's not a thief," Barbara responded to Mr. Carter. Quietly, she asked, "What's wrong, dad? Is it your glasses again?"

Alfred grunted and nodded.

"No one can see anything wrong with them," she rolled her eyes. "Well, except the fact they broke, and you wrapped a whole roll of tape around them."

Alfred nearly shouted at his daughter for her disrespectful jab. However, it was so similar to what his wife would have said that he froze. And then a new thought pricked him and made him feel even worse. Jose had never blown up at Marie, and he showed no signs of ever doing so. The Mexican would probably take the time to explain to his daughter what the problem was and how he was going to fix it. Alfred had done nothing but try to hide his problem with the insults appearing and blow up at those who wondered what was going on.

"He doesn't look entirely well," Mr. Carter observed. "Maybe he should go to the hospital. He's favoring his right side like he's got a broken rib or something."

Alfred met Barbara's eyes briefly. His daughter looked genuinely concerned, yet he couldn't shake her fear from that evening in the kitchen when the ambulance had been called. He also couldn't shake how he'd caused her to trip into the tub at the motel. He placed his glasses and pushed them up on his nose. This was not a little thing like getting his pants dirty or dropping an apple on the floor. She needed him to be strong and deal with his problem out of sight.

"It'll all be fixed when I get my new glasses." Alfred held out little hope that would be the ultimate resolution, but maybe it would help. "These old ones must be causing too much strain on my eyes."

Seemingly satisfied, Barbara trotted up beside Jose and tickled Marie's armpit. The little girl pulled away, giggling. Alfred tried to remember teasing Barbara in such a way, but the only memory that surfaced was of Mrs. Featherbomb scolding him and lecturing him about how a lady is to maintain poise, posture and grace.

"So," Mr. Carter broke the silence, "the office still treating you swell?"

Alfred cleared his throat, thankful for a topic with which he didn't have to fear additional insults scrawling across his glasses. "There's plenty of clients in need of our expertise. You'd be surprised at how many people look for loopholes."

Mr. Carter grunted, "Sometimes the world feels a bit like my boys. They're always trying to get an edge on each other and push one over me and the misses. If the world's going to hell in a hand basket, that basket is going to burn up a long time before it ever gets there."

"Greed and debauchery," Alfred summed up Pastor Meyers' opinion of the consumerism that prevailed all around them. Not wanting to discuss his own views on such subjects, Alfred followed the normal pattern of his conversations with his neighbor. "How about the industrial front? How's the automobile assembly looking?"

"It ain't no picnic at the park," Mr. Carter scowled. "Annie likes that the hours are a bit shorter now, but it makes it a bit harder to climb the ladder. That corner office isn't gonna just drop into my lap, you know."

268

"How long have you been supervising?"

"It took some adjustment after the war—World War II," Mr. Carter scowled again. "I hope this war in Korea is over soon. It's got the misses all tied up in knots. Then there's the tensions with the Soviets and the communist threat. It's all tough on a woman, you know, when she's got sons."

Alfred nodded. This was a common observation of Mr. Carter's. He was glad he didn't have to worry about Barbara being drafted and sent to the frontlines. However, the Red Scare affected every aspect of life.

"Your boys are what? Ten?"

"Right'O," Mr. Carter chuckled. "Another eight years of worry for the misses." They took a few steps and then he added, "It's not bad for a boy to get drafted and serve his country. Teaches them some discipline and respect. It's hard on the womenfolk who don't understand that sometimes it's what a man has got to do. It ain't swell how they get all worked up over it."

Alfred thought of his most recent experiences with Mrs. Featherbomb. He didn't think women understood much of what made a man a man and all the expectations men had to put up with. But then, Barbara had taken care of him, cooking him breakfast and such, when his wife wouldn't. He grew conflicted and didn't know whether to agree with his neighbor or to contradict him.

"That's what we're here for," Alfred settled on a middle-ground response. "We're supposed to provide and protect."

"And sometimes we die as a result," Mr. Carter observed. "It's too bad so many of the army boys don't get appreciated when they come back."

Suddenly, the behavior of the two girls with Seargent McCoy made sense to Alfred. He couldn't condone it because it wasn't right, from the way they were dressed to how McCoy treated them, but he understood their desire to be with a man who wasn't going to lose a limb or his fire for life.

"You're getting real thoughtful these days," Mr. Carter stated. "You're behaving like an old codger."

He was indeed taking more time to think about the deeper meaning of things that he was only just beginning to notice. Old codger was an apt description he realized.

"See what I mean," Mr. Carter declared.

"A lot's been happening lately," Alfred excused it as a temporary state. "I've got more to think about."

"Well, I prefer to leave the smoke pouring from my ears stuff for when I'm working."

Alfred tried to suppress the heat climbing his neck into his cheeks. His bruised side, the one Mrs. Featherbomb and smacked with the broom, throbbed and ached. He pulled his glasses off and set to cleaning them.

"Dad," Barbara called back to him, "can we get elephant ears and hotdogs?"

"That will be fine. It's about lunch time."

The rodeo grounds grew more and more crowded as they wove their way to the food stands. Most were simple wooden shacks with a grill where sweaty cooks flipped hamburgers or rolled hotdogs.

The smell of roasted peanuts filled the air with salty anticipation, and garish signs looked like a paint bomb had been detonated. Lines of young couples and exhausted-looking parents with rowdy children stretched down the sort of aisle or street that had been formed by the food vendors.

Barbara led them to a trailer made to look like a Conestoga wagon. The gold embellished sign proclaimed "The Chuck Wagon" in old west lettering. They joined the line, and Alfred read through the short menu.

"May I get a soda?" Barbara asked, a hopeful grin brightening her face.

Alfred nodded.

Mr. Carter said, "It was swell catching up with you. I'm going to find the misses. She wouldn't take it kindly if I bought lunch without her."

Alfred was about to return the goodbye when Mr. Carter's boys raced up and asked for money for sodas, peanuts and cotton candy. He breathed a sigh of relief. The performance that everything was fine could end for the time being.

Barbara grasped his hand. "There's Will and James," she said, peering down the packed food street. "I don't want them to see me yet."

Alfred scanned the direction his daughter indicated. He couldn't deny his relief that she was staying with him where he could protect her, yet if they were friends, why didn't she want to go hang out with them right away? He didn't see the two boys.

Jose pulled a handful of coins from his pocket, paid the man at the window and, with a smile, handed his daughter a hotdog wrapped in brown paper. Tucking two lemonades under his arm, he escorted Marie to the side and bit into his own hotdog.

Alfred couldn't help but think that Jose was the perfect picture of a father providing for his daughter. He and Barbara followed suit, and soon they were walking back the way they'd come with Barbara leading once again.

Jose reached for the remainder of Marie's hotdog that she didn't finish and handed her a lemonade. "Señor," he addressed Alfred, "mi hermanos, brothers, vendir...sell— cotton candy. ¡Vamos!"

Marie squealed with delight and exclaimed, "¡Gracias, Papi! ¡Vamos!"

Alfred turned to his daughter for a translation. "Vamos means let's go," she informed him. "Here, I'll throw our trash away."

Before he could refuse and say he'd do it, Barbara had their trash in hand and wove her way to a waste bin.

They turned a corner, and a tall, old west style storefront greeted them with "Fashions for everyone!" Beside the door, a smaller sign listed the open hours and the times of the old west fashion shows.

"This is where Donna and I are supposed to meet. What time is it?" Barbara lingered in front of the door.

Alfred checked his wristwatch. "It's a quarter after noon."

"Okay. Donna's probably not here yet, but we need to come straight back here after the cotton candy."

Alfred peered into the store. Boots, belts, cowboy hats and neckerchiefs dripped from every display. By the counter he glimpsed a door with "Photobooth" written on it in black lettering bordered in gold foil. He wondered whether his daughter would remember their deal about the photo with cowboy hats. It was probably too much to hope for, but he did not want to embarrass himself by putting one of those things on his head for a photo, immortalizing his disgrace and black eye.

The cotton candy vendor was an old man with a gap-toothed smile and wispy strands of candy floating around his ears. He put on a small show as he spun and looped the stick around as the candy seemed to magically stream toward it.

Marie jumped and clapped as the man handed her the first cloud of cotton candy. Barbara accepted the second, thanked the candymaker and then rushed them toward the Old West Mercantile and the fashion show.

"Donna's gonna be here any minute," Barbara hurriedly picked a dark brown cowboy hat with a black leather hatband studded with silver from the display. She handed it to Alfred and grabbed a cream colored one with a caramel hatband for herself.

Alfred's heart dropped as she pulled him toward the photobooth.

"Ah, Señor," Jose laughed, "no te gusta, no like, the sombrero vaquero."

Alfred's face throbbed as it flushed red in addition to the black, blue and yellowish green. Already, he was being made fun of for the hat.

Barbara held the door open for him, but what Jose did next made him pause. The Mexican placed a white hat with gaudy turquoise stones on the hatband on his own head and whirled his arm in the motion of throwing a lasso, then, with a lunge, he wrapped his arms around Marie. His daughter giggled and demanded he do it again as she turned and sped around the display.

"C'mon, dad," Barbara pressed. "We don't have much time."

She ushered him into the box. A cord hung from the ceiling, and a single, dark hole revealed the glint of a camera lens. Barbara reached up for the cord at the same time she grabbed his hat and helped him place it on his head.

Inspired by the joy he'd seen in the interaction of Jose with his daughter, he raised his hand and slowly spun an imaginary lasso. For the moment he forgot about his bruised and battered face.

A minute later, they exited the photobooth, and Barbara raced toward the display to replace her borrowed hat. Alfred stepped to the counter to ask when the photos would be developed.

"I'm going to check if Donna is at the fashion show already," Barbara called as she sailed past.

Alfred turned to acknowledge her, but she was already disappearing down the hallway to the back door. He heard Jose speaking softly in Spanish and wondered what he was telling his daughter.

Marie pointed to the photobooth. Jose shook his head apologetically. Sorrowfully, the little girl took off her hat and gave it to her papi to put back on the rack.

Something tugged at Alfred's insides. It wasn't like the guilt he felt at having falsely reported Jose as a communist spy. It wasn't heavy in that sort of way, but he felt like he should do something. His photo session with his own daughter had cost him only twenty-five cents.

"Here, Jose," Alfred held out a silver coin.

"Ah, no, Señor," Jose said when he saw it. "Is too much. Cost only twenty-five."

"No," Alfred grabbed Jose's hand and placed the fifty-cent piece on top of Jose's callouses. "I insist. Take some photos with your daughter."

"Gracias. Gracias, Señor," Jose grinned and grabbed the hat for his daughter. "Yeehaw, cabelleros, Chiquita," he cried as he and Marie stampeded to the photobooth.

Alfred smiled and studied the leather handbags on display below the counter. Perhaps, Clarabelle would enjoy a new purse. He had eight minutes to wait before the assistant had the photos ready, plenty of time to choose one without too much turquoise or fringe.

Happy squeals and the hummed tune of *The Lone Ranger* emanated from the photobooth as he bent to pick up a tooled handbag with silver clasps inlaid with turquoise. He tried to imagine Mrs. Featherbomb wearing it to church.

Instead of appreciating it and sporting it everywhere however, Alfred saw her pat her hair and scoff, "Did you steal that old thing off an Indian? You're a real drip and know nothing about modern fashion."

He dropped the bag as if it was a revolver that would shoot him if he held it any longer and rubbed his eyes.

His glasses settled back into place on the bridge of his nose, and he froze. In the small space of vacant glass remaining on the lenses, a single word formed as if written by an invisible hand with ink that took some time to coagulate.

The insult Mrs. Featherbomb had just given him in his imagination stared back at him.

Tearing his glasses off, he scrubbed at the word as the realization set in. It wasn't Jose who had been tormenting him. It had never been him. All along, it had been his wife. She could easily pretend not to see insults she'd written on the windows and his glasses and lie about it. Barbara was probably in on it with her. Afterall, Barbara hadn't been able to see anything on the kitchen window or on his glasses when she'd put them on, but maybe she was just lying the way her mother was.

His brain flashed through snippets of the interactions he had had with his family recently. They were like flashbulbs popping one after another in a dark room first from one side and then the other and then from behind and then in front. Then, the flashbulbs transformed to rifles, and gunfire drowned out all rationality. He was a soldier, hunkered alone in a fox hole. His squad told him he was the enemy. No amount of begging and pleading convinced them otherwise. They circled him and shot him until he bled like a sieve in a waterfall.

"Excuse us, sir," a young, male voice echoed at the edge of Alfred's consciousness.

He blinked and staggered to the side.

A young lady gasped, "Oh, Ed, it's Alfred from work."

"It sure is," Alfred recognized Ed Albright's voice. "You don't look so good, Mr. Featherbomber. Is everything alright?"

He needed to smile and say everything was fine, and that he had merely stubbed his toe. No smile made it to his lips just as no words smoothed everything out. He stood, scrubbing his glasses in a frenzy.

"Ed," Sunny said in her accented drawl, "he's gone pale. Help 'im sit down."

"Easy does it, Featherbomber," Ed said softly. He wrapped his arm around Alfred's shoulders and eased him onto a barrel that Sunny cleared of a tiered display. "You look like you met the wrong end of Yosemite Sam's temper. What happened to you, man?"

Alfred could do nothing but scrub his glasses and stare straight ahead. Then, his head began to shake. Back and forth it went. He couldn't stop it.

"¿Amigo?" Jose called.

Alfred looked at him. The blurry figure moved toward him. Alfred mumbled, "No, it wasn't you. It wasn't you. I'm sorry. I'm sorry. It wasn't you."

"What's he going on about?" Ed demanded.

"He's been beaten silly," Sunny said, dabbing at Alfred's forehead. "But that black eye isn't fresh. It must have happened after work yesterday. I would have noticed something like this if he came to work with it."

"Amigo, I bring you daughter. I bring Barbara," Jose declared.

"N—n—no," Alfred stammered. Fear darkened the edges of his vision.

"Si, amigo," and with that Jose tore off down the hall, Marie trotting after him.

"What's going on, Featherbomber? Who is that?"

"Ed," Sunny cried, "he needs help not an interrogation."

"What if he's the one that did this?" Ed countered.

"That Mexican?" Sunny asked incredulously. Then she tilted her head, "Stranger things have happened."

"Who did this to you?" Ed asked.

"He walked into a door last night," Barbara's voice was laced with worry and dread.

She grabbed Alfred's hand gently, stilling his frantic cleaning. He stared at her. His daughter who acted like she loved him but was really working with her mother to make him go mad.

"Ed, maybe we better call an ambulance or the police," Sunny said.

Alfred was about to vehemently shout no to that idea, but Barbara beat him to it, "No, he doesn't need an ambulance.

He's just having some issues with his glasses causing him stress, is that right, dad?"

Did he accept his daughter's lie, which was really his lie he'd told her earlier, or did he make a bigger scene and shove Barbara away?

At last, he spoke, "It was nothing. I overreacted to a news bulletin on the radio."

The group surrounding him listened to the strains of a western song for a moment before relaxing, seemingly satisfied.

"But who did this to your face? You apologized to this Mexican and said it wasn't him," Ed pressed. "Was it another Mexican? Someone that looked like him?"

Alfred shook his head, "No. This is Jose. He's done some work for me at my place," a pang shot through him when he called the house he'd been forced out of "his place." "That's his daughter Marie. I'm a bit clumsy at times." He gestured to his black eye, "I left a door open and walked into it in the dark. Broke my glasses too. See?"

He extricated his hand from Barbara's and held up his repaired glasses. The taped repair did indeed look like he had used a whole roll of tape.

"Last name Featherbrim?" the clerk called from the counter. He glanced back at the photo strip. "Sorry, Featherbomb," he corrected himself.

Barbara raced to the counter and returned with the photos. She studied them closely and then held them for him to see.

Alfred peered through the remaining clear bits of his glasses and wondered what an appropriate response would be.

"You look hilarious, dad," Barbara grinned. "Look at this one. You look ready to fall off your horse."

Heat flushed his face once again, and he found he wanted to rip the photos away and tear them into little pieces. That would definitely not be an appropriate response.

"This is proof that some squares can be fun, dad," Barbara earned a laugh from Ed and a nervous giggle from Sunny.

Jose also glimpsed the photos for he said, "Very nice, amigo. You are natural with the sombrero vaquero."

Ed laughed harder and slapped Alfred on the back. "Sunny, we need some copies of that for the office."

Sunny cleared her throat and came to Alfred's rescue, "I think we had best give Alfred some space and stop barging in on his family and friends the way Codgens would."

"You ain't sayin' I'm like that bloke, are ya darling?" Ed worked mock sweetness and innocence into his voice.

"Well," Sunny threw up her hands in exaggerated exasperation, "when you put it that way, you're just like him."

"You don't mean that, Sally," Ed grinned broadly and plunked a gray ten-gallon cowboy hat onto his head.

"Why you—"

Sunny caught herself and addressed Alfred calmly, "Please excuse us. I need to kiss some sense into this specimen of a tease until he forgets all about ever seeing a girl named Sally."

With that she selected the same hat Barbara had chosen for herself and rushed at Ed. He wrapped her in his arms and spun her around.

"Now, you fine folks pardon us while we step into the adjoining accommodations," he said in a western drawl.

Sunny squealed and wrapped her arms around Ed's neck as he swept her into his arms and carried her to the photobooth. She reached for the handle, and they disappeared.

"Ah, how you say, amigo, love birds?" Jose asked with a grin.

Alfred nodded. He had never seen Ed be anything but shy and reserved. Sunny was certainly pulling him out of that.

Marie gazed at her papi and fiddled absently with the fringe on a pouch hanging beside the cowboy hat display. "Ellos like papi and mami."

"Chiquita," Jose laughed and tickled her on her neck until she giggled and shoved his hands away.

"She said her parents behave just like those two," Barbara offered a translation for Alfred. "You work with them?"

Alfred nodded and set to cleaning his glasses, "Sunny's the receptionist and Mr. Albright works on the simpler cases. He's coming along quickly though."

"Is he the one you told mom gets called Bright-as-a-Light-Albright?"

Alfred nodded again. He'd forgotten he'd told Mrs. Featherbomb that little snippet from work. It was the first nickname Codgens came up with for the man. On top of that, it had been within the first two or three hours that Albright had started. Remembering how Mrs. Featherbomb had laughed and then demanded to know his own nickname at work before abruptly brushing the topic aside, sent a pang through him. He longed to have some sort of closeness with his wife that simply wasn't there.

"I'm sorry, dad," Barbara said, "I forgot that's still a touchy subject. Will you come to the Old West Fashion Show with me?"

"I thought you were meeting Donna here for it," Alfred stated. He felt as if he'd been lowered into the dumps, and he didn't want to socialize anymore.

"She's not here yet," Barbara frowned. "I hope her parents didn't change their minds. Maybe we could go pick her up?"

Alfred pushed his glasses back onto his nose, "I don't think that would be a good idea. If her parents don't want her to come, we shouldn't try to smuggle her here. Besides, we left the car at home."

Barbara looked down. "Right. Okay. I really wish she was here."

Alfred glanced at his watch. "It's still five minutes before it starts, I think."

Jose pulled a program from his pocket and offered it to him.

"Yes," Alfred confirmed. "She still has time to meet you here."

"Thanks, dad," Barbara smiled. With a saddened expression, she stepped slowly through the displays of leather goods.

Jose's little daughter said something in Spanish. Alfred looked quizzically at Jose. "She say to find mama," he said, scooping her into his arms. He winced as he did so. "Ella, she, here," he motioned to the left, "or maybe she there. Necissito buscar—need make search for her."

Alfred gave a nod of understanding. They were going to look for his wife who was at the rodeo somewhere. An empty sadness welled up inside him. He had grown to like having the Mexican and his daughter hanging out with him and his own daughter. It wasn't that he felt lonely around Barbara, but it was that the additional company, the friendship he now had with Jose, made him feel complete in a way he couldn't remember ever feeling before. Further, he had no words to describe it, and he had better not try to talk about it anyway. He shuddered. If he started talking about stuff like that, he would be ridiculed and viewed as a weirdo—more so than he already was.

He looked up. A gray smudge he couldn't quite make out worked its way across his glasses. It wasn't as dark as the black smudges, so it was harder to follow as it traced what could only be another insult describing him. Was it still an insult if it was true? He pulled his glasses off and set to scrubbing them with his shirt. It wasn't the frantic frenzy of just a couple minutes ago, but it was intent.

"What do you think, dad?" his daughter called from the far side of the little store. She took three steps toward him and spun on her heels like a fashion model on the runway.

Alfred replaced his glasses slowly and stared. His daughter's ponytail bounced beneath a wide-brimmed, acid green hat with a sparkling ostrich feather sticking out of the hatband. She had to be joking about liking the hideous thing, right? What was the correct response? Jose's daughter was barely more than a toddler, but he found himself wondering how Jose would respond if Marie had chosen to sport the hat.

"You would probably be sent to an asylum if you wore that around town," Alfred called and forced a playful chuckle. He winced. He hadn't meant to make fun of her.

Barbara spun, a horror-struck expression giving way to a sheepish grin. She snatched the hat off. "Yeah, it's not my style."

Alfred tried to save face, "It's probably designed to be a jest."

Barbara silently selected two more hats and placed the brown one on her head. It blended perfectly with her dark hair. Alfred watched as she pulled her short ponytail to where she could just see it and compared it to the hat's color.

"Look at my little cowgirl," Alfred smiled. There. That sounded more like something Jose would say.

Barbara cringed, "Dad, I'm not five anymore."

Heat rose and anger simmered. She was right. That did sound like a childish compliment.

"It matches my hair too closely," Barbara declared and placed the other hat on. It was a light tan with a snakeskin band. "What about this one?"

Alfred frowned. He needed to think about what a teenage girl wanted to hear her father say.

"You're right. I'm not too keen on the snakeskin either. What about the color?" she grabbed the brim and tipped the hat back the way cowboys did in the westerns on television.

Just then, Sunny and Ed spilled out of the photobooth still locked in one another's arms. Alfred scooted to the side to avoid acting like a bumper in billiards.

Barbara placed her hand on her hip and pretended to chew.

"Um…" Alfred tried to focus. He was failing miserably.

Barbara rolled her eyes, "I should know better than to ask a square." She turned and flashed a playful smile over her shoulder, "Sorry, dad, but you have no sense of style."

Alfred ground his teeth and forced himself to not look at the words on his glasses.

"Okay, what about this one?" Barbara pulled a cream hat with a plain, brown leather band off the display and held it in front of her.

"Um…can you put it on. I think I need to see it on you to decide," Alfred stuttered.

Barbara grinned broadly, "There you go, dad, you're getting the hang of this."

Was that another mockery or was she being honest? Was it possible to be honest and mock someone at the same time?

Barbara placed the hat on her head and struck a pose. Alfred exaggerated his assessment by grabbing his chin and gazing at her from different angles. He was determined to do this shopping thing correctly.

In response, his daughter smirked, a glimmer sparkling in her eyes, and struck a new pose, turning partially away and tilting her head back so the hat was more visible.

"Well," Alfred said decisively and pulled his glasses off. He couldn't pretend not to be nervous. His daughter was fully capable of biting his head off the same way Mrs. Featherbomb was. "I have to say I like the face beneath the hat."

"Dad!" Barbara wailed.

"And the hat looks good with it," Alfred finished. He replaced his glasses and reached for the hat. "Is it the one you want?"

Barbara grinned warmly at him, "Can I have it?"

"Only if you promise not to wear it with the price tag tucked into the hatband," Alfred replied, plucking the handwritten price tag from the band.

"Thanks, dad," Barbara hugged him, knocking the hat to the floor. "You're the best," she said as she snatched the hat and placed it back on.

"You're welcome, Sweat Pea," Alfred smiled at her.

"Sorry I'm late," a teenage girl called from the door. "Oh, gangbuster hat!"

Barbara hurried over to her friend, Donna, and laid a hug on her before striking a pose similar to the ones Alfred had noticed on billboards. The two girls exchanged a few more breathless greetings and then made their way toward the fashion show.

"I'll just pay for the hat and meet you back there," Alfred said quietly. He didn't think his daughter heard him over the story Donna had launched into, but it made him feel a little better having expressed his intentions.

"Okay. After the show, can Donna and I use the photobooth?" she replied.

Alfred wondered how long that would take but nodded. As he turned toward the counter, he caught Donna's expression wrinkle up in disgust. She whispered to Barbara, and Barbara whispered back.

It was easy for him to imagine the whispered conversation about him looking like a prize fighter who had lost and then the explanation that he had walked into a door.

"Quite the snapper you've got there, mister," the man at the counter commented.

Alfred nodded, clutched his glasses against his wallet and counted out the money for his daughter's hat.

Chapter 30

Alfred straightened his back, trying to find a comfortable way to sit on the hard, wooden grandstand bench. Bob Wills and His Texas Playboys were on their second song, and a small group of both young and old formed on the ground in front of the stage. They stirred dust into the air as they danced and stomped to the music.

The song ended, and Bob informed them that they would be playing again for the square dance that evening. Barbara looked at him with imploring eyes. He nodded that they would stay for the dance.

Then, Donna, who had stuck with them since the fashion show, looped her arm through Barbara's and tugged her down to the tangle of dancers. At the center of the dancers, several boys kept the tempo by switching the girls they danced with. He wanted to warn his daughter about them but didn't, knowing she would probably call him a square or roll her eyes and keep going.

That was a concerning behavior he'd been noticing in a lot more teenagers lately. Pastor Meyers often commented on it as well, saying that the younger generation was destined for a fiery end unless they made a U-turn. That always earned him a wide slew of head nods and murmured agreements from the older parishioners, while eliciting the condemned behavior from the younger parishioners.

Alfred watched his daughter and her friend until they were indistinguishable from the other dancers. He tapped his foot along to the violin, enjoying the music alone until the band ended their set in thunderous applause and a standing ovation. The band bowed and ducked off stage.

He scanned the crowd for his daughter as the announcer thanked the dancers for returning to their seats.

A brief clown act entertained them while the stage was pushed away. Next, came calf roping and trick riding and then trick shooting followed by bronco busting. Bull riding finally provided a climax to the thrills. The crowd cringed and cheered collectively, and the popcorn, peanuts and lemonade flowed cheaply the whole afternoon.

Finally, the announcer declared a respite and encouraged attendees to grab some more grub and their dancing shoes and reassemble at the arena for square dancing and a ten-minute slot of slow dancing for all the tuckered-out cowboys to recoup, otherwise known as the old-timers who helped build the traditions.

With the excitement and danger of the rodeo at an end for the time being, Alfred found himself wondering whether he and Barbara would be welcomed home or whether he needed to save a little cash for another night in the motel.

"Dad," Barbara held her hat down against the gusty breeze, "Donna's parents are taking us to Jiminy Slim's."

Alfred grunted and nodded. She hadn't even asked whether she could go. He wasn't Mrs. Featherbomb though, so he wasn't going to demand she tell him who would be there.

"Oh. I didn't think about it," Barbara looked downcast. "You'll be all alone, dad. May I still go with them?"

"How much money do you need for a meal?" Alfred avoided confronting the issue.

Barbara looked torn for a moment like she knew she shouldn't abandon her father but also excited to hang out with her best friend. "Donna said her parents are paying."

Alfred tucked his billfold back into his breast pocket. "Very well. Will they be bringing you back here afterward?"

Barbara wrapped him in a quick hug, "Thanks, dad! Yeah, Will asked me to dance the slow dance with him."

She bounded off with her friends before Alfred could process what she'd revealed. A slow dance with a boy. He raised his eyebrows and shrugged. Could he, or even Mrs. Featherbomb, keep her from being interested in boys? It wasn't like she would be alone in a car with him. Alfred considered the dance. Whole families would be surrounding the young couple. Couple?

"No cussing, dear," Mrs. Featherbomb's voice—

"Oh, shut it," Alfred murmured. The dance was as safe a place as any, if not safer, due to the countless adults who would jump in as chaperons if need be.

Alone, he walked toward the food wagons. Discarding an empty bag of roasted peanuts, he considered what to drink to rehydrate his throat after the salty treat.

Barbecue and orange soda, he decided.

A familiar figure held hands with his daughter and wife in front of a small shack with a weathered board declaring they had tacos, burritos and churros.

"Jose," Alfred called and strode up to the family.

A broad grin spread on the Mexican's face, "Hola, Señor."

They shook hands. Marie offered her little hand to him, and he grasped it without hesitation. Then, the little girl ducked shyly behind her mother's leg. Jose's wife smiled at him and also offered to shake his hand.

As Alfred shook her hand, Jose said, "Mi mujer, my wife name Marta."

Jose laughed with his wife as if they were sharing an inside joke, and then Jose asked, "You want tacos picante—spice?"

Alfred held up his hands, "No, no. I don't want anything that'll burn my tongue."

"Ah," Jose refused to take no for an answer. "I buy one for you. You eat or no eat, no problema."

Alfred imagined his tongue having a considerable "problema" if he chose to eat the spicy, Mexican food. Jose would not take no for an answer though.

A few minutes later, they sat on the ground beneath the shade of a large maple. Several others sat around them, enjoying the reprieve in the rodeo. Marie accepted a plateful of food from her mother and folded the tortillas with practiced fingers. Jose held his own plate of tacos and a small boat of churros.

Alfred took a swig from his orange soda and relished the sweet, tangy coolness as it chased away the desert the peanuts had made of his throat. He opened his eyes, which watered immediately at the aroma of an impending forest fire built from hot peppers. Jose held his plate of tacos and limp, green grilled peppers up for Alfred to scoop a taco off.

"No," Alfred held up his hand to reject what could only spell torment.

"For you, Señor," Jose bobbed his head.

Marie took a big bite of her taco and smiled shyly at him. Her eyes were clear without a hint of watering from pain. Alfred relented and scooped the smallest taco onto his palm.

Behind him, whispers rose in a hushed chorus about him being friends with a greaser and eating greaser food. He felt the need to clean his glasses, but with the taco in his hand he couldn't. He pushed the urge away.

"Mira, watch," Jose instructed. He set to folding up a taco slowly and lifted it without spilling a single piece of meat. Then, he took a grilled pepper and placed it on top. He gave a quick smile to his student and took a bite, chewing in delight. Then, he kissed his fingertips and opened his hand expressively. "Ah, Señor, perfecto. Muy rico."

Alfred felt the held breaths of all watching him as he copied Jose and took a much smaller bite than his mentor. An explosion of melted cheese and spices enveloped his taste buds. He'd never tasted anything like it before in his life. Mild heat drew a thin film of water to his eyes, but the previous image of his head turning red with smoke and fire pouring out of his ears like a cartoon proved unfounded.

Apparently, his lack of spontaneous combustion was a letdown for his audience because conversations picked back up, and someone whooped and called, "You wet rag. We wanted to see you split your wig."

Jose looked imploringly at him. "Is good?"

Alfred nodded, "I've never tasted anything quite like it."

Jose gave his wife a victorious smile and set to eating with gusto.

Alfred finished the taco and washed it down with orange soda. A pleasant tingling remained in his mouth after the shock of the carbonation dulled. His barbecue tasted bland and excessively sweet after the complex flavor of the spices in the taco. He ate with a growing wish that he had purchased tacos instead of barbecue. He eyed the churros, wondering whether Jose would let him taste one of the fried, bready sticks plastered in cinnamon and sugar.

Marie picked up a churro and offered it to him. He hesitated a moment and then accepted it with a thank you. The little girl grabbed her own churro and leaned against her mother as she nibbled at it, savoring every bite.

Alfred thought he'd gone to heaven as the sweet cinnamon caressed his tastebuds.

Struck by remembering a question his daughter had asked, Alfred leapt up and hurried to the Mexican food shack. Jose's family had shared with him despite not having much money. He needed to repay them somehow. He felt people eyeing him, but he resisted the urge to glance around like he was doing something wrong. He adjusted his glasses and waited to be addressed.

When the cook looked at him, he said, "Churro."

The cook looked at him blankly and then held up a finger for him to wait a moment. A minute later, Alfred paid for the boat of churros and found his seat again. He held the boat out to Jose's family, and Marie quickly grabbed one in each hand. Marta said something in rapid Spanish that sounded like scolding to Alfred. The little girl placed the one in her left hand back in the boat.

"Gracias, Señor," Jose picked up the discarded churro. "Ah, thank you."

Barbara doesn't know what she's missing, Alfred thought.

Jose's wife stood and picked up her family's used napkins and other trash. Next, she held out her hand for Alfred's trash. He tried to refuse, but Marta smiled and insisted.

"Grah—gracia," Alfred attempted the Spanish word he assumed meant thank you.

Marta smiled again and backed away with a bow of kind deference.

Alfred watched as Jose gestured all around as he wove a story for his daughter in their native language. The little girl laughed and added her own ideas to the tale. A thought crept out from the dark recesses of Alfred's mind as he found his mouth twitching, fighting to smile along with the family.

Would every day be like this for him and Barbara if Mrs. Featherbomb wasn't always holding them to her ideals? Obviously, they couldn't attend a rodeo every day, but sadness muddied his thoughts as he contemplated leaving the rodeo with his daughter and returning to the house where he'd taken a thrown plate to the face. He and Barbara had felt something new. They had never been able to spend so much uninterrupted time together, and they had smiled together more than he remembered ever doing.

As he ruminated, he realized he didn't even feel worried about the pictures of him and his daughter with the cowboy hats. In fact, he was satisfied, even glad, he had let his daughter drag him into the photobooth.

"Ah, Señor," Jose said. "Hour for make dance." He mimed dancing and clapping to a rapid rhythm, "Bailando."

Alfred glanced at his watch and then noticed how low the sun had sunk. Grunting, he pushed himself up and stood.

Marie raced by with two other kids, playing some game only they could see. Jose called to his daughter, and she ran into him with a gleeful hug. Jose winced and patted her on the back. He murmured to her in Spanish, and she grabbed his hand and then reached for her mother's, tugging on both of their hands.

Alfred strode quickly to catch up. "Are you hurt?" he asked, pulling alongside Jose.

A brief flash of pain contorted Jose's face causing the sinking rays of sunlight to cast shadows on his weathered skin. "Is nothing, Señor," he made a brushing away motion with his free hand.

"This morning, when that horse pushed you against the fence," Alfred was certain that was when Jose had gotten hurt. "You've been wincing every now and then since then."

"Si, Señor," Jose admitted. "Is nothing. Small pain." He winced as Marie swung on her parents' arms.

Alfred knew he was right, but also that there was nothing he could do. He couldn't force Jose to get checked out at the hospital, and he himself hadn't even gone after Mrs. Featherbomb blackened his face with the plate.

"Okay," Alfred stated. "I'm going to find my daughter, and we'll meet you at the arena."

Jose smiled and bobbed his head, "Si, Señor."

Alfred wove his way through the streams of people moving this way and that way. He was self-conscious of his black eye, but no one else seemed to notice. Glancing at his wristwatch, he figured Donna's parents would have the girls back any minute.

"Dad," Barbara called from behind him a few minutes later. She hugged him, pinning his arms to his sides, "I'm sorry, dad."

Alfred pulled his right arm out from under hers and asked, "Sorry for what?"

"I still feel like I abandoned you at dinner," Barbara's voice held a raw edge to it. "I should have just gotten something here with you instead of leaving with Donna."

Alfred analyzed his daughter's apology before replying, "You never turn down an opportunity for Jiminy Slim's. Besides, I had a good time with Jose and his family." Barbara looked up at him with apologetic, round eyes. He met them and continued, "You won't guess what I tried."

He had never talked this way with anyone since he'd grown up. It was too late to turn back, however. Also, he really did want to tell his daughter he had tried a new food.

"What? Aren't you going to tell me, or are you just going to hold us up from going to the dance?"

"Your old man tried tacos for the first time."

Barbara stared at him. "Ha, you haven't tried anything new for...for as long as I can remember. Are you feeling alright?"

Alfred laughed and nodded in admittance. He turned and pulled Barbara close, wrapping his arm around her shoulder. "It's true no matter how hard it is to believe, and they're quite good." He squeezed her shoulders, "We'll have to discuss your disrespectful disbelief later."

Barbara looked up at him, an appalled expression creeping onto her face. She didn't say anything, but Alfred could tell she was trying not to be devastated.

"Sorry," it was his turn to apologize, "I was—"

"I didn't mean it that way," Barbara interrupted.

"—joking more than being serious," Alfred finished.

Barbara stopped abruptly. She scrutinized him carefully. "My dad doesn't joke like that," she said. "Are you feeling alright? You've been a bit weird lately."

It didn't feel nice to have his behavior called out, but she was right...again.

"I think I've been too much of a grouch," Alfred replied quickly. "I really haven't felt better than I have today for..." he trailed off deep in thought.

"How is that? You and mom have been fighting, and she hasn't talked with you except to yell at you about the rodeo. She gave you that black eye too."

Alfred glanced around nervously, "I don't think we should talk about it here. Yes, all those things are true."

Barbara pulled away and furrowed her brow. "Well, there's got to be something I can do to help you and mom stop fighting," as she said it, her voice transitioned to a more self-reflective thoughtfulness.

Alfred wrapped his arm around her shoulders again, "Let's keep enjoying the rodeo. We haven't had a time like this in ages."

Barbara smiled and snuggled tight to him for a moment, "You're right, dad. Let's enjoy it while we can. Can I still dance with Will?"

Alfred met his daughter's questioning gaze. He felt like laughing—not because he thought she was funny or because he wanted to make fun of her but because the question struck him as absurd.

"It's a square dance, Barbara. Partners are changed every time the caller says to."

"Oh, right," Barbara blushed. "I guess I forgot. Still, we might be able to dance the entire slow dance together."

And so, they probably would be able to, but Alfred chose not to address the likelihood. He kept his gaze fixed straight ahead.

They entered the arena immersed in the flow of people talking and joking loudly with each other. Many couples joined up and danced in brief spurts as the surrounding people clapped their hands to an energetic beat.

"I'm going to go hang out with Donna before it starts," Barbara called.

Alfred acknowledged with a nod and a final squeeze of her shoulders.

"Are you going to be alright?"

"Don't worry about your old man," Alfred replied. "But," he paused, trying to put it into his own words instead of repeating what he'd heard Mrs. Featherbomb say, "don't make me wish I had a shotgun."

"Dad!" Barbara wailed.

Alfred rubbed his eyes and cleaned his glasses quickly as his daughter wove through the crowd away from him. He saw Donna on the far edge talking with Will and James and a couple other girls, Paula, Kendra and the Wyman girl. That protective edge boiled to the surface again, and part of him wanted to shoulder his way through the crowd and bring his daughter back to his side.

"Ladies and gentlemen, lasses and lads," the announcer called. The crowd immediately settled. "May I present to you Bob Wills and his Texas Playboys."

Cheers drowned out the announcer's attempts to continue.

Finally, he was able to proceed, "Over here we have the square for dancing, and over there we've got ice cold water and lemonade free to everyone. Now," he launched into a quick refresher on the calls for the dance and then walked off the stage as the band struck up their opening rhythm with rapid violin parts full of double-stops.

Couples flowed around the arena like leaves in a bucket of water stirred by a young child. Alfred, not having a partner, found himself standing alone on the edge. Several others, mostly those with infants or those too old to keep pace on their feet, swayed and clapped to the rhythm beside him.

A couple burst past as he kept time with the violinist. Then, Bob stepped to the side, raised his violin to his shoulder and added a harmony. Alfred couldn't tell when the song changed except that the banjo line was faster and there were a lot more violin parts. Dust clouded into the air, and it formed streaks of mud on some of those sweating profusely. Everyone was smiling, and not a single body was still.

Alfred scanned the arena for his daughter and spotted her on the other side. She and Donna were part of a teenage square with other couples he didn't recognize.

The caller called the ladies to the center. Barbara and Donna twirled in the center of the square with the two other girls while the boys grasped hands and pulled themselves past each other. Barbara's feet pounded the dirt in perfect sync with the violins.

Before he knew it, he was one of the few on the edge of the teens' square. Barbara never missed a call, and she moved with fluidity and grace.

Three songs later, Barbara bounced to a stop beside him. She panted and accepted a cup of lemonade from Will as he skidded to a stop. Glancing at him, she drank thirstily.

"Haven't you found a partner, dad?" she called over the music.

Alfred shook his head.

"It would be fine, dad. Mom wouldn't be caught dead here."

His daughter was right. Mrs. Featherbomb always patted her hair and turned on her heel to make a quick exit whenever Alfred had a western show playing on the television.

Ignoring his daughter's concern, he changed the subject. "You know what I saw?"

She looked uncertain.

"I saw my daughter having the best time she's ever had if that smile on her face says anything," Alfred found himself grinning uncontrollably as Barbara flushed and smiled. "And," he continued, "she has incredible timing. She'd probably be able to take Bob's fiddle and make this place go nuts."

Barbara beamed, "It's already nuts, dad! Or as your generation might say, it's hoppin'."

They shared a laugh before it was cut off by one of the other girls pulling Barbara back into the square so she could take a break.

Alfred rubbed his brow. He wasn't mad at his daughter and had seriously begun to doubt her involvement with the plot to make him go crazy. He just couldn't rectify his daughter joining in willingly and then behaving so genuinely warm toward him. Either she wasn't part of the scheme, or he was madder than he thought. Either way, it let his daughter off the hook, and he found that he preferred that.

As he continued watching his daughter dance, Alfred's heart soared higher than it had since...well, it didn't matter that he couldn't think of a time to compare it to. Seeing his daughter enjoying herself with such wholesome and unpressured fun, did something deep inside him. Years later, he would realize it had been cathartic, leading to healing he hadn't known needed to happen.

"Hey, Featherbomber," a breathless Ed Albright pulled up beside him, "you're taking my place while I get some refreshment."

Alfred felt Ed's hand on his back, and before he could protest, he was propelled toward a square with all ages. Sunny broke rhythm for a moment as she looked for her date. Ed made a drinking motion and then pointed to Alfred. She smiled and scooped up Alfred on the next call.

The caller slipped into a string of calls requiring partners to change every two steps. Alfred found himself dancing with Sunny one second and then hooking his arm with a young girl with buck teeth taking up her whole smile to holding the hand of a gray-haired woman who looked old enough to be his mother as she spun like a merry-go-round around him.

Some time in the wildness, Ed came back, but Alfred remained sucked into the dance until much later, well after the arena lights flickered on.

The caller made a call for the last slow song. Many of the men ran to the lemonade stand and came back with their hands full.

The slow dance song was a slow waltz tune with a bit of country flair. Couples swayed to the rhythm as they followed the step pattern.

Had Mrs. Featherbomb been present she would have demanded that Alfred keep an eye on the boys around Barbara even after she would have encouraged their daughter to wear a skirt much too short. The thought was gone nearly as quickly as it rattled through his brain.

He'd been fighting with himself about whether or not to attempt to go home, and as the time approached to leave the rodeo, he knew he couldn't keep Barbara out of the house multiple nights in a row. Never mind if Mrs. Featherbomb didn't talk to him, he needed to look after their daughter. But what if Mrs. Featherbomb threw the broom at her again? What if the window hadn't been fixed yet? Jose could install a new windowpane, couldn't he?

Alfred dumped the last swallow of water from his cup and plucked his glasses off his face. Instead of scrubbing at them, he swiped his shirt sleeve across his brow, soaking away the remnants of perspiration. His feet yelled at him to change out of his shoes, and his legs told him to sit down. He felt something inside he hadn't felt in many years—a deep satiation of his spirit.

"Good evening, Mr. Featherbomb, sir," a young male voice interrupted his reflection. Will stood in front of him with Barbara clinging to his arm and looking up at him with admiration shining in her eyes. "I've been lucky enough to dance with your daughter tonight, sir." He took her hand from his arm, and, with a slight bow, presented Barbara to her father. "And I thank you for allowing us to dance, sir."

Alfred took his daughter's hand and met Will's eyes, "Thank you for bringing her back to me."

"You're welcome, sir," Will stood straight and tall and extended his hand.

Alfred took it and shook the boy's firm handshake. Will turned to leave, but a glance at his daughter made Alfred say, "Son, you're welcome to call on her at our home."

Will's face lit up with an enormous, sheepish yet elated smile, "Thank you, sir. I won't do anything to hurt her, Mr. Featherbomb, sir."

Alfred nodded, "See that you don't."

Barbara clutched tightly at Alfred's arm as her crush turned courter made it only a few steps before punching the air victoriously.

"Well," Alfred patted his daughter's hand, "let's get home."

"Sure, dad," Barbara's voice was wispy.

Alfred let her stare after Will for a few moments longer. Then, he took her by the hand and led her toward the exit.

"Buenos noches, Señor y Señorita," Jose fell in beside them. Marie rode on his shoulders while his wife leaned on his arm.

Alfred puzzled for a moment in a futile attempt to understand the Spanish. "Uh, good night to you too," he said, hoping he had deciphered the drift of what Jose had said.

"You are dancing man crazy," Jose's teeth flashed in a smile.

"These old legs still have something in them," Alferd adjusted his glasses. He wasn't sure whether being called a crazy dancing man was a compliment or a jab, but he was going to run with it being a good thing.

They paused at the lemonade stand. Alfred poured a cup for his daughter and one for himself. Jose picked up another pitcher while Marie balanced on his shoulders.

"Take your greasy hands off that," a loud, slurred voice yelled.

Before Jose could react, Seargent McCoy placed an unsteady hand on the pitcher and shoved Jose. He winced, and Marie clung tighter to her papi's head. Jose shuffled sideways and regained his balance with noticeable pain. He panted and looked at the drunk McCoy with fear and apprehension.

Alfred couldn't fathom where McCoy had found booze, but he was clearly so drunk he was on the verge of collapsing. He attempted to pour himself a cup of lemonade, but most of it spilled onto the table. Raising the cup to his lips, he gulped it like a shot of hard liquor.

"We don't need their kind around here," he slurred, throwing his empty cup at Jose. Then, he lurched an aggressive step toward Jose and his family.

Marie whimpered, fear making her eyes shine white. Jose remained crouched and reached up to comfort her. Marta slipped beside him and attempted to pull the young girl from his shoulders. Marie shrieked and fought to stay in place despite the impending danger.

McCoy took another provocative step, flaring his arms as if loading for a punch.

"C'mon, man, he doesn't want to fight you," a bystander called.

"You and all that booze is the only problem here," another bystander joined in.

The crowd formed a ring around McCoy and Jose's family. No one made any move to step between them or to escort McCoy away. Alfred squeezed his daughter's hand and stepped toward the drunk man.

"Dad, don't. He'll hurt you," Barbara snapped out of her dreamy revery.

"Barbara," Alfred responded firmly, "let me do this. No one should be afraid to attend a public event."

Alfred stared at the back of McCoy's head as he continued to stare down at Jose.

"McCoy," Alfred said cooly.

"I ain't finished yet," McCoy slurred.

"We need to get you home before you pass out," Alfred reached out to touch McCoy on the shoulder.

Just before his hand landed, McCoy spun, swinging with his right hand. In his drunken state, he forgot to move his feet and tumbled forward onto his side, his fist having flown wide. His breath shot out with a whoosh, and he lay gasping for a moment before going limp.

"Let 'im sleep it off," someone commented.

Two men broke from the crowd, scooped McCoy up under his armpits and dragged him toward a barn.

Alfred staggered, suddenly exhausted as relief flooded his veins. He wasn't sure how much more punishment his face could take, and he was glad McCoy's punch hadn't landed.

"Gracias, Señor," Jose said.

The crowd stared as Alfred led his daughter and the Mexican family to the exit, but none of the bystanders said a thing.

Once they pulled abreast of the parking lot, Jose tapped Alfred on the shoulder. "Mi coche, car here," he said.

Alfred looked at him blankly.

"I think he means they drove here," Barbara offered.

Alfred nodded and extended his hand for Jose to shake.

"How are we getting home? We left the car for mom."

Alfred wiped his eyes and replaced his glasses. He had failed his daughter. He was supposed to supply everything they needed. That was as far as his thoughts were able to go, however. Marta spoke in rapid Spanish with her husband and made numerous gestures at him and Barbara.

"I think she wants to offer us a ride," Barbara translated.

Jose glanced at Barbara and then looked at Alfred with a smile, "Si, Señor. Need a—¿Como se dice? A lift?"

Alfred stumbled over understanding the Spanish words, but his daughter bobbed her head and replied, "Si, muchas gracias. No tenemos nuestro coche porque...porque se lo dejamos a mama."

Jose's eyebrows shot upward, and he exchanged a look of surprise with his wife. "¡Vale! ¡Vamonos!"

Barbara tugged Alfred as she set off with Jose's family.

"Wait," Alfred said, "what did he say?"

"He said let's go," Barbara said. "He's going to drop us off at home because I told him we left the car for mom."

Alfred tried to carry on a conversation with Jose for the first couple minutes, but it did nothing to distract him from worrying about Mrs. Featherbomb and more flying saucers and plates.

Barbara and Marie played and talked like sisters. He wondered whether Barbara would have liked to have a younger sibling.

Alfred scrubbed his glasses and attempted to steel himself as they drew closer to their house. Faint smudges squiggled across the lenses, but the only word that stared back at him was

Coward

Taking a deep breath, he replaced his glasses and looked at his driveway as Jose stopped his rundown car.

Their Buick sat in the driveway and another car was parked next to it. Anger flared inside but gave way to fear when he recognized it.

"What's Pastor Meyers doing here?" Barbara voiced the question gyrating in his own mind.

Without looking at her, he shook his head and said, "I don't know."

"All is good, Señor?" Jose asked.

Alfred nodded and turned to his friend, "Yeah. Thank you for the ride."

"Buenos noches," Jose and his family chorused as Alfred and Barbara stepped toward their house.

They both turned and waved and then proceeded to the front door. Barbara clutched Alfred's hand.

"It'll be fine," he said mostly to reassure himself. "With Pastor Meyers—or more likely his wife—here, your mom won't attack us."

He felt her shudder and winced at his choice of words. Naming Mrs. Featherbomb as "your mom" was a not-so-subtle way of shifting blame onto Barbara as if she were responsible for Mrs. Featherbomb's actions.

He walked up to the door and hesitated, his hand on the handle.

"Maybe we should knock," Barbara's voice was shaky and thin.

"Nonsense," Alfred rolled his shoulders. "This is our house."

He cracked the door open. When no porcelain or broomsticks flew toward them, he pushed it open all the way. Dim light leaked from the kitchen. Alfred and Barbara both froze. Pastor Meyers and his wife were both seated at the table.

Alfred's voice disappeared, and he swallowed.

Pastor Meyers rose tiredly from the table. His wife, who had been facing away from the door, twisted to look and then stood too.

"I'm sorry, Alfred," Pastor Meyers said. "There was nothing that could be done."

"Where's mom?" Barbara's voice broke. She pulled free and raced forward to the hall.

Alfred let her go, knowing something was dreadfully amiss. The pastor exchanged a glance with his wife. She walked slowly down the hall, following Barbara. Alfred closed the door without looking away from the pastor.

Pastor Meyers stood in the archway. "Alfred, your wife collapsed at the store. She was taken to the hospital immediately, but there was nothing they could do. She was gone before they got there. I'm sorry."

Alfred's vision swam. Darkness intruded at the edges. The emergency responders should have been faster. He shouldn't have left.

The room tilted. He had been having fun at the rodeo as his wife died.

She was gone.

He shouldn't have taken Barbara with him.

He didn't have to worry about flying plates or saying the wrong things anymore.

Mrs. Featherbomb had died without hearing him say he still loved her.

He let his body be guided to the sofa. Pastor Meyers sat beside him. What was the man saying? Alfred heard his voice but couldn't make out the garble.

She was gone. His life had just changed irrevocably. Barbara's life had just changed.

"No!" Barbara shrieked. "Mom! Mom?" She descended into a wailing sob of crying and calling for her mother.

After some minutes, Mrs. Meyers, escorting Barbara, came into the living room. They sat and Mrs. Meyers clasped Barbara's hands as she continued to sob and shake her head.

Chapter 31

Alfred lost track of time. He pulled his empty stare from the chair and beheld his daughter. She was still denying that her mother had died, and Mrs. Meyers was not able to comfort her.

Alfred shuffled to her and knelt on the floor. As he reached around his daughter to hug her, her eyes met his for a brief moment, and then she latched onto him and sobbed into his neck.

He should be crying too, right? He should be crippled with grief.

He was experiencing neither.

He pressed his hand against his daughter's heaving back. She slid off the overstuffed sofa and landed on his lap. He held her as if she were a toddler who had just scraped her knee. Any minute she would suck her tears back in and run off to play again. Only she wouldn't. He hardly felt anything, but Barbara was sobbing with no end in sight.

Alfred sat like that until his legs fell asleep, and then he stayed there until Barbara stopped crying. Her breath came even and deep with only an occasional whimper.

Mrs. Meyers was preparing something in the kitchen. Pastor Meyers clasped a hand on Alfred's shoulder.

"We'll go to the hospital tomorrow," he said softly. "We should get her to bed."

Alfred shifted just enough to see his daughter's face. She looked peaceful apart from the dried streaks on her cheeks and the crusted snot at her nose. He shook his head, "She can't wake up alone."

Pastor Meyers nodded, "Of course. We'll make up a bed for you next to hers."

As the pastor rose and took a step, Alfred turned to him and asked, "H—how did she die?"

Pastor Meyers looked more tired than ever as he met Alfred's gaze. "They suspect a cerebral aneurysm."

Alfred's mind raced to remember the context of the medical term. A pocket of trapped blood had burst in Mrs. Featherbomb's brain. It could have left her alive with or without possible partial paralysis. Since she had died, it must have been a large amount of blood.

"They said she was gone before the ambulance arrived," Pastor Meyers rubbed his forehead. "It was so quick, she wouldn't have felt a thing."

Alfred dropped his gaze to the floor where it became unfocused once again. He nodded and dully noted the pastor's footsteps as he stepped out of the room.

He and his daughter were alone again. Alone just like the previous night when they'd stayed in the motel. Alone just like they would be for the rest of their lives.

Correction, he would be alone. Barbara had a suitor who was going to stop by.

He blew out his breath. So much still needed to be done. He ran through a mental list. It was so dauntingly overwhelming that he felt like he was sinking beneath spiraling waves.

"We've got your beds made up," Pastor Meyers said gently.

Alfred nodded and looked down at his daughter. She deserved so much more than he had ever given her, and now, he was certain he could never give her what she needed. He would be gone at work, while she would be gone at school. At least she would be surrounded by friends.

He shifted his feet. They stung like thousands of porcupines had spent a day using them as practice targets. Pastor Meyers helped him stand, pulling him up underneath his armpits. Then, with the precious daughter he had let down so often, he staggered to Barbara's room.

"We covered the broken window," Mrs. Meyers was saying, but Alfred barely registered her voice.

Barbara moaned as Alfred laid her gently on her bed. Mrs. Meyers pulled her shoes off and drew the covers up.

"Poor child," Mrs. Meyers whispered. "You'll take good care of her though. She's got a good father. We'll be here if you need anything."

Alfred nodded and thanked her. The pastor and his wife left the room and turned out the light. He sat in silent darkness interrupted only by the light filtering in from the hallway and the slow, steady inhale and exhale of his daughter's breathing.

He took his glasses off and rubbed his eyes. Not stopping there, taking both hands, he rubbed his face—a silent prayer that he was enough; that he could raise his daughter alone.

What kind of fool was he? He knew he wasn't a good father. He'd been too absent. Mrs. Featherbomb had done all the raising. He tried to be like Jose because he was a good father to Marie. Barbara had seemed so happy at the rodeo, but what would she think of him when she woke up? Wouldn't she blame him for letting her mother die?

Alfred slumped fully to the floor and leaned his back against his daughter's bed. The numbness he felt gave way to something that crept into him like a snake slithering into a hole. Fear, no...terror, gripped him. Of all the possible fathers in the world, Barbara had him.

He knew he should pray because that's what people did when they went through hard times. The only syllable that formed in his mind, however, was the timeless question of curious children and devastated adults. The irony was lost on him. Why? Why was he the father his daughter had?

It started in his pinky fingers and then worked its way through his hands and up his arms. Then, his whole body succumbed to shaking. It wasn't gentle shivering of a body trying to warm itself in the cold. Rather, it was the violent convulsions of a man told he would die a gruesome death by the hand of the thing he feared most.

Blankets rustled behind him and then a snap sounded harsh and hard in the stillness of the room. His shaking turned into rocking as he grabbed his knees. Bare feet smacked the floor beside him. He turned to see his daughter, draped in a blanket, lowering herself beside him. He couldn't help but stare as his bottom lip quivered. His mouth was pulled into a silent scream. Barbara said nothing as she wrapped half of the blanket around his shoulders and leaned into him.

After several minutes of silence, she said softly, "We'll make it through, dad. I love you."

Father and daughter cried together. He knew her tears were for her mother, and he knew his tears were a silent plea for help.

Sometime in the night, they had climbed into their beds. Barbara's bed was against the wall on one side and Alfred's cot on the other side. She hadn't stayed in her bed for more than five minutes before she had climbed onto his cot and snuggled onto his shoulder. She'd cried silently and sniffed back tears for several minutes before drifting off.

Alfred woke first and sat up. Barbara lay peacefully swaddled in a cocoon of blankets on the cot. He pulled the corner of one blanket and tucked it under her chin. Then, he turned and held his face in his hands. He had no idea what he was supposed to do. The only thing he knew for certain was that he couldn't leave his daughter's room until she woke up. He could think of nothing worse than her seeing an empty room and an empty house when she awoke. He needed to use the bathroom though, so he debated with himself whether to wake her up.

No, he decided, *better to let her sleep in tranquil oblivion a bit longer.*

His blurry gaze shifted around his daughter's room. It was funny how he didn't recognize it. Apart from occasional entry for correction, he hadn't had any need to enter her room for years and, thus, had missed the little bits of decoration and the photos and sketches she'd tucked into picture frames or placed on her dresser. It wasn't his space at all. He was invading.

How would a good father handle his daughter's need for him at a time like this?

He stared at a spot at the foot of his daughter's bed until he identified the black smudge on the floor. His glasses. He kept staring and saw they were snapped on the right temple and over the nose where he'd wrapped the frames in tape. He felt like such a failure for Barbara that he didn't want to reach for them and try to put them on. Undoubtedly, he would see nothing but a reminder of his incompetence as a father.

Barbara jerked awake behind him. Slowly, he turned and watched her as she rubbed her eyes and slowly pieced together her surroundings and the events of last night. Her gaze landed on him.

"Dad, I'm so sorry. I should have been up already to make breakfast."

Alfred reached for her hand as she threw the blankets off to jump out of bed. "It's okay, honey. Mrs. Meyers will probably have breakfast ready for us."

"They stayed for us?" Barbara sounded amazed.

Alfred nodded, portraying more calm than he felt. "I bet Pastor Meyers left for church already—"

"Church?" Barbara wailed and then clasped the blankets with both hands and pulled them to her chest. A distant look entered her eyes.

Alfred didn't see his teenage daughter scared to have to explain to her friends that her mother had died. Instead, he saw a young girl staring at the scariest monster she had ever seen. He reached forward and wrapped her in a hug.

"I don't feel like attending either," he said simply.

Barbara sniffed at tears, yet Alfred felt some soak through his shirt. He rubbed his daughter's back and racked his brain for something to say that would offer more comfort than just his physical presence could offer.

"I don't want her to be gone," Barbara sniffed. "Who's gonna do my hair? Or take me shopping?"

"Shhh. We'll figure it out," Alfred said quietly. "She did a lot for our family."

He stopped. A familiar guilt crept up inside him. The type of guilt he felt when he was saying more than he knew to be true. Something wasn't right. Something in him was *glad* Mrs. Featherbomb was gone. He was sad, angry and such a failure as a husband that he had let her die, but he felt some sort of relief beneath it all. There would be no more endless fights, no more silent treatments for days on end and no more constantly wondering if he was measuring up to the impossible standard Mrs. Featherbomb held for a husband.

He stifled a sigh and forced out, "I miss her too."

"I know she and you were fighting," Barbara cried freely, "but I thought we'd come back from the rodeo and everything would go back to normal."

Alfred wondered if the normal would have been Mrs. Featherbomb standing up for her daughter's choices in short skirts or throwing brooms through windows and plates at faces.

"I wish I hadn't made her mad about the rodeo," Barbara added when Alfred didn't say anything in reply for several seconds. "I wish I could have been a perfect daughter. I wish I hadn't been so stubborn."

Alfred marveled at what his daughter was saying. She was making statements so close to the ones circling in his own mind that he dared not reveal that he found himself afraid he may have talked about all the things in his sleep. What she said also sounded remarkably close to the types of things he felt when he read the insults and descriptions that showed up on his glasses or on the windows.

"Dad, you're squeezing me too tight," Barbara gasped for breath.

Alfred immediately loosened his hug.

"Barbara," he admitted, "I'm scared too. I want to be the father you need me to be, but I don't know how to do that. I've been so wrapped up in work that I haven't," he paused. Realization, or maybe naked honesty, marched into his consciousness. "I haven't treated you like my daughter. I've been distant and haven't been here for you.

"Yesterday, at the rodeo, was the first time since you were a toddler that I think I've actually been a father to you. I'm sorry." Tears worked their way out of his eyes.

He was alone as a parent now. He was all his daughter had for immediate family. He had blown it for all those years as he pursued what he thought made him a good father and what society said made a good husband. No, that didn't settle quite right. If that had been all, he would have felt some sort of justification, but he didn't feel release from the guilt. He could see it now. He had taken a step back from being a father so that he didn't cross Mrs. Featherbomb. He had withdrawn from his daughter in an attempt to maintain peace in his family. What Barbara needed more than ever was a warm and caring father full of smiles the way Jose was with Marie. He had been so cold for so long he didn't know if he could do that.

"Dad, it's okay. You've done what you needed to," Barbara comforted him. "We've always had a house and food and money for clothes and other necessities."

Alfred interjected, "No. Something has been missing. Something I didn't know what it was until just now. I've seen it with Jose and his daughter."

"Dad," Barbara negated his revelations, "I'm fine. I've never needed anything I don't have."

Alfred looked at his daughter blankly. Maybe he was wrong. Maybe he had been making stuff up with all the stress of the words he'd been seeing and with Mrs. Featherbomb's death. There would be a funeral service and a burial. He would need to help make the arrangements. His glasses were broken, and the eyeglass doctor hadn't yet called to inform him that the new ones were ready. He needed to figure out who would cook for him and Babara—he certainly couldn't do it. He needed to let his boss, Mr. Davis, know that he would be taking some time off to settle everything.

"It's alright, dad. Like you said, we'll figure it out."

Alfred refocused his gaze. Barbara's eyes were pooled with unlet tears. She shouldn't be the one trying to comfort him. He was her father. She should be able to cry and wail and throw whatever attitude kids her age did, but here she was behaving like an adult to comfort him.

"Barbara," Alfred said, "it's okay to cry and be upset."

The dam burst, and tears trickled down Barbara's cheeks. "Then why aren't you? Are you glad mom's not here?"

Alfred blinked. Her words cut deep, yet they were not malicious. His daughter was scared and demanded to know why he hated her mother. Hated her mother? He swore in his mind. He had loved Mrs. Featherbomb.

Her question was not unfounded. He still hadn't shed a single droplet in sadness. She had no right to speak so disrespectfully to him, but wasn't this what he had realized only moments before? That she should be allowed to release any ugly actions and attitudes? He was glad his glasses were broken so he couldn't see confirmation that he was insensitive and uncaring.

"Get away from me," Barbara shrieked and swung a pillow at his face. The pillow connected, and she stared at him with her face frozen mid-sob. She lunged at him and buried her face in his neck.

"Why? Why is she gone?" she whimpered.

Alfred sat too stunned to move or reply. His daughter picked her head up just enough to look him in the eyes. Her red-rimmed eyes were blurry to his poor eyesight.

"Why did mom die?" she whispered before her lip curled and she went back to sobbing against his neck.

Finally, Alfred moved. He wrapped his arms around her and pressed a hand against the back of her head. "I don't know. I don't know," he repeated in a whisper.

Something inside yelled and berated him for admitting it, but what could he do but tell the truth? He argued with himself internally. The truth would be more comforting than a comfortable lie, wouldn't it?

It was several minutes before Barbara calmed down and sniffed back the slowing flow of tears. She sat back, looking at the floor.

Alfred was about to suggest they go see what Mrs. Meyers had made for breakfast when Barbara leapt from the cot.

"Dad, I'm sorry," she cried. "Your glasses. I didn't mean to." She picked up the pieces of his broken glasses. "I can fix them. I'll glue them back together or tape them for you. I'm sorry."

She sank to the floor, the glasses in her hands like an offering to appease some king or deity. "I'm so clumsy. I'm sorry, dad."

She lowered her hands and futilely stuck the ends of the frames together as if fitting them would make them magically stick.

Alfred crossed the floor and gently took the glasses from her worrying hands. "I've got new ones ordered," he said, placing the pieces in a pocket. "They will probably be ready to pick up tomorrow."

Barbara looked at him, gnawing on her lip. "You can't drive without them."

Alfred nodded and forced a smile. There was no warmth in it he knew, but he hoped his daughter would understand the attempted gesture, "But I can walk, and if a blind man has a guide...well, he's a lot less likely to walk into a light pole."

Barbara sniffed and nodded glumly.

Alfred leaned down and took her hands, drawing her to her feet.

She rubbed her arm, "I'm sorry. I didn't mean to break them again."

"Breakfast," was all Alfred said.

Mrs. Meyers smiled at them as they stepped into the kitchen. She had bacon and eggs staying warm in the oven and asked how they liked their toast after a brief inquiry about how they slept and how they were doing. She had a quick hug for Barbara and an apologetic explanation that Pastor Meyers had already left for church.

"They'll miss you at the piano," Alfred offered as a sign he did not expect or need anything more.

Mrs. Meyers smiled with a bob of her head and turned abruptly, muttering something about forgetting the coffee.

Alfred reached for a plate, but Barbara cut him off, "I got you a plate, dad."

Alfred said, "Thank you. Can I pour you some orange juice?"

They ate in silence; Mrs. Meyers having retired to the armchair in the living room and pulling a pile of yarn and knitting needles onto her lap. Alfred found himself worrying through the logistics of how he would get his daughter to school, go to work and then pick her up from school.

"It's too quiet," Barbara whispered, setting her fork down. "You and mom always argued about something, and you would crinkle the paper."

Alfred swallowed and rested on his left elbow. His daughter didn't look at him, but he didn't need his glasses to see the glitter of fresh tears dripping from her eyes. He glanced out the kitchen window. His gaze never made it past the words scrawled on the glass.

You never loved her

glared at him like a challenge from a lifelong enemy.

"I did too," he muttered. He rubbed his eyes and looked back at the windowpane. The silent glass held the words that shouted at him and made his blood boil.

"I did too," he shouted, slamming his fork down with a sharp clink.

Across from him, Barbara flinched and doubled over as bigger sobs added to the erupting chaos. Mrs. Meyers tossed her knitting to the floor and rushed to comfort her. She draped her arms around her and spoke softly into her ear. Then, she looked at Alfred, but he rose from his chair and stepped menacingly toward the window.

"Mr. Featherbomb," Mrs. Meyers barked shrilly, "what's gotten into you? You're scaring your daughter. Lord knows she's been through enough already."

Alfred heard her as if she were merely a small mouse in the midst of a raging storm. The window continued to hurl its accusation. He hadn't yet shed a tear for his late wife, and the relief and freedom he hadn't yet fully identified felt like a cool breeze in the midst of a scorching desert.

"I did too love her," he growled at the window. He stood directly in front of it, snatched a towel and scrubbed furiously. "I loved her you—" He cursed the window with words he'd never uttered in his home before.

"Alfred," Mrs. Meyers called sternly. "Why on earth are you taking the Lord's name in vain? What's gotten into you? There's nothing on that window, and I don't see anyone outside. Who are you talking to?"

Alfred raged on. Arguing with the window and—the thought slowly formed that he was fighting to convince himself that he was indeed telling the truth. He felt the pastor's wife beside him. Her calm hands closed over his frantic ones, slowing his scrubbing.

Barbara bawled from the table, "He sees things, messages I think, on windows and mirrors and his glasses. He doesn't say what they are." Her voice succumbed to gasping sobs. She hiccupped and continued, "Can you help him? He saw something the night we were at the motel after mom kicked us out.

"She threw a plate at dad. That's why his face is black and blue. She—she," Barbara stuttered as she forced herself to say it. "She threw the broom at me. That's why my bedroom window's broken. We went to the rodeo. Mom didn't want us to. She and dad were arguing, but mom hadn't talked to him for days.

"It's all my fault. I ruined everything. They didn't want me. I've been a terrible daughter. It's all my fault. It's all my fault."

Barbara wept uncontrollably and didn't bother trying to sniff the snot back from dripping from her nose.

Mrs. Meyers stared on with her hand frozen in midair, an appalled look leaving her mouth agape.

The declaration that he loved his wife died on Alfred's lips. He rushed to his daughter's side, stubbing his toe on a chair leg. He sucked in his breath and lowered himself next to Barbara. He was going to say the wrong thing, he always did, but he knew he had to try.

"Barbara, what your mom and I fought about was never because of you."

She glared at him incredulously. "Is that why mom stopped talking to you when you told her Mrs. Wyman was taking us to Piper's Pier?"

Alfred thought hard to recall the scenario that had led to Mrs. Featherbomb refusing to talk with him. It felt all of a year ago. His daughter was right. That had been a fight because of what she wanted to do. Mrs. Featherbomb had even said she wouldn't have needed to be so hard on Barbara if she didn't insist on bringing so much trouble on herself.

But no...it hadn't been Barbara's request, had it? It had been his attempt to convince Mrs. Featherbomb that Mrs. Wyman was driving the girls with no boys in the car.

Barbara's tears renewed, "See, it's all because of me. I'll bet you and mom didn't fight before I was born."

"Barbara," Mrs. Meyers interjected. "You're talking to your father, young lady."

Barbara screamed and cried harder, "Don't say that! Don't say what mom says."

Alfred rested his hand on his daughter's shoulder. She jerked away, slamming herself into the wall. She was like a cornered animal that had lost its instinct to fight and thought only of running away. He pushed himself away and snatched a box of tissues from the counter.

Barbara stared at the offered tissue. "You expect me to pull myself together and ignore the truth?"

Alfred beheld the tissues and then set the box on the table. He'd done the wrong thing again. How would he have felt if someone had tried to make him wipe the problem away and hide it? That was easy to consider. As a man, he was supposed to do that with everything. And it was frustrating and lonely.

One of Pastor Meyers' sermons came to his mind. He had taught on how to weep with those who weep and mourn with those who mourn. The words from the sermon made sense, but he didn't know how to put action to them. Then, he considered Señor Jose with his daughter. He would change his actions and his voice depending on what Marie was doing.

Alfred stared at the table, unable to risk meeting his daughter's glare. "Barbara," he began softly, "I'm sorry. I can see why you would see it that way."

His daughter sniffed, "Why did you and mom fight all the time? Why isn't mom here?"

He felt her gaze on him, but he still couldn't look up, "I don't know. I guess we disagreed on a lot of things."

Barbara reached for a tissue, "Did you want me?"

Alfred felt an invisible force, like a lasso drawing tight around both steer and saddle horn, pull his gaze to meet his daughter's eyes. The look of pain and frozen anger nearly paralyzed his vocal chords. "I know I don't do a good job of showing you, do I? Being your father is the best thing that's ever happened. I could lose my job or have to move out of town, and that wouldn't matter, but if I lost you, I'd be lost."

Barbara sniffed and blew her nose, "I'm not very quiet, am I?"

"Oh, you're completely fine," Mrs. Meyers said.

Alfred ventured out on a limb, "If I crinkled the paper, I don't think you'd hear it."

Barbara sniffed and offered a quick smile, "You and mom would be able to drown me out."

She looked down, and fresh tears dripped from her eyes, pooling on the table. Alfred rested his hand on her shoulder, and she leaned closer to him.

"I wish she was here," she whispered.

"I do too," Alfred said. He was still trying to work out what he was feeling and whether he truly missed Mrs. Featherbomb or if he simply wanted to have things normal and familiar.

Chapter 32

Sunday evening had seen Mrs. Meyers receive countless dishes and casseroles for Alfred and his daughter. Pastor Meyers had driven them to see Mrs. Featherbomb's body and promised to make all the funeral arrangements for them. He only needed to know what type of flowers and what family to invite that didn't live in town.

Alfred was thankful for the help and sat at the table nursing a cup of coffee the following morning. He spent a couple of minutes debating whether to make oatmeal for breakfast before deciding he wouldn't wait for Barbara to get up. He wasn't going to rely solely on her cooking skills for nutritional sustenance. He was the parent and needed to be the one to care for his daughter.

He ground his teeth and pressed on despite the kitchen window's posted litany of nasty remarks about his inability to cook.

Mrs. Meyers promised to stop by and drop off a couple cookbooks and an apple pie. Until then, the fridge was bursting with food, and he and Barbara would manage with some help from the women at church stopping over to help around the house. He'd also insisted that he did not want extended family moving in to help even if for only a week or two. Having Mrs. Meyers stay with them as long as she had had been helpful but also exhausting.

Pastor Meyers also promised Alfred he would call Mr. Davis and report the family matter so that Alfred would have time for bereavement and to settle things for Barbara.

This left Alfred free to contemplate Mrs. Featherbomb's death completely alone with no friends or family to interrupt. He had not revealed any emotion upon seeing the body. Barbara had wept uncontrollably and latched onto him for comfort. He told himself it was necessary to be strong for her. The question remained, however: why did he feel less pressure and fear at simply existing and going through his day as he wanted now that his wife was gone?

The window reported once again that it was because he never loved his wife. He glared at the letters, the only thing in the whole house that showed up in sharp focus for him.

He hadn't bothered to get the paper yet because he wouldn't be able to read it without his glasses. Barbara had offered to tape a stick to them so he could use them like a Victorian era aristocrat with a mask, but he had refused. He didn't want to be any closer to the accusations. The kitchen window was doing a bang-up job of force-feeding them to him already.

Further, he didn't feel like waving to Mr. Riley or dealing with condolences from the Carters. He was still afraid they had heard and maybe even seen some of what had transpired the night Mrs. Featherbomb forced them violently from the house.

"Dad," Barbara stood beside him. He hadn't heard her. She hugged him around his shoulders. "I'm sorry I slept so late. You must be hungry."

Alfred turned to her. The life had gone out of her voice, and the usual brightness in her eyes hid behind redness. He set his coffee mug down, only then realizing he had never risen from the table to start on the oatmeal. "I thought about fixing some oatmeal, but I can't read without my glasses."

"I shouldn't have slept so late," Barbara chided herself. Her hand lingered on his shoulder as if she was scared he would disappear if she didn't keep close tabs on him. "I'll get some oatmeal made," she yawned and rubbed her eyes with one hand.

Alfred stood, "May I help you with it?"

An expression he couldn't decipher blew across his daughter's features like a leaf blown across the yard in the fall. He had never offered to help her cook anything before.

"Um, sure, dad," Barbara shrugged. "Can you get the medium pot?"

Alfred shuffled to the cabinet beside the stove. After rummaging for a minute, he pulled out the first pot he found.

"Not that one," Barbara called as he set it on a front burner. He moved the pot to a rear burner. Then, Barbara was there taking the pot gently from him.

"This is a cake pan, dad." She said it like a schoolteacher instructing a very young pupil.

"Oh, it's round so I thought it was a pot," Alfred muttered. Heat climbed his neck and cheeks.

Barbara knelt and bobbed back up, "Here," she handed him a pot with a long handle, "this is the one we should use. See how it has a handle and feels heavier and thicker?"

Alfred accepted the pot and hesitated, scared to make another wrong move.

"The front left burner," his daughter called.

A knock echoed from the front door. Father and daughter both stared at it as if a monster lurked on the other side.

"I can answer it. You can sit tight, dad," Barbara said lifelessly.

Alfred clasped and unclasped his hands. He was useless at home.

The smell of dew on growing things wafted in before being joined by a light voice he recognized instantly.

"Good mornin', sweetheart," Sunny said. "I'm so sorry to hear about your mother. You must be all blown to pieces inside."

Barbara received a hug from her father's coworker and nodded. Sunny wore her customary yellow in the form of a knee-length dress that cinched around her waist with a thin, brown belt. In her hands she carried a plate of cookies and a seedling of some kind.

"Well, it's okay to be all jumbled up," Sunny went on. "A mother is the closest thing to an angel here on earth." She went on without noticing Barbara's glance at her dad at Sunny's comparison. Alfred had used the nickname "Angel" to try to smooth things out with Mrs. Featherbomb.

Sunny clasped Barbara's hand, "I don't mean to go on and on. Here," she held up the seedling. "This is a crimson maple. It'll grow the closest thing to purple leaves I know of. You can plant it and let it remind you of your mother. When it's big enough, it's shade will feel like your mother watching over you from heaven."

Barbara accepted the seedling and voiced her thanks quietly.

"Here," Sunny held up the plate of cookies. "Oatmeal raisin cookies always help me when life is hard. I ate a whole batch in one day when I lost my own mother." She looked down, "I still miss her. She taught me how to make these when I was six."

Barbara accepted the plate. Alfred stepped forward to help, but Sunny turned to him. "Oh, Alfred, I can't imagine how you're feeling. You're doing so well with your daughter."

Alfred swallowed and nodded once. "We'll make it through," he offered.

"Mr. Davis called me and let me know. The cookies are the least I can do. Ed and I can stop over this evening to help you with dinner," she paused with a glance at the refrigerator and the bread and pound cakes stacked on the counter. "You don't need any other concerns on your plate right now."

"Thank you," Alfred tried to sound warm and much less deflated than he felt.

"Oh, look at me. I've done nothing but talk. How are you doing—really doing?" Sunny glanced between them both.

Barbara placed the cookies and the seedling on the counter and stood by Alfred. She looked tired and as if she may start crying again at any second.

Alfred thought of several responses, but they all sounded sharp and unfriendly as he considered them.

Sunny said slowly, "There's an ache and a longing for her that doesn't let itself be spoken. She should be here loving you both instead of me running my mouth. It's a pain that makes everything feel like nothing will ever be green and bright again."

Barbara's eyes leaked as she nodded. Alfred stared into nothing as he wondered what that would feel like. He couldn't picture it, but somehow, what Sunny had described was what he knew to be the right response.

Sunny took them each by the arm and said, "You two have each other and the memory of your mother and wife. It'll be the most painful thing you've ever endured, but you'll make it out the other side."

Barbara reached out to hug Sunny. She wrapped Barbara in a tight embrace and rubbed her back as tears flowed. After a few minutes, Barbara withdrew and sniffed.

"I don't want to spoil your pretty dress," she said.

"Sweetheart, you don't need to worry one tiddle about my dress." Turning to Alfred, she held her arms wide to give him a hug. As she embraced him, she said, "You're doing a great job. If you need help with anything, and I mean *anything*, let Ed and me know."

The hug ended, and Alfred stared at the floor, hardly believing what he was about to do. He cleared his throat.

"There is one thing," he said. "My glasses got broken, but I have new ones at the eye doctor. It'd be easier to have someone drive me there to pick them up."

"Oh, of course," Sunny said. "I'll call and see when they can be picked up. We can use Ed's sedan. We wouldn't all fit in my little coupe."

"Thank you," Alfred said.

"Like I said, if you think of anything you need, Ed and I will be more than happy to help. Mr. Davis sends his regards as well. He would have called, but he thought you probably wouldn't want to be tied to a phone."

"Yes, that's thoughtful of him," Alfred confirmed with a straight-lipped smile.

"I'll let you know what I hear on your glasses," Sunny said, giving Alfred a brief hug and then wrapping Barbara tight for a moment. "Ed and I will come help you get dinner prepared. No need to worry about entertainin' us. We'll stop over and then be out of your hair once you're set."

"Thank you, Sunny," Alfred smiled. He found he felt lighter and a bit brighter too. The responsibility for preparing at least some of the food for the day did not rest solely on his daughter and neither did it rest on his own lack of skills. He also had help picking up his new glasses.

Sunny stepped to the door, "You know how to get ahold of me if you need anything."

Alfred nodded and stepped forward to close the door. "Yes. We'll see you tonight. Thank you again."

When he turned around, Barbara was eyeing the cookies.

"Cookies for breakfast?" he asked.

"I wasn't going to," Barbara replied hurriedly. "They're still warm and smell really good though."

"No, I meant let's have one or two along with our breakfast," Alfred said.

Barbara's eyes grew round, "Mom, won't like that."

Alfred stepped to her side as she caught herself, and her eyes welled with tears. Part of him was angry that they couldn't do as they pleased without Mrs. Featherbomb's fussiness elbowing in. Another part of him was sorry he had suggested doing something that reminded his daughter of the emptiness where her mother had been.

Before he could change his mind, Barbara scooped two cookies from the plate and held one out to him. The warm, moist treat melted in his mouth, the sweetness complementing the bitterness of his coffee growing cold on the table.

The oatmeal was just beginning to let off steam while Barbara stirred it when another knock sounded on the door. Alfred called that he would answer it and hurried to the door.

"Hola, Señor," Jose stood on the step with his hat in his hands. "Lo siento. Sorry, Señor, for late—lateness—I being late."

Alfred blinked. Of course, it was Monday. Jose was showing up to work because he had no idea that Mrs. Featherbomb had died.

"¿Señor?" Jose looked at him nervously.

Alfred still made no reply except to motion the Mexican inside. Jose greeted Barbara and then looked between them.

"What happen?" he asked. The whites of his eyes seemed to glow against the darkness of his skin.

Alfred sat at the table and said flatly, "My wife died Saturday while we were at the rodeo."

A blank expression flitted across Jose's face as he struggled with the words. Then, he took Alfred's hand, "I am sorry, amigo. This is not easy thing," he said enigmatically. "¿Y su hija? And you daughter?" He turned to Barbara who stood motionless at the stove. "Dios mio," he shook his head.

The oatmeal bubbled, demanding Barbara's attention. Alfred stared at her as she swept the pot off the stove and onto a potholder. She was half an orphan now without her mother.

"I intend not be happy when you have pain, Señor," Jose lifted a grocery bag and placed it almost ceremoniously on the table. "Marta make empanadas. This thing before I know."

Barbara showed more curiosity than Alfred felt. She placed the oatmeal and bowls on the table and peeled open the paper bag. A sweet, fruity aroma overpowered the earthier scent of oatmeal. Alfred rubbed his forehead, suddenly exhausted.

"Is too much to think about, this thing," Jose observed. He gestured to his heart, "Have rock huge crushing su corazon—you heart."

Barbara sat and scooched her chair closer to Alfred's, yet Alfred had nothing to say. He couldn't help but believe that what Jose said should have been true, but it wasn't true for him. His pain was in his mind where he couldn't decipher why he was relieved and not devastated.

"Something more, Señor, I see," Jose observed. "Ah," he murmured as if seeing the answer that had eluded him. "You are confused. Confusion written all over you face."

Alfred nudged his coffee mug. "I don't want to talk about it," he mumbled.

"Si, si, Señor," Jose responded quietly. "It is thing we hide that make confusion into pain."

"I said I don't want to talk about it."

Barbara laid her hand on the back of his and asked, "How much would you like, dad?" When he didn't answer, she turned to Jose, "Señor Jose, thank you for coming. I'm sure dad will have some work for you in a few minutes. Can I get you coffee?"

Jose nodded, "Si. Gracias, Señorita."

"I don't feel the way everyone seems to think I should," Alfred said. Barbara paused halfway out of her chair.

326

"For some reason, I'm glad I don't have to expect fights and cold shoulders and," he gestured to his face, "plates hitting me in the face."

He felt Barbara staring at him and glanced at Jose, who stood with a thoughtful expression. He'd finally said something about it. His daughter would never forgive him, and it wouldn't be long before everyone in town knew he'd hated his wife.

"Ah, understand, Señor," Jose grunted and played with his hat. "You and she not get along so well. I see this thing when I work. I see that she not like you."

"That isn't true," Barbara erupted. All pretense of domestic deference slid from her features. "That isn't true. Mom and dad argued, but they loved each other. Right, dad?"

Her question was not a request for him to back her statement up but a plea to keep what little remained of her world intact. Alfred looked at her. He had no control over the pained expression he felt creep into his eyes.

"Right, dad?" she asked quietly.

"Barbara," Alfred forced himself to speak, "I loved your mother with everything I had. I don't think it was ever enough to satisfy her."

"You don't mean that," tears streaked down his daughter's face. "She loved you too. She just made some mistakes like we all do. She probably didn't mean to hit you with the plate."

Alfred didn't think about his next statement. It was out before he realized what he'd said, "Just like she didn't mean to throw the broom at you that broke your bedroom window?"

"That isn't true," Barbara screamed and ran from the kitchen.

Her bedroom door slammed, and Alfred stared at the table in silence. He had blown that big time. Once again, he was glad for his lack of glasses. The insult or description of his shortcomings could not be blared like a truck horn. However, it was still there, still demanding attention.

Jose shifted his hat around in a circle. "Is not my place, Señor," he said quietly, "pero ella...she need you talk with her. I know this thing difficult."

Heat continued to build in Alfred's cheeks. The bruise throbbed with a dull ache. "What do you know about it?" he spat.

Jose lowered his hat to his side in one hand and laid his other hand on Alfred's shoulder, "Marie, mi hija, is not my first daughter. She is my only sobrevivir... how you say this thing... surviving daughter."

Alfred turned to look at the man standing beside him.

"I had other daughter, but she die quando ladrones shoot her," grief colored his voice, and his eyes misted over. "She had same years as you daughter."

Alfred swallowed, "I...I'm sorry."

"Ah," Jose made a dismissive gesture but continued. "I wish always I never lose her. Ah, Zoribel."

"What do I say?"

"I not know English well," Jose looked him in the eyes. "She need padre," he squeezed Alfred's shoulder, "love her. She know truth, but she need padre walk side by side with her." He linked his hands together as if to help Alfred visualize what he was saying.

"I always say the wrong thing," Alfred objected.

"Walk side by side not always saying right thing. Marie, muy joven, but she need feel love in corazon," Jose placed both hands over his heart, "before hear truth with ears just like Zoribel. You hija, Barbara, same way. She need this thing."

"You're telling me my daughter doesn't know that I love her?" Alfred asked, eyebrows lacing together.

Jose closed his eyes and ducked his head, "Si, Señor. This thing."

"She won't listen to me now."

Jose laid his hand back on Alfred's shoulder. "You think you are man who make only mistake." He pointed in various directions, "Mistake. Mistake. Mistake."

Alfred found himself nodding. Jose was finally saying something he understood.

"Forgive me, Señor," Jose continued. "I think you mujer, wife, she tell you this thing every day. I think you believe this thing many year. Bueno, Señor, todos los gente, all people make many mistake. People of love correct mistake, pero ellos, they correct mistake in head first," Jose touched Alfred's temple lightly, "and then correct mistake in life."

"So what mistake are you saying I need to correct in my head?" Alfred tried to brush Jose's words away, but something was taking root. He knew what he was hearing would help, but he resisted it instinctually. It had always just been easier to believe he was always the one who messed up.

"Oh," he murmured and glanced at Jose who nodded and raised his eyebrows as if to tell him he was beginning to understand. "I need to stop thinking that all I can do is make mistakes, don't I?"

Jose grinned and nodded.

"That still doesn't help me know what to say to my daughter."

"Si, Señor," Jose nodded again. "When you know you can do more than make mistake, you will find right thing to say. I know this thing."

"So, do I apologize to her? Or do I tell her how much I love her and that I loved her mother?"

"Si, Señor."

Alfred cut Jose a side-eyed glare as he pushed himself up from the table. The man was unfazed, however, and continued to smile.

Alfred walked heavily down the hall and stopped at his daughter's bedroom door. After lifting his hand to knock, he paused. He had only a vague idea of what to say, and it was probably the wrong thing yet again.

"I don't want to talk about it, dad," Barbara's muffled voice came from inside.

Alfred cleared his throat and rubbed his eyes. "Barbara, I'm," he cleared his throat again. "I'm sorry. I shouldn't have snapped at you like that. I shouldn't have tried to force you to see things my way."

A long pause followed, and then Barbara's footsteps stopped on the other side of the door.

"Is that how you really see mom?" she asked quietly.

Alfred swallowed at the gravity of what his next words could do to his relationship with his daughter. He knew he had to plunge ahead. He just wished he had some surety, some signal, that he would say the right thing.

He slid his hands into his pockets. "I made a mistake with you this morning. That was no way to talk with my daughter whom I love with all my heart."

"But is that how you really see mom?" came the reply. An edge of raw emotion and frantic need tinged her voice.

"Barbara, your mother and I fought. I can't hide that fact from you. I think you're also old enough to see that even when people fight, they can still love each other."

"Mom didn't act like she loved you very much...or me."

Alfred, unable to think of a response, stared at the door.

"She always wanted me to dress like her and talk like her. She'd get frustrated if I didn't think and act just like her— her little copy. In her eyes, I don't think I ever did anything right."

Alfred's mind scrambled to steady itself. His daughter couldn't say such things.

"Dad, what's going to happen to us now?"

Alfred shifted from one foot to the other. "We're going to figure out how to live," he said at last. "I'll be here for you. I'll need to work, and you'll need to attend school, but I'll always be here for you. When I cook, I promise it won't actually be poison even if that's what it tastes like."

Barbara gave a single, snorting laugh and sniffed back tears, "Can you just take me to Jiminy Slim's until you get good enough at cooking to not starve a goat?"

Alfred smiled, "Deal."

A warm place, like a candle in a dark room, ignited in his heart. Perhaps it was just the feeling that he had made things up to his daughter, or maybe it was the growth of a real heart to heart connection between two souls looking at a rough road ahead and agreeing to help each other.

Chapter 33

"No, we've had way too much food dropped off," Alfred held up his hand as he declined Sunny's offer for her and Ed to take them to the supermarket.

True to her offer to help with anything, Ed was driving the four of them to the eye doctor to pick up Alfred's new glasses. Barbara rode in the back with her face buried in a book. Sunny sat beside her while Ed drove and Alfred rode shotgun.

"You can come over and cook again. Dad's not getting any better," Barbara looked up from her book long enough to share the laughter that followed.

Alfred laughed as well. It had been only a few days since they had buried Mrs. Featherbomb's body, but already, with the closeness he and his daughter shared, he didn't feel the incredible weight to perform fake grief. Some days were still hard. Sometimes, Barbara needed to be held while she cried, and she had several friends that stopped over and helped her when she needed them instead of a prickly-pointed square.

Will even visited. He had been dressed the sharpest Alfred had ever seen any of the young men in town dress. He'd brought condolement, flowers and a book he said was his favorite. While he was visiting, Sunny and Ed had arrived to cook dinner, and they had helped Will's visit stay free of the awkward tenseness that had threatened repeatedly.

Barbara had devoured his favorite book and then gone to the library with Donna to check out the whole series.

Jose kept showing up for work, as well. He would most often start working in the yard until Alfred made it out of the house to talk with him. Marie would often accompany him in the mornings and play with Barbara until Marta came by later to pick her up. Their conversations were halting, but Alfred was getting better at deciphering Jose's broken English and spattering of Spanish injected into his sentences. They sometimes talked about nothing more than what the house and yard needed. However, Alfred found himself seeking Jose's counsel about why he didn't feel and express grief the way it seemed everyone around him assumed he should.

"Señor," Jose added another weed to the pile pulled from the overgrown garden behind the house, "you are not a man who cries. I know this thing. When woman fight against man, man no have sad when relationship finished."

"But she was my wife. I should be struggling to hold myself together and not thinking about all the things my daughter and I can do since she's not here to throw the proverbial wrench in the gears."

"Ah, Señor, I think that you not understand." Jose grabbed some of the weeds he'd pulled and a handful of small rocks. "This thing is like this flower," he grabbed the stem of a daisy. "When woman tell hombre, man, she not like him or she not happy with what he does, her words like these stones." Jose dropped them on the daisy. One of the white petals tore off and fell to the ground beside the green leaves that were pinned to the ground by the weight of the stones. "Then," Jose held up the weeds, "she act like she not like him and give no beso o brazo, understand?" He crushed the daisy with the handful of weeds laid on the stem.

"Like this, el hombre wilt and die like flower." Jose pantomimed wilting and dying and being buried. "But think, when woman gone, maybe dead or maybe moved on to different man, flower have no more stones and no more weeds." He removed the weeds one by one and then brushed the stones off the leaves. The daisy sprang back almost to where it had been.

Alfred considered Jose's lesson as Ed turned into the parking lot. Then, he pulled his glasses off, stating, "I won't need these things anymore." He placed the patched up glasses on the dashboard and glanced back at his daughter, "Not that I'm not grateful for them."

Barbara flashed him a quick smile before diving back into her book. She had taped a toothpick to the inside of the frames to make them wearable. She had still seen nothing on the lenses even though he had asked her about it.

Rubbing his eyes, he stretched and closed the car door. Suddenly, he didn't feel like going into the optician's office. He remembered the woman who had accused him and yelled at him. His troubles had only increased after going here the last time.

"You alright?" Ed called through the open window.

Alfred shrugged, "Yeah."

"We all get older and need some help with things sometimes."

Alfred nodded, knowing Ed was talking about the glasses. Was he ashamed about needing glasses to see clearly? He couldn't be sure. The one thing he knew was that he feared the same messages showing up on his new glasses and never being free of the feeling that everyone else could see how despicable he was. He still harbored a sneaking suspicion that others could see what was written on his glasses and the windows, but they were too polite to acknowledge the truth and tell him to his face that he was those things the writing described him as.

He blew out his breath and walked in.

Ten minutes later, he walked out and took his seat in the car. Barbara looked at him curiously.

"Oh, they look the same," she said, spooning vanilla ice cream into her mouth.

Alfred glanced around. All three were working on ice cream.

"We'll get you one too," Sunny giggled. "We weren't goin'a sit here and do nothin' while we waited for you."

Alfred felt heat rise to his face. The bruises from the plate Mrs. Featherbomb had thrown were nothing more than a few dime-sized yellow spots that persisted in their job of discoloring his face.

He felt like a little kid as he ordered a malt and Ed paid for it.

"Dad," Barbara called from the backseat, "can I try your malt?"

Alfred let go of the straw and passed it back. When he received it back, a quarter of it was gone. He twisted to look at his daughter.

"What?" she said, wiping her mouth. "It's really good. I'll have to get one next time."

Ed and Sunny laughed. Alfred ducked his head and pulled on the straw. The tangy malt tickling his tastebuds dissipated some of the anger that rose as they laughed at him.

"No. No. No," he muttered as terror widened his eyes. On the left lens of his new glasses, the word

Pinhead

scrawled in bold, black lines. On the right

Square

formed like black mist coagulating into brush strokes. He ripped the new glasses off and held them, frozen. He couldn't clean them because of the malt in his other hand.

"You alright?" Ed asked.

"I'm fine, Codgens, I mean, Albright," Alfred ground out. His attempt to sound normal vanished as another insult formed on the car's windshield. "Does no one else see that?" he shouted.

The car lurched to a stop in the driveway. Alfred heard Sunny comforting Barbara. He had done it again. He'd scared her and made himself look crazy, but how could no one else see the insults?

Ed helped him out of the car, and all four entered the house. Alfred didn't stop. He led them all outside again into the backyard and paced back and forth. He set his malt on the steps and cleaned his glasses.

"Hey, we didn't mean to make fun of you," Ed fell in step beside him. "I know you're going through a lot, and, I guess, it probably wasn't funny to you."

"No, you don't understand. None of you do. I want to be free of these insults. Someone's writing them on my glasses and the windows, but no one else admits they're there." Alfred stopped and stood still.

"I'm sorry for laughing at your expense," Ed offered.

The mature part of Alfred's brain fired, dragging at the part that still thought like a little kid. He was acting like a fool, a spoiled brat, in front of other adults who happened to be coworkers.

"I just want it to stop," he muttered.

"Grief can do a lot of funny things to a man," Ed said. "We're here to help you."

Alfred glanced at Ed and then at Sunny and Barbara. He wiped his eyelids and replaced his glasses, "I'm sorry. I let my imagination get the best of me."

Barbara pushed away from Sunny and descended the steps. She hugged him and said, "Dad, I know things aren't the way you always wanted them, but Mr. Albright is right. We're here for you."

A tear pricked Alfred's right eye. He wrapped his arms around his daughter and replied, "I should be the one here for you. I shouldn't get so riled up about nothing."

"Dad, Jose tells Marie, whenever she throws a tantrum, that it's okay to be mad or sad or whatever it is she's feeling. It never changes the fact that he loves her." Barbara paused to take a rattling breath. "I think he's right. Even when you have these episodes, I might get scared, but I still love you."

Alfred sniffed back another tear and rubbed his daughter's back. He tried to end the hug and push her away, but a hand on his back kept him rooted.

"You need this," Jose's accented English sounded softly behind him. "Health, this thing is."

Alfred stopped fighting the urge to end the embrace. "I love you too. I'm sorry I'm not a very good father."

"Shh, dad. We all make mistakes now and then." His daughter's voice was soft and apologetic, "I can see now how you've tried to do things, but mom stood in the way." Her voice caught, "She wanted me to be just like her and always get my way which was actually her way."

"Big sister Zoribel crying," the small voice of Marie interrupted the silence. "She sad?"

Barbara nodded and reached out to hug the little girl.

"I know you're not my real sister, but you're kind just like she was." Marie latched onto Babara's leg. Alfred knelt with Barbara so his daughter could more easily hug the little girl. "I miss her, and I'm sad she's gone, but I have you for a sister now."

Barbara wiped her nose and nodded, her sobs turning into a snippet of laughter.

Jose patted him on the back, "All is okay, Señor."

"No," Alfred released his daughter and turned to him. "No, it's not all okay." He placed his glasses on. Sure enough, across both lenses in big letters

LIAR

glared at him. He could pretend something else was bothering him and avoid confronting the truth. Maybe he could live, knowing that Jose still didn't know who had reported him as a communist.

Alfred swallowed and plunged ahead, "Jose, it was me."

Jose stood unfazed.

"I didn't want you coming around my house. I hated how good you were at the things that I was supposed to be doing. And...and I thought you were the one painting the insults on my glasses and windows."

Alfred took a breath and met Jose's steady gaze, "I called the authorities on you. It was me who told them you were a communist. I'm sorry for doing that, and I'm sorry for separating you from your family and sending you to prison."

Jose stood perfectly still, a placid expression not betraying any emotion. Then, he nodded slowly, "Si, Señor. I know this thing. This thing was terrible thing."

Alfred hung his head. He had hoped beyond hope that Jose would overlook what he'd done and the inconvenience to his family. It'd been too much to ask for.

"Hermano, brother," Jose said, extending his arms. "I am no mad at you. I forgive you."

Alfred let Jose hug him. After several seconds, he wrapped his own arms around the man he had falsely accused. He felt the weight of what he'd done wash over him again. He closed his eyes at the realization that he would live with that weight for the rest of his life.

"One question," Jose said. "Do you forgive Alfred?"

Alfred's face screwed up in confusion. Then, he had his answer. As long as he carried the weight, he would not forgive himself.

He shook his head. "I can't."

Jose nodded, "Maybe it take time. I still carry weight of Zoribel's death. No culpa mio. Is not my fault, but I thinking it is. Ah...is heavy." He glanced at Alfred. "Sometimes I hear words that say is my fault." He shook his head. "It like the words on you glasses. They say I am not good; that I make my daughter be killed. These words are wrong, but them remind me to forgive me every time they come against me."

Alfred glanced around the yard. Marie swayed and bounced around in a dance. Barbara followed her, trying to copy each move while Ed and Sunny sat on the steps leaning into one another and watching with peaceful smiles on their dreamy faces.

"So, you're saying they'll never leave?" Alfred asked.

Jose nodded and held up a finger, "But I have seen this thing only when I not forgive me."

Alfred nodded, understanding slowly dawning in his mind like a droplet of ink dropped into a bowl of water. Slowly, the black words on his glasses faded. Maybe he could see the ghosts of the letters. Gray ghouls that slipped from view when he tried to focus on them only to show up at the edge of sight. Or maybe he was just making things up. He didn't know.

"Dad," their daughters danced up, "can I have some money to take Marie to Piper's Pier?"

A look passed between Jose and Alfred. They smiled, and Jose let his daughter pull him into a playful dance while Alfred reached for his billfold and withdrew a couple of bills.

"Get yourself a malt this time, Sweet Pea."
Barbara grinned, "Oh, I'm gonna. Thanks, dad."

341

The End

If you enjoyed *The Writing on the Window*, please share it with your family and friends. Also, please consider rating it and writing a review. This not only encourages me and helps me know you enjoy my writing but also helps my work become more visible so that other readers like you can find it and live in an alternate universe for a short time too. Thank you for joining in the adventure. Happy reading!

Find the author and his other works at:

moleculesofstory.wordpress.com

T. M. Bennett on Facebook

Timothy M. Bennett on Goodreads

About the Author:

T. M. Bennett grew up in the worlds of *The Lord of the Rings* and *Star Wars*, running through the woods with a homemade bow, a stick for a sword (or lightsaber), and occasionally a cloak. Those childhood adventures taught him that the best stories are built on characters worth following into darkness. Now, he crafts brutal, character-driven stories that don't shy away from the cost of heroism. He lives near the west coast of Michigan with a shy spren and is always hunting for the next story that makes him feel like that kid in the woods again.

The Writing on the Window was inspired by the author's ongoing journey after the abuse he survived and is, therefore, a true heart project, one that needed to be written despite its drift from T. M. Bennett's usual genre preferences.

If you find yourself in an abusive situation, remember that you are not alone and there is life on the other side of abuse. Search for those who can help you in your area and reach out to them. An abuser is typically a person who needs therapy, yet those around him/her are the ones who end up going to therapy.

Also by the Author:

Short Stories:

A Unicorn Named Nothing

Remember

Jupiter's Child

Novels and Novellas:

Star Sky Series:

(#1) The Trouble with Dragons and Strangers

(#2) A Journey of Unknown Skies

(#3) The Cycle the Shadow Came

(#4) A Constellation in Ashes